REVELATIONS OF A TIME TRAVELER

DOUG MOLITOR

THE ALTADENA
PRESS LLC

Revelations of a Time Traveler
by Doug Molitor

Copyright © 2018 Doug Molitor

The Altadena Press
www.thealtadenapress.com

Cover Design by Kristin Bryant at Kristin Design

Publication date: July 2024

Third Edition

All Rights Reserved

ISBN: 978-1-965057-04-9 (EBOOK)
ISBN: 978-1-965057-05-6 (PRINT BOOK)

PRAISE FOR DOUG MOLITOR

"You couldn't ask for a finer guide to the future, or the past, than Doug Molitor. Having so thoroughly enjoyed his 'Memoirs of a Time Traveler,' the next book I read is, without a doubt, going to be his 'Memoirs of a Time Traveler' again."

LARRY GELBART, *M*A*S*H, TOOTSIE, A FUNNY THING HAPPENED ON THE WAY TO THE FORUM, CITY OF ANGELS*

"For Pete's sake, do not wait for the inevitable Major Motion Picture! See Doug Molitor's 'Memoirs of a Time Traveler' NOW, as it was meant to be seen: on that giant screen between your ears!"

RANDALL WILLIAM COOK, WRITER, DIRECTOR, AND OSCAR™-WINNING VISUAL EFFECTS ARTIST (*THE LORD OF THE RINGS*)

CONTENTS

1. The Past Is Prologue 1
2. Call Me Unreliable 10
3. April Eleventh, 1865 15
4. Back To The White House 21
5. Fare Well, Two Arms 24
6. Seems Like Old Times 28
7. Future Tense 42
8. Late Moments With Mr. Lincoln 46
9. Dietary Issues 53
10. Double Doppelgangers 59
11. Nice Workout If You Can Get It 63
12. Judgment At Harrisburg 68
13. Black Gold 76
14. Third Time This Week 82
15. Eight Fingers 94
16. O, Tannenbaum! 98
17. The Times, They Are A-Changin' 107
18. Late Again 112
19. Just My Daguerreotype 125
20. At The Circus 132
21. Hercules vs. The Christians 137
22. The Bestiarius Of Our Lives 151
23. The Invincible Woman 157
24. The Arrows Of Time 168
25. Empressive 176
26. Decline And Winter 188
27. Mr. Kobayashi 193
28. The Chaplin Studio, 1933 199
29. GreenAcres Is The Place To Be 202
30. The Gambling Den 216
31. Designated Driver 226
32. Richfield Tower 231
33. Cornered 241
34. Like Father, Unlike Son 250
35. Mopping Up 257
36. The Party's Over 263

37. The Single Changeable Timeline   270
38. Meet The Family   278

Historical Notes   289
Acknowledgments   291
About the Author   293
Preview: Chronicles Of A Time Traveler   295
Also by Doug Molitor   299

For Mike Moberly

"What have my books been from The Time Machine *through* World Brain, *but the clearest insistence on the insecurity of progress and the possibility of human degeneration and extinction? I think the odds are against man but that it is still worthwhile in spite of the odds."*

H. G. WELLS, 1939

1

THE PAST IS PROLOGUE

"YOU SOCKDOLOGIZING OLD MAN-TRAP!" concluded the actor on the Ford's stage. The line brought down the house. President Lincoln opened his mouth to let out a huge laugh. Someone knocked me down, leaping from the next box to land beside us, making the floorboards shudder.

Time slowed to a crawl. I saw a series of magic lantern slides, each a frozen fraction of a second:

John Wilkes Booth, instinctively turning to face the intruder at his left—even as his right hand tightened on the trigger.

Ariyl, her biceps dramatically sculpted in the gaslight, delivering a sledgehammer uppercut.

The gun barrel discharging flame, setting fire to Lincoln's head.

Booth flying outwards.

Ariyl's fist turning his head at a weird angle.

Mary Todd Lincoln turning to her husband with a quizzical expression.

Then time resumed its regular pace, as Booth landed headfirst below with an audible crack. The uproarious laughter went out like a candle, replaced by a chorus of shrieks. Mainly from women in the orchestra seats, who recognized their idol.

Lincoln leapt up, swatting embers from his singed hair. The rocker of his chair rolled onto my finger, but I was too electrified to feel the pain.

I sprang to my feet and stared down at Booth—now a broken doll sprawled on the edge of a marionette stage, his smoking gun still clutched in one hand, and a dagger in his other. He was minus a couple of teeth. Remarkably, he was still alive.

The First Lady screamed and swooned. The president's guest, an army major, sprang to her aid and caught her at the last second. Mrs. L gone limp was heavier than she looked; the major staggered. His date hastened to help him support the load.

"Mr. President, are you all right?" shouted the major.

"I am half-deafened," exclaimed Lincoln above the panic. "The report of the gun came right beside my head!" He cupped a hand to his injured left ear, wincing.

"Arrest that man! He just tried to murder the president," the major hollered at the gallery below.

A soldier jumped from the audience to train a pistol on Booth.

"Don't you even twitch, you rebel dog!"

But twitching would be all Booth would be doing from now on, judging from the sharp tilt of the actor's head on his neck and the scarlet pool spreading from the back of his skull.

The only things I could see move on Booth were his bloody lips, and he sure wasn't yelling *"Sic semper tyrannis."* He seemed to be mumbling over and over, "All for nothing."

Lincoln touched the back of his head again, saw there was no blood on his fingers, then glanced at Booth's twisted form below. Then he gave me a curious look, and finally raised his gaze to Ariyl. It wasn't often old Abe found himself at eye-level with someone.

"Young lady...?"

She rolled her eyes, amused. "Oh, please, call me Ariyl."

"Ariel? Like the sprite in Mr. Shakespeare's play?"

"Sure. Whoever he is. And this is Professor David Preston. He's with me."

The great man nodded at me. "Professor. Well, Miss Ariel," he smiled wryly, "if it was your intention to gain an audience with me, you have found the surest way."

Ariyl beamed at me in triumph, apparently expecting congratulations.

I just stared back, wondering what the holy hell was going to happen now.

THREE SOLDIERS BURST into President Lincoln's box with rifles aimed at Ariyl, and as she smacked their weapons aside and punched them out, it seemed life was not going to get dull anytime soon.

The audience below was a riot of excited shouts and screams resulting from Booth's misfired shot and abrupt descent.

The house lights came up. More soldiers barged through the door, barrels waving every which way.

"Put up your weapons, gentlemen!" shouted their Commander in Chief. "This lady has just saved my life!"

"It's true!" agreed Major Henry Rathbone, the president's guest.

Every soldier who was still conscious obeyed Lincoln's order, except one keyed-up type who kept his rifle aimed at Ariyl's heart. In an eye blink, she yanked the firearm from his grip and broke it over her thigh.

Lincoln gaped for a second. Recovering, he addressed the remaining soldiers.

"Sergeant, I shall require an armed escort for my party back to the Executive Mansion. Please wait for us outside the box."

"Yes, sir!" gulped the sergeant. He pushed all the soldiers (including those who'd just come to) out into the hallway. "You men, take up posts at every door! No one is to enter this corridor!" He turned back to the president. "We are at your disposal. Whenever you're ready, sir." He closed the door behind him.

Lincoln knelt by his wife, who was still in a swoon on the floor. Major Rathbone's fiancée, Clara Harris, was fanning her, to no avail.

Lincoln patted her wrists. "Mary, dear, are you all right?"

"Permit me, sir," I said, kneeling beside her. I checked her pulse.

It was steady. "She just needs some smelling salts. We should get her out of here."

Major Rathbone pulled Lincoln aside for some urgent whispered words.

There was a knock at the door. Rathbone opened it, spoke to the sergeant, then returned to his president.

"Mr. John Wilkes Booth just died."

We had crossed the Rubicon, history-wise. We were headed into the unknown. But if I'm being completely honest, I enjoyed seeing Ariyl smash Booth's face in.

"God rest his soul," sighed Lincoln, who was a lot more forgiving than I was.

Below, soldiers were carrying Booth's body out of the auditorium, which was still bedlam.

Lincoln stepped to the front of the box and held up his hands. "I beseech you all to be calm!" he announced.

The panic in the room subsided, and he went on.

"The young lady you see beside me prevented an assassin from killing me. She has my profound thanks."

Someone clapped, and Lincoln took up the applause. The whole house began clapping and cheering. Ariyl blushed and waved.

Finally, as the ovation faded, Lincoln signaled for silence and went on: "The man is dead, and we are all safe now. I bid you, please return to your seats and allow the players to finish their performance." There was an awkward pause. No one was really in a mood for a comedy now.

I could see Lincoln taking the temperature of the crowd. He continued: "I am reminded of the circus owner whose tiger escaped. After it was recaptured, the owner said, 'the show must go on.' In that case, the tiger had eaten no one, and thus it was still possible for every single member of the audience to get his money's worth."

The audience broke into relieved laughter. It got a bigger laugh than "you sockdologizing old mantrap!"

"Please, let the play resume," he urged at last, and sat down in his rocker.

The actors came out of the wings and applauded Lincoln, an

ovation that was taken up by the cheering audience. It went on for some time, but Lincoln just nodded then gestured to the players.

The house lights finally went down, and *Our American Cousin* resumed.

Once it was dark, Lincoln murmured to Ariyl and me, "We must depart."

Lincoln started to help his wife up, but Ariyl whispered, "I got her," and scooped the hefty Mary Todd Lincoln up in her arms as if cradling a child.

Abe looked more impressed by this feat than any other she'd performed.

* * *

Outside Ford's Theatre, Major Rathbone and Miss Harris stood at the carriage door and bade the president a reluctant good-bye.

Six cavalrymen galloped up to offer an escort. They had their sidearms out and were scanning the darkness for any possible attack.

"Mr. President, may I recommend that you deploy a couple of these men to Secretary Seward's home?" I said. "In a few minutes Booth's fellow conspirator, a man named Lewis Powell, will try to stab Mr. Seward to death and will severely injure several others."

Rathbone gave Lincoln an alarmed look. Now he really suspected me.

But the president said, "Major, have two men ride to the secretary's residence on Madison Place at Lafayette Park, and offer him protection." Then he turned to me. "What about Vice President Johnson?"

I shook my head. "He's in no danger. George Atzerodt, the conspirator assigned to him, lost his nerve and is out getting drunk."

"I hope not with Andrew," Lincoln said under his breath.

Rathbone swallowed his objections and barked orders to the mounted men.

The presidential carriage lurched off toward Pennsylvania Avenue, with four cavalrymen in escort, as the other two raced ahead to Seward's house.

As we departed, I looked back at Clara Harris and her husband-to-be Major Rathbone, and shuddered. Henry Rathbone's suspicions were more than mere caution. I knew later in life he would grow insanely jealous and paranoid. I knew of Clara's sad fate, and I also knew there wasn't a chance in the world she would believe me if I warned her.

MARY LINCOLN LAY on the floor of the carriage, her face covered with a handkerchief, her feet raised and resting on the seat beside me. She was still in shock.

"I just want to go home," Mary kept murmuring to herself.

Abe stroked her brow reassuringly. "We'll be there soon, Mother."

She fell silent. Lincoln turned his gaze on us.

"Professor, Miss Ari-el..." (he pronounced it to rhyme with "merry hell") "...the uncomfortable duty falls to me, to inquire how you knew that Mr. Booth would be in my box, intending to murder me."

I exchanged a silent look with Ariyl, but neither of us felt ready to answer.

"Major Rathbone urged on me his theory that you two must be conspirators yourselves. Your further knowledge about an attack on Secretary Seward certainly supports that contention. However, it does not explain why you have acted to foil our assassinations."

"We're not in any conspiracy! I just happened to see Booth go in with that gun," began Ariyl.

I cut her off, annoyed. "Forget it, Ariyl. You just changed history in a radical way. It doesn't *matter* what you tell him now, or whether he believes us. There's no way this world results in you being born, or me!"

Ariyl shrugged. She knew it was true.

"When you say you just changed history, I suspect you are not merely employing a poetic turn of phrase. Am I correct?" pressed Lincoln.

"Yes, Mr. President. I meant it literally," I said. "I come from a hundred and fifty years in your future. Ariyl is from a century beyond that. In her era, science will make it possible to revisit historical events. Your assassination at the hand of John Wilkes Booth tonight at 10:15 P.M. is a fact every school child learns."

(Well, maybe not in Ariyl's world, but certainly in mine...well, in better-funded schools, anyway.)

Lincoln pulled out his watch and opened it. It read 10:22 P.M. He quietly closed the cover then gazed into my eyes as he pondered what I had said.

I was surprised at how haggard he was—even more than at his final sitting for a photographer, just two months before Ford's Theatre. It wasn't just his dry unkempt hair, such a contrast with the neatly trimmed chin whiskers. It wasn't the bony face with its exaggerated nose and ears, drooping eyelids, cadaverous cheeks, and deeply etched lines in his face: That was the beloved ugly Lincoln whose face I'd known from childhood. Tonight he looked worse—truly unwell and in desperate need of sleep.

Yet old Abe's gaze was magnetic. I'd met a few politicians in my day who had a similar kind of charm, but none whose charisma approached Lincoln's. For all his palpable exhaustion, his eyes sparkled; his voice and face radiated warmth, kindness, and intense curiosity. I instinctively trusted this man. I could not lie to this man. And there really wasn't any point.

At last he spoke.

"Forgive a possibly foolish question...but how could children of the future learn the alleged fact of my murder, since you have prevented it?"

"Because that's now another future," explained Ariyl. "We came from it, but we've branched off it."

"And can no longer return to it," I added, trying not to sound peeved.

"I know it sounds incredible, Abe," Ariyl said.

I cringed at her familiarity.

"But it really is the truth," she assured him.

Lincoln nodded then rubbed his eyes. "A few nights ago, I dreamt that I heard weeping in the White House," he began.

"And you went to the East Room and found a body lying in state, and you were told it was the president who had been assassinated," I replied.

The president looked astounded. "I have told no one of this dream, except my friend Ward Lamon. I am thunderstruck that he should breach such a confidence."

"I've never met Lamon, sir. But years after the assassination, he revealed the story of your dream. It's been common knowledge for more than a century."

Lincoln shook his head, marveling. "The fabled razor of Brother William of Occam would have me shave away everything but the simplest explanation. I confess I am unable to conceive of a simpler one than yours, however fantastic its premise. Might I inquire how you make such a journey into history?"

Ariyl showed him the torus-shaped gem around her neck. "A Time Crystal. Don't ask me how it works. I'm no scientist. I couldn't even tell you how your telegraph works." She paused. "You have those right? The clicky things?"

"Indeed we do," chuckled Lincoln. "Would you be willing to demonstrate your device?"

"Uh..." she began.

I cut in: "The problem is, sir...the nature of history is such that if, by way of demonstration, we were to journey away from this era, we have no guarantee that we can return to this precise moment, or anytime near it."

Lincoln nodded. "No man can step into the same river twice. I'm familiar with Heraclitus."

"You have a great understanding of philosophy, sir," I said, genuinely impressed.

"I was always more keen on reading than on rail splitting," he said wryly. "Alas, I have a Cabinet full of skeptics, and I had hoped I might be able to assuage their doubts."

Secretly, I was glad we couldn't do that—while I trusted Lincoln's judgment, that confidence did not extend to telling all his appointees about the existence of time travel.

"Well, there's more than one way to skin a cat," the president mused. "It occurs to me if the date of my assassination was history to you, you must know the dates of other dire events yet to come."

"I could predict some major earthquakes, Mr. President. But nothing in the next few years. And as for anything that relies on human decisions—elections, assassinations, wars—Ariyl has just changed the direction of history. I'm confident your men will find Lewis Powell at Secretary Seward's home. But in the days and years beyond that, your actions and others' will make the world increasingly different."

The president said nothing, so I ventured some advice: "Perhaps, sir, it is better that only you know our secret. After all, we are once again headed into an unknown future."

Lincoln looked dissatisfied with my answer. I knew how he felt. We were on this journey together now.

"But at least now you'll be at the helm, sir," I added. "In the history *I* grew up learning, you died from the bullet that you just dodged."

"I did not dodge it, Professor. It dodged me, when Miss Ari-el slew my assassin." He gave an admiring grin. "With one blow. I've seen many a fight, young lady, but never a man hit that hard, nor knocked that far."

"He had it coming," said Ariyl.

"I am in your debt. I do find it awkward to admit that I admired Mr. Booth's thespian ability greatly. More than once, I invited him to come see me."

"Well, he wasn't an admirer of yours," I said. "I saw him three nights ago, outside the White...uh, the Executive Mansion, listening to you speak."

2

CALL ME UNRELIABLE

TRIGGER WARNING: IF YOU SLIP INTO A COMA reading backstory and exposition about how time travel could and could not work, this chapter is not for you. The story picks up right where I left off, in the chapter after this.

That said...

If you read *Confessions of a Time Traveler*, I fear I have an additional confession that did not make it into that book.

Ariyl Moro did not, as I wrote, confiscate the wasp-sized flying drone camera ("dram") that I had taken off Lon Chaney's discarded Wolf Man makeup. Why is that important? I'll get to that.

But first let me get this off my chest: I lied to you about that. Which makes me the proverbial unreliable narrator.

At the time, it seemed that I had good reason. Although what liar doesn't feel that way?

In my case, the goal was to protect history from further alterations.

I say "further" because I have some possibly distressing news for you: the history you currently believe is yours is not original history. You'll have to take my word for that, since I no longer have a shred of proof aside from my memories, which I recorded in the first two books.

There was a first draft of history, in which my ex-roomie from UCLA Andy Graise scored a record five home runs in a Dodgers-Braves game in May 2011. He died that same night in the crash of his private plane. And in that original timeline, I eventually gained a measure of fame for discovering the long-lost Minoan Temple of the Dolphins in a sea cave on Santorini on October sixth, 2013. I was famous enough that certain people in the future knew (will know) the date of my find.

But don't bother looking for either of these events in your history books—no one on this earth remembers them but me. Well, two if you count Ariyl Moro. And maybe three.

My discovery was never announced by the Greek government, which seized control of my dig, my phone, my laptop, and all my notes. Maybe my find will be published someday. I can only hope.

More definitely, Andy Graise never hit five homers, and never will—he was cut from the team, and forced to sell the plane he was originally fated to crash in. He wound up teaching high school P.E. and living in the same West Los Angeles apartment building that I do.

Additionally, certain names have been changed to protect the innocent. And the guilty, like me.

But here's the thing:

In the first draft of history, the world of 2109 A.D. was—or rather, will be—well, actually, *would* have been—a utopia populated by gene-tooled superhumans like Ariyl Moro, Jon Ludlo, and Dylila Duprae. War, poverty, crime, disease, aging, and even death had been banished by N-Tec, the artificial intelligence that was supposed to run planet Earth for the benefit of all humanity. N-Tec wielded the godlike power of nanotechnology, with microscopic molecular assemblers capable of creating any physical object humans desired in virtually limitless supply, almost instantaneously.

The only real drawback to the world of N-Tec was that paradise was ultimately boring for people.

N-Tec then invented time travel.

Worse, it allowed humans to visit past eras for recreational purposes. And, I suppose, research.

The idea was that N-Tec had built-in safeguards that monitored the two Time Crystals worn by pairs of time tourists, and the instant any traveler made a non-negligible alteration to history, N-Tec would instantly erase the trip and auto-return its wearer to 2109. Essentially, he or she would never have left 2109, though as long as they had followed the rules, they would be permitted to retain the memories of their adventure.

Sounds foolproof, right?

Alas, one of the Time Travel Agency's clients—its very last client—was Jon Ludlo (b. 2086, d. 1954). He took his time tour with Ariyl Moro.

Ludlo managed to prove that even the smartest artificial intelligence can still be fooled by sociopathic human madness. Armed with a backdoor password bequeathed to him by his software engineer grandfather, Ludlo disabled N-Tec's safeguards, and as soon as he was back in time, he began messing with history.

He got Ty Cobb to sign a baseball in 1908 then traded it to Andy for a ball autographed by Andy; then he stole a golden minotaur figure from the Temple of the Dolphins and buried it nearby so that I found it some 3,600 years later.

Emboldened, Ludlo then began stealing crucial objects from the past like the Declaration of Independence and Einstein's atom bomb letter to FDR. This created warped versions of history in which there was no America, or in which the Nazis won World War II.

Ariyl and I discovered that by visiting the same eras and stopping Ludlo from stealing these things, we could short-circuit the changes and get history back on track.

But we never did figure out what it was that Ludlo stole, or did, that erased Ariyl's home era—that took paradise and put up a post-apocalypse parking lot.

It wasn't the Declaration or the Einstein letter.

Nor was it when Ariyl and that other formidable future female Dylila Duprae abducted Ralph Nader and threw the 2000 election to Al Gore. All that did was land Gore in federal lockup, make George

W. Bush president-for-life, and destroy civilization with a green-house climate: Los Angeles in 2109 became a blistering desert, while New York drowned under the rising seas.

Neither was it when Jon Ludlo attempted to make an all-star snuff film out of the 1948 Oscars: that resulted in a reactionary America which elected segregationist Strom Thurmond as president. We encountered that mutant timeline in 1954, and with the aid of three actors named Karloff, Lugosi, and Chaney, we derailed that disaster.

But crucially, Ariyl dragged the 1948 progenitor of the Thurmond timeline—Ludlo—into that warped future where she was then forced to kill him to save my life.

That entire timeline then dissolved into impossibility...and nearly took us with it.

As a result, Time Travel Agent Dylila Duprae made a command decision: to get back her and Ariyl's N-Tec era, she must erase Jon Ludlo's entire trip through time, starting at his first destination in 1908. That, of course, meant that Ariyl and I would never meet at Dodger Stadium in 2011, nor go off exploring time in 2013.

I refused to accept that decision. Before Dylila could accomplish her mission, I convinced Ariyl to drop me off on Santorini in 2013 the instant after we left on our time travels. I assumed that when Dylila diverted Ludlo, her doing so would forever wall off my timeline from their version of 2109, and I would never see Ariyl again. But my one solace was I would remember our time together.

But those memories came at a price.

The timeline somehow shifted around me.

I AM STILL GRAPPLING with the logic of what happened.

I stepped into my own footprints in 2013. When I'd left, Andy was a dead baseball legend. The instant I returned, he'd never had his big day, or died at the end of it.

How could history transform itself around me, leaving me the only witness?

· · ·

My friend, neighbor, ex-physics prof, and time-travel-fiction fanatic, Sven Bergstrom, age ninety-two, explained to me that there are three types of universes in which time travel is possible:

1) The Single Unchangeable Timeline: You can only visit the past or the future, but you cannot change history in any significant way. Whether you know it or not, whatever has happened and will happen, including your time travel, is already predestined. The implication of this timeline is that free will is an illusion. (This would be the universe of *The Time Machine, The Time Tunnel, Berkeley Square, The Terminator,* and *Terminator 3.*)

2) The Multiple Changeable Timelines: Also known as "Multiple Worlds". Any act of time travel branches off a new timeline whose outcome will be at least slightly different, and perhaps radically different, from the time traveler's own history (*Terminator 2, Déjà Vu, Source Code.*)

3) The Single Changeable Timeline: There is only one ultimate history. The past can be changed multiple times, information can be brought back from the future to alter the present, and the time traveler can witness and even experience physical changes resulting from those alterations: A changing family photo, a scar appearing, someone vanishing because they were killed in the past (*Back to the Future* trilogy, *Looper, Frequency.*)

I thought we were in the Type 2 multiverse, where there were infinite possible histories. But Sven thinks it's Type 3...and that history is shifting around me because I'm a time traveler. I didn't buy it, at first.

Then on Election Day 2016, my world was turned upside-down. I don't mean the election results; I'm talking about my entire place in history.

Because Dylila Duprae showed up—in my timeline, not hers—and told me I had to stop Ariyl from saving Abraham Lincoln, to rescue humanity from extinction.

3

APRIL ELEVENTH, 1865

A FTER SHE'D MANHANDLED ME AND NEARLY totaled my car on Election Day 2016, I had promised Dylila Duprae to use the Time Crystal she gave me to go back to 1865. My mission, which I knew was more important than my legitimate beefs with Dylila, was to prevent Ariyl's interference with history. In that, if nothing else, Dylila and I were of one mind.

Departing modern Los Angeles, I experienced the spatial move as if I were flying eastward across North America while a hundred and fifty-two winters and summers flickered white and green-brown beneath my feet.

The world snapped back into focus as I stood beside a tree on the north lawn of the White House on the foggy evening of April eleventh, 1865. The smell of lilacs and wood smoke hung in the air.

No one saw me, except for a stray goat that looked up from her supper then went back to grazing.

The Time Crystal was programmed to minimize any change to history by my presence, so my sheltered arrival spot was to be expected. But I also knew a rogue time traveler named Jon Ludlo had removed the most important safeguards—the ones meant to instantly erase any measurable change to history. That was why I'd deliberately arrived three days before the Lincoln assassination, to make sure I had a head start on Ariyl.

I was also aware that this evening, April eleventh, Abraham Lincoln would make the most fateful speech of his life. As a historian —yeah, we archaeologists are partly that—I wanted to be there for it.

The North Front of the White House was blazingly lit by hundreds of torches, candles, lamps, lanterns, and a large bonfire. An iron fence and army guards kept the massive throng off the portico steps. The trees were much shorter than those we see today. Nevertheless they held dozens of people who had clambered into them for a better look; observers also climbed onto the statue of Jefferson at the center of the circular drive.

I found a shadowed spot over to one side, near the back of the crowd, where I could watch.

In the second-story window, just over the front door, stood the Great Emancipator, reading his speech in his high Illinois twang while a full-bearded man held a kerosene lamp for him.

Lincoln was arguing for the acceptance of a newly-formed Louisiana state government: "The amount of constituency, so to speak, on which the new Louisiana government rests, would be more satisfactory to all, if it contained fifty, thirty, or even twenty thousand, instead of only about twelve thousand, as it does."

As he finished each page, he let it flutter to the floor, and twelve-year-old Tad Lincoln, dressed in a miniature Union army uniform, snatched it up.

"It is also unsatisfactory to some that the elective franchise is not given to the colored man. I would myself prefer that it were now conferred on the very intelligent, and on those who serve our cause as soldiers."

There! Limited as it was, this was the very first time an American president had endorsed the right of black men to vote.

"God damn him!" whispered a voice four yards to my right.

I automatically turned and saw three, maybe four men in their twenties standing in the shadows a few feet back from the edge of the crowd. The speaker, unshaven, with beady eyes and greasy black hair, looked like he'd dressed in a hurry. Then to my shock, I recognized his stylishly clad, thick-mustachioed companion: John Wilkes Booth, his classical features twisted into a snarl of pure hatred.

I really had a front row seat for this bit of history, a lot closer than was wise. I knew what was coming next.

"That means nigger citizenship!" growled Booth. "You've got a pistol, Lewis. Shoot him now."

The third man had to be Booth's fellow conspirator, Lewis Powell. He couldn't have been more than twenty-one; he was clean-shaven and wore a low-crowned hat over a mop of hair. The ex-Confederate soldier reconnoitered the crowd with a practiced eye.

"You must be mad, John," he softly drawled. "This mob would tear us to pieces."

"Now, by God, I'll put him through," Booth muttered to the first man, whom I now realized was yet another member of the conspiracy, David Herold.

"That is the last speech he'll ever make," spat Booth, shoving his way through his companions...and right past me. He stopped, staring into my face. Belatedly I realized I must be glaring at him with as much hate as he had for Lincoln.

Now Herold noticed me. "Was he listening to us?"

"I certainly was not!" I scoffed with disdain. "Why should I care what a passel of drunken ruffians are mumbling about?"

Booth eyed me with lethal calm. "I think we must assume he was."

I felt a pistol barrel jab my kidney. It was gripped by Powell, who murmured, "Come with me, and do not utter a sound."

"No!" I barked. My strident refusal startled them. They looked around to see who else heard. I continued loudly: "You're right, Mr. Powell. If you do anything untoward, this mob *will* tear you and Mr. Herold here limb from limb."

"Booth, he knows our names!" hissed Herold.

"Shut your fool mouth!" snapped the actor.

Powell opened his long coat and held his 1858 Whitney revolver inside it. His gun was masked from the rest of the audience, but I could see it was aimed at the window where Lincoln stood.

"You love Father Abraham, do you?" he whispered. "Then do as I say, or I will risk the mob's vengeance here and now."

That shut me up. I certainly hadn't come back in time just to move Lincoln's assassination up three days. That would still cause enough historical changes that Ariyl and I would never get home. But I knew if I walked into the night mist with these fanatics, my personal history would end in minutes, with me face down in a pond. There were four of them, they were armed, and Ariyl wouldn't arrive for three days. I didn't have a lot of options.

Booth tugged down his hat and turned up his collar. "See to him. I shall meet you back at Mrs. Surratt's house," he whispered, then strode off.

The fourth man, whom I could not recognize in the dark, departed with him. I suspect it was his friend Louis Weichmann, who would later attest to Booth's words tonight.

Now it was just Powell and Herold.

Powell cocked the hidden pistol he still had aimed at Lincoln. "Make your choice, sir. Will you come?"

Words were the only weapon I had.

"Booth just left you two holding the bag," I said. "And he will again. He'll catch a bullet, but you two will hang. Slowly. They'll botch the job at the Washington Arsenal, so you'll both kick and squirm for five minutes before you finally shit your pants and strangle."

Powell tried to laugh, but it died in his throat. I'm a lousy poker player—one look at me, and he must have seen I wasn't bluffing.

"You shut up!" seethed Herold, grabbing me. That was all the break I needed. I leg-tripped Herold backwards into Powell, who dropped his pistol. I swung my fist at Powell's nose. Powell dodged, and instead I hit the man who had just run over to us, and who immediately hit me back a lot harder.

* * *

WHEN I WOKE up in a cell in the Washington, D.C. police station, I learned I was under arrest for assaulting an officer.

The other men in the fight had escaped, the policeman had no idea who they were, and I couldn't exactly tell him about the Lincoln conspiracy. So I apologized. I blamed my errant blow on strong drink and unsavory companions. I threw myself on the mercy of the court.

The magistrate sentenced me to three days in jail, which would mean I'd be released on the morning of the fifteenth. Hours too late to stop Ariyl from altering history.

My guard on the night shift was Ernest, who wasn't the sharpest knife in the drawer, but he *was* the heaviest club on the pile.

At dinnertime on April twelfth, I saw that Ernest hung the keys on a peg four feet from my cell. Too far to reach with just my arm, but not too far if I undid my bowtie and fastened it to the end of my spoon, which I then bent into a U-shape. With just the right upswing, I would be able to hook the keys with it. Simple.

On my thirty-sixth try, Ernest returned, confiscated my neckwear, and announced I would have no more utensils for my meals.

At dawn on April thirteenth, Ernest entered my cell to find my bunk empty. "Help! He escaped!" cried Ernest.

But while Ernest was not himself sharp, his peripheral vision was. His gaze strayed up to where I was suspended over his head, my feet pressed against the wall and my hands gripping the tops of the bars—not so easy with my fingers still greasy from eating supper without a spoon.

Ernest yanked one of my feet off the wall and I landed on the floor. It would be a while before I would be able to inhale.

"Never mind," Ernest announced to the other guard as he locked the cell door.

The evening of April fourteenth, Ernest found me lying on the floor holding my stomach. "Oww, I'm dying! Get me a priest!"

Ernest bent close enough for me to break my supper dish over his head. He laid me back on the floor with one punch. Unlike in the movies, a thick ceramic bowl cracked across his skull did not render him unconscious. It just gave him a painful bump on his head—one that he promised he'd return with interest once we were alone on the night shift.

Did I mention the guy outweighed me by eighty pounds?

Ariyl was right; I should not try to fight my way out of these messes.

Fortunately, my final escape attempt was successful: During his late supper break at 10:00 P.M., Ernest left the jail for more whiskey to medicate his injury.

Distracted, he forgot to lock the cell door. I was gone before the other guard realized it.

* * *

OF COURSE, I was too late to prevent Ariyl from saving the life of Abraham Lincoln. I'd been conflicted about that mission from the beginning. Maybe I failed because on some level I wanted to fail.

The point was, we were now headed into a different future that would never result in my home era. I might not be born in this version of history; my parents might not be. Or maybe they'd have married different people. Or maybe I'd be born, but with a different first name, a different calling in life, completely different memories. Regardless, there would be no place for me in the 2016 to come. Thomas Mann was right—I couldn't go home again.

4

BACK TO THE WHITE HOUSE

" A ND THAT'S WHY I HAD TO SAVE YOUR LIFE, Abe," explained
Ariyl as the carriage clip-clopped up Pennsylvania Avenue.
"David said it was because you were killed, that black people in the
South were practically slaves for another century. Right, David?"

Lincoln looked at me for an explanation. This was my punish-
ment for teaching Ariyl history: I now had to explain a timeline that
she had just rendered completely moot.

"In 1877, in a backroom deal to win the Electoral College, the
Republican Party agreed to immediately end Reconstruction. Something I'm sure you would not have stood for if you were alive."

"As yet, we haven't even agreed upon what Reconstruction will
encompass, much less passed that law," said Lincoln.

"It will include federal troops guaranteeing blacks' safety and
voting rights in the South. Congress passed the act in 1866 after
armed whites massacred eighty black people in New Orleans and
Memphis and burned their neighborhoods."

"Dear Lord," breathed Lincoln. "Will this bitter war never be
done?"

"With the end of Reconstruction, the South began what we call
the Jim Crow era: disenfranchisement, segregation of the races, white

terrorism, and lynchings. It took until the 1960s to begin restoring blacks' civil rights."

Lincoln was devastated. "Six hundred thousand lives it cost to end slavery. I had thought our peace might amount to something better than what you describe."

"Sir, that was *our* history," I reminded him. "It doesn't need to be yours."

Ariyl squeezed Lincoln's arm, imploring: "And it won't be! I did what I did because this country, this *world*, needs you. You'll show them the...you know. The better angels of their nature."

Well, she'd learned something from that Civil War vid she played, after all.

At that, Lincoln looked up and managed a wry smile. "I admire the strength of your conviction." He glanced at his wrist. "And of your right arm."

"Oh, sorry!" she said, releasing her grip.

"No need to apologize, Miss Ari-el. That arm, after all, was my deliverance. I do not favor the phrase 'the weaker sex' for I have seen many a strong woman. I know how much work it takes to forge such an arm. May I inquire, did you ever split rails?"

"No, but I work out a lot."

He seemed bewildered.

She explained, "That means I lift weights."

Huh? In our several days together, I'd never seen Ariyl work out. Unless we were counting her fights as workouts. I guess throwing men around *was* a bit like pumping iron. God knows she was sure jacked when the fights were over.

Like she was now. She flexed her chiseled biceps for Abe.

"Back in my early days, I was also an arm wrestler of some repute," mused Lincoln. "I wonder, Miss Ari-el, which of us might fare better in such a contest."

"Only one way to find out," smiled Ariyl.

"Oooohhhh!" moaned Mary Lincoln, possibly fainting in her sleep.

· · ·

As the carriage crunched up the gravel drive to the North Face, shots echoed in the night.

Lincoln stepped out of the carriage listening intently. More pistol shots.

"That sounds like it's coming from Lafayette Park." He turned to me. "I pray I sent enough men."

"We must get you safely inside, sir," said a cavalry officer.

Abe turned back and saw Ariyl was carrying the unconscious Mary Lincoln. He walked along with them, and I followed.

At the door of the White House, Mrs. Lincoln revived. "Put me down, I pray you," she told Ariyl. "I can walk now."

Ariyl set her on her feet.

We all turned at the sound of horse hooves galloping up. A heavyset Washington policeman in black uniform and bobby-style helmet leapt off the horse and puffed up to the Lincolns at the doorway.

"Mr. President," he slurred through a prodigious mustache, "I am here to protect you."

Mary Lincoln stepped between Abe and the cop. "Mr. Parker, is it? Our supposed bodyguard who was three hours late for duty tonight? Where were you when my husband was nearly murdered? In a saloon, I'll warrant, to judge from your breath."

"Now, Mother," began her husband.

"Leave these premises, you miserable sot," she declared. "You may consider your position on the police force at an end if I have anything to say about it." She gave Abe a stern look: "And I shall."

She turned on her heel and went inside. Abe went after her, with Ariyl and me bringing up the rear.

John Frederick Parker stood there looking poleaxed as the butler shut the door on him.

5

FARE WELL, TWO ARMS

THE OLD RAIL-SPLITTER WAS IN FOR QUITE A contest. He had stripped to shirtsleeves, and now focused all his formidable will and muscle on putting Ariyl's right arm down. She truly looked like she was having a hard time. A bead of perspiration rolling down his brow, his arm shaking with the effort, he slowly pushed her hand toward the tabletop. I was glad that, for once, she was letting a man win. If anyone deserved his pride left intact, it was Abraham Lincoln.

But with her knuckle a quarter inch above the polished walnut, Ariyl reversed the direction, brought his hand up, and then firmly pressed it down to the table.

He let out an exhausted breath. "Miss Ari-el, you have the strongest arm of anyone I have ever seen."

"Thanks, Abe. You want to try the other arm?"

He shook his head. "I fear my right arm is my stronger one."

"No, I meant, you can use both." She put up her arm again. "Let's see how you fare!"

I cringed.

After a second, Lincoln threw back his head and laughed loudly.

. . .

WE WALKED out of Lincoln's second-floor office—which one day would be known as the Lincoln Bedroom—only to find most of his Cabinet assembled, waiting for him in the anteroom, looking flustered.

William Seward, his Secretary of State, was a hawk-beaked man whose pillow-head mane made it evident he had spent the last few days in bed. Still, he had managed to get properly dressed, despite one broken arm in a sling, and the neck brace that served as a cast for his fractured jaw. He looked quietly appalled at the spectacle of Lincoln in his shirtsleeves. Lincoln took the hint and shrugged his coat back on.

"I apologize, Mr. Secretary," said the president. "Allow me to introduce Professor David Preston and Miss Ari-el Moro, the young lady who prevented my murder." We politely shook hands with half a dozen Cabinet officers as their names were mentioned.

"Where's the Vice President?" Lincoln asked.

"Indisposed," scowled Seward.

Lincoln shook his head, understanding all too well.

"Miss Moro and I, we were trying to establish who was the superior arm wrestler."

"Evidently," fumed Seward.

"It turns out, she is," allowed Abe.

"But in any event, I thank God you are safe, sir."

"And I, you," said Lincoln. "It's been quite a week for you. I heard of your unfortunate accident the other day."

"You were thrown from your carriage, I believe," I ventured solicitously.

Seward's gaze drilled into me. "I nearly suffered worse tonight, Professor. I understand you alerted the president to my peril. Might I inquire as to how...?"

Lincoln held up his hand. "Suffice it to say, their information saved both of our lives. As is often the case with those who spy for us, I'm afraid I am not at liberty to divulge its source."

"Not at liberty...?" sputtered Seward. "May I point out that this city is still full of *Confederate* spies?"

"I can give you a complete list of the conspirators," I said.

"No doubt," snapped Seward.

Secretary of War Edwin Stanton said, "Our men have already apprehended this Powell character and his landlady, a Mrs. Surratt."

"She's actually innocent," I put in.

Seward really gave me the stink-eye. "Is she indeed?" He turned to Lincoln. "Mr. President, may we converse in private?"

"I am satisfied that these people can be trusted," said Lincoln mildly.

Seward grew exasperated. "Then may I reiterate my private advice to you—that you not speak of Negro enfranchisement while we still have troops in the field and no legitimate governments in most of the rebellious states? The situation is a tinderbox. If you think the late Mr. Booth was alone in his implacable opposition, you are greatly mistaken."

"Nevertheless, Bill, we must move in the right direction, however cautiously we do it."

"The South will never stand for it!" exclaimed the secretary.

"They wouldn't stand for losing the war, either," remarked the president. "And yet they have. Nor losing their slaves. And yet they will."

Attorney General James Speed put in, "Mr. President, the Thirteenth Amendment has yet to be ratified. We're not even in full agreement as to how many states constitute the required three quarters under the present circumstances. In my judgment, it is far too soon to speak in public about Negroes voting."

Lincoln looked at Seward and the other Cabinet officers, who all nodded.

"Well, perhaps you are right," he sighed, wearily. "It *has* seemed to rub salt in wounds all too recently received." He turned to us. "Professor, Miss Ari-el, please allow me to express my heartfelt gratitude once more...and to bid you goodnight."

This was it—we were getting the bum's rush. If I were smart, I'd keep my mouth shut. But I'm not.

"Mr. President, you were right to speak for the franchise. Ending slavery is not enough. You will need a fourteenth and a fifteenth amendment, to guarantee former slaves citizenship and the right to vote."

"And don't forget women!" said Ariyl.

Every jaw dropped as they all turned to her.

"Women *are* gonna get the vote, guys," she said. "Why not do the right thing now, instead a hundred years from now?"

"Fifty," I murmured to Lincoln.

There was a lot of shocked huffing and puffing and "Why, I never!" from the assembled collection of muttonchops and Old Testament beards.

But I saw the ghost of a smile on Abe's face. He put his hand on my back and escorted me to the door.

"If a woman can save a president's life, I think she might well be entrusted with a vote. I shall consider your words, both of you," he said, opening the door for us to leave.

The young fresh-faced soldier posted outside saluted the president.

"Corporal, please arrange conveyance for my dear friends to wherever they wish to go."

"Yes, sir!" replied the corporal.

"Please come and see me tomorrow evening," Lincoln told us. "I shall leave word to admit you."

"Thank you, sir," I replied

"Goodnight, Abe!" said Ariyl.

The door between us closed.

6

SEEMS LIKE OLD TIMES

O UTSIDE THE WHITE HOUSE, WE THANKED THE young soldier— who gave his name as Corporal Calvin Ross—but assured him we did not need a carriage; we'd rather take the night air.

"In that case, goodnight, sir...ma'am. And thank you for saving our president."

WE WANDERED through the parkland that half a century later would become the National Mall. Tonight, it was a strange amalgam of landscaping, marshes and ponds, greenhouses, businesses, and in the distance, a railroad crossing. Aside from the White House and the Capitol, there was little that reminded me of today's assortment of grand public buildings and polished stone memorials.

We were heading toward a giant marble stub that was the quarter-finished Washington Monument, which had been stalled for two decades for lack of funds.

We said nothing as long as we were in earshot of other strollers, but finally we found ourselves alone. I opened my mouth to speak, but Ariyl beat me to it.

"You were right, and I was wrong."

That was a pleasant surprise. "About...?"

"Abraham Lincoln is awesome. He's nothing like the racist jerk in *Abe's War.*"

"Thank you," I said. We'd had quite an argument over that vid she'd played as a girl, which was her only exposure to the history of the Civil War. "That's why I said he was our greatest president. It's why he's my personal hero." I paused for a second. "Now, what the hell were you thinking, saving his life?"

"*Excuse* me?"

I lost my temper. "Do I have to explain to you again how time travel works? You *just* got N-Tec back; I can't believe you did something this, this—"

She lost hers right back. "*You're* the one who said it was a tragedy for America that Lincoln was murdered!"

"And it was, but—"

"You're the one who called me stupid for not knowing what he did!"

"I never used that word!"

"No, but that's what you meant!"

"You have no *idea* what I meant!"

"So you *do* think I'm stupid!"

"Oh, don't be an idiot!"

She seized my lapels and lifted me in the air. "David, sometimes you make me so mad I could just...GRR!" With that last frustrated growl, she swung me up in her arms, carried me over to the pond, and dropped me in.

The water was cold and stagnant, with a fishy smell.

"Ariyl!" I sputtered. "What the fuck?!"

She kept fuming for a second...then she burst out laughing.

"Very funny!" I snarled.

"Oh, come on, you needed to cool off. Here." She put out her hand to me, but I ignored it and tried to climb out on my own. The muck grabbed at my shoes, and the bank was too slippery.

"Stop being so stubborn," she said.

I kept trying to climb out, and finally slipped back and fell on my ass in the water.

"Oh, David, I'm sorry!" she said, stepping in and sweeping me up in her arms. Her apology would have been more convincing if she could have suppressed the giggle at the end.

She set me down then noticed she'd gotten wet and muddy from holding me. She touched her shoulder and told her SmartFab outfit, "Clean up and dry."

Her programmable clothing did just as it was told. Now she looked spotless—and gorgeous as ever. But my non-computerized wool suit was still muddy and soaked.

"Oh, look at you! I really am sorry," she said, now sounding genuinely penitent.

She gave me one of those patented long kisses of hers that made me feel like a Tex Avery wolf, with my tie spinning and smoke coming out my ears.

"It's fine," I shivered. "I just need to get these clothes off."

"You read my mind," she said as she carried me into the bushes.

* * *

AN HOUR LATER, we lay on the soft grass where the Daughters of the American Revolution's Constitution Hall now stands. I tried to picture the look on the DAR ladies' faces if they could see us now.

It was a chilly spring night, but I was lying atop her and Ariyl's bodacious bare bod put out beaucoups of BTUs to keep me warm.

She twirled a stand of my hair with her finger. "I've really missed you, David."

I'd missed her too, but I wasn't about to admit it.

"Forgive me?" she asked.

"For what?" I said absently, staring dreamily into her eyes. "Oh, right. Dumping me in that grody pond."

"Tsk! I knew it. You haven't forgiven me, have you? Sweetie, you called me an idiot. Please forgive me." She began kissing me again. "Please? *Please?*"

"Okay, okay, I definitely forgive you. I forgive the living shit out of you." I kissed her back, tenderly. "But..."

"What, David?"

"Nah. Forget it."

"Something's bothering you. I know it."

"It's nothing."

"Tell me," she urged. "You'll feel better."

"It's just...have you noticed that every time you lose your temper and toss me around, you try to make up for it with an epic screw?"

"Only *try* to?" She sounded a tiny bit hurt.

"Okay, you *do* make up for it. God, how you make up for it. But...doesn't that aspect of our relationship strike you as...I dunno, a little kinky?"

"Kinky?" She chuckled softly. "Honey, tossing you around gets me in the *mood*." She nuzzled my ear and breathed in it. "Doesn't it you?"

"Ariyl, I'm always in the mood for you. But we come from very different eras, with different *mores*. In my time, women don't carry men around in their arms."

"You didn't answer my question."

"And they don't toss their boyfriends in the drink over a little spat. That didn't 'get me in the mood' at all."

"Really?" she looked at me, then at our surroundings as we lay naked on the grass. "You could've fooled me."

"Ariyl, I *love* you. I accept things from you I wouldn't accept from anyone else."

"Not even Princess Shining Moon?"

"That was different. Khutulun was a Mongol warrior. I couldn't say no to her, or she wouldn't have helped me find you."

"Or Dylila Duprae?"

"She took me unaware!"

"For a guy who doesn't like getting womanhandled, it seems to happen to you a lot."

"The point is, there's nothing cute about getting dunked. It's humiliating!"

"You know, David, since I last saw you, I did a little research on your time. I spent a week in the year 2010 and saw a bunch of your flat-flix...the new ones and the so-called classics. I saw men dumping *women* in pools all the time, and everybody laughs!"

"Pools are not the same as a filthy pond."

"And why is it romantic when a man carries a woman, but you guys never show it the other way around?"

"It's just...how it is. Women aren't stronger than men in my time."

"A lot of them are."

She quickly stood up with me cradled in her arms, and kissed me a full minute. Finally we came up for air.

"Now, isn't that romantic?"

"Yeah," I panted. "At least, I like it."

"I mean, in your movies women are carried off by men constantly. Even when they're not happy about it! Even when they say no. Even when they resist, slap the guys' faces, pound the guys' backs. And then they always give in the end. Happy to be carried off! Like that was the moral!"

"Let's keep it down," I whispered.

"And that was the *comedies!*"

I felt like I had to defend twentieth-century cinema. "Okay," I murmured, "but that was the reality of courtship in the Thirties, and the Forties. Maybe Fifties at the outside."

"Men threatening to spank women, David. In comedies! And actually doing it!"

"Okay, make it the Sixties. I think John Wayne was the last guy to get away with that."

"You mean *Duke*?" she asked. We'd both met "Duke" Wayne in 1945. "Huh. I wish I'd known that. I'd have set *him* straight, fast."

"I just bet you would."

"And then there were all those films where the girl gets in a fight with a guy and *he* always wins."

"Okay, that's action flicks. James Bond movies. Seventies, Eighties, Nineties. I mean, chivalry kind of went out of fashion when feminism came in. But they really did try to do female action pictures where the girls win. They just never catch on."

"What about *Wonder Woman*?"

"Well, that's coming out next year, 2017. I predict it'll tank too." Then it hit me: "Wait, you know about *Wonder Woman*?"

She just smiled.

"But you guys don't know any of our pop culture!"

"A few things stuck with us."

It struck me that Ariyl was still carrying me in her arms, like Diana did Steve Trevor in the old comics. Would the new *Wonder Woman* dare to show that?

"So, I should buy stock in that studio?"

"David, I don't know what stock is, and you know I'm not supposed to tell you anything about your future." She went right back to her rant. "And don't get me started on fairy tales like *Beauty and the Beast*, where she falls in love with a bully who kidnaps and abuses her. I mean, your whole pre-Change culture going back to *Taming of the Shrew—*"

"You voluntarily watched Shakespeare?" I interjected.

"—romanticizes men dominating women. And *Gone With the Wind* was supposed to be your grand love story? He rapes her!"

"That's only the tip of the iceberg of what's wrong with *that* film," I said.

"And your men have taken their cues from that stuff for centuries. To me, *that's* kinky. And not in a fun way."

"Okay, I shouldn't have said kinky."

"Or called me stupid."

"I did not call you stupid!"

"Sh. Don't yell."

"You throw *me* in the swamp, and I'm not supposed to y—?"

She clamped her hand over my mouth.

"Who goes there?" called out a man's voice.

Silhouetted in the gibbous moon, we could see a short, stout, bushy-bearded Union soldier, rifle at the ready.

THE NEXT THING I KNEW, Ariyl was running through the woods with me slung over her shoulder. We were both naked as jaybirds.

"Halt!" cried the soldier, hearing her running footsteps.

A rifle shot echoed through the trees but missed us.

"M-may I suggest that we use our T-time Crystals?" I said as I bounced along, able to see nothing but the swampy ground fly by beneath her powerfully pumping legs.

"About that...I'm not so sure we can sync up our Crystals anymore."

"Seriously?"

"Yeah. Dylila told me not to sync with hers. Last time we tried that, we got separated in time by three hours. She said we were lucky it wasn't years."

Ariyl was now bounding from rock to rock, leaps of a dozen feet or more each time.

"You're saying—ooof!—the Time Crystals are malfunctioning?"

"Dylila called it a software glitch. I think it's smarter if you just hold onto me like you did at first, and let me do the navigating."

At that moment, her foot landed in a deep puddle that splashed my face.

"Yeah, you navigate," I sputtered.

She had outdistanced the soldier. We could hear him shouting to a comrade far off. She entered a thicket where she could set me down.

Actually, I wasn't completely naked—I still had on my soaked period-leather shoes. The water would probably ruin them.

Ariyl had thoughtfully grabbed our clothes. She put hers on—she looked sensational. Mine were still wringing wet and mud stained. I was starting to shiver.

"Let me see if I can borrow some dry clothes for you," she said.

"Th-thanks," I shivered. "But please don't beat anyone up."

"You know *me*," she winked.

The fat, bushy-bearded private and a taller, thinner African-American one were double-timing it down the path toward our location, rifles at the ready.

Ariyl tapped her shoulder and whispered, "More boobage." The neckline of the period gown restraining her phenomenal bust obediently widened and plunged to expose the expanse of cleavage you'd see at a RenFaire. She then squared her shoulders and stepped out of the tree line to make our pursuers' acquaintance.

"Halt who goes—?" repeated the stubby soldier.

"Oh, b-begging your pardon, ma'am," said the taller one, touching his cap.

"Did you happen to see a pair of people running past you?" asked the short one.

Ariyl took a very deep breath. "Goodness, no!"

They tried to keep their gaze at polite eye-level, but the law of gravity was unavoidable, and as soon they took in her décolletage, it took them in.

Her hands clamped the backs of their heads and buried their faces in her bosom so tightly that they couldn't breathe, let alone aim their rifles. They yelled, but it sounded like they were a couple rooms away.

The little bearded guy fumbled for his Colt sidearm.

"David, get their guns, please."

That wasn't hard. Hypoxia was already setting in. I heard their muffled cries of panic diminish and their struggles weaken until they passed out.

She gently laid them on the path.

I shook my head. "*Must* you do that?"

"You said don't beat them up. See? No bruises, no pain, and they wake with a smile on their face." She opened her arms to me. "Sure you don't want me to show *you* how it feels?"

"No. I mean, yes, I'm sure!"

I BUTTONED up the tall soldier's wool jacket, whose sleeves nearly covered my fingertips. At least his shoes fit me. I was forced to wear the little fat soldier's pants, which I had to hold up. I left some of my silver coins with them—I didn't like the idea of robbing soldiers who had just won the Civil War. I had plenty left to buy new clothes and get us lodging till we saw President Lincoln again.

As we briskly walked away, Ariyl asked, "So, what do you think Abe wants to talk to us about tomorrow?"

"If I were him, I'd want to know everything I could about how to make Reconstruction work. The problem is, everything is going to be different now. You heard it tonight—his Cabinet nearly talked him out of the Fifteenth Amendment."

She looked blank.

"The right to vote." I explained.

"They weren't too crazy about women voting, were they?"

"No. Maybe you could wrestle them into agreeing."

"What's that supposed to mean?" she demanded.

"It means you can't go too fast with these people. They do not have anything approaching a modern mindset. Lincoln is the only one with vision."

"But we can help him!"

I nodded. "Assuming we want to spend a big chunk of our lives in the nineteenth century as his advisors." Then I remembered. "Well, a big chunk of my life, anyway. You're immortal. You've got nothing but time."

"Are you trying to pick a fight with me?"

"I'm just repeating what you told me before you left me. My situation hasn't changed. Has yours?"

She couldn't meet my eyes. "No. But, David, I never meant to hurt your feelings."

"I know. But listen, Ariyl, my last stop before I got here was the year 2109, where L.A. is now at the foot of a glacier."

"Glacier? The last time I was there, L.A. was like the Sahara!"

"History changed and Earth entered a new ice age, sometime between 2016 and 2109."

She looked like she expected me to say more, but I was waiting for her reaction.

"Well, it's news to me," she said finally. "What caused it?"

"Something cut off the sunlight, obviously. Endless snowfall, glaciers form...the fossil record says the world can shift into an ice age in a matter of decades. Now, this ice age might have been caused by a gigantic natural disaster, but I don't see how any change to human history causes it, unless it's a nuclear holocaust."

"How'd you even find out about this? And how did you *get* here? You didn't have a Time Crystal when I left you in 2013."

"Dylila tracked me down three years after you left me and gave me your old Crystal. She sent me back here to stop you from changing history."

Ariyl stopped and stared at me. "That can't be right. 'Cause she sent *me* back to 1865 to save Lincoln."

"What is *with* you women?" I said, exasperated.

"You *women?*" she repeated, putting her hands on her hips and cocking her head.

"You just got your N-Tec world back, and you go and pull a stunt like this?"

"You said that before. What did you mean, we got N-Tec back?"

I mansplained it patiently. "Your pal Dylila told me how she busted Ludlo at his first destination, at the Mount Lowe Railway in Altadena in 1908. She said she took him back to 2109, erased his whole trip, and you guys got your world back."

"She told you that?"

"Yeah! Why? Isn't that what happened?"

"No, David. It's not. Ludlo is still dead. She *tried* to erase Ludlo's trip, so that you and I would never meet. But it didn't work."

"What do you mean?"

"She canceled his trip. N-Tec was fine. But the minute we went back in time again, we lost the thread. We couldn't get back to N-Tec. Dylila thought it had to do with that consistency-thingy."

"The Novikov self-consistency principle?"

"Right. It was on the tip of my tongue."

"Well...I can kinda see why there might be safeguards for that. We've seen what happens when a timeline doesn't make logical sense. Like when you brought Ludlo into that insane white supremacist future he was creating...then crushed him with a TV camera."

"To save your life," she reminded me.

"As you might recall, Ludlo's timeline then came apart at the seams. We were lucky to get back to normal history."

"Fine. Next time, I'll just let him shoot you."

"I'm not complaining. I'm grateful!"

"Oh. Good thing you told me, because you don't sound grateful."

I tried not to tear my hair out. "Ariyl, can we stick to the point here? Your Quality Control officer told me that she succeeded, and then something *else* happened, and it changed our future *again*."

"Wait, I'm getting confused. Why did you think all this might be because of me? I mean, you ran into this new ice age before you even got to 1865."

"But not before *you* got to 1865. Dylila and I were visiting the future you produced. And tonight, I failed to stop you. So apparently, we're still on course for that ice age."

"David, I just don't believe a world where Abe Lincoln survived tonight, ends in a nuclear holocaust."

"Well, come with me then, and let's see if I'm crazy."

I started to pull my Time Crystal out from under my uniform jacket.

Ariyl pushed it back inside and took out her own.

"I do the navigating, remember?"

"Okay, but let me tell *you* when to stop. We have to take this step by step. First, let's see how Lincoln's second term ends and who's president next."

"Fine."

I took her hand and gave her the coordinates for Washington, D.C. on Inauguration Day, 1869. I figured we could hit a library or maybe just ask people about current events.

Unfortunately, Ariyl's Crystal wouldn't take us there.

I told her to take us to 1889, 1909, 1929, 1949...we couldn't reach any of them. We were still stuck in 1865.

We tried my Crystal: same result.

"Novikov strikes again," I said to myself.

"Meaning?"

"Meaning I half expected this. Look, you and I are going to help Lincoln have a successful presidency, right?"

"You mean it?"

"Hell, why not?" I was stuck in a completely different history; I might as well make the most of it.

"David!" Delighted, she kissed me. I kissed her back. It was a beautiful moment.

Then she frowned. "But...why can't we get to any of these dates we want?"

"Sven Bergstrom and I discussed this scenario before I left. Right now, you and I aren't trying to travel into our own established past: We're trying to check out a future that we're still changing."

"You mean it's like trying to jump into tomorrow and find out what you're going to wear the next day?"

"That's an excellent analogy. When we get back to Lincoln, we'll be in a position to influence hundreds of major decisions that will form a specific, consistent future. Right now, there's no definite future for us to go to. We haven't created it yet!"

Ariyl gasped in realization. "That must be why the Time Crystal never lets us travel into our own future. I mean 2109 is as far ahead as we can go!"

"Yep! The fact that you're always changing your present makes your own future unknowable and unreachable."

"But then...how did you and Dylila get to that new ice age in 2109?"

"I think because it's a dead future. Humans are extinct. So we can't bring back any information that will change the details of it. It's binary—that ice age either exists, or it doesn't. Our job is to see to it that it doesn't."

"So you're saying, as long as we *can't* travel to any specific date in our future, that's a sign we're actually doing okay."

I thought that over. "Um...yeah, I guess I am saying that. Or actually, *you* are."

She grinned. "*Told* you I had a logical mind."

"That you do. So the thing to do is try to get to that dead future I saw in 2109. If we can't get there, it's not dead anymore, and we can stop worrying."

"Well, let's go!" She took hold of her Time Crystal as she held me with her other arm.

"Wait. First, put me down."

She clucked her tongue in disappointment, but complied.

"Second, take us to Cavendish Laboratory, Cambridge England, 1928. Make it Christmas Day. We want the place to ourselves."

"Why?"

"We're just going there for a minute, to borrow the world's first Geiger counter. Then we go to 2109 and estimate from the radiation what date the nuclear exchange was."

"And then all we have to do is stop World War III," she said wryly.

* * *

FORTUNATELY, we got into the lab and were successful in locating the primitive Geiger tube. In a few minutes, I'd hunted up some batteries and wired them together to power it.

Then I searched for some radioactive substance to test it. I finally came across a lead-lined drawer, labeled "Pitchblende." I held the Geiger tube up to the dark stone, and got the familiar clicking sound.

"Okay, we're good to go."

"How is it we can get to *this* date?" Ariyl wondered.

"My guess? It's not Washington, D.C., or anywhere in America that our actions could affect. Whatever Lincoln did during his presidency, Cavendish Laboratory in 1928 was going to be pretty much the same. And we only came to borrow this little gadget; we have no intention of finding an American history book to look up the details of Lincoln's second term. If we had those plans, we probably never could have arrived in the first place."

"But what if we change our mind now?"

"Don't! We're having trouble enough."

"So you're saying what we *plan* to do actually affects whether we can get to somewhere in time? Like if you're planning to kill your grandmother, your Crystal won't work?"

"Yeah. I'm not sure if it's the Crystal's safeguards, or just what Stephen Hawking calls chronology protection. Obviously, it didn't prevent Ludlo's changes to the past. Or stop you from saving Lincoln. Pastward travel seems unprotected. But it seems like intent affects time travel into the future."

"That's weird. I mean, even for time travel, that's weird."

I took her hand. "Now, give the Crystal the coordinates of when you and Ludlo left the Time Travel Agency. With any luck, it'll be an alive, potential future that we won't be able to travel to."

She held the Crystal and spoke into it: "Time Travel Agency, L.A., noon, June fourth, 2109 A.D."

IN AN INSTANT, we were freezing between the snowy slopes of half-buried Los Angeles City Hall and that same damn glacier from the Hollywood Hills.

We said it at the same time:

"Shit!"

7

FUTURE TENSE

ARIYL STARTED TO CRY. THE WIND WAS SO cold, the tears actually turned to ice on her face. I'd never been this cold in my life. We were being flash-frozen.

Ariyl wailed, "It's not fair! It's like humans blow ourselves up no matter who was president!"

Meanwhile, I was shivering so hard I was practically having convulsions. "Get SmartFab to make something warm! And big!"

Ariyl sniffed and touched her shoulder. "Blizzard clothing, with a double-size warm cape!"

Her high-button shoes morphed into fur-lined waterproof boots and her 1860s gown grew into a voluminous, white fur cape. She threw it around us, which immediately cut the wind-chill factor.

"Can it make boots for me? My feet feel like they're in a block of ice!"

"No, but long as you're with me, honey, you don't need boots," she said, scooping me up in her arms. "I mean, if you don't mind my taking such an unseemly liberty," she added archly.

Only our faces, chummily cheek-to-cheek, protruded from the cape hood into the Arctic blast. I ducked down inside the cape and fiddled with the Geiger tube. It wasn't cooperating. But at least it was warm inside. I inhaled Ariyl's scent...and something else.

"What kind of fur is this, ermine? Or polar bear?" I wondered aloud.

She pulled her head inside to watch me work.

"SmartFab doesn't use fur," she said.

"If you say so. But it feels real. Even smells like an ermine coat."

"You've smelled dead ermine fur? Eww!"

"I'm just sayin'."

"David, SmartFab is some kind of nanotech. It moves atoms around. So I guess it duplicates what fur is. But we don't kill animals!"

"That's very humane. I guess N-Tec makes your food the same way?"

"Of course. I wouldn't touch meat if we killed animals for it."

"But you ate..."

"I ate what?"

Suddenly I realized this was not a productive or smart avenue of conversation with her.

"Never mind. I think I have this working."

I stuck my face out the cape hood again and pushed the Geiger counter out into the blowing snow.

"I don't hear anything. Does that mean we're safe?"

"This doesn't make sense!" I said. "Can you take us somewhere else, same date?"

"Where to?"

"Try New York."

MANHATTAN WAS THE SAME STORY: Abandoned skyscrapers poking out of a polar snowscape. But barely a click from the Geiger counter.

Moscow, Beijing, Paris, Jerusalem, Lagos, Rio, Sydney: all of them showed us a dead world locked in ice but scant evidence of radioactivity.

"Well, the war must have been quite a while ago. Probably decades. Try jumping us back in five year intervals."

. . .

THAT DIDN'T WORK. We were stuck in 2109 with no way of telling when the disaster had hit. I gave up.

"Get us back to the Cavendish Lab in 1928."

AS BEFORE, there was no problem with Cambridge—we arrived a few minutes after we'd left. I replaced the Geiger tube and its components.

"Does this mean we can't stop the apocalypse?"

"I don't know. But it means that Lincoln surviving Ford's Theatre will not prevent that ice age. It means your mission for Dylila is ultimately doomed to fail."

"Are you sure?" She looked crestfallen.

I hated to crush her hopes. "Well...maybe not. Maybe if we actually go to work for Lincoln and change that society around, all this can be avoided. We might as well try."

Encouraged, Ariyl spoke the coordinates for Washington, D.C. on Lincoln's fateful night in April.

INSTEAD, we found ourselves in a snowbound Washington. It wasn't the ice age world we had just left, but it certainly wasn't April 1865, either.

I picked up a freshly discarded newspaper. The date was December twentieth, 1866.

We tried jumping back to the previous year—it didn't work. Neither would my Time Crystal take us back.

Either some subtle programmed safeguard, or Hawking's chronology protection conjecture, or just plain fate was refusing to let us get back to the night we'd left Mr. Lincoln.

The newspaper's content was even more disturbing: Both the Reconstruction Act and the Fifteenth Amendment were stalled in the House of Representatives while anti-Negro race riots wracked the South.

In the Senate, a newly-appointed Republican "moderate" named Octavius Johnson, from California of all places, argued for a "Grand Compromise" in which only Negroes who could establish their "mental competence" would be granted citizenship and the vote. The issue threatened to split the ruling Republican Party.

"And nothing about the women?" frowned Ariyl.

Most concerning of all was the absence of any news about President Lincoln, other than that he had not appeared in public for months, and the rumor was he'd been suffering from acute melancholia over his attempted assassination.

"That doesn't sound like Abe," said Ariyl.

"We need to go see him," I agreed. "Like now."

8

LATE MOMENTS WITH MR. LINCOLN

THE WHITE HOUSE WAS PACKED WITH WAITING dignitaries, officials, and lobbyists. There wasn't a place on a divan or a chair to be had. So we stood in an alcove, awaiting approval from persons unknown, to see the president.

I kept looking at the stairway. Maybe the thing to do was make a run for it. If we could figure out the right room and get in to see Abe Lincoln before the guards caught up to us, I was sure he'd dismiss them.

To my chagrin, Major Henry Rathbone, Lincoln's guest at Ford Theatre, walked up to us and bowed, courtly.

"Professor Preston, Miss Moro. It must be fate that our paths have crossed again. It gives me the opportunity to offer you my sincerest thanks for your saving the lives of the president and Secretary Seward. And to tender my abject apologies for having treated you with such suspicion that night."

I didn't bow back. "That's quite all right, Major. It's already forgotten."

Then I turned back to Ariyl and ignored him.

"Well, good afternoon, then," he said with an awkward, second bow.

"Goodbye, Major," said Ariyl warmly, hoping to make up for my boorish behavior.

I continued to look the other way.

Ariyl watched as Major Rathbone withdrew, then she turned to me. "Wow. The glacier in L.A. wasn't as frosty as you were to that guy."

"Did it show?"

"Only the way you glared at him. And clenched your teeth. And balled up your fists. Why do you hate that guy so much?"

"What's to like? The bastard accused us of conspiring to kill Lincoln."

She looked at me then shook her head. "Nope. That's not it."

"I don't know what you're talking about," I said, checking the stairway again.

She put a finger alongside my jaw and turned my head back toward her. "I can read you like a book, David."

"Except you don't read books."

"I can read you like a comic book. Every time you turn your eyes away from me, I know you're keeping something from me. Now, what is it?"

"I just don't like him."

"You might as well tell me now. You know I'll get it out of you one way or the other."

"Don't be stupid!"

She rolled her eyes. "And now you're just trying to make me mad, so I'll forget what we're talking about. Not gonna work."

"I really don't care to discuss it. Okay?"

She got an impish smile. "What if I were to pick you up right now, like Dylila did? In front of all these people?"

My ears started to burn. "You wouldn't dare."

"You know me better than that."

"We're trying to blend in here!"

"Or maybe lift you way over my head, carry you around the room like that for a while?"

"You're the one who wants to help Abe Lincoln! You think

47

making a public spectacle of ourselves will do that? Those guards'll throw us right out!"

"They could try."

"I am not discussing this."

"Okay," she said. She slipped her hand through my belt in the back, took hold, and lifted me a couple of inches off the ground. "Last chance," she whispered in my ear.

One of the soldiers across the room looked over in my direction. It must have seemed odd to him that I was now eye-level with Ariyl, when before I'd clearly been shorter.

"Put me down and I'll tell you," I murmured.

She smiled and complied.

I spoke under my breath. "Two years from now, Major Henry Rathbone and his theater date Clara Harris will be married. In 1883, Henry will be a U.S. Consul in Hanover, Germany. Two days before Christmas, Henry will fly into a jealous rage and attack his children. When Clara tries to protect them, he'll shoot her and stab her to death."

"That's horrible," she gasped. "But why?"

"There was no reason. He died in an insane asylum."

"David, we have to warn her."

"No. This is exactly why I didn't want you to know."

"Then I'll tell her!"

"She won't believe you."

"She'll believe Abe Lincoln when I tell him."

"*Abe* may not believe you. Not about such a shocking event two decades in the future. And if he did believe it, what could he do? Arrest Henry for a murder that he won't commit for seventeen years?"

"Then how about I warn Clara so she doesn't marry that psycho?"

"If you *could* convince her, then their three children will never be born. You'd erase their lives. Is that what you want?"

She shook her head, downcast. "Of course not."

"And one of those children grows up to be a congressman."

She lifted an eyebrow. "Well, now you're gonna make me change my mind."

I gave her a wry smile. That was the girl I knew.

"Miss Ari-el?" said a familiar voice.

It was Corporal Calvin Ross, the young soldier who had escorted us downstairs the night we met Lincoln.

"You two are lucky I'm on duty today. The president did tell me you were to be admitted. But that was more'n a year ago. Every month or so, the president draws me aside, and he always asks if I've heard from you two."

"We were unavoidably detained," I non-explained.

"Well, never mind. Come this way, please," said Calvin, leading us up a stairway to the second floor.

"How is he?" asked Ariyl.

The soldier looked abashed. "I could get in a heap of trouble for telling you this, but...he's in a bad way, Miss Ari-el. He ain't been out of his bedroom in weeks. Them folks downstairs? Ain't none of 'em getting in. And I couldn't help hearing his doctors outside the residence. One said Mr. Lincoln would not finish out his term."

"What's wrong with him?" I asked.

"Don't rightly know. But Mrs. Lincoln took to her bed too. 'Course, I don't think she's been right since they lost their little boy Willie. But she cries so much now, the doctors only let her see her husband for a short while."

Corporal Ross knocked gently, then a bit louder. There was no response. He screwed up his courage and opened the door for us.

When we entered Lincoln's bedroom, my heart sank.

The great man was pale and emaciated, his dark hair now sparser and turning white. He looked a decade older than when we saw him last year. There was a large growth on his neck and a bloodied dressing over what I assumed had been exploratory surgery to determine its extent.

The corporal spoke softly. "Mr. President, I brought you those visitors you were asking for." Then Calvin left us, closing the door.

Lincoln stirred. He blinked at us through rheumy eyes...but when he recognized us, he smiled and his face became animated. He visibly drew strength from our presence.

"My friends, you have returned at last!" His voice was hoarse, barely above a whisper.

"We're sorry we couldn't get back sooner. But..."

He weakly waved off my explanation. "I understand. We must blame the river of our friend Heraclitus. I am much obliged that you were able to ford it at all. Had you come much later, I fear our conversation would have been entirely your responsibility." He tried to sit up but lacked the strength. Ariyl gently pushed him back onto his pillow.

"Don't tire yourself. You have to get well," said Ariyl, choking back tears.

Lincoln wearily shook his head. "I have cancer in my thyroid glands. To remove it all would be fatal to me. And no doubt, would end my public speaking career even sooner than my prognosis indicates."

I indulged him with a smile—God love him, he was trying to cheer *us* up. But it was a gloomy wit that he was showing. He was depressed, and the man's once-indomitable energy seemed spent.

"David, couldn't we take him into the future with us, for treatment?"

I nodded, "In my era, we can cure this kind of cancer. But we have no assurance we'd get there, or get him back to this year, or this decade," I warned her. "Not with the Crystals on the fritz."

Lincoln shook his head again.

"To restore my health would achieve nothing," he rasped. "I have lost the public argument. You were right, Professor. We needed those other amendments. I fought for them until my strength gave out."

"I read in a newspaper about Senator Octavius Johnson's Grand Compromise," I began.

"We have tried compromising over human liberty before. Either all men are free, or none are. I once felt that I had my finger on the pulse of public opinion, but I fear Senator Johnson is now my superior in that. Perhaps I have too many fingers in the way."

I assumed that was a joke at the senator's expense, but I didn't get it. "He was not a senator in our original timeline," I told Lincoln. "This is what I meant about how history would quickly become unpredictable."

"Indeed it has. There have been massacres even worse than you foretold. I wanted citizenship and the vote for the Negro. And for the ladies, Miss Ari-el. But I have failed. I hope I have not proven too great a disappointment to you."

Her eyes filled with tears. "You're the greatest man I ever met, Abe. You could never disappoint me."

I told him, "If it's of any consolation, sir, the man who is now my president—in 2016—is a black man. And he's a very great admirer of yours. He was sworn in with his hand on your Bible."

Abe's eyes welled up in pride. "Thank you for telling me that. How strange...it makes me now wish that you had not saved my life last year."

"Don't say that!" gasped Ariyl.

"Please do not think me ungrateful. You did it with the purest of motives. Yet I cannot but believe, that in death, my wishes might have carried more weight with the Congress than they have with me alive."

"That's not true," she insisted.

"On the day Mrs. Lincoln and I went to the play, I had to decide whether to pardon a deserter, or let him hang. In the end, I said the boy could probably do us more good above ground than underground. A year later, I seem to be in the opposite situation. Or do you think I am mistaken, Professor?"

I had to tell him the truth. "No, sir, I think you're right. In my timeline, your assassination outraged the conscience of America. Maybe there never was any other way to pass those amendments."

"If it took your world another century, even with those amendments to commit to racial justice, I tremble to think how long it will take us without them." He lay silent for a moment. "When you first told me of this alternate history, I confess that I thought the notion madness. How can things both be true and not true? It seems to rob all meaning from life."

"I have a mentor in my era, sir. An old scientist named

Bergstrom. He believes that alternate timelines are temporary; that eventually, the most logical version of history prevails, and the others cease to exist, except in the memory of the time travelers who witness them."

I glanced at Ariyl—she wasn't going to like what I said next. "He says there is a way we can undo our changes to events like this. I'm willing to give it a try."

Ariyl was speechless. But for the first time since we walked in the room, Lincoln looked genuinely hopeful.

"If that is so, and you can undo what you have done," he said, "then I pray you let history follow the course in which my death will have the most meaning."

Ariyl was aghast. "You want me to let Booth kill you?"

"Yes, Miss Ari-el, I do." He swallowed, and could not suppress a wince of pain. "You have a most compassionate heart. Will you not do me this favor?"

She began to cry. "I *can't.*"

"But you must, my dear. I see now that things must be as you said they were. Perhaps you could think of it as a kindness: I do not imagine that I suffered much on the night that I was shot."

"No, sir," I said softly. "You lost consciousness immediately and never awoke."

"It is ironic. I was so enjoying myself that night. I suppose if we should meet in the hereafter, I might thank Mr. Booth for generously allowing me to enjoy so much of that wonderful comedy," he said wryly.

"That wasn't generosity, sir," I said bitterly. "Booth knew the play, and to aid in his escape, he fired the shot during the biggest laugh in the show."

"Then that is how it must be," whispered the great man.

Tears were streaming down Ariyl's face. Mine too. But Lincoln managed a chuckle as he squeezed her hand.

"My dear, brave young woman, do not weep for me. Please take comfort from the words of our late poet, Mr. Edgar Allan Poe. He wrote, 'To die laughing, must be the most glorious of all glorious deaths!'"

9
_____

DIETARY ISSUES

W E HAD MADE A DIFFICULT PROMISE TO THE dying president. Carrying it out would be even more problematic.

The Time Crystals were continuing to malfunction. We couldn't jump back from 1866 to April fourteenth 1865, nor any date for a week back. We finally managed to reach April seventh. Which meant we had to spend seven days in Washington, trying to keep out of sight, out of trouble, and out of any timeline-ending paradoxes.

I hadn't budgeted for a one-week stay, but a chance conversation in another saloon led us to the farm of Josiah and Rebecca Perkins, just outside the District, in Maryland. Rebecca looked after the farm while Josiah ran Perkins General Store. The Perkinses agreed to one dollar per week rent (in silver—thank you, Sven, for the donations from your coin collection) on their upstairs bedroom, meals included.

Ariyl snickered at the Victorian propriety of the era, but she agreed that we must pose as husband and wife. I purchased a pawned wedding ring for her that turned her finger green within hours.

Our first night with the Perkins family was uneventful, other than Rebecca's shock at Ariyl's food intake; she was particularly fond of Rebecca's chicken and dumplings, having six helpings. I had to renegotiate terms, paying another dollar a week for meals. Considering the silver content of a dollar, that was a bargain. Even for the modern numismatic value, it was a fair price.

On the following morning, I awoke an hour before dawn to find Ariyl gone from the room. Then I became aware of a wooden squeaking sound. It seemed to be coming from outside the farmhouse.

I tiptoed downstairs to find Ariyl out in the dark barnyard.

She was doing sets of squats with the back of Josiah's sturdy buckboard on her shoulders. The wagon was fully loaded with sacks of flour, cords of firewood, casks of ale, kegs of nails, and the rest of Josiah's merchandise for delivery. It probably weighed half a ton; Ariyl was knocking off sets of ten but barely breaking a sweat.

She was dressed in what was as close as SmartFab could come to an 1865 gym outfit: A fancy corset, plus open-top drawers that, while technically more modest than bare skin, were skin-tight, displaying every muscle group of her mighty legs, the same as if she'd painted her limbs off-white.

"You weren't kidding about working out," I observed.

"Of course not. If we're stuck here for a week, I need to keep my strength up."

"I just thought you future people were engineered to be strong."

She kept squatting with the wagon, whose wooden structure creaked in protest at each dip. She was breathing hard but able to keep up a conversation as she pumped wagon. Obviously, this was nowhere near the limit of what she could lift.

"Well, we're way stronger than you. But our bodies still work the same way. We eat, we sleep. If you want to stay strong...you have to exercise. You want to get stronger...you exercise more."

"So is everybody in 2109 as strong as you?"

She chuckled. "I hope not. I'm a competitive athlete."

"You?" I half-laughed.

She set down the wagon and got out from under it. "You say that like you don't believe it." She grabbed her towel off a fencepost to mop her face.

"No, no. I just...you never mentioned what you did."

"You didn't ask."

"You gave me the impression that life in the future was one big vacation."

Now she took a folded horse blanket and laid it across a low tree stump in the barnyard. "God, wouldn't that be boring? Most of us like to work at something." She picked up the wagon yoke and dragged the buckboard over the stump. "Music, art, writing, vidz design, theoretical math, scientific research, gardening, cooking, travel...we even have a few people who are into archaeology, believe it or not. In my case, it's powerlifting."

"Why?"

"Why? Why do *you* dig up old ruins?" She slid into the narrow space between the stump and the wagon, with her back on the blanket.

"That's my job."

"Well, we don't have jobs. We just do things that are fun."

She got a good grip on the axle and began bench-pressing the wagon. (I mentioned this was a fully loaded wagon, right?)

"Is lifting weights fun?"

"Is digging up ruins fun?"

"Not exactly, but finding things is."

"Well, so is finding out how strong I can get." She did eight more reps then slid out from under the wagon.

"Huh. I just never figured you for a jock."

She shrugged. "It's what I do. I'm good at it. I like it. I like being stronger than anybody else." She hit a double-biceps pose. "Why, don't you approve?"

"You know I do. You're awesome, Ariyl."

"Gee, that's a relief," she said dryly.

"Why wouldn't I approve? I'm a fencer."

"You don't strike me as a jock, either." She slipped her fingers under my belt buckle and lifted me up for a kiss. "Maybe you can come at me with your sword sometime, and we'll see who wins."

"You really are competitive," I commented.

"Mm-hm." She kissed me.

There was some attitude beneath all her banter, but I couldn't quite put my finger on it. I decided not to get into it. She finally set me down again.

"So...do you do any other sports?" I asked.

"Oh, some field events."

"Like you did at the Olympics? Javelin, discus, shot put?"

"Yep. All the strength sports."

"So who's stronger...you, or Dylila?"

"Now, why do you want to know that?" she asked, sounding suspicious.

"I'm just trying to figure out who I can least afford to piss off," I smiled. I didn't add that I was still disturbed that Dylila was clearly telling the two of us very different stories.

"When she was young, Dylila used to powerlift. These days she's more into combat sports. Boxing, jiu-jitsu, karate. But the answer to your question is: me. Don't piss *me* off."

She kissed me on the forehead, and went back to doing something she called heel-raises, where she gripped one wheel of the wagon and raised it simply by rising up on tiptoe. Apparently, it worked her calf muscles, because those were soon bulging right through her tights.

"Judas Priest!" exclaimed Josiah Perkins, who had just emerged from his house.

Fortunately, he hadn't seen Ariyl tipping his buckboard. It was simply her outfit that scandalized him.

I apologized, explained that my bride was a sleepwalker, and guided her back up to our room.

* * *

OUR IDYLL at the Perkins farm came to a crashing end the following afternoon, when I heard Josiah hollering blue murder from the barn. I ran downstairs, across the yard, and into the barn to find Ariyl holding Josiah in the air with one fist, ready with the other to punch his lights out.

"Mister, help me! Your wife's gone crazy!"

"Ariyl, what on earth is wrong?"

"I caught this bastard killing a chicken!"

"It's for your dinner!" screamed Josiah. "Put me down!"

Ariyl looked at me. "What does he mean, it's for my dinner?"

"Put him down, and I'll explain," I told her.

She set the man down, and he backed out of the barn with a look on his face as if he'd just met Satan himself. Or herself.

"Uh, we'll be packed and out of here in three minutes, Mr. Perkins," I yelled after him. Then I turned to Ariyl, "Come on, before he can get his shotgun loaded."

* * *

HALF A MILE down the road to Washington, I watched Ariyl go in the woods to throw up. She emerged looking disgusted.

"When were you planning to tell me that you've been feeding me dead animals?"

"I've been...? Ariyl, we don't have N-Tec to make our meals. You've been eating real meat ever since you went back in time."

"That's horrible! Oh, God, I'm going to be sick again!"

I waited by the road. She came out again, ashen-faced.

"Ariyl, how could you go back in time to all these primitive eras and not know where your food is coming from?"

"How would I learn that? It's not in the vidz. Do *your* movies show people killing chickens and cows and pigs?"

"Uh, not really a lot of slaughterhouse scenes, no. We just kind of don't pay attention to that."

"You people are monsters!"

"I know how you must feel, but you're judging us by a pretty unrealistic standard. Nobody in the world of N-Tec goes hungry or malnourished. Back in 1865, there weren't unlimited protein sources. People raised animals for food and hunted in order to live."

"I am not eating any more meat!" she declared.

"Okay, I respect that," I told her. "But I suggest you cut back on your workouts, because I have a rough idea of how many calories you burn a day."

"Thanks for the training advice. Now, can we get something to eat that doesn't have a face? I'm starving."

10

DOUBLE DOPPELGANGERS

O N APRIL FOURTEENTH, 1865, WE MADE OUR way to Peter Taltavull's Star Saloon. We sat there from eight o'clock on, nursing our drinks, waiting for the fateful hour to roll around again.

The saloonkeeper was clearly scandalized by a woman's presence —we were breaking a pretty serious taboo (and probably a law or two) by her being there at all. Fortunately, Ariyl's imposing size made the idea of ejecting her impractical.

The fact that she wasn't touching her alcohol probably unnerved Mr. Taltavull even more: She might be a temperance fanatic, ready to bust up his saloon. Certainly she wouldn't need a hatchet to do it.

I suppose we should have ordered water, assuming we didn't mind a case of typhoid. Buying whiskey we didn't drink really made us stand out, but we needed our minds absolutely clear tonight.

I made a point of telling Taltavull to keep the change from Sven's 1865 Seated Liberty silver dollar. The barkeep kept his objections to himself.

Shortly after nine, the intermission crowd from *Our American Cousin* spilled in. When I saw Lincoln's alleged bodyguard John Parker deserting his post to come in and get plastered, it took all my willpower not to break his gin-blossomed nose.

Finally, it was ten minutes after ten.

Ariyl and I headed next door to the theater. My pulse was pounding, because I really had no idea whether this would work or not, nor what would happen to us if it *did* work.

Logically, there was a big fat chance that by meeting and deterring our earlier selves, our current sadder-but-wiser selves would be erased. It was like knowing right before it happened, that you might suddenly get amnesia. And that wasn't even the worst-case scenario.

Worst-case was that the entire history of N-Tec would become impossible, and cease to exist. We'd seen something like that happen in an alternate 1954 where Ludlo had made Strom Thurmond president; Ariyl then pulled Ludlo from 1948 into the future he was making, and he died there. With no Ludlo to bring it about, we saw that reality literally dissolve around us, nearly taking us with it.

But this was the only move we had left, so we made it.

Marching toward the far side of Ford's Theatre, we saw one-week-younger Ariyl, bent on saving Lincoln. She had almost reached the army officer at the door, when older Ariyl—my Ariyl—grabbed her arm and dragged her into the alley between the saloon and the theater.

"What the hell?" said younger Ariyl.

"You can't do this," said Ariyl.

Younger Ariyl stared at herself, speechless.

Meanwhile, one-week-younger me shouted from down the street as he ran toward us. "Ariyl!"

Younger Ariyl suddenly vanished. As did younger me.

I felt myself. I was still there. So was the Ariyl I came with.

"Where'd they go?" she breathed.

"You mean where did *we* go? Our younger selves? I don't know. We still have their memories, right?"

Ariyl nodded. "I remember saving Lincoln."

"So maybe those selves still exist in a parallel universe," I said. "The main thing is they're no longer in this version of history."

"But which version is the real history?"

There was a loud laugh from within the auditorium, and a muffled shot. Then shouts and screams.

"This one," I said.

We held each other a long time.

"I need a drink," said Ariyl.

I did too.

We returned to the Star Saloon and told Mr. Taltavull to leave the bottle.

* * *

I'M NOT sure how long it was before we left the saloon. It felt like forever, but I think it may have been less than ten minutes; in any event, we'd managed to get pretty hammered.

As we stumbled along, at the door of Ford's Theatre we literally bumped into Clara Harris, whose fiancé Major Rathbone was supporting the hysterical Mary Todd Lincoln.

"Murder! My poor husband has been murdered!" wailed Mrs. Lincoln.

"Perhaps the doctors will save him!" said Clara with desperate cheer. But I could see in her eyes that she knew the wound was mortal.

Rathbone was white as a sheet, and tears rolled down his cheeks. "I was so close...why couldn't I stop him?" he cried.

His fiancée tried to comfort him: "No, Henry, he had that dagger —oh, look at how you're bleeding!"

Clara was right. Henry's left hand was soaked with blood flowing down his arm. I could see a hideous cut from his shoulder down to his elbow—right through his uniform. It looked like it went to the bone.

Rathbone ignored the wound as he wept bitterly. "I have failed my president! What kind of man am I, who couldn't even stop his assassin?"

Clara took his face in her hands: "Listen to me, Henry Rathbone. No man ever behaved more bravely!"

That much was true—I knew that, despite Rathbone being severely slashed, he had grabbed the actor's coat as he leapt to the stage, causing him to fall. Booth could thank the major for the broken leg that led to his being tracked down and shot dead twelve days hence.

The couple glanced at us. For a moment, I could have sworn they recognized us. But of course, they couldn't have.

Rathbone wiped his eyes on his unbloodied right sleeve. "Clara, dear, forgive me. I-I must help Mrs. Lincoln!"

"Of course, Henry!" said Clara.

Rathbone escorted the sobbing Mary Lincoln across the street and into the house where her comatose husband had just been carried.

Feeling implicated in Clara Harris's tragic end, I could not return the young woman's gaze. I looked down as I mumbled our apologies and tried to escort Ariyl away.

Instead, Ariyl took her hand, urgently. "Miss Harris...Clara?"

Clara was taken aback. "Pardon me, but do I know you?"

"No," said Ariyl, "but I have to warn you."

I looked at Ariyl, aghast. She was going to derail history *again*?

"Warn me?" Clara looked mystified. "Of what?"

Ariyl searched the young socialite's eyes for an answer that she would not find there. Finally, she squeezed Clara's hand. "Just...protect your children."

Clara stared at Ariyl as if she were a madwoman. Then she turned and hurried across Tenth Street and into the house where in nine hours, President Abraham Lincoln would pass into history.

11

NICE WORKOUT IF YOU CAN GET IT

THE NEXT DAY, ARIYL WAS IN A RUSH TO DEPART 1865 Washington, the time and place that had brought her so much grief. But I insisted on spending that day in town, so that I could check out one more historical lead.

Over the past week, Ariyl and I had been ordered to leave every boarding house we'd stayed in, and it seemed our current (fourth) one would be no different. We would almost certainly get the boot at dinner tonight.

We were at that awkward stage in our relationship: We essentially had started living together, but in extremely cramped, penurious, and primitive conditions which just exacerbated the getting-to-know-you pressures.

Ariyl's dietary demands, while fortunately not pure vegan, now limited us to houses that would serve her heaping helpings of the most available non-meat protein: mainly eggs, chickpeas, cheese, and beans. Also, she had to eat in our room, since she could no longer stomach seeing carnivores eat...and after a week on her new diet, she in turn would not be welcome downstairs anyway. It was sub-freezing out and still we had to keep our window open.

The one thing Ariyl would not compromise on was her workout.

Since we didn't have access to a buckboard or anything else particularly heavy, she had to make do with the heaviest thing in our tiny room, which as it turned out, was me.

I'm only 180 pounds. That's up six pounds from my mid-twenties but certainly not obese. So Ariyl's routine of necessity changed, from low reps with maximum weight, to maximum reps with a light weight (no cracks, thank you).

She would warm up with fifty squats carrying me across her shoulders, then move to sets of forward lunges. Then she'd drop to the floor for a hundred pushups, with me sitting atop her shoulders to maximize her difficulty.

I had no idea how much Ariyl weighed—all I knew was, I could not possibly lift her. But our combined weight was making the floorboards squeak with each rep.

"Can I ask you...a question?" she puffed as I rode her up and down.

"I don't know, can you?"

"Clearly I can," she panted. "Why are we still...hanging around...this nasty...dirty...bloodthirsty...little town?"

"Because I love history."

"Yeah, well...I don't...not anymore." She finished her hundred. "'Kay, get off."

I stood up and she got to her feet. She took hold of the back of my belt, with both hands lifted me to her shoulder, then with one arm pumped me toward the ceiling in an overhead dumbbell-raise (again, no cracks).

"Where...have you...been going...every day...this week?" she grunted between lifts.

"Libraries. Newspaper morgues."

"Oh, David...not again..." She ended with a long-suffering sigh: "*Why?*"

"I went to school in California. I learned all about my state's history in the fourth grade. I made a kick-ass model of Mission San Juan Capistrano. Whoa, careful, you almost banged my head on the ceiling."

"Oops," she said, not sounding particularly sincere.

"For extra credit, I did a report on California during the Civil War."

After twenty reps, she set me down. "Fascinating. I guess sometime before my workout's over, you'll tell me how that's relevant." She grabbed my belt with her other hand, raised me to shoulder-height, and began another set of one-arm lifts.

"Remember Senator Octavius Johnson, who Lincoln said had opposed him over the Negro vote?"

"Do you have to say Negro?"

"It's historically correct and way better than the most frequent alternative in this era."

"Wouldn't use either one...around Dylila," she grunted.

"In the alternate 1866 we just came from, the newspaper said Johnson was appointed to fill out the term of a California Democrat named James A. MacDougall, who was killed in a botched robbery in May of 1865."

She rolled her eyes in boredom as she hoisted me skyward again and again: "You wanna solve...a murder of someone...no one but you...ever heard of?"

"Nope. As I reported to Mrs. Pitts in the fourth grade, in original history, Senator MacDougall retired from Congress in 1867. He drank himself to death six months later."

"You put that in your school report?"

"I actually did. So if anyone killed MacDougall, it was John Barleycorn."

She set me down on the floor again. "Who the hell is...?"

"Demon rum."

"Aww," she clucked her tongue in mock sympathy. "So, no murder to solve?"

She lay on her back, pulled her right knee up to her chest, and angled the sole of her foot at the ceiling. As instructed, I sat on that foot, and she began doing leg presses with me.

"We're not in that timeline anymore. MacDougall won't be murdered, since we put history back the way it was. But the only change *we* ever made to history was to save Lincoln's life. Yet one month later, there was a *second* change: A senator who was destined to retire is instead assassinated, by person or persons unknown, and his replacement just happens to be a Republican who votes against his own party and president on a historic issue."

"Switch legs," she said, lowering me and pulling her left knee up. "What's your point?"

"Something stinks."

"Blame the chickpeas."

"I'm referring to Senator Octavius Johnson. I've been reading up on him in every old paper I can find. There's something fishy about this guy."

Her leg kept powering me up and down. "But didn't you say he's not even a senator in this timeline?"

"That's right. But he's still rich as Croesus, even though no one seems to have heard of him before 1859, when he made a fortune leasing land he bought just one year earlier...in *Titusville, Pennsylvania*," I concluded dramatically.

"Where they make chocolate?" she guessed.

"You're thinking of Hershey, Pennsylvania. Titusville was America's first oil boom."

"Well, I was close. Same color." She took me down off her foot and sat up. "This is ridiculous."

"Yeah, that's how I feel."

"I mean, you weigh less than I do. I should just do one-legged squats holding you."

"Oh. Good thinking. So, workout over?"

"You're saying Octavius Johnson got rich investing in land nobody knew would be worth anything?"

"Nobody, except someone who knew their history."

"Oh, no. *David*."

"What?"

"You can't possibly think it's Ludlo!"

"No, I don't."

"I threw a TV camera on him! You saw me! He couldn't possibly survive that!"

"He didn't. You gooshed him like a roach. Plus, you have his Time Crystal. But we know someone *else* who has one."

"Dylila?" Ariyl got to her feet. "Telling this Johnson prick how to get rich? No. That I refuse to believe."

She grabbed my belt buckle underhand and bent her elbow, slowly lifting me off the ground till we were nose to nose...then she let me down...then lifted me again...then down, then up...

Doing biceps curls with me really made that floor squeak.

Ludicrous as I felt, I kept on talking: "It could explain why she told us two completely opposite stories. She told you that you had to save Abe Lincoln, and she told me I had to stop you."

"I know, you told me that. But this makes zero sense. Why would Dylila help someone who's against black people voting?"

"I can't figure that part out. Yet."

"Seems like a pretty big part."

"Look, maybe I'm wrong, and nobody whispered in Johnson's ear. Maybe he just got lucky. That's why tomorrow I want to go up to Harrisburg and check the public records of Pennsylvania incorporations in the last few years and talk to his attorney. To see if our Mr. Johnson has made any more suspiciously prophetic investments."

She switched me to the other hand. "All right," she sighed, resigned. "One more day, David. But then I really want to kick this popsicle stand. *Okay?*" she asked, her voice rising plaintively.

I couldn't help chuckling.

"What's so funny?"

"Oh...the way your nose wrinkles. The way your programmable clothes are always a little small. The way you sound like a little girl asking permission while using me as a human barbell."

She curled me close to her and held me there, her lips a tantalizing millimeter away from mine. "Admit it, you love it."

I leaned in and kissed her.

BAM-BAM-BAM!

The owner of the boarding house was pounding on the door. She'd had it with the indecent creaking floorboards and told us to find other quarters.

12

JUDGMENT AT HARRISBURG

W E TOOK THE MORNING TRAIN UP TO THE State Capitol in
Pennsylvania to meet Alden Linthicum, a Pennsylvania
state representative whom I had learned was also the attorney of
record for Mr. Octavius Johnson.

Wearing a tailored suit and affecting a fusty British accent, I
invited Mr. Linthicum out for a lavish lunch that was long on liba-
tion and short on answers regarding my own background.

I convinced Linthicum that my name was Aubrey Smythe, and
that I was England's answer to Alexis de Tocqueville, writing an
authoritative tome about great American captains of industry,
among whom I had heard that Mr. Johnson was preeminent. I
suggested that my work would, of course, mention this captain's
steadfast legal advisor.

His tongue thus loosened by spirits and flattery, Mr. Linthicum
informed me that his mysterious client was indeed a business
genius, having bought fortunate land parcels in advance of not only
the Pennsylvania Oil Boom, but the 1858 Pike's Peak Gold Rush and
the 1859 Comstock Silver Strike.

Another round of drinks yielded the news that Mr. Johnson had invested in a large parcel of land that Mr. Linthicum fretted would never amount to anything, a few miles due west of some tar pits near a sleepy California cattle town called Los Angeles.

Mr. Linthicum departed our luncheon for his rooming house, where I expect he slept it off, and I headed back to meet Ariyl at the depot.

* * *

"WELL, MAYBE HE LOVES TAR," shrugged Ariyl as we walked into the depot.

"He didn't buy the La Brea Tar Pits!" I pointed out. "He bought land two miles west, which in my time will be a hundred million dollars' worth of real estate in Beverly Hills. Where they strike oil in fifty years. He got it for three cents an acre. That's on top of buying claims just before three major finds in two years. I'm telling you, somebody from the future is tipping this guy off."

"I don't believe it's Dylila who told him."

"Who else could it be?"

"She would not interfere in history like that!"

"Of course she would! She sent you back to..." I stopped, and looked around to be sure we weren't being overheard. I gestured to an out-of-the-way pair of chairs and we sat down there.

"She sent you back to save Lincoln," I concluded quietly.

"That was different. Remember, the Agency has a Quality Control rule: if you're in a mutated timeline, you try to nudge it back into the historic groove."

"You weren't in a mutated timeline. That was original history. And anyway, that rule sounds nuts to me."

"'Cause you're pre-Change."

"What's that supposed to mean?"

"That you're a product of your time. We've had a century of progress since you were born."

"You call a world buried in glaciers progress?"

"David, she sent me to create an alternate timeline to see if things work out better. Where racists don't run America, 'cause black people got the vote when they should have."

"And women," I pointed out.

"Sure, why not? And where history doesn't end in a dead greenhouse planet."

"So instead it ends in a dead ice age!"

"Okay, it didn't work! Now we've undone it. Lincoln's dead again. You happy?" She was starting to cry.

"No, I'm not happy. Not until we restore history the way it *was!* Altered history cannot lead to your world or mine. I'm telling you, we are in a single, changeable timeline. So what we change, we have to either live with, or undo."

"David, we tried everything else! We can't get home if we don't change things!"

"According to Dylila! Who sent me back to stop you! Don't you get it? You can't get home if you *do* change things! Either she's lying to one of us, or to both of us."

"How do I know you're not lying? You didn't exactly tell me the truth about where these people get their meat."

"I didn't tell you because I knew you'd freak out!"

"I don't freak out!"

"Sh."

"Don't shush me!"

"I didn't shush, I just said 'sh'."

"David, you are making me really mad with you."

The big depot had great acoustics. Heads were turning in our direction.

"I love you, Ariyl. I am not lying to you. Dylila is."

"Why would she do that, David?"

"Because...she's a crazy bitch! I don't kn—"

"What did you call her?" This was accompanied by a cock of the head that suggested how much trouble I was in.

"Ah...I've been thinking about my word choice for the last five seconds or so," I began. "I believe I might owe you both an apology."

"Then make it."

More heads craned to eavesdrop on us.

"This is ridiculous," I whispered. "It's just a word. People say it all the time."

"Not in my time, they don't."

Ariyl stood up. She was six-six in those high-button boots and close to seven when you counted the piles of Lillian Russell curls atop her head. And that tight Victorian traveling suit could do nothing to disguise her impressive physique.

"Um..." I explained.

She put her fists on her hips. Calmly.

"Darling..." I reasoned.

She walked over to my chair. Slowly.

"Don't even think about it!" I warned.

She put her hands under my armpits. Gently.

"We're in public," I pleaded.

She lifted me into the air till my feet were dangling by her waist. Easily.

"Will you calm down!" I hissed.

"Has that phrase ever calmed *anyone* down?"

"Uh, not in my experience, no," I admitted.

Everyone in the depot was staring at us now. A guy who for all I knew might be Matthew Brady started to set up his camera. I had to end this fast.

"I'm very, very sorry."

That last phrase seemed to work better on her. She set me down and smoothed out my coat.

"I'm sorry too, David. But please don't use that word again."

Everyone was still staring.

"We're discussing when women will get the vote," Ariyl informed the crowd with a sunny smile. Husbands quickly escorted their astounded wives and daughters and sons to less dangerous environs.

One craggy-faced man bustled out of the crowd.

"Madam, would you entertain an offer to perform that feat of strength at my American Museum in New York?"

"Sorry, I only do that when I get angry," she said, turning to go.

"We could build a show around you. You could deliver a lecture on women's suffrage."

Ariyl turned back, intrigued.

"Darling, we do have to get home," I reminded her.

Ariyl sighed. "Okay, killjoy."

We walked out of the depot at a fast clip.

The man who was lugging a heavy bag couldn't keep up with us. "If you should change your mind, look me up at the museum," he called out. "The name is Phineas Barnum!"

"David, you know I could put on one hell of a show," Ariyl said. "Maybe my lecture would catch on, and..."

"Ariyl, don't be a sucker."

* * *

Harrisburg was bustling, so we walked toward the woods at the end of a street, where we could depart unseen.

"We should have at least listened to his offer," she pouted.

"His offer?" I scowled. "That firetrap museum of his burns down three months from now. You don't want to know what happens to his exhibits."

"Well, not if we warn him. I mean, he'd let me lecture on women voting!"

"He's the most famous con man in American history. You can't rely on anything that old fraud says!"

Ariyl gave me an impatient look: "You really are judgy, you know that?"

"About a crook like P. T. Barnum? Yeah, I am."

"About everybody! Me. Dylila. Even how cold you were to Major Rathbone when we saw him at the White House."

"You mean the guy who's gonna murder his wife in front of their kids? What should I have done, shaken his hand?"

"We met him when Lincoln didn't get shot, remember? Maybe in that history Henry didn't kill Clara, either."

"How do you figure?"

"Didn't you see him after the shooting?"

"Yeah. I saw him." She had a point. The guy was devastated. "He *was* pretty broken up."

"Broken is right. I bet he'll spend the rest of his life blaming himself for Lincoln's death. I think I know a little bit how he feels now."

"Okay, but that doesn't excuse..."

"I didn't say it did. I just said you're quick to judge."

"I can't wait to be proved wrong about Dylila. Let's see if we can get back to 2109."

"Shouldn't we go in steps, make sure history's on track?"

"We can skip to June fifteenth, 1954."

"But we've been there, and it was nuts!"

"That's exactly what we're checking on."

I knew that the first, unaltered draft of history would land us in a sleepy Eisenhower America ready for summer vacation, on a Tuesday night with Red Skelton hosting a trio of horror stars at eight-thirty on CBS.

"The Time Crystal will never take us *there*," she protested. "Oh, my God, an entire timeline self-destructed there!"

"If it refuses to send us to June fifteenth, at least we'll know this Crystal is actively preventing paradoxes. Either way, we'll know more than we do now."

"What if it's still the mutant timeline? What if we see President Strom Thurmond again? And Dylila? And *us?*"

"Can't happen. You killed the man who created that timeline before he could create it. It's nothing but a memory. But that same erasure can happen to us if you and Dylila keep messing with history."

"That timeline only failed because I created a paradox. To save your life, by the way. My bad. It was no reason not to try and save Lincoln."

"But will you admit that didn't work out either? Ice age!"

"So we try something else!"

"You two are assuming there can be any number of alternate

universes—that a time traveler can change whatever he or she wants and it costs the multiverse nothing. But that doesn't make sense—nothing is unlimited. It takes energy to create a universe, and if there's one thing I know, there's no free lunch!"

"You're wrong. N-Tec gives us free lunch all the time. Dinner and breakfast, too."

"What if you're wrong? What if in the end, there can be only one history? What if by creating these branch-off points, you're making *our* history less and less likely to be the true one?"

"Why are *you* freaking? Didn't I put history back the way it was?"

"Yes, you did."

"You're welcome!"

"Thank you! Now can we please leave it that way?"

"Let's just make sure we can get home. Once we do, I can smooth things over with Dylila."

I didn't believe that for a second. But there was no point arguing about it now.

Ariyl took hold of her Time Crystal. It was visibly dimmer than before. She tapped it. I found it strangely comforting that even in the twenty-second century, dealing with nanotech devices created by an artificial intelligence whose underlying principles we couldn't begin to follow, the human urge to jar machinery to get a better result still endured.

"Damn, my Crystal is out of power."

"I sat in the sun for a couple of hours; I think mine's good to go." I put out my hand. "C'mon, I'll give you a lift."

"That'll be a nice change," she smirked. "But look, I told you we had trouble doubling up with Dylila's Crystal. I think it'll happen with any Crystal Ludlo hasn't reset."

"Like mine?"

"Yeah. So if you take *me* through time with yours, I have a feeling I'll arrive about three hours later than you. So don't panic if that happens."

"But you show up at the same location?"

"Yep," she said. "So far."

"Uh..."

"If I'm not with you when you get there, just stay put. Okay?"

"Sure, that'll give me time to verify that history hasn't made any changes. I'll meet you at that newsrack out front of the Good Samaritan Hospital. The one you broke open last time."

I took her hand, held my Crystal, and spoke the coordinates.

13

BLACK GOLD

I FELT THE USUAL INVERTED SENSATION AS North America spun eastward under our feet, flashing green-tan-red-white through nine decades of solstices and equinoxes. As the world returned, my hand was suddenly empty. As she'd predicted, Ariyl was gone.

Hopefully, to appear in this same spot in about three hours.

I was on Wilshire Boulevard, just south of the Good Samaritan Hospital. And according to the clock outside the jewelry store it was two o'clock.

This was the very same hour Ariyl and I had arrived in the 1954 that Ludlo had mutated. Who was the president? I had to know!

There were no discarded newspapers in view, but there was the infamous newsrack she'd attacked. And "Ike" was featured in the headline as president. So overall, history looked correct. But there was a detail I needed to be sure of.

I reached into my pockets for change. I found a shiny new 1865 half-dime—the small and skinny forerunner of our big fat modern nickel. I happened to know this particular date was a rarity worth hundreds of dollars in 2016, but I was in a hurry and would gladly have sacrificed it for a quick news fix. Unfortunately for me, and the news vendor, the half-dime wasn't heavy enough to operate the rack and fell through into the return tray.

I didn't have a dime, yet I did have ten cents; it was in the form of that silver half-dime, a big copper two-cent piece, and a small nickel three-cent piece: oddball denominations used for postal change back in Civil War times.

Miracle Mile Coins was just a block down the street. I hurried over...only to find a "Closed For Lunch" sign, with a plastic clock that indicated he'd just left.

I tried to get passersby to trade me a humble modern dime for these rare coins, but no one recognized them as real money. They treated me like the world's dumbest counterfeiter.

After a few minutes, I gave in and offered to trade my 1858 silver dollar for a dime. I finally got one taker, who was probably a numismatist, judging by the way his face lit up at the offer. He must have thought I was developmentally challenged, though no doubt he'd have used a meaner word for it. He hurried off, having taken obscene advantage of me.

I yanked the *Los Angeles Times* out and unfolded it to the back pages. Just as I'd hoped, the TV-Radio page listed Red Skelton with the exact guest cast he was supposed to have on his show tonight on KNXT: our erstwhile time-traveling companions Bela Lugosi and Lon Chaney...plus Vampira, the hourglass-figured horror hostess.

Thus, I was safe from paradox. I would not meet Dylila or Ludlo or Khutulun, or anyone else that I knew had been at this hospital today, in the other timeline.

History was still on course, nine decades after Lincoln.

But now I had a three-hour wait for Ariyl.

That was a long time to sit. And I was curious about whatever happened to that property Octavius Johnson bought on Wilshire.

The nurse at the admitting desk lent me their phone book.

There was an Olga Johnson, an Oliver Johnson, and an Otto Johnson. No Octavius. But under O, I found in all caps (as businesses were listed) OCTAVIUS CORP.

The address was at 555 Flower Street, Suite 1200.

I'll grant you, the sensible thing would have been to wait there for Ariyl to materialize in three hours. That way there would be no chance of missing each other.

But it was a warm day to be wearing a wool suit with starched-collar shirt.

I took out my pencil—the one useful thing I still had from 1865—and wrote "ARIYL, WAIT HERE BACK AT 5 PM" across the top of the *Times* TV-Radio page, and stuffed it into the chain link fence beside the newsrack.

I told myself leaving the hospital grounds would be like washing my car to bring on a rainstorm—it would more or less guarantee that when I got back, Ariyl would be there, albeit fuming. Then my eye was caught by the striking black tower a mile away. My destination.

I strolled east on Wilshire Boulevard toward it.

The state had recently completed the Harbor-Pasadena Freeway to America's first four-level interchange. I turned north then crossed the freeway on the narrow sidewalk of an overpass, amazed to see traffic flowing at over thirty miles an hour on a weekday afternoon.

I headed east again, past the once-elegant Victorian mansions atop Bunker Hill; by this point, they had aged into the peeling-paint flophouses you can see in mid-century *noirs* like *Kiss Me Deadly*.

At Olive and Third Streets, I bought a round-trip ticket for five cents, earning me a nostalgic "Gee whiz!" from the nonagenarian in the ticket booth. He happily accepted my two-cent and three-cent pieces. I then boarded the funicular car named Olivet and rode it down Angels Flight to Hill Street.

I bought a pastrami sandwich at the Grand Central Market then strolled south and stuck my head in the door to sample the steampunk charm of the Bradbury Building, with its tile, Italian marble, polished wood, ornamental iron, and cage elevators. All these delightful relics of the city's past are still there today, but it was fun seeing them a lot closer to their heyday.

The infamous L.A. smog of the Fifties stung my eyes, and the ozone I'd been breathing felt like someone had dropped a lit match into my lungs. But at last I reached Flower and Wilshire to behold a sight that was worth the long walk, if not all the pollution that had financed it: The Richfield Oil Building. Alongside the new freeway that its product made possible, stood that legendary Streamline Moderne landmark, clad on all sides in shiny black terracotta with golden accents.

(Black gold, oil company headquarters, get it? It was even topped by a tower shaped like an oil well. The façade also featured sculpted chevrons, even though that was the name of the competition.)

The interior of Richfield Tower was just as spectacular. The gleaming rococo brass elevator doors alone were works of art.

Alas, suite 1200, which bore the brass plate identifying it as Octavius Corp., did not respond to knocking. The office had a glass entry door, and stout doors stood open, revealing inner offices. The place was empty of furniture or furnishings. And had been for a while; there was an actual spider web across the door handle.

Meanwhile, I realized I'd been gone from the hospital for over an hour, and I should get back to the Good Sam and see if Ariyl had materialized yet.

I went back up Angels Flight and made my way past the seedy rooming houses.

As I walked, I became aware I was being watched by three large punks in pompadour haircuts with ducktails in back; all three wore T-shirts, faded blue jeans, and leather motorcycle jackets. It was like their uniform.

They fell in behind me as I walked.

"Hey, mister!" called out their ostensible leader, a blonde with a scowl that would curdle milk. "What are ya, mister, an actor?"

Great. I'd forgotten I was still in my Civil War era clothes; my odd outfit had now singled me out for the special attentions of these juvenile delinquents. Except they weren't that juvenile. More like twentysomethings with a case of arrested development.

"Something like that," I said, keeping a steady pace.

"Nice job, workin' in a theater," the blond guy said. Those hard Rs and "job" pronounced like "jab" made me place the kid as a Chicago transplant. "Or are you in the movies?"

"Buzz off, junior," I said, trying to sound older than twenty-nine.

"Tough guy!" said one of the blond guy's wingmen.

"Yo-ou duhty rat, you killed my brotha!" said the other, in a vague approximation of Cagney. The other two laughed themselves sick in appreciation.

I glanced around. No cops or witnesses. Suddenly, Bunker Hill in 1954 seemed like a mean street. I decided to pick up the pace.

They picked theirs up too.

I decided to run instead of walk.

But in no time they were gaining on me. I ducked around a corner into an alley and pulled out the Time Crystal. If I had to, I could always go to my previous destination and hope to God I could get back to Ariyl later. I watched the corner like a hawk.

Until I heard a spring-loaded click and turned to see the blond punk was right behind me, with his switchblade half an inch from my eye.

He had slid through a narrow passage between buildings and gotten behind me.

"Not a sound," he instructed me. His two friends rounded the corner and flicked their switchblades too.

"I have money in my pockets, if I you'll let me reach for it," I began.

The blond guy yanked the Time Crystal off me and held it up with a curious eye. I lunged for it, but the punk stepped back, keeping the blade between us. His henchmen gave a sarcastic "Oooh!"

"Nice jewel, mister," said the towhead punk. "Hey, fellas, how much you think I could fence it for?"

"Twenty bucks, Jerry. Easy."

The other wingman swatted the first wingman. He was only a minion, yet even he knew it was a dumb idea to use names.

Meanwhile, I was at triple knifepoint, while my Barlow knife was still in the custody of the Washington, D.C. police, rusting for decades in a property room or a police museum somewhere. That meant dueling the three of them à la D'Artagnan was out. So was making another grab.

"You don't want that thing. It's a stage prop," I said. "I'll give you all my money if you just give it back."

"If it's not worth anything, why do you want to give me all your money for it?" said Jerry.

"'Cause if I show up at the theater without it, I'll get canned."

"Aw, yer breakin' my heart."

"C'mon, fellas."

"Naah, I think I'll keep it. *And* your money." Jerry snapped his fingers and stuck out his palm.

The less-than-discreet wingman peered at the Crystal.

"Hey, doesn't this kinda look like the thing Mr. Eight-Fingers is looking for?" he opined.

"Shaddap!" snapped Jerry.

"Who's Eight-Fingers?" I asked. "You work for him?"

"We work for nobody. Now hand over the dough!"

Jerry gave a "do-it" look to his smarter compadre. That guy closed in on me.

"Okay!" I said, reaching into my pocket for my last dollar. "But you guys really should take this to a coin shop..." I held it up with my forefinger encircling the heavy metal disk. "...'cause it's really RARE!"

With a flick of my finger, I flung the heavy coin right at my attacker's forehead. It pinged off the bridge of his nose—he groaned in pain and went down. Jerry and Mr. Namedropper came at me, ready to do some serious ventilation.

I took off running.

14

THIRD TIME THIS WEEK

I RAN THROUGH THE EERILY DESERTED SLUM without knowing where I was going. I flew through alleys, down a concrete stairway, across a termite-riddled porch, under a trestle, up another stairway. The ozone was working my lungs like a boxer on a heavy bag.

Eventually, I wound up back where I'd started, on Olive Street.

I rounded a corner and flattened myself against the wall of a rooming house, trying not to pant so hard, so I could hear if my pursuers' running steps were getting louder, or fainter.

I cursed myself for being unprepared. I had set off walking through a major American city without anything I could use as a weapon. Now I was on the run from three dangerous thugs, one of whom I had to let catch up to me at some point, since he was carrying my ticket home.

I listened. All I heard was a single set of footsteps. Leather-soled shoes. Walking.

I prayed that they had split up, and that this was Jerry, the asshole who took my Crystal.

One on one, I might be able to take him, knife or no knife.

Curiosity would kill me even more surely than those switchblades would, but I had to take a look.

Peering around the corner, I saw....

An Asian-American schoolgirl crossing the far end of the alley, hugging her books to her chest. It must have been a parochial school, since she had the uniform: White blouse, tie, pleated plaid skirt, kneesocks, polished black Mary Janes. Sauntering, barely noticing her surroundings.

She wasn't after anyone.

I relaxed. I must have lost them.

Then I realized I didn't want to lose them all. I needed to find Jerry. But how the hell was I going to do it?

I looked at the girl again. I had the oddest feeling I'd seen her before. I couldn't place her, though.

Then I saw Jerry and the others again. But they didn't see me. They weren't following me. They were crossing that same alleyway.

They were following the girl.

I had a pretty good idea what they intended.

So I started following them.

As I did, I kept looking for a beat cop or a patrol car or anyone I could get to help me

At the end of the next block, the girl kept walking, paying her three stalkers no heed. She turned right, and headed into an alley. They did the same thing.

I hurried along closed-up brick storefronts. As I ran, I looked up and down the street: nary a soul in sight, let alone a cop. There was a payphone, but I didn't have any workable coins. I scanned the sidewalk, desperate for a piece of pipe or stick or even a rock.

I saw not so much as a pebble.

There was a half-used book of paper matches. I scooped it up. Who knows, maybe I could somehow set one of them on fire.

I was so busy looking for a weapon that I almost missed the alley entrance, nearly blocked off by trash cans, but then I glimpsed daylight at the end of the narrow passageway.

I dashed into that dark alley.

Suddenly, I found myself in a trash-strewn vacant yard that backed onto a sheer drop. I was facing the guy with a bruise where

I'd beaned him with the dollar. The other wingman was with him. Their knives were open.

I turned to run, but my escape route was blocked by Jerry, switch-blade in hand.

"Okay, come *on!*" I yelled with as much bravado as I could muster. "Maybe the three of you can take me!" There was no maybe about it, but I planned to make a lot of noise before they took me down.

Jerry laughed. "Get the Jap girl. I'll handle the play-actor."

They ran around the corner of the building after her.

I heard the girl cry out.

Jerry lunged at me with the knife.

I heard a grunt as a body hit the ground.

She cried again, higher. I kept dodging Jerry's blade.

Some impacts that had to be body blows, and again, a body hit the ground.

They were killing her!

I looked back and saw just the tip of a plank sticking out of a trash can in the alley. I ran for it.

Jerry figured I'd turned yellow.

"Yeah, you better run while you still can!" he snarled.

I grabbed the plank from the can and went after Jerry, ready to do some serious damage.

I was too late.

As I rounded the corner of the building, I realized I had pictured the scene all wrong.

Jerry's two wingmen were sprawled on the ground, whimpering and holding their bruised faces; the schoolgirl, barely mussed, was facing off with Jerry. He was jabbing at her under-hand with his stiletto, just looking for an opening. He wouldn't find it.

"Hee-yah!" she cried, kicking the knife out of his hand. It landed on a sewer grate then dropped inside.

Jerry threw three fast punches. She dodged the first, blocked the second—but the third caught her on the lip.

Blood started to trickle down the side of her mouth.

He came in to finish her off. But she blocked both punches then delivered three of her own.

Jerry staggered back, blood now running out of his nose. Furious, he came at her again and grabbed her throat. She immediately brought up her hands between his, broke the hold, and then did simultaneous neck chops.

The blond punk grunted in pain but shook it off. With a furious growl, he charged. She met him with karate chops.

"Yah! *Hep! HAAH!*" she barked, each cry louder, just as each blow landed with more force, knocking him backward step by step.

Suddenly, the first gang member was on his feet with his arm around her throat. For a second. Before I could even move, she put her palm on the back of his head, dropped down, and threw him over her shoulder: "Hi-YEEE!"

She stomped his midsection and he was out of action.

The schoolgirl turned back to Jerry. Instead of him advancing on her, she began driving him backwards with chops, punches, and backhands, while she blocked every jab he threw. She kept up a running commentary with each blow.

"Whatsamatter, Jerry?" (CHOP!) "Didn't go like you planned?" (PUNCH!) "Thought I'd be easy?" (SMACK!) Then she landed a kick to his chest that threw Jerry spread-eagled against a board fence. He stared at her in uncomprehending terror.

"Look, I give up. Just lemme go!" pleaded Jerry.

"No way, champ!" she crowed. "I'm just getting warmed up!" She hit a karate stance then beckoned to him with her fingers.

"Biff! Tony! Help me!" he yelled in panic. But his pals were in no shape to respond.

Jerry charged her in a desperate rage and got a kick to the groin and a knee to the face for his trouble. He swung a haymaker that she ducked; she snapped a side-kick to his face and sent him sprawling.

Suddenly she pivoted—out of nowhere came one of his battered pals. She must've seen his shadow from behind her. Biff (or Tony) got his own face-kick that sent him back to the ground, limp.

Meanwhile, Jerry found a four-foot piece of lumber.

He nearly brained her on the first swing—but missed by half an inch. On the follow-through, she kicked him in the side, and he dropped the beam against the alley wall.

"You won't be needing this. Hee-YAH!" she yelled, snapping the two-by-four with her foot.

"You lemme alone!" he roared as he swung his fist at her face.

She ducked and resumed punching and chopping.

"Where'd I hear...those words...before?" she mused between blows. "Oh, that's right. Me, six years ago." Face punch. "Begging you to stop." Neck chop. "Cermak Road. Five blocks from my school!" Gut punch.

Oh, my God, I finally understood.

"Stop!" he groaned.

"I said that, too. I even said 'please.'"

He swung at her. She ducked. Two more chops to either side of his neck.

"Please!" he moaned.

She paused then shook her head.

"Turns out that word doesn't work either. Does it?"

Face punch. He fell to the ground, his nose leaking like a rusty tap.

She stepped over him. "Get up," she commanded.

Jerry just lay there, shaking his head. Shaking all over.

"Okay. He's had enough," I said, stepping into the sunlit vacant lot.

She whirled and glared at me.

"I'll call the cops," I told her. "I'm your witness. They started it."

"Where'd you come from, sport?" she demanded.

"I was following them. I could see they were following you."

"Who asked you to help?"

"Nobody. But you were in danger."

"Was I?" She surveyed the trio of moaning men on the ground.

"Well, obviously not as much danger as they were."

"That's right. But Jerry here is in even worse danger." She gave me a challenging look. "And so are *you*, mister, unless you're smart enough to just walk away."

"That's what *he* just told me to do."

"Both times, good advice."

"They're not going anywhere. Let me get the cops."

I turned to go, but she grabbed my wrist and bent it at a painful angle. I gasped and fell to my knee.

"No cops," she said in a low, angry voice. "They don't do shit."

The blond guy on the ground stirred. She released me, bent over, seized his shirt in her fists, and pulled him in close. "Remember me yet, Jerry?"

His eyes went wide. "I-I never saw you before!" Her next neck chop broke his collar bone. He wailed.

"If you keep this up, you're going to kill him!" I warned.

"I'll just have to risk it," she said, bringing up her hand for another karate chop.

Instinctively I grabbed her hand. I say instinctively because if any thought had been involved, I would not have done it.

She dropped Jerry, seized my finger to pry my hand off her, then with a "Ha!" she chopped *me* on the neck. My whole left side went numb. "Ha!" A gut punch took my breath away.

Before I knew what was happening, she grabbed my arm and threw me over her shoulder. I landed flat on my back. I struggled to turn over, but she jumped on me, grabbed my shoulders, and straddled me, her knees on my shoulders. With every ounce of strength, I rolled her over, got on top, and pinned her shoulders to the ground.

"Stop!" I told her. "I don't want to fight y–"

I couldn't finish that word because suddenly I saw the heels of two black-leather Mary Janes as she brought her legs up behind me and locked her ankles at my throat. Then her calves compressed my neck and pulled me off her.

I landed on my back, my neck still held between her legs. Before I could free myself, she slid close and put me in a figure-four hold, holding my arm trapped beneath me, my head clamped between her thighs, her calf pulled up against my windpipe. Her plaid skirt fell across my eyes so I couldn't even see. I couldn't move an inch. I gasped for air.

She pulled up the skirt. Now I could see her face, upside-down, leaning over me as I lay trapped in her lap. She was furious. And pretty. And pretty furious.

"Listen, big man," she snarled. "You're in *way* over your head. Either you let me finish this creep, or I put you out. You want that?"

"No!" I moaned.

"I'm dead serious, mister. I could leave you in a wheelchair."

"I know!"

"Do you?" She flexed her thighs and instantly my trapped arm ached and my head was like a sub at crush depth.

"Definitely!" I yelped.

"Otherwise *yours* are the next bones I break."

"Got it!"

At last she relaxed those killer quads, and my head began to resume its original shape.

"I'm just saying don't kill him."

She turned up the pressure again as she gave an exasperated growl. "Maybe I should just give you a neck that predicts rain the rest of your life."

"No, no! Not necessary!"

"'Cause I can do that for you, no problem."

"Please don't!"

She slightly lowered her thigh pressure, but kept glaring down at me. I was aware of a lull in the conversation.

"Did anybody ever tell you you're a very angry girl?"

Her calf bulged inside that white cotton sock and cut off my windpipe. "My ex-husband, all the time. It always pissed me off," she muttered. "So you just made me a teensy bit angrier."

"Sorry," I gurgled.

At last, she let me inhale. "Are you going to do exactly what I say?"

"Yes. I would like to keep on being surprised by the weather."

She didn't crack a smile.

"I swear to God, I won't interfere," I added.

"You won't run for a cop?"

"I won't even limp."

She held me a few seconds longer, appraising me. Finally she gave me a smile that was half sneer: "Good boy."

Jerry rose up behind her with my plank in his hands.

"Look out!" I yelled.

The Japanese girl leapt up, spun, kicked the board from his hands, and went back to work on Jerry. With insistent karate cries, she chopped him left and right. I heard her blows break bones and heard a punch that must have fractured his jaw. In seconds he was on his hands and knees, weeping.

"No more," he begged.

"When I cried, did *you* stop?" demanded the girl.

"I'm sorry! I'll never do it again! Please don't hit me anymore!"

"Okay, Jerry, no more hitting," she said. She stepped back, and then yelled "Ha!" as she did a leaping roundhouse to his head.

"And that was my last kick," she told the senseless form bleeding into the dead grass.

As she strode back toward me, her angry face relaxed slight-ly...into a contemptuous smile.

"You can get up now, hero." She offered me her hand, which is to say, she pointed a deadly weapon in my direction. I hesitated, but I didn't want to look as scared as I felt. I took hold, and she pulled me right up. I surveyed her whimpering victims.

I cleared my throat. "Well, at least you got that out of your system," I said, still having trouble using my larynx.

She shook her head. "I got a *lot* more where that came from."

I walked over to Jerry and retrieved my Time Crystal from his jacket.

"Ooh, pretty," she said dryly. "Really sets off your eyes."

* * *

She bought me a Coke at a taco stand two blocks away. Maybe she felt a little bad for working me over. She watched me as I sipped it.

"Why do you keep looking at me like that?" she said, suspi-ciously.

"Sorry, I don't mean to be rude. You just...look familiar. Like I've seen you somewhere."

"Oh, *brother.*"

"No, no, I'm not feeding you a line. It's just there's something about your face...you don't have any Mongolian blood, by any chance?"

She shook her head. "I wish. Mighta kept me out of Manzanar. No, I'm Japanese. And Filipino, Cheyenne, Scotch-Irish."

"Well, it's not that you look like her, and she was taller. But she had your build and moved like you."

I took another swallow of Coca-Cola. I sipped it gingerly, but still winced.

"First time you're ever beaten up by a girl, sport?"

"Third time this week," I said.

"Ha!" This time it was a laugh.

I put the cold Coke bottle on my aching neck. My gut still hurt, and my whole left side was sore. "Note to myself: before rescuing damsel in distress, always ask if she knows karate," I said.

"And aikido. Black belt in both, so don't get cute," she replied. This girl had attitude to burn. "Now, who the hell are you?"

"Professor David Preston. I'm a historian at UCLA." That was true, at least in a future tense. "And what's your name?"

"Why? So you can tell the cops who beat up those creeps?" She was getting mad again.

"Never mind, it's none of my business."

She cooled off. "Smart boy. So why were you following me again?"

"I wasn't. My Crystal was stolen an hour ago, by your friend, Jerry."

Her voice went ice cold. "He's no friend of mine."

"I figured. But you knew him years ago? In Chicago?"

"Good guess, champ," she nodded.

"What are the odds you'd run into him here in L.A.?" I asked.

"A lead-pipe cinch. I tracked him here."

"He's not your ex-husband, is he?"

"Naah, Johnny wasn't bad. Just immature. We only lasted nine months. He couldn't handle me dancing in clubs. I divorced him a couple years ago."

"So you're not really a schoolgirl."

She shook her head. "But I was when Jerry raped me. Men like him don't change. I knew if I walked his neighborhood long enough dressed like this, he'd spot me and try something." She shook her head. "After all that, the creep didn't even recognize me."

"You must have been young," I realized. She didn't reply. She didn't need to. "I'm really sorry," I added.

"Don't be. Sorry don't do shit. Ask Jerry, if he ever wakes up. But don't worry. I'll find each one of them; no matter how long it takes. And then I'll make *them* sorry."

"Them? How many were there?"

"Five."

"Jesus!"

"Yeah, I was yelling that name a lot. And his dad. Guess they were too busy to help."

"Did you go to the police?"

"Oh, sure. But one of those punks' daddy paid off the judge, so they all got off with a slap on the wrist. Not a day in jail. That's when my dad started teaching me karate. I got my black belt in five years." She gave a contemptuous smile. "Now *I* decide where they get slapped. And how hard."

I turned, hearing a rising siren. An ambulance raced past us, down the street in the direction of where she'd left Jerry and his pals. She barely paid it any mind.

"Do you have any idea what Jerry's doing here in L.A.? Like, who he's working for?"

"Nope. I found the first of his gang back in Chicago. Dewey. Now, Dewey only held me down, so I went easy on him. I only broke his arms. Maybe a couple other things. Between spitting out teeth, he agreed to tell me where Jerry was living in L.A.—on Bunker Hill."

I eyed the seedy hotels. "Nice spot for him."

"You live around here?" she asked.

"I'm just kind of passing through. I'm supposed to meet a friend at the Good Sam hospital."

She laughed. "Say hi to Jerry for me. But I don't think you should walk around this town by yourself. Not after today. Tell you what: I'll walk you over there. Just in case anyone else tries to get rough with you." She gave me a condescending smirk.

"Thanks, but that's not necessary."

"It's right on the way to my bus."

"I'll be fine."

"Don't be a hero, Professor. You're not cut out for it. I have a hunch if I hadn't taken out these punks, they were going to gut you."

"Your hunch is right on the money."

"See? You need someone to take care of you."

A second ambulance went by on the street, siren wailing.

"You already took care of three guys. That's enough. I should get going. Thanks for the Coke." But as I started to rise, she took hold of the rope-like metal chain of the Crystal.

"So...what's with the bauble?"

"It's something they thought was worth money, but isn't. I told them it's just a prop, but losing it would get me in big trouble. They didn't care."

"Why do *they* want it?"

"Near as I can figure, they don't want it. Some rich guy they call Eight-Fingers wants it."

"Hm," was all she said.

A third ambulance screamed past.

"They talked about him like he was some kind of rackets boss. I have a hunch he hangs out in Beverly Hills," I said. "And that sure is a hoodlum's name—Mr. Eight-Fingers."

"You sure about that?"

"Not entirely, but it feels like that's the way to bet. If I'm right, this guy is as dangerous a crook as you ever met."

She smacked her palms on the table and got up. "Well, sport, I gotta blow. Don't try to save any more fair maidens."

"You're not gonna walk me back to the Good Samaritan after all?"

"I *was* your good Samaritan," she said.

"That you were. I'd like to thank you."

"Forget it. I also kicked your ass, so we're even. So long, Professor." She strode off with a determined look on her face.

For a girl who had been taking her time and enjoying needling me, all of a sudden she was in quite a hurry to get rid of me.

Was it my imagination, or did that start as soon as I mentioned Mr. Eight-Fingers?

THE ONLY ONE who might know the answer was walking north.

I got up from the bench and began following the girl. At a discreet distance. I sure as hell didn't want Little Miss Black Belt to catch me at it.

15

EIGHT FINGERS

I T WASN'T EASY KEEPING UP WITH THE ASIAN girl. She walked fast. She caught a crosstown bus at Sunset. She moved to the back of the bus and took a seat. I patted myself down and found one more antique quarter in my rear pants pocket.

"No change," the driver warned me.

"It's fine," I muttered, ducking into a seat behind the driver. I checked his interior mirror: I could see the girl, and as far as I could tell, she hadn't seen me.

The traffic wasn't as bad as it is in our era; there were occasional stops to let one of the last remaining streetcars by—in a handful more years, those would be history.

The bus rolled through Echo Park, Silver Lake, Los Feliz, Hollywood, West Hollywood, and the Strip, and finally into Beverly Hills. I felt a little more justified about my suspicions of Mr. Eight-Fingers, recalling that Octavius Johnson had, with remarkable foresight, purchased land in that city—half a century before it was founded.

We stopped in front of the big pink Beverly Hills Hotel at Benedict Canyon Drive. The girl got off at the back door of the bus. She looked all around her—caution born of dire experience. It meant I couldn't get off as long as she was facing in my direction.

Finally, she headed up the canyon road. But by that time, the bus was moving. I begged the driver to let me off, but he was a stickler for the rules.

So I clambered out an open window.

"Hey!" he yelled at me as I dangled my feet above the fast-moving concrete roadway then dropped off.

I managed a decent landing, rolling as I fell.

Then I loped back east on Sunset to Benedict Canyon. By this time, the girl was a quarter mile up the road, nearly out of view. I hurried to try and close the distance between us.

Way up the hill, I saw her pick up a phone at a fancy gatepost. The electric gate rolled open for her, but it had closed by the time I got there.

I suppose I could have phoned from the gate as well and come up with some great story about why a guy dressed like Ashley Wilkes needed to talk to a very rich man who, I was pretty sure, would never admit to being "Mr. Eight-Fingers."

Apparently I had writer's block, since I couldn't come up with one.

On the other hand, I could have easily climbed it, but scaling the front entry at the compound of some criminal robber baron seemed foolhardy at best, even if he didn't have a time traveler feeding him intel.

Carefully, I worked my way around the downhill side of the property and found a tree I could climb to drop down on the other side of the wall.

THE PLACE WAS UNBELIEVABLE. And vast. It went on for acres. I literally got lost trying to figure out where the house was.

Imagine Jack Woltz's estate in *The Godfather*, then add Michael Corleone's spread on Lake Tahoe, as revamped by Walt Disney.

There was a hundred-foot high waterfall cascading down into a stream a block long, with a brace of canoes stacked along the head of the stream.

There was a nine-hole golf course, complete with an old mill as a clubhouse. I don't mean to say that the grounds lay alongside this golf course—they *contained* it.

There were a dozen gardens: sunken gardens, terraced gardens, Italian gardens, rose gardens. A long ridge down to the golf course, with its center divided by a series of cascading fountains.

Some kind of tropical forest.

Stables, greenhouses, orchards, farmland.

An open-air pavilion with a bandstand.

Tennis courts, a handball court, a green set up for lawn bowling.

Most strange of all, a child-sized little English village, with a four-room fairy tale cottage playhouse, pony cart, stable, and a wishing well. Whoever and whatever else Mr. Eight-Fingers was, he must have doted on his little girl.

And a double-Olympic-size swimming pool. Of course.

But aside from the manicured golf course, the place looked down at the heels: dead trees, untended gardens, dusty walks. The stables were empty, the orchard was dropping unpicked fruit, and lawns were in need of cutting. I hate to say it, since I loathe the gasoline exhaust and the noise that blasts me awake every Monday morning in my West L.A. neighborhood, but the place sorely needed a team of mow-blow-and-go guys.

Keeping to the tree line that fringed the estate, I made my way toward the house: a mansion styled like some Florentine villa.

There wasn't a soul on the property that I could see.

I reached the house, my hand clutching my escape vehicle. I still didn't have a plan, but I wasn't going to blow my chance to find out who this guy was who had thugs out looking for a Time Crystal.

I peered into one window and was startled to see an enormous lit-up Christmas tree. It took up the entire end of a barrel-vaulted sitting room, and every square inch of it was covered in glittering metal and glass ornaments, some of them the size of casaba melons, plus enough lights to illuminate a small town, and pounds of tinsel.

In the middle of June. I idly wondered when was the last time it was watered.

I shifted my gaze, and then I saw the man. His back was to me. He was bending over a woman who lay supine on the floor at his feet. With a jolt, I saw that it was my black belt savior, now cringing, naked, and helpless, with livid red gashes down her belly.

He gestured at her, and that's when I saw his right hand was mutilated, missing the forefinger and thumb and a chunk of the palm.

But he had eight fingers left.

16

O, TANNENBAUM!

I STILL DIDN'T HAVE A WEAPON. EXCEPT FOR one thing in my pockets, which I prayed I wouldn't have to use.

I burst in the door nearest the giant Christmas tree.

"Get away from her!"

The man turned. He was sixty or so, well-dressed, graying, bushy-browed, bespectacled. Grandfatherly, was my first thought. My second thought was that clearly, not every monster looks like one.

"Who are you?" he demanded.

"You heard me! Back off, Eight-Fingers!"

"I *beg* your pardon!" he exclaimed, drawing himself up. "Do you know who I am?"

I noticed a strange camera with three lenses on a tripod near the girl.

"Some perv who photographs his crimes, it looks like!"

He slipped his good hand into his pocket. "Let me show—"

"Ah-ah!" I held up my book of matches, tore one out, and held it to the striking surface, near the Christmas tree. "Take your hand out empty and real slow!"

He did as instructed. "Wh-what are you doing?" he gasped.

"It's been six months since Christmas, pop. I bet this thing would go up like the Fourth of July if I strike a spark."

"Now, let's just calm down," he said. "There's no need to do anything crazy."

Little Miss Black Belt sat up and stared at me.

"*Professor?*"

"Can you walk?" I asked her. "Are you hurt bad?"

She stood up. "Not as bad you're gonna be."

I had my pack of matches poised beside the tinder-dry branches. "Don't worry, kid, Mr. Eight-Fingers is going to behave himself. He's going to sit down quietly while you dial the police. Because he knows it beats calling the fire department."

And the man did sit down, staring at me as if I were an escaped lunatic.

The naked girl ran over to me, like she was going to hide behind me. Except instead, she grabbed my hand with the matches, yanked it away, and threw me over her shoulder with one of her patented karate yells.

I literally flew into a grandfather clock, which started to topple over on me.

"Judas Priest!" cried Eight-Fingers, who leapt up with astonishing agility to grab his falling antique. As I looked up at him, holding onto the ponderous timepiece as it leaned crazily forward, I suddenly recognized him.

And why not? He embodied the most famous image of the silent movies: The bespectacled man clinging to a damaged clock on a skyscraper in *Safety Last*.

"Oh, my God...you're Harold Lloyd!"

"Why, yes, I am!" he said, pleasantly surprised to be recognized.

I must've landed on my head, because I then put out my hand to shake his. He automatically put out his left hand in response—but the clock slipped, nearly crushing me, and it took the two of us to push it back upright.

* * *

We sat, appropriately enough, in Harold Lloyd's sitting room. I had to keep reminding myself it was June 1954. Time had stopped in Harold's world. It wasn't just that potentially explosive *Tannenbaum* looming over us at the far end. Every piece of furniture in the room seemed to have been bought before the Depression. But if anyone had a reason to keep on living in the Roaring Twenties, I guess it was Harold. It was his decade.

"Mr. Lloyd, I'm a major fan. Your films are just...masterpieces of comedy. *Safety Last, Girl Shy, The Freshman...*" I left it hanging like I'd seen more, but those were actually all I'd seen. I'm not nearly as up on silent cinema as I am on talkies; but I definitely knew Lloyd was one of the three comic geniuses of the era.

"Well, I'm pleased to hear such a nice compliment, young man. Not a lot of people your age know my work. Now, would you mind explaining why you broke into my home and tried to burn it down?"

As mild-mannered as he seemed, there was an edge to his voice. I could tell he was still pretty upset with me. But since he had his butler serving us tea and cakes, I got the idea he wasn't ready to call the cops on me quite yet.

"I wouldn't really have struck that match, sir...but I thought you might have a gun. It was all I could think of."

"Well, that *was* inventive," he allowed, with a flicker of admiration. "But why would you think I had a gun?"

"You see, I thought you were the mobster who sent some thugs to try and steal...well, some property of mine."

"I am not in the habit of employing 'thugs', as you call them, Mister...?"

"Professor," the girl put in. "He says."

I nodded. "Professor David Preston."

"And this property of yours is what?"

I started to dissemble, but quick as a flash, the girl yanked the Crystal out of my shirt and over my head. She handed it to Lloyd.

My heart started pounding. If there was any chance that this reclusive genius *was* secretly after a Time Crystal, he now had it in his hand and could depart for 1925 at any second.

He held it up to the light.

"This isn't a real gemstone," he opined. "No flaws."

"No, sir. It's a theatrical prop."

"Are you an actor, then? I thought you said you were a professor."

"In my spare time, I do community theater, and it's a real shoe-string production. I'd hate to lose something they'd have to replace. May I have it back?"

He shrugged and handed it over.

I relaxed.

"And how do you know my model?" he asked.

Before I could answer, she did: "The same punks who tried to rob him tried to attack me."

"And you handled them, I'm guessing," said Harold.

She nodded.

The old comedian chuckled. "I'd have paid money to photograph that. Maybe next time?"

"It'd be my pleasure," she grinned.

"So, you photograph nude models at your home?" I asked.

"I most certainly do. And yes, my wife Mildred approves of my hobby. I've been experimenting with stereo pictures." He pointed to the camera. "You know, 3-D. I have some polarized glasses if you'd like to see them. My work is published in the leading photography magazines. Some very famous women have posed for me. Marilyn Monroe, in that pool right out there. Bettie Page."

He gestured at the Asian girl, "And of course, the beautiful—"

She cut him off, "He doesn't need to know my name, does he, Harold?"

"Not if you don't wish it, of course," he said.

She gave me a sidelong glance. "I was gonna warn you about him, Harold. I'm still not sure we can trust this guy."

"Look, I admit I followed you here," I told her. "But those thugs were talking about a 'Mr. Eight-Fingers' and when I mentioned it, you suddenly took off, and I figured you were my only lead to find him. And when I saw him standing over you with what looked like blood on you..."

Lloyd burst into laughter. "I can only imagine what you thought!

Oh, boy, wouldn't that be a wonderful gag for a movie?" Then the smile faded. "If I were still making them."

The girl drew her finger through the "blood" on her tummy and licked it off. "My hero."

"Raspberry sauce," said Lloyd.

He went over to a light stand and brought back a large stuffed toy tiger. "The Lady and the Tiger was supposed to be our theme. And as for 'Eight-Fingers', I can assure you no one I know has ever referred to me by that charming nickname."

I wished I could sink through the floorboards. "I am so embarrassed, sir. It's all an awful coincidence. I meant no disrespect to your accident."

"Well, don't give it another thought. I never do. It was thirty-five years ago."

I did the mental math.

"You mean you did all those movies—dangling off moving streetcars, climbing a skyscraper—with just one good hand?"

He beamed. "And I didn't use stuntmen or double exposures or studio tricks. It was all done outdoors in real settings." Then he leaned forward, confiding. "Except we built that skyscraper set on top of a real building. Our background was very high up, but I wouldn't have fallen more than twenty or thirty feet, onto some mattresses."

"Even at twenty feet...you're a braver man than I am," I confessed. "I'm scared of heights."

"Oh, so am I!" he said. "But to this day, I still take a lot of hair-raising photos. I force myself."

He pointed to a color print on the wall, looking down from the top of the Golden Gate Bridge. I got vertigo just looking at it.

"You have to get the shot, but you do it carefully," he concluded.

"I had no idea what you went through for your movies."

"Audiences never knew. I didn't want them feeling sorry for me. I used a prosthetic glove for my right hand."

I had to ask: "How'd it happen, Mr. Lloyd?"

The girl shot me a how-could-you look.

"Well, since you know my films, *and* have threatened me with arson, I guess we should be on a first name basis now, David. You may call me Harold."

"Thank you...Harold."

He raised his mangled right hand to his chin, as if it were holding something round.

"I was doing some publicity poses for Hal Roach, and we hit on the idea of me lighting my cigarette off a burning bomb fuse. We didn't realize I was holding an actual explosive." He grew somber. "It also burned my face, and for a time I was blind in one eye. I thought I'd never work again."

Then he tapped my Time Crystal with his disfigured right hand. "So take it from a professional actor: If you don't know everything about a prop, it can cost you your life."

I nodded. If he only knew. If *I* only knew.

"Now, tell me," Harold said. "You can't be more than twenty-five."

"Twenty-nine."

"Where did you see my films? I haven't released anything in nearly twenty years, except that god-awful thing I did for Preston Sturges and Howard Hughes. Nobody saw that."

Oops. I'd have been too young. And I hadn't seen any of his talkies.

"Maybe, *Professor Beware*?" he suggested.

The girl glared at me suspiciously. "Yeah, he should."

"I saw *Safety Last* at the Silent Movie Theatre," I said.

"Oh, of course," he nodded. "The Hamptons. Nice people. I'd like to get my films on television like Charlie and Buster have, but the networks haven't yet met my price. After all, I have expenses," he said, gesturing at his own personal theme park outside the window.

"Maybe you could charge admission, like Disneyland," I suggested.

"That place? Walt's going to lose his shirt, believe me. Well, maybe not. He's making pictures. People still know *his* name."

He stared off at his little hermit kingdom, wistful. "It used to be, I could go around this town unrecognized till I put on the glasses." He took off his prescription glasses and picked up a pair of his trademark lensless round horn-rims and donned them. "Then I'd be mobbed!" He smiled at the memory. "Nowadays, I can wear these *and* a straw boater—and nobody knows me." He took them off and put on his real glasses again.

"It won't be long before everyone knows you as a comic genius the equal of Chaplin and Keaton," I said. And I meant it.

He bristled. "Well, I should hope so! You know, thirty years ago, we were the big three, all producing our own films. Those boys were always over here for this party or that. There was no ego, no jealousy."

He showed me a silver tray, piled high with embossed party invitations. I saw dates from the late 1920s through the 1940s. Nothing recent, and all covered in a fine dust. Did this guy ever throw anything away?

Harold pulled one out and showed me. It was dated 1925.

"This was a wrap party for Charlie's picture *The Gold Rush*. As a surprise, Buster and I even did a short film for him, along with Jackie Coogan, Doug Fairbanks, and poor old Roscoe."

"Roscoe?" asked the girl.

"You'd know him as Fatty Arbuckle. If you know him at all," he added quietly.

The girl plainly didn't.

"Of course, my pictures always made more than Buster's. Now, Charlie's were bigger hits than mine, but I made three *times* as many as he did. That's how I could afford to build Greenacres."

So that's what this sizable principality was called, I thought to myself.

He showed me a 1929 invitation to his open house.

"I made fifteen million dollars in the Twenties. Charlie only made ten million." (About $210 million versus $140 million in today's dollars.)

"Does the money matter that much, sir?"

"How else do you keep score?"

"I mean, all three of you made great comedies people will be laughing at centuries from now."

"I suppose. But look at us now: I can't get a picture made, Charlie got himself chased out of the country, and poor Buster drank himself out of a career."

"Oh, is he the guy you showed me on TV?" the girl asked.

Harold nodded. "I saw that show he did on Channel 11. Great stuff. But instead of filming it, he did it live! Then when he finally wised up and did it all over again on film, it just wasn't as good. Everyone had already seen it."

Lloyd shook his head. "Buster was never a businessman," he sighed, as if that said it all. "But from the start, I always liked him. Maybe because I had a dog named Buster when I was a kid. He even took falls like Buster did. That dog was fearless. I trained him to dive off a bridge into the Big Nehama River. But one day, Buster jumped off the bridge...it wasn't even that strong a current. I don't know what happened. But he never made it to shore."

He turned his back to us, removed his glasses, and took out his handkerchief. He pretended he was cleaning his specs. Finally, he turned back with his glasses back on.

"I never told anyone about that little dog," he told me and the girl. "So if I hear anyone else repeat that story, I'll know one of you betrayed me."

He said it jokingly, but it was clear he meant it.

He rose and began packing up his lighting equipment.

"Aren't we going to do the Lady and the Tiger?" asked the girl.

"No, I'm not in the mood anymore."

The girl looked daggers at me.

Harold took money out of his wallet and offered it to her.

"Harold, you don't have to pay me. I'm the one who ruined the shoot, letting this bozo follow me."

"I insist. You showed up, and your time is worth something. If you're going to have a career in Hollywood—and with that lovely face, I definitely think you will—you must never let anyone take advantage of you." He pressed the bills into her palm.

Touched, she kissed him on the cheek. "You are the sweetest man I ever met." She gave me a look that said I wasn't even in the top fifty.

"Now get dressed, and I'll have Ferdinand drop you two wherever you need to go."

She went out in the corridor, to another room.

"Mr. Lloyd..."

"Harold," he corrected me.

"Harold, I have to ask you one other question."

"Go ahead," he said patiently.

"Do you know anything about the Octavius Corporation, in the Richfield Building?"

"Octavius?" He actually went pale. "No. Nothing about a corporation, at any rate. But I know the name Octavius. Octavius Johnson."

I was electrified. A century later? "Who is he? Have you met him?"

"It's been twenty years, twenty-one actually. It started the night of that wrap party I threw for *Duck Soup*." He shook his head as the unwelcome memory washed over him.

"What can you tell me about him?"

"Nothing."

"Was he a guest at your party?"

"Yes. At least he was supposed to be. You have to remember in Hollywood in Prohibition days, everybody drank like a fish. Now, I usually don't drink much, but that party was a blur for me...well, anyway, I can't recall his face, or why it is that his very name fills me with dread."

"Why would he have been there?"

"I'm not sure. It was mainly a party for the cast. As a nod to the Marx Brothers, I invited every working comedian in town. But Octavius was definitely not a funny man."

None of this made sense. "Then you're not even sure if you really met this guy Octavius?"

He gave me a haunted look: "I'm not sure I did. I only know ever since that party, I've had a recurring dream that's all about someone with that name. I never remember the details...but I always wake up in a cold sweat."

17

THE TIMES, THEY ARE A-CHANGIN'

HAROLD LLOYD WAS DEFINITELY RATTLED BY what I'd said. He left the room to summon his chauffeur. It seemed he couldn't get me off his estate fast enough. I quickly sorted through the dusty invitations on the tray.

Within a minute, a horn beeped. Lloyd's uniformed chauffeur Ferdinand drove up in a mint condition Rolls-Royce: Ferdinand proudly informed us it was a 1929 Phantom I Riviera Town Brougham Brewster.

The girl, back in her bogus school uniform, joined me in the passenger compartment.

"And remember, back up, don't go around the fountain!" Harold instructed.

It was a lovely Italian antique with stone lion heads spurting water.

"The boss is superstitious about that thing," Ferdinand explained, cautiously backing down the long driveway.

I couldn't help noticing that with its long shiny black body accented by gold-tone radiator, hubcaps, and free-standing windshield frame, the Rolls would have made a perfect car to park out front at Richfield Tower. For Ferdinand's sake, I hoped the sunny weather would hold, because he sat up front of the passenger compartment, in the open-air driver's seat. Yep, it was that kind of car.

First he dropped Harold's model off at the Sunset Strip club where she danced—she didn't clarify whether it was a Strip club or a strip club—and I sure as hell wasn't going to press my luck by asking.

Looking out the window of the Rolls, my eye strayed to the club's marquee. The girl walked over to my side of the car, to lean over me and block my field of vision. She narrowed her eyes.

"Never mind trying to figure out which name is mine, Professor," she said. "You did come to my rescue, which is the main reason you're still walking. But from now on, you leave me alone—*and* that nice old man. You got me?"

"I got you," I said.

"Better drop him off and get back to Greenacres fast," she told the driver, indicating some clouds to the west. "It looks like we might get some rain. What do you think, Professor?"

I was rubbing my still-sore neck. "Feels like it," I sighed.

FERDINAND DROPPED me at the Good Samaritan at quarter to six. Ariyl was impatiently waiting on me. She lifted an eyebrow at the Rolls. "Where have *you* been, a parade?"

"Gathering information on our friend Octavius."

"I thought we were just checking the timeline to be sure everything was back to normal."

"I was, until—"

She showed me the *Times* TV listing. I looked at the newsrack, but this time she hadn't mangled it to get her copy.

"It's all changed back to how it was before Ludlo derailed things, right? Now can we go home?"

"I don't think it's exactly the same. That guy Octavius—or at least the corporation that bears his name—is still operating here, ninety years after the Civil War."

"And?"

"And someone here named Eight-Fingers hired some thugs who stole my Time Crystal."

Her eyes went wide. "You lost it *again?*"

"Calm dow...uh, take it easy. It was only for a minute. I got it right back." I showed it to her. "What I'm saying is, someone who knows about Time Crystals is here, in 1954, and has people out looking for them."

"What people?"

* * *

ARIYL AGREED to wait outside while I checked with the admitting nurse. It was the same one Ariyl and I had met in the President Thurmond timeline, but of course she didn't know me from Adam.

Yes, she remembered the three young men who had been brought into the emergency room a few hours ago. Two had been treated and released; the third was in intensive care with numerous broken bones. Seeing him was out of the question. No one but immediate family.

I snuck into Jerry's room anyway.

When he saw me, he flinched. I believe he'd have jumped out of bed and run if not for all the casts.

"She's not with you, is she?" he gasped, peering around behind me.

"Who's not with him?" asked Ariyl, who apparently decided not to wait outside after all.

"No one," I said. Ariyl had doubts enough about my ability to hold onto my Crystal. I didn't want to explain that someone else had gotten it back for me.

"Just keep that Jap chick away from me!" snarled Jerry.

"What Jap chick?" asked Ariyl. "And by the way, that is so racist."

"Never mind!" I snapped.

"The one who beat the crap out of me and Biff and Tony! She's crazy!"

"I won't tell her you're here, Jerry...as long as you tell me where I can find Mr. Eight-Fingers."

"I can't!"

"Who's this *girl?*" Ariyl asked me. I gave her a "later" head shake.

"She beat up all three of you?" Ariyl asked Jerry, intrigued.

"Who's *this* bitch?" Jerry asked me.

"What did you call me?" demanded Ariyl.

I leaned between her and Jerry. "You never learn, do you, Jerry? How do I find Eight-Fingers?"

"You don't find him, he finds you," said Jerry.

"Where did he find you?"

"I never saw him. I know people who know people who saw him. He put the word out all over town he was looking for your crystal-thing with the hole in it. Offered a grand for it. That's all I know, I swear."

"Okay." I turned toward the door. I wasn't about to thank this creep.

"By the way, Jerry?" said Ariyl. She picked up his hospital bed. "Don't say 'bitch' anymore. It's disrespectful."

* * *

THE SUNSET at the end of Wilshire Boulevard was an intense orange, thanks to all the hydrocarbons in the mid-century atmosphere.

"I don't understand," said Ariyl. "Are you saying this Eight-Fingers is somehow the same man as Octavius Johnson?"

"It would explain a lot."

"But he'd be like a hundred and twenty years old! You pre-Changers don't live that long."

"He wouldn't have to be that old. Not if someone is hopscotching him through time. The way you did with me."

"By 'someone', you mean Dylila?"

"Again, it would explain a lot. Like why she lied to both of us."

"She didn't lie to *me*. Maybe she doesn't trust you with the truth.

Which reminds me, when were you going to tell me about your new girlfriend?"

"She's definitely not my girlfriend. I don't even know her name. And she's too young for me. And she's divorced."

"Still being judgy, huh?"

"And she's a black belt, she poses nude for Harold Lloyd, and she's on a crusade to put the guys who raped her in traction. So far she's two for five."

Ariyl stared at me for a moment. "And you don't know her name?"

"She wouldn't tell me."

"And you didn't recognize her?"

"Should I?"

Ariyl almost fell down laughing.

"Would you mind letting me in on the joke?" I asked.

"No, Mr. Movie Expert. I'm going to enjoy watching you unravel this little mystery."

"Fine, don't tell me. We've got a bigger one to solve. We're going to my apartment on November eighth, 2016, so I can jump on the Internet and check out Octavius Johnson."

She waited.

"If that's agreeable," I added.

"All right, but do me a favor. When you get there, stay home. Don't wander off till I show up, okay?"

"Deal." She took my hand.

I held up my Crystal. "Destination: 1155 North Bundy, West Los Angeles, Apartment 212." I decided to arrive four hours after I'd left for the Civil War. "Five P.M., November eighth, 2016."

Again, Ariyl's hand vanished from mine as I appeared. I was alone. But in the downstairs hallway, not the upstairs.

18

LATE AGAIN

ANDY GRAISE, WHO IN THIS TIMELINE WAS married, had a small child, and taught P.E. at University High, was just coming out his door in his underwear with a trash bag. I apparently had materialized in his peripheral vision. He did a double-take.

I stuffed the Time Crystal down my shirtfront.

"Whoa, Preston! Don't sneak up on me like that, bro."

"I didn't sneak—"

"Where the hell you been?"

"Uh...I went out to vote."

He broke up like I'd just cracked the best joke of the day.

"Hey, I bet you loved the president's tweet this morning," he smirked with a superior air as he opened the trash chute.

"I know, I know, he's gonna win," I sighed.

"*Gonna* win? Dude, it's been more than a year. Get over it, libtard!" He dropped the bag and let the chute close.

"More than...? What's the date today?" I stammered.

Andy laughed louder. "Sven told me you were in Greece or some shit. They don't have calendars there?" He shut his door, still cackling.

Sven's door, which was next to Andy's, opened. The old man's jaw dropped as he saw me.

"Dafid!" he said, reverting to his *svenska* roots. He beckoned me into his apartment, urgently.

"Sven, do you know me?" I said with great relief.

"Do I ever!" He pulled me in and shut his door.

I SAT down on his big comfy couch. "Man, am I glad to hear that! I can't tell you how many times I've come back to L.A. and found you treating me like a total stranger and living in my apartm..."

My voice trailed off as I saw my Ansel Adams posters stacked in a corner of his living room. My fencing trophies were crowded onto Sven's fireplace mantel alongside his family photos. My plants were hanging all around his kitchen like banners on someone's birthday.

"Sven, are we roommates in this timeline?"

Sven looked bewildered then saw what I was looking at. "Oh, no, no. This is just my apartment."

"Then why is my stuff in it? Why isn't it in *my* apartment?"

"Uh, you don't have one anymore."

"I lost my place?"

"I'm sorry, David. I didn't know what to tell the manager. You've been gone sixteen months. I had your key so I got your personal property down here, but I couldn't move the furniture. The manager donated it. I saw some of it at the Salvation Army store, if you're interested..."

I sank farther into the couch. "I loved that apartment."

Sven nodded. "I miss it too. Such a great view."

I held up my Time Crystal. "This goddamn thing. It's getting less and less accurate. It's like it has a mind of its own, and it loves messing with me."

"Or maybe, it's because each time you make a choice of when to go and what to do, you are closing off avenues for logically possible futures."

I chewed that over.

Sven leaned in close. "By the way, would you please call your parents? They've been out of their mind with worry, and I didn't know what to tell them except that you told me you were on a top-secret dig and couldn't be reached."

"Why'd you do that?"

"Wishful thinking, I guess. I just hoped you'd be back."

Sven helpfully handed me my phone. I tried it—No Service.

"Oh, yeah," he realized. "I got your phone bills over there. They finally went to collection. Here, use mine."

Sven passed me his old corded phone.

* * *

AFTER AN HOUR of genuine apologies and fictitious excuses and half-sincere promises never to scare them like this again, my parents finally let me hang up.

Mom in particular was convinced that my failure to find the Temple of the Dolphins back in 2013 had finally sent me into a nervous breakdown, and that was why that nice Moira Shea broke up with me back then. Dad offered to help me find a good shrink and a better health insurer to cover it. My mental instability was probably the only cover story that they could ever believe. So I thanked them and agreed to look into it.

Finally, I agreed to a family meeting in three days with Mom, Dad, and my older brother Ben, the stockbroker. The successful son.

But I insisted on doing it at the local steakhouse in Brentwood. Being out in public would prevent what I knew would otherwise devolve into a scene.

Sven couldn't help eavesdropping, nor refrain from offering advice: "It's good that you love your family, David. But remember: they can't live your life for you, and you can't live it for them."

But they had me over a barrel. I was wracked with guilt. It had never occurred to me that I wouldn't be able to get back to my life at the point that I'd left it, even though I have repeatedly been close to not getting back to *any* life.

• • •

WHAT ELSE COULD I DO, though? A climate catastrophe would destroy my parents' world and mine in a few decades' time. Maybe only a few years off...there was no way to tell.

I didn't dare look at the stacks of my mail. Sven had my duplicate mail key too, and I was sure I had a lot more bad news from my (no doubt former) employer UCLA, my bank, the utility companies. My credit rating was presumably lower than a Death Valley septic tank. I likely had a letter or two from the IRS, since I hadn't filed taxes for nearly two years.

"I drove your car once a week, to keep the battery charged," Sven said comfortingly. "I park it in my space. I just knew you were coming back."

I patted him on the shoulder, grateful that I had one true friend in this timeline.

Then I felt a sharp card in my pocket. "At least, I didn't come back empty-handed," I said as I took it out and showed it to Sven. He gave an admiring gasp.

It was an embossed invitation to the Harold Lloyd estate in August 1933: a wrap party for the Marx Brothers' hilarious satire, *Duck Soup*.

AFTER THE GREEK government confiscated my laptop in 2013, I bought a new one, and Sven had loyally kept it charged. I now sat on Sven's sofa and used his Wi-Fi to log on and do a search for Octavius Johnson.

"Make sure you check all the spellings," Sven kibitzed.

I held up my hand. "One sec."

I pulled out the tiny dram that I'd been carefully moving from pocket to pocket each time I changed clothes. (See? I told you I'd get to this detail.)

"Follow and record us—include computer screen," I told the bee-sized object. A tiny red light went on as it hovered over my shoulder.

I found several Octavius Johnsons online, with a variety of spellings and middle names: Athletes, performers, musicians. None looked anywhere near a hundred and seventy years old.

But as for an investor who had made several fortunes before the Civil War by leasing or buying land where gold, silver or oil was soon found, and who (in one recently canceled timeline) had dabbled in politics and possibly murder, in the aftermath of Ariyl killing John Wilkes Booth—that Octavius Johnson could not be found online. Not a trace.

If Harold Lloyd had actually met that man in 1933, instead of just having nightmares about him, not a shred of proof still existed.

There were, of course, libraries and public records I could check, given weeks of time. But if ol' Octavius had ever been on the Internet, he had been surgically scrubbed from it.

Octavius Corporation was a different case.

Closely held, Octavius stock wasn't listed on any exchange. Yet it was a ghostly presence in private trades among those aware of its existence. It focused on a few specific industries: Mining, metals futures (oddly, selling precious metals short), robotics, and private space exploration.

Who owned Octavius Corporation? Who knows?

As for Mr. Eight-Fingers, that could refer to a musician, a video game villain, or a number of hideous accidents...but there was not a single hit for a mysterious gem buyer in 1954 Los Angeles.

Yet I knew that he existed and had thugs doing his bidding. Six decades ago. Could he still be out there?

DUNK-dunk! went the cheapo mechanical doorbell on Sven's door.

I jumped out of my skin and back in again. Sven went to the door. "Who is it?"

There was no answer. Sven shrugged then peered out the fish-eye lens peephole.

"What do they look like?" I hissed, quickly closing my search windows and deleting my browsing history.

Sven looked at me, mystified: "Two Zeppelins docking." He'd actually seen that, by the way. He was born in 1926.

I gave an exasperated sigh, motioned Sven back, and whipped open the door. As I figured, it was Ariyl standing with her bosom at the lens. Such a kidder.

She was laughing as she entered. "By the way, there's a strange woman in your apartment now. She never heard of you. Lucky for me, I found Sven's name on the directory."

Sven stared up at her. "This is her?"

"Sven Bergstrom, meet Ariyl Moro."

"You weren't exaggerating," he marveled.

"Hello, again!" she trilled.

"Again?" asked Sven.

"We met before, Sven. In Nazi L.A. Of course, you don't remember that."

"You kicked down my door, bent my fireplace poker, and beat up a roomful of cops."

"How can he remember that?" Ariyl asked me, amazed.

"Well, I didn't live it. I read it in David's book."

She looked at me. "You wrote a book about me?"

"Two."

"Aww!" She started to kiss me then realized: "But I warned you not to write your memoirs! It could change the future!"

"More than saving Abe Lincoln? I don't think so."

"Oh, about that, David," Sven began. "When I read your second manuscript, I realized you and whatshername, Dylila? You were wrong, thinking that the ice age could have resulted from Ariyl preventing that assassination."

Ariyl gave me her patented superior look.

"How do you figure?" I asked.

"Because the day you left, you and I both knew Lincoln was supposed to be shot on April fourteenth, 1865. *Our* history hadn't changed. Ergo, the frozen future that you then visited was caused by something after 1865."

"Damn it. You're right. How'd I miss that?"

Ariyl crossed her arms, which wasn't easy with her build. "Well. Seems like someone owes me an apology for blaming the end of the world on me."

"Okay. I'm sorry. Truly. I don't know why I didn't figure that out myself."

"Well, Mr. Archaeologist, it *might* be that the second you heard 'danger to history' you just went off on your mission half-cocked, without really thinking it through."

"That does sound like me," I conceded.

"*Or* it might be that Dylila is a very persuasive girl, and so you went off full-cocked."

"Ariyl, I told you, there's nothing between Dylila and me! There never has been!"

"There was something the night I saw you two hugging," she said, inspecting her nails. "I saw it in your eyes."

"No, you didn't."

"Okay, in your pants."

"She hugged *me*. About three feet off the ground. I'm a man, all right? What did you expect me to do, run home and take a cold shower?"

Ariyl rolled her eyes...and that was when she noticed with alarm the tiny red light hovering over us.

"David...is that a dram?"

"Yeah. I found another one tangled in Lon Chaney's Wolf Man fur. I kept it from you. Sorry."

"Why did you do that?"

"Right before I left for the Civil War, it occurred to me I might not see Sven again. At least, not the version of him who knows me."

I turned to the tiny hovering dram. "Replay my conversation with Sven, November eighth, 2016."

A semi-transparent hologram of me standing at Sven's door appeared in the middle of the room:

IN THE HOLOGRAM, *Sven opened the door.* "Come in, David! I was just finishing your manuscript!"

Hologram Me entered, and Sven shut the door. Sven's hand suddenly became huge as he reached for the tiny camera recording the scene.

"What is that, a firefly?"

"It's a dram, Sven. Just like I wrote about. Only they're real. I was really back in time. It's all real: Ariyl, Ludlo, N-Tec, Time Crystals."

"David...I think you've been working too hard."

"Sven, I have to go back to the Civil War, but every time I return to my present, you're different. Sometimes you don't even know me. This recording is to prove to any other version of you that I meet, that we're friends—"

"Of course we are! And neighbors. Since 2007!"

"—and that I'm a time traveler."

"Uh...that you might need to prove a bit more."

*Hologram Me turned to the hovering camera: "Dram, remain on Sven."
Then, I put a hand on Sven's shoulder: "Now, don't be startled. I'm going to
vanish." Hologram Me held his/my Time Crystal and said: "Same location,
ten seconds in the future."*

*Suddenly I vanished from the hologram. Sven almost leapt out of his
loafers. "Jumping Judas!"*

He started looking all around the room, calling me.

I told the dram, "Fast forward to three minutes later."

*Hologram Sven jumped comically around his room in sped-up
fashion.*

Ariyl laughed merrily at the spectacle.

*The hologram resumed normal speed as Hologram Me materialized in
the exact spot I'd left, right before Sven's eyes.*

"Jumping Judas!" exclaimed Hologram Sven.

"END PLAYBACK," I told the dram, and the ghostly images of Sven
and me vanished. "As you can see, ten seconds turned into about
three minutes. These Crystals are getting really unreliable."

"And after all that trouble, you didn't need it," chuckled Sven.
"You managed to restore the timeline so closely that I still remember
that last conversation, exactly."

"Better to have it and not need it," I said.

"But you were supposed to turn all the evidence of our travels
over to me!" protested Ariyl. "That dram is from, like, 2030!"

"I was *going* to give it to you...but then I realized Dylila would just destroy it."

"Uh, yeah! That's her *job*."

"Well, my job is to preserve history. So I kept it. And I lied in my book that you took it with you."

"Oh, *thanks!*" she exclaimed. "So if some bad guy wanted it, they'd come after me for something I didn't even know existed?"

"Who could come after you? Up till a week ago, I assumed you were in a completely different timeline that nobody could ever get to again. I just didn't want anyone in *this* timeline to know I had a record of that mutated 1954. And for that matter, of me telling Sven everything you and I and Dylila and Ludlo had done to the timestream."

"You told Sven all *that?*"

"Don't be mad with David," soothed Sven. "At the time, he told me it was all a science fiction story he was writing. I didn't know the truth until an hour before he left for 1865. That was an emergency."

Ariyl was still upset, but I could tell she was warming to the idea.

"Oh. So, your book's a novel? Am I an important character?"

"Yes, very. Well, not the protagonist—David told it in the first-person. But I would say *you're* the hero."

Ariyl beamed. "Me? Ohh, David!" She slipped her arms around me, kissed me a long, long time. I looked over at Sven, who gave me a wink and turned his gaze elsewhere.

I no longer wear glasses, but my contacts were steaming up. And as usual, my shoes were dangling above the carpet.

We paused for air.

"You know, in my era, when a woman kisses a man, she keeps his feet on the floor."

"Such a primitive time," she breathed. "How do you stand it?"

Sven cleared his throat. "I'd tell you kids to get a room, except I think all David's credit cards have been canceled."

"You mean he hasn't got any money?" Ariyl set me down again. "Well, that's a turn-off."

I gave her an incredulous look. "You said you don't use money where you come from!"

"Yeah, but it's how *you* guys keep score, right?"

"Oh, so you keep score now. Well, there's a silent movie comic I need to introduce you to."

"Hey, it was no fun almost running out of money in 1865." Then she brightened. "Maybe you'll make a fortune on your books about me. That'd be hot. Even if it does mess with the future."

"On the contrary," mused Sven, "I think it might actually make your original future more likely to come about."

"How would that work?" I wondered.

"So far, each future you time travelers have created has resulted in humanity's extinction. But you've witnessed several *different* extinctions—nuclear holocaust, runaway warming, ice age. That shows that humanity has no single fate: you can change the future. So logically, there must be at least one change that results in normal history up through N-Tec and 2109. Otherwise you, my dear, wouldn't have been able to travel back here in the first place."

Ariyl nodded admiringly. "I love smart men." She stroked Sven's white mane. "And old people are just adorable. We don't have them in my world. Are you going to look like him someday, David?"

"If I keep hanging out with you, I'll probably look like him by next week. If I live that long."

"You act like we're always in danger! You know I'll protect you."

"I know you *mean* to...but somehow you always get distracted." Then I turned to Sven. "What did you mean, 'at least one change' that leads to normal history? How could any change lead to the same future?"

"Not the same one, but so close as to be almost indistinguishable. Some changes actually reinforce certain futures—for instance, N-Tec knowing that Ariyl traveled back and met you might make it more likely that N-Tec would allow her trip in the first place."

"But Ludlo and Ariyl came back to see Andy hit five homers— and in this timeline, he doesn't."

Sven leaned forward, warming to his topic. "Andy's record was not necessary to produce their era. Yes, it was a detail that got them to meet you, but once you started time traveling, they could change that event and not affect their era significantly. Those two futures are nearly congruent. Essentially, your published memoirs take the place of Andy's homers in motivating their time travel to meet you. Maybe their historical records are incomplete and all they know about Andy's career now comes from your memoirs. The point is, for her specific era to come about, one way or the other, she always had to meet you."

"Aww, isn't it romantic?" said Ariyl.

I saw the logic: "That's why whether Andy gets cut from the Dodgers, or blows out his knee falling in the dorm and never made the team, he still winds up a high school gym teacher."

"What else would he do for a living? Like Dylila said, history has inertia," said Sven.

"But that also means that a future where civilization survives disaster might be as unlikely as Andy hitting five homers. Any little change could upset the whole apple cart."

"Regrettably, that's logical. It seems civilization is an extremely unstable state," concluded Sven.

Ariyl shook her head. "I still think you guys are just making this stuff up as you go along."

"We're formulating a hypothesis," corrected Sven. "Now you can use a Time Crystal to check experimentally whether it works."

"I don't get you," said Ariyl.

"Neither do I," I admitted.

"Of course you do, David. You already anticipated this little experiment when you swiped that invitation to the party at Harold Lloyd's house."

"Sven, I only did that so I could find out who Octavius is, whether he's a time traveler...and whether he somehow caused an atomic Armageddon."

"You're assuming it was nuclear war."

"What else could cause a global winter?"

He shrugged. "Solar irradiance variation. Supervolcano. Asteroid impact."

"But those are all beyond human control."

"You told me there was very little radiation in 2109. A nuclear exchange would leave significant radiation for decades."

"But maybe not if the war breaks out in the next few years. Given our current government, does that seem so unlikely?"

Sven snorted. "No. I'd give you even money. Except if I win, money won't be worth a plug nickel."

Ariyl put an arm around each of us for a powerful group hug. "Think positive, you guys! There has to be a way we can stop this thing."

"But first, you need to prove my theory," winced the old physicist.

"Explain this theory to me, Sven," I said. "I'm still not getting it."

Ariyl's eyes started to glaze over. She let us go, sat down at my laptop, and started fiddling with it, as Sven outlined the possible outcomes of his experiment.

"Universe Type One: single, unchangeable timeline, like *The Time Machine*...well, we already know that one is out. Octavius couldn't have made all those canny investments on his own. But if that were the type of universe we had, whatever Octavius did at Harold Lloyd's party has already happened and cannot be changed.

"Universe Type Two: multiverse with unlimited changes and new timelines possible, like *Terminator 2*. Octavius attended the party, then you two go back and prevent that...but you would head into a different future than this one. I—this me—would never see you again. You might return to tell *your* future's Sven how it went, but that wouldn't be me. He'd be a different person who hadn't had this conversation we're having."

"Why not?" put in Ariyl, who had been listening after all.

"Because in his timeline, there was no mystery about Octavius Johnson to unravel. You would have solved that in *that* Sven's timeline."

"Sorry I asked," said Ariyl, returning to her Internet search.

"I mean conceivably, you might make such a horrible mess of Lloyd's party that the United States seals off its borders and young Sven Bergstrom is never allowed to emigrate."

"We won't do that," I assured Sven.

"Doesn't matter. I don't buy an endless multiverse in any case.

Where does the energy to power all these universes come from? There's no free lunch!"

"I already did that joke with David," said Ariyl, preoccupied.

"So, we're left with Universe Type Three: single, *changeable* time-line. Like *Back to the Future*. That's the one I'm convinced is true. The reason Harold Lloyd in 1954 doesn't remember clearly what Octavius Johnson did at his party in 1933 is that you intend to travel back to that party and *cause* whatever happens—which will then retroactively give the older Harold a definite memory. So, assuming you survive..."

"That's a big assumption," I put in.

"...then you should return to 1954 and ask Harold what he remembers. My prediction is that he will remember the changed timeline, regardless of what happened the first time. And then, of course, you report the results to me. If *I* still remember this discussion, our universe has a single, changeable timeline." Sven turned and addressed the dram. "I hope you got all that."

"David, did you look at all these Titusville pictures?" Ariyl said, flicking through them with inhuman speed.

"Yeah, but you can close that tab. There's no one named Octavius there."

"No, but there is a guy with only eight fingers."

19

JUST MY DAGUERREOTYPE

I SAT DOWN BESIDE ARIYL LIKE A SHOT. "EIGHT fingers? Where?"

She showed me a group of pioneering oilmen, stiffly posed in a field studded with derricks. Ariyl zoomed in: "See, that guy is missing his middle and ring fingers on his right hand."

"Good eye, Ariyl!"

"Thank you."

"Those old daguerreotypes had incredible resolution," noted Sven. "Better than a digital camera."

"Now, what else do you notice?" asked Ariyl.

"He also has a patch on his right eye."

"Duh. One other thing."

"Uh..."

"Don't you think he looks a lot like Jon Ludlo?" she prompted.

I peered closer. "No, that's not Ludlo."

"And I didn't say it was. I said it looks a lot *like* him. Enough to be his brother."

"Did Ludlo have a brother?"

"Nope."

Most photographic subjects of the day stared at the camera like deer at an approaching semi. But this Octavius Johnson—if that was his name—seemed undaunted. A guy who knew all the answers. He glared out of the 1857 daguerreotype, daring me to do something about him.

"So what are we talking about? Ludlo's ancestor who somehow knows what his descendant knows? Someone Ludlo jumped back and met that we don't know about?"

Sven went to his computer, excited. "David, I'm sending you a facial-recognition app that Cheryl Williams came up with."

"Cheryl from your Physics Department?"

"She's kind of a polymath."

I downloaded it, cropped the facial image of the eight-fingered man, and did the search.

"Now X out everyone who definitely isn't the same man," instructed Sven. "From what you reject, it will learn to refine its search."

It took a while, but pretty soon, we had historic photographs of the man we were pretty sure was Octavius Johnson, not only in Titusville, but Pike's Peak, Virginia City, and Washington, D.C. The latest picture was 1881, where he was starting to go gray.

"Now expand the date range," Sven told me.

I did. There were some more pictures, but from the 1890s through the 1910s.

"He's younger. And not quite the same in these photos," Ariyl pointed out. "Same dark hair, same eye patch, same missing fingers, kinda similar face...but his hairline is lower."

"Maybe his son? Octavius Johnson, Junior?" I suggested.

Then some new photos cropped up, the subject's clothing placing him in the 1920s and early 1930s. He was good looking, in a rugged way. Black curly hair, a surly expression. He was powerfully built and a head taller than anyone else in the picture—probably six-four. Same eye patch, same eight fingers.

"I'm assuming this is the grandson. Octavius Johnson III," I said.

"This Octavius parts his hair on the other side," said Ariyl. "And what's that on his left finger?"

"A wedding band," said Sven. "None of the others had one." We clicked back and forth. Sven was right.

Then we came across several where Octavius III was at a gathering in Rome.

"This looks like the early 1920s," I said. "Some kind of corporate/industrial conference, Octavius sitting with a bunch of Italian big shots in expensive suits...and Benito Mussolini!"

Ominously, the next one we found was one of Octavius and Adolf Hitler, both in 1930s business attire.

We exchanged a worried look and kept searching.

"Whoa, go back to that one!" I exclaimed. "Who *is* this guy—Zelig? Octavius is in the background and look who's in the foreground!"

"Charlie Chaplin," said Sven. "His hair's nearly white, but he looks about forty. And I think that's his brother Sydney."

"Where was this?" asked Ariyl. "And when?"

"Looks like that Japanese restaurant in Hollywood, on top of the hill behind the Magic Castle. Uh..." The name was on the tip of Sven's tongue. "What's it called?"

"Yamashiro's," I said. "It was just up the hill from Chaplin's studio. Looks like this was in the early Thirties."

"But where's his mustache?" wondered Ariyl.

"He didn't wear it offscree—" I stopped, surprised. "You know who *Chaplin* was?"

"You were always talking about your favorite flat-flix," replied Ariyl. "One of the ones I watched was *City Lights*. You were right, it was wonderful." She flipped to the next picture.

I gulped. "Do you see who Octavius is standing near?"

"Franklin Delano Roosevelt, shaking hands with a man in a donkey suit," laughed Sven. "I guess this is when he was still the Democratic candidate."

"No, Sven," I shuddered, suddenly feeling cold. "This is afterward. FDR is president-elect. This is February fifteenth, 1933. He's in Miami, and the man behind him, Anton Cermak, is the mayor of Chicago. About a minute after this photo is taken, a gunman named

Giuseppe Zangara tries to shoot FDR but misses and kills Mayor Cermak instead."

"Here's another picture of Octavius. Looks like the same event," said Ariyl. "Only, who's that little guy Octavius is talking to?"

"That," I said, "is Zangara."

"My God," said Sven. "Octavius *was* trying to change history."

"Or maybe just change the future, like any assassin does."

"We have to stop him!" declared Ariyl. "Don't we?"

"No, because he failed," reasoned Sven. "He must have, or we wouldn't remember FDR's presidency. If you go back to February 1933, you might actually change that fact. No, I'd say leave this alone."

"But since this Johnson family knows the future, one or more of them may be *trying* to change it," I said. "It must be that at some point, Octavius—or one of his descendants—succeeds, and causes the ice age. We have to find out what they're after."

"Why is he hanging around Charlie Chaplin?" asked Ariyl. "I mean, what if he was out to kill Charlie like he was FDR?"

"Haven't you been paying attention?" I sighed.

Ariyl looked annoyed.

I explained, "He can't have been after Charlie. Chaplin lived till 1977. But I'm sure that family is up to *something*."

Ariyl finished her photo search. "Well, we'd better figure it out in 1933. 'Cause I don't find any other photos of Octavius after then."

"He *could* have wised up and stopped letting them take his picture," I suggested.

Ariyl shook her head, not buying it.

"Maybe I'm wrong about there being no Fate," mused Sven. "It seems like you don't have much choice but to go to that party at Harold Lloyd's estate."

"Sven, would you print out the photos of Johnson with FDR, Zangara, and Chaplin?"

"All right, but make sure they don't fall into anyone else's hands."

"Now, one other thing," I said. "Just in case the invitation doesn't get us in...we need to fake up a couple FBI identification cards from 1933."

"I don't think it was called the FBI back then, but I'll fix you up," said Sven.

* * *

OUR TIME CRYSTALS had gotten four hours of solar charge. Ideally, I'd want more, but I had the nagging (if irrational) feeling that the longer we delayed our trip, the more damage could be done by whoever was using a Time Crystal. I didn't tell Ariyl I still strongly suspected Dylila, because there was no point starting that argument again.

We were as ready as we would ever be. I was wearing a smartly cut, light 1930s linen suit (thanks to my costumer Cheryll Lee!) and Ariyl's SmartFab was programmed for a cocktail dress of the era. She looked more Mae West than Carole Lombard, but she would definitely pass.

Before we left, I asked Sven to catch me up on the sixteen months of history that I'd overshot since November 2016.

Big mistake. After twenty minutes, I made him stop playing me Internet clips.

"David, you look kind of green," worried Sven.

I took a deep breath.

"He pulled out of the Paris climate deal because climate change is a hoax. He threatened a nuclear war with North Korea. He gave away intel methods to the Russians. In the Oval Office.

"He says the FBI and the CIA are conspiring against him. He fired the head of the FBI because it investigated Russian collusion. He tried to fire the Special Counsel investigating him. He calls the press 'enemies of the people' and says everything is 'fake news' unless it's from Fox or *The National Enquirer*. He starts every day posting boasts and threats on Twitter like a disturbed ten-year-old. He insulted the widow of a dead war hero. He says there are good people marching with the KKK and the Nazis. Everyone in his inner circle is either being investigated or indicted for obstruction, perjury, failure to register as a foreign agent, money laundering, breaking campaign finance laws, and/or wife beating.

"He falsified business records to pay off a porn star he screwed. He's being sued for sexual assault. And the only person he hasn't got a single bad thing to say about is the journalist-murdering dictator he colluded with."

"'Fraid so," nodded Sven.

"All that happened in just sixteen months?" I exclaimed. "How is he still president?"

Sven shrugged, sympathetic. "It's not like we weren't warned. Bottom line, some very rich, powerful people are going to get far richer, and that's how America is run at the moment."

"I swear to God, Sven, I'm tempted to go back and save Lincoln all over again. That *can't* turn out any worse than this."

"You know both timelines lead to the ice age. Chin up, David. America will get through this. You just focus on this Octavius Johnson."

Ariyl and I donned our respective Time Crystals.

"Let's use mine," she said, taking hold of hers and taking my hand. "It'll be more accurate."

"At least for once, we're going to a party instead of some monstrous historic disaster," I said.

"Yeah, but I still want a real vacation with you when all this is over."

"Sure, anywhere you want."

"You know what I'd really like? I loved that flat-flick *Roman Holiday*. I'd like to spend New Year's Eve in Rome."

"Why not?" I said. I pulled out Harold's invitation. "May I do the honors?"

"Knock yourself out."

I put my other hand to her Time Crystal and read the address of Harold Lloyd's estate in Beverly Hills and the date.

· · ·

THE BACKWARD TRAVEL took longer than I expected, with the years flickering by so fast that the strobing gave me a headache. Worse, I could tell we were moving across an ocean.

Worst of all, when I arrived, I once again had lost Ariyl's hand. I had arrived alone.

WHEREVER I WAS, it was a dark, dank stone tunnel that reeked of sweat, blood, urine, feces, and death.

20

AT THE CIRCUS

"Ariyl?"

No response.

I called her name again, louder.

I heard only an excited crowd cheering. I walked toward the light at the end of the tunnel and squinted out into an arena.

It was a partly cloudy, cold and windy day. But I immediately knew I was in Rome, because I'd already been to this particular tourist destination in 2005, on a trip after college.

Like virtually every sightseer in Rome, I have visited the Flavian Amphitheater—alias the Colosseum. But these days it's a ruined skeleton of brick, concrete, volcanic tuff, and pockmarked sandstone.

It certainly did not look like the marvel I now beheld: finished in beautiful Italian marble, with bronze plaques and statues and details, and colorful banners, and a decorated cloth *velarium* for shade drawn across the sunny side of the stadium, and crowds of people in tunics and togas filling its marble seats.

What. The. Hell.

I was making my second visit to the Colosseum two thousand years before my first visit.

My mind was reeling—how could this have happened? I had read precisely the address and the date off Harold's invitation.

Then I recalled Ariyl musing about New Year's Eve in Rome. But she never named a year. She'd been talking about a film from 1953— a couple of millennia in the future. Could her Crystal possibly have misunderstood her this badly?

Stupid question. Obviously, it had, and here I was. But where was Ariyl?

I took hold of my Time Crystal, ready to yell escape coordinates. But that would be only as a last resort. I didn't want to leave this time period unless I was sure I wasn't leaving Ariyl stranded.

"Ariyl?" I called out into the tunnel again.

I heard an angry male voice bark in Latin: "*Quo vadis?*"

I hoped he wasn't yelling at me; in any case, my answer would have been that I had no idea where I was going. Or when.

I wished I knew what date this was.

I heard a heavy footfall behind me. I turned too late—someone struck me on the back of the head.

Now I really didn't know what day it was.

I lay dazed on the dirty brick floor as excited voices fought, and a dozen rough hands tore my jacket off me, then my shirt. My linen pants would have been next, but then a loud voice of authority asserted itself:

"Back, you scum!" A whip cracked, and my assailants parted.

"Get him up!" barked the whip-wielding *lorarius*. I grabbed my Time Crystal for one second, but before I could yell "previous destination" his fellow guards seized my arms and yanked me to my feet. He stared at my light-colored trousers, which actually weren't all that light anymore, thanks to rolling on the filthy floor. Then his eye lit upon my Time Crystal.

"No!" I yelled. "Ariyl!"

But she wasn't there to save me. Two strong arms held each of mine. I was helpless. The *lorarius* chuckled and donned the Crystal. "You won't be needing this where you're going, prisoner!"

"I'm no prisoner! I am a free man!" I insisted.

"Me too!" said another.

"I'm a free man!" said the guy wearing my ripped-up linen jacket.

"*I'm* a free man!" said the guy in my shredded shirt.

Now they were all shouting it. It was as close to a Spartacus moment as I was going to get. I certainly felt like crying, but not for the same reason as Kirk Douglas.

Another crack of the whip, and the *lorarius* and his men lined us all up single file. Aside from the guys who had my jacket and shirt, there were two men who were hobbling because each was missing a foot, one who was minus a forearm, and one guy who was literally a raving madman, and half a dozen other unfortunates.

Apparently, my fellow convicts and I were the next act in the arena.

Outnumbered and weaponless, I forced myself to bide my time. Sooner or later, that *lorarius* would let his guard down, and I would have to make my grab for the Crystal then...or die trying.

In the meantime, in an effort to slow my pounding heart, I tried to reason out just what date these Romans wanted to carve on my tombstone. Maybe then I could figure out what had gone wrong.

At the tunnel's mouth, through the archways to the northwest, I could see a huge turquoise-green statue, a hundred feet high—a colossus in oxidized copper. Which, by the way, was the reason the Flavian Amphitheater became better known as the Colosseum.

The figure itself was almost in silhouette against the gray sky: it looked like a half-naked man with an umbrella, spearing an orange. But I knew from historic descriptions that it was meant to be the Emperor Nero, steering the globe with a rudder.

Just goes to show, you can burn down the city and burn up the Christians...but if you erect a mammoth monument to yourself, you'll still be remembered. However, by the time I took my post-graduation trip, the Colossus Neronis would be long gone, melted for medieval scrap, leaving only its namesake arena behind.

So the statue meant I had arrived sometime during or after the reign of Nero, which began in 54 A.D.—though the date might conceivably be as late as the last gladiatorial fight in 404 A.D.

To one side of the arena, workers with pails, shovels and rakes were scooping up large red-stained clumps and dumping out bucketfuls of pristine sand in their place. Essentially, they were cleaning up a slaughterhouse. I realized with a turning stomach there were two bodies left—a giraffe and a decapitated ostrich.

More workers struggled to load the large carcasses onto carts for removal.

I knew that some Roman gladiators were *bestiarii*—or animal-fighters. If you can call beheading an ostrich a fight.

I started to count the red sand spots they were shoveling up and replacing. I stopped at forty. This was a different brand of sadism than from Nero's crucifixions and incinerations.

I looked again at the Colossus. There was something large on its head that I couldn't quite make out in the shadows. A helmet?

Then a golden shaft of afternoon sun broke through, illuminating the face of the giant: a curly-bearded young man inside the open mouth of a lion's head.

Well, I knew from history there were a number of Roman emperors so vain that they would put their own head on another man's statue. But there was only one who insisted that any likeness of him wear a lion skin to convince everyone he was Hercules incarnate; this had to be the sword-happy, sadistic Caesar who made Nero look like a nerd and Caligula like a clodhopper.

Embroidered purple cloth draped the imperial box, where two score Praetorian Guard stood by, but the emperor's throne was empty. Instead, a balding man in a gold-trimmed toga stepped up to a big brass megaphone to address the audience.

"Citizens of Colonia Lucia Annia Commodiana! I, Gaius Lucian, editor of this spectacle, welcome you to this afternoon's Plebeian Games!"

The announcement confirmed that my location wasn't actually "Rome" this day. I now knew exactly what year it was: 192 A.D., when the Eternal City—temporarily—bore the name of the gladiator emperor Commodus, the murderous megalomaniac whose reign would end with his assassination this New Year's Eve.

And as a barbarian prisoner, I was here to be sword fodder for this self-styled Hercules. I was unlikely to survive long enough to sing "Auld Lang Syne" over his corpse.

"Arm yourselves!" growled our *lorarius*, cracking his whip at us and pushing us farther out into the arena, toward a pile of wooden swords.

21

HERCULES VS. THE CHRISTIANS

THE FEVERED MOB CHANTED THE NAME OF THE god of strength, over and over. The courtiers and hangers-on in the imperial box were cheering like their team was winning the Super Bowl.

Six of my cellmates already lay dead on the arena floor: Three convicted murderers (two wearing my blood-soaked jacket and shirt), two deserters (one with a peg-leg), and one raging lunatic, all with their wooden swords by their corpses.

Tall, brawny, blond-bearded "Hercules" had made short work of them; they never stood a chance, even if they'd had real weapons. I saw now that Commodus was every bit the expert swordsman that history said.

I'd puked into the sand at the first slaying. I had nothing left in my stomach now.

But I still thought I might be able to take him.

The man with the lion's head for a helmet beckoned me forward.

Instead, I cast aside my wooden *rudis*.

"O, mighty Caesar, surely you do not fear your humble subject so much that you give him a toy to fight you with!"

Commodus gave a sharp look to his editor.

I hastened to add, "I pray you, give me a real sword, that your victory over me might bring you truer glory!"

"What glory? You are no gladiator!" scoffed the editor.

"Give me a *gladius*, and I will show you that I am!"

"Pick up that *rudis*, or I will cleave you where you stand!" declared the emperor. He strode toward me.

I could tell he meant business.

I'd studied his moves against the convicts and the madman— even a wooden sword might allow me to show him there'd been advances in the art of fencing after he was dust. If I could just hold him off long enough to impress him with my skill...

I did a rolling dive for the *rudis* and came up ready to fight.

I was hoping his first move would be a thrust that I could deftly parry. Instead, he slashed at me and I instinctively ducked as I countered with my *rudis*—which meant his blade sliced right through the wood. Game over.

"Aw, Christ!" I swore, bitterly.

Commodus, winding up for my decapitation, paused in mid-swing.

"You are a Christian?"

My bad luck streak just kept getting hotter.

"Why, you got a hungry lion?" I snapped. Instantly, I regretted it, since Commodus almost certainly had one. I wondered if it was too late to request a nice quick beheading.

Then the emperor began laughing. It went on for a lot longer than my joke had been worth.

"This is a fortunate day for you," he said at last. "My mistress made me promise not to execute any Christians today."

"Really?" I hadn't been a churchgoer since childhood, but I made a mental note to take Mom to Easter services this year. Assuming I ever got home.

"Indeed it *is* fortunate, mighty Caesar!" I gestured to the prisoners in line behind me. "For we are all Christians!" With my right thumb I made the sign of the cross on my forehead, like the minister does on Ash Wednesday, a move my fellow sacrifices all imitated with varying degrees of accuracy.

Commodus found that even funnier.

"Free them," he at last said to the editor, between bouts of laughter. The crowd cheered this rare display of imperial mercy.

My luck had just done a fast 180. I'd stumbled across the one monster Caesar who wasn't all that into persecuting Christians. I wondered if this lover he spoke of might be Marcia, the Christian woman who would poison him on New Year's Eve before his personal wrestler strangled him in his bath.

Like me, Marcia was a sinner who fell way short of the mark. But in this case, I couldn't really hate the sin. This guy needed to go.

The *lorarius* shook his head, disgusted, but gestured with his bull-whip for the arena gate to be opened. My fellow prisoners made a mad dash for the exit. Their former tormentor cracked his whip at them again, but they were already running (or those with a missing foot, hobbling) at top speed into the city formerly known as Rome.

I bowed low. "O, mighty Caesar, truly are you renowned for your mercy!" I was amazed I could say that with a straight face. I turned to follow my fellow parolees—as I passed him, I would jump the thieving *lorarius* and grab my Crystal for a vanishing act they'd remember all their days.

"Not so fast, gladiator," said Commodus, wiping the blood from his *gladius* and the smile from his lips. "I promised that I would slay no Christians. There are others here who have made no such vow. One of them is eager to test your skills."

Commodus went over to the imperial box and spoke to the editor. They both gave me a look of amused contempt.

A different *lorarius* brought me over a *gladius*—a Roman sword about two-and-a-half feet long—and a *scutum*, a tall rectangular shield covered in bronze. Last, he handed me a *galea*—a broad-brimmed helmet with a cage over the face.

He put the helmet on me, but it made me instantly claustrophobic. I was sure any protection my skull enjoyed would be paid for when my side was pierced by an opponent I couldn't see. I took it off and let it drop. I actually got applause from the crowd for that bold act.

Commodus, I felt sure, would pick his most formidable gladiator to take me on. As it was, I was out of practice at dueling. I began praying for a miracle, though I was even longer out of practice at that.

Suddenly, I heard organ music.

Not a heavenly or church variety. But it was some kind of forced-air organ, no doubt hydraulic-powered. Up in the stands, I saw the organist working the valves of a big boxy instrument. It had water pipes leading into it and air pipes of ascending heights rising out.

As he played, the buzzing crowd gulped cups of wine and beer and ate bread and sizzling sausages that I could smell from a hundred yards away.

For a weird second it felt exactly like where all my adventures had started—the game at Dodger Stadium in 2011. Well, you know, if the Dodgers and the Braves had gone at each other with baseball bats.

As the organist's tune reached its crescendo, out came my opponent.

She was female. But she definitely wasn't Ariyl.

The gladiatrix wore a Samnite helmet with wide forward brim and the usual cage over her face; she wielded a *gladius* and carried a *scutum* like mine. Her armor was a throwback to the Spartacus-era gladiators of the Republic, rather than typical of imperial Rome.

She had dark, shortish hair and was muscled much like the male gladiators; her relative lack of body hair and her broad hips were the only real tell that she was female. Well, that and the fact that her breasts were bound, where a true Samnite would have been bare-chested.

The crowd knew her by that retro helmet. They chanted her name, "Hippolyta! Hippolyta!"

The Amazon raised her sword to her fans. Then she looked me over...and contemptuously cast aside her shield. The audience cheered her bravery.

I held onto mine. The mob booed and catcalled me for my cowardice. Big deal. Sword or knife may end my life, but Latin words won't hurt me.

We began to circle each other.

I am a pretty good amateur fencer, but I'm used to the Olympic saber (or sabre, for you non-Americans). The *gladius* was a foot shorter and nearly twice as heavy. It felt like I was fencing with a sharp lead pipe.

Hippolyta began a shrill ululation and charged me, sword swinging. I fended off her first few strikes with my *scutum*, but my arm stung with the power of her blows. This babe was no pushover. Her last one was so hard that I lost my grip on the shield.

Now I had only the *gladius* to counter her strikes.

Aside from my duel with the late Jon Ludlo in Atlantis, I had zero experience with an opponent who was out to cut my head off.

Luckily, I had a couple millennia of improved tactics to use against Hippolyta. I was able to parry each of her thrusts and block her swings, but I was at a disadvantage: I wasn't trying to run her through or hack her limbs off. She had no such compunctions about me. She'd keep going until I got too pooped to parry.

At some point, I was going to have to disable her. A slice to one of her legs seemed the quickest way. I didn't want to do that—call me chivalrous—but if I didn't, sooner or later I'd make an error and she'd cut me down. I couldn't think of a third option. Meanwhile, my weary arm was sore from fending her off.

I had one last trick up my sleeve: Back in college, a rotator cuff injury had forced me to fence left-handed for a time. Since Hippolyta was right-handed, this might be my chance to really throw her off— so I tossed the *gladius* to my left hand and engaged her again.

She retreated, clearly flummoxed by a suddenly left-handed opponent. I could see a spot on her upper leg that did not have armor or padding. A slashing cut there would force her to stop.

But as I made my way in to deliver the *coup de grâce*, she showed that she'd been paying attention to my tactics: She vigorously parried my blade the same way I'd been parrying hers—and as my left hand was not my stronger one, I lost my grip on the sword.

Then she stepped on the blade, so I couldn't retrieve it.

Eyes riveted on the Amazon, I backed up to get my *scutum*, only to find it was not where I'd dropped it. What the hell?!

I was well and truly screwed.

An excited walla ran through the crowd, though neither I nor my would-be slayer had done anything to warrant it.

Hippolyta was staring past me, seemingly at someone behind me.

Did that look-behind-you gag really go back to ancient Rome?

"Get behind me, David," I heard Ariyl say.

I turned and saw my miracle had finally arrived. She was wearing that impractical, skimpy "fighting armor" she'd worn at the ancient Olympics. Apparently, she had walked out of the tunnel just beyond her and picked up my shield.

"Ariyl! Thank God!"

"Take my hand. We'll jump out of here."

"We can't till we get my Time Crystal back. One of the guards took it."

Ariyl gaped at me in disbelief. "Which one?"

"Uh...I don't see him right now."

"Okay," she fumed. "Guess we have to do this the hard way."

Commodus stared at Ariyl from his box. He and the editor had a hurried exchange of words. It was clear both were bewildered by her presence, but they could tell the crowd was eating it up.

Ariyl walked up to Hippolyta, who backed away as she repeatedly whacked her sword on Ariyl's shield. I could now reach my *gladius*. But the second I snatched it up, the crowd really started booing us. Ariyl looked around, a bit hurt.

"What'd I do?"

"I guess they think two against one is no fair."

"If you want to finish her off..." she began, offering me the shield.

I waved it off. "No, no. I've had my fun," I said, and tossed her my *gladius*.

Ariyl appraised the weapon. "I don't need this," she said, and jammed it into a post, embedded to the handle. I wished she'd asked my advice before her impressive gesture—we might need a sword sometime in the near future.

Next, Ariyl frisbeed her *scutum* at Hippolyta, who ducked it.

"You are mad!" the gladiatrix marveled.

"No, just annoyed," said Ariyl. "Let's get this over with."

"Then stand your ground, sister," said Hippolyta. "I will make your death quick."

"You can try," said Ariyl.

Hippolyta began ululating again, raised her sword, and ran at Ariyl.

Ariyl grabbed the gladiatrix's wrist in a grip of iron and wrenched away her sword, then jammed it deep into the same post as mine.

Hippolyta now realized she was in serious trouble. She dashed back to where she'd ditched her *scutum*.

Ariyl strode toward her, fists up in a boxer's pose. Hippolyta held up her shield with both hands and tried to block Ariyl's blows. Ariyl punched it, denting the bronze. She bashed it again and again, driving the Amazon backwards until the *scutum* was pockmarked junk. Ariyl swatted it from her hands and picked up Hippolyta by her hips.

"Be smart, little sister, just stay down," she murmured in Latin. Then she threw Hippolyta five yards backward.

There was a collective gasp from the stands.

The gladiatrix landed on her back on the sand; if she wasn't knocked out, she did a good job of faking it.

Commodus stood, and silence fell on the crowd. He held out his fist...and after what seemed an eternity, put his thumb down.

The multitude cheered.

Ariyl shot me a stern look. "I am not killing that woman."

"No, no," I said, *sotto*. "The movies have that wrong. I guess your vidz do too. Thumbs down meant spare their lives. Thumbs up meant finish them off." I imitated an upward sword thrust against her abs—which were firm as ever.

"Well, he'd better keep his damn thumb down," she growled.

Commodus conferred with Lucian. The editor then stepped up to his megaphone for the big announcement:

"Most noble Caesar has declared that if the barbarian giantess wins her next two bouts, she and the Christian shall be granted their freedom!"

The organ took up a new tune, and the long brass tubas chimed in. Something big was in the offing. Suddenly, two guards grabbed my wrists and tied me to the wooden post, while a third kept his *gladius* pointed at my throat.

Ariyl looked ready to mop the floor with them, but I yelled, "No, don't risk it. Commodus won't go back on his word. Not in front of this audience. No matter who they send against you, you can take him."

Another gladiator entered the arena, this one male. He was a lot bigger than Hippolyta. He was on eye-level with Ariyl.

Ariyl folded her arms and waited.

Then another gladiator emerged from the darkness of the tunnel. And a third, and a fourth.

Ariyl now faced this quartet of large, brawny, bare-chested, heavily armored gladiators, each with a similar face-covering helmet, with padded iron armor (a *manica*) on at least one arm, more armor (*greaves*) on their shins, and each carrying a short sword.

The first was a *hoplomachus*, whose helmet crest was studded with bird plumes; he carried a *hoplon* (small round shield) and a *gladius*.

Next was the *secutor*, in a smooth, rounded helmet with no crest or other ridges; he too wielded a *gladius* but had a legionary's tall rectangular *scutum*.

Third came the *dimachaerus*: He was a dark African, had mail armor, and was the only one without a shield. Instead, in each hand he held two short, curved *siccae*. This type specialized in carving up his foes at close range.

The fourth was a *murmillo*, with the leaping-fish crest on his helmet like all *murmillones* had. Don't laugh—it was a fierce-looking sea creature, and this particular merman looked like he could punch out a shark. Like the *secutor*, he carried a rectangular *scutum*.

Then to complete the sea-monster-versus-fisherman theme, the traditional opponent of the *murmillo*, the net-wielding *retiarius*, was the fifth gladiator to walk out into the arena. A universal cheer went up: he was obviously the star of this group. His supporting cast gave way so that he could walk directly up to Ariyl.

He was a lean, weathered, but well-muscled redheaded Celt with no helmet or armor or even sandals; just a shoulder guard, leather belt, and loincloth. Besides his stout rope net, he carried a trident with a thick bronze shaft and long thin prongs, from which he apparently never cleaned the blood of his previous victims. Nice theatrical touch.

"Seriously? I have to fight all five of you brave men at once?" sighed Ariyl.

"She's unarmed!" I protested.

"And you are tied to a post," noted the Celt. "But the editor expects blood. As does Commodus. As does the crowd."

"Commodus is insane," I hissed. "You all must know that. He calls himself your fellow gladiator, but today you've watched him butcher prisoners and cripples, for G—uh, for Jupiter's sake!"

"Even a damned giraffe," agreed the *dimachaerus*, also keeping his voice low.

"What true gladiator does such things?" I looked each of them in the eye.

"He killed *what* now?" asked Ariyl.

I ignored her. "He put his own name on the noble Roman Senate. He renamed Rome itself."

"What do you care? You're no Roman," scoffed the *hoplomachus*.

"And you Romans, he calls you Commodianus," I shot back.

"And the legions, Commodianae," nodded the *secutor*.

"And the navy," said the *murmillo*.

"Don't forget renaming all twelve months after himself," muttered Hippolyta a few yards away, eyes shut, still playing possum.

The *secutor* growled bitterly: "I saw him abandon the empire that Marcus Aurelius won for us. Now Rome's word means nothing to our allies or our foes—the world laughs at us. The traitorous cur."

My guess? The *secutor* had been a soldier under Commodus's father Marcus Aurelius, last of the Five Good Emperors. I had struck a rich vein of discontent.

"He keeps taking silver out of the money," said the gloomy *murmillo*. (I knew that a lot of gladiators survived to retire on their savings.) "My children will be paupers. While the treasury pays him a million *sesterces* for every appearance in the arena."

"Really?" That was news to me. "That's just like paying him for his golf outings," I mused.

"What is golf outings?" wondered the *hoplomachus*.

"So you people are making your ruler wealthier. Isn't it supposed to be the other way around?"

The gladiators exchanged dissatisfied glances.

But the *retiarius* was having none of it. "You talk like a Greek, bemoaning your precious, dead *dēmokratía*."

"What was this about a giraffe?" insisted Ariyl.

Commodus couldn't hear what we were saying, but it was clear he disapproved of our discussion. He beckoned to Lucian, the editor.

I had to drive my point home fast: "Your nation is in the hands of a vainglorious Narcissus obsessed with slapping his name on everything in sight. A cowardly bully who boasts when he wins against powerless opponents. A lying, cheating, perverted, treasonous incompetent who thinks of nothing and no one but himself."

"And is your wonderful homeland any different, barbarian?" bristled the *hoplomachus*.

"Uh...at the moment, no," I admitted. "But we're talking about Rome. Which Commodus is looting and disgracing!"

"Begin the combat!" boomed the impatient Lucian through his megaphone.

"Stand up for yourselves," I urged them. "Tell him you will not kill unarmed opponents!"

"You make a pretty speech," the Celt muttered. "But every man who defied Commodus has died a horrible death. Is that not true?" He stared down his comrades. "I intend to live to spend my money. Do any of you feel different?"

They all shook their heads and gripped their weapons tightly. They still had a living to make.

"Look, I don't want to hurt anybody..." Ariyl warned.

"That is where we differ, *amica*," the Celt grinned. "I enjoyed holding that giraffe for Commodus."

Ariyl's eyes flashed. The next instant she fetched the Celt a slap that knocked him off his feet.

He lay on the sand, stunned for only a moment. He got up slow, licking blood off his lip, and chuckled sadistically as he waved his trident near her face. "Thank you, *pulchra*. You just made this much easier."

Suddenly the *hoplomachus* came at her from behind. Ariyl whirled at the last instant, dodged his blade, and slammed her fist down on his helmet. He bit the dust, literally. The throng in the stands tittered as he got to his hands and knees, dazedly trying to shake the sand out of the grate covering his face.

The Celt could see brain was needed more than brawn here. He moved in, expertly whirling the net over his head as if it were a lariat. He feinted this way, that way, and another, then suddenly leapt forward and flung it on Ariyl.

She sidestepped it with her usual speed, but by the time it hit the sand, the *retiarius* was already thrusting his trident to impale her. She yanked it from his fingers, held it over her head, and grinned as she bent the bronze shaft into a U-shape. The crowd gasped.

There wasn't time for the Celt's Plan C, which was to run. As he turned to flee, she threw his own net over him. Tangled, he tripped and fell.

She reached down by his feet and bunched the mouth of the net in her fist. Then she hoisted her frantically wriggling catch of the day into the air and swung him playfully.

The crowd roared with laughter.

The *murmillo* took his colleague's predicament personally. With a growl he charged Ariyl.

She immediately leapt back and began to whirl the Celt in the net around and around her as if she was in the Olympic hammer throw and he was the hammer. Once she had him up to speed, she raised her arms over her head. Now only he was spinning. She'd essentially made him her human mace.

This, even the battle-hardened *retiarius* was unprepared for—he began hollering like he was stuck on the Zipper ride at the county fair.

The *murmillo* backed away, but not fast enough. Ariyl swung her man-mace at his helmet and the net snagged on that piscine crest. The momentum yanked him off his feet and headfirst into the nearby wooden post, flattening his fish like a flounder. He collapsed.

The *secutor* came at her next. She lowered the whirling *retiarius* each time he got close. The agile gladiator ducked as the net audibly brushed his head twice; his helmet was designed to be too smooth to snag. Meanwhile, he timed his sword thrusts to miss his captive colleague.

He was wasting his time: Ariyl made a sudden low feint then brought her human blackjack up hard, a pop fly that knocked the gladiator six feet in the air. The duo's combined *"OOF!"* was in perfect harmony, but thereafter they parted ways—the *secutor* was unconscious before he hit the ground, while the revolving *retiarius'* ordeal would go on and on.

Next came the *hoplomachus*, who'd finally gotten the grit out of his grille. Ariyl just sped up her spin—then lunged forward and bashed him. Shedding helmet feathers, he flew fifteen feet—and might have gone farther if not for the wall below the imperial box. Apparently this time she was going for distance.

The Colosseum mob cheered her astounding power.

Ariyl now faced her final opponent, the *dimachaerus*, his twin mini-scimitars slashing toward her flesh.

"Die, Amazon bitch!" he said. In Latin, but I knew she'd still take offense. He was not concerned for his net-bound buddy. He was out to kill her no matter the cost, so he thrust his blades again and again, each time slicing his Celtic comrade, who responded with ripe curses.

Ariyl abruptly leapt behind the *dimachaerus*, swung for his feet, and knocked him heels over head. He backflipped onto his helmet and fell beside the *secutor*, insensate upon the sand.

At this point the only one in worse shape than the four downed gladiators was the poor battered schlub she'd used to take them out. Now that the *retiarius* had served his purpose, she extended her arms back into hammer-throw mode, gave him a couple last spins for momentum then let go of the net. He gave a vanishing cry as he sailed thirty feet then landed in a tangled heap on the arena floor.

The audience went insane with hilarity and cheers.

"*Amazon vivat!*" became their chant.

Commodus noted the crowd's fervor with a grim expression. He again gave the thumbs-down for the defeated. Attendants with litters rushed from the tunnels and carted off Ariyl's unconscious victims.

Then the emperor murmured an instruction to the editor, who hurried down a staircase that must have led to the subterranean tunnels of the arena.

"For my second bout, I want to challenge Commodus," said Ariyl.

"Uh, no. That's a really terrible idea."

"You say that about all my ideas, David. It's starting to piss me off."

"I've seen Commodus fight. He's better than any of those clowns you fought. He's an expert, with a lot of military experience."

"You said it yourself—you've only seen him take on cripples with wooden swords. And from what I saw, *you* could have taken him if you'd had a real sword."

"Wait a sec, you were here for that?"

She nodded. "I was watching with a javelin in my hand. I would have speared his sword arm before he landed that last blow. But then you got him laughing, so..."

"So you just kept quiet and let me fight that Amazon?" I said, my temper rising.

"Well, I didn't want to injure your manly pride," she smirked. "I only stepped in when I could see you were going to lose. Anyway, Commodus doesn't scare me."

"He scares *me*. I don't want to see you dead!"

"Aw, you're worried about me! That's so sweet!" She kissed me. "But you *do* remember my little sword fight in Atlantis with Ludlo?"

"Who almost killed you!"

"Only 'cause I tripped. I was doing great till then, and Ludlo was a lot stronger than any pre-Changer."

"Take it from me, strong is all that Jon Ludlo was. He was a lousy swordsman. Commodus was a champion gladiator, according to Gibbon."

"And who's he?"

"Edward Gibbon. He wrote *Decline and Fall of the Roman Empire* in 1776."

"Which means I've seen more of Commodus than he has!"

"Cassius Dio was a senator who *knew* Commodus. He's probably up in those stands, and he's Gibbon's source. Trust me, all Commodus needs is one good swing and your head is rolling on the arena floor. That's something not even *you* can heal from!"

"David, I just beat five of their best gladiators. At once."

"That's the *other* downside—if you defeat the emperor, he'll have us both killed. See them?" I pointed to the Praetorian Guard in the stands: two dozen armored archers stood by in the back of the imperial box.

"They could cut us down from a hundred yards away. And let's not forget those guys." I indicated another detachment of Praetorians, farther down the stands: two score legionaries with shields and spears and brass breastplates and purple horsehair bristles in their crests.

"Nice outfits. I still think I..." she began.

We were interrupted by a brace of long brass *tubas* and curved *litui* announcing the second bout.

"Forget it. Your next opponent is up," I said, relieved. "Whoever they could send now, is better for us than you fighting the emperor, believe me."

She rolled her eyes, bored. "Fine. How many do you think it'll be this time?"

We heard ropes creaking, and a square patch of sand unexpectedly rose from the arena floor.

The sand lay atop the wooden frame of an elevator cage—and inside the cage was a huge, ravenous lion.

"Just one," I said, my mouth going dry.

22

THE BESTIARIUS OF OUR LIVES

A ROPE FROM THE TUNNELS BELOW PULLED THE catch, and the wooden door of the cage dropped down. The lion leapt out onto the sand, about fifty yards from us.

I will confess I was scared.

The *tubas* frantically broadcast the thrilling news that we were about to be torn to shreds.

The mob above us was hooting in bloodlust.

The lion was big, but thin. I could count his ribs.

I will confess I was trembling.

"If you were ever going to tell me who the karate girl at Harold Lloyd's house was, now's the time."

Ariyl ripped apart the ropes holding me to the post.

"Run. I'll handle him."

I looked. Every tunnel was blocked by guards with whips or swords.

"That's not gonna happen. The emperor wants me here for this."

"Then stay behind me."

Leo shook us with a basso roar that bounced off the far end of the Colosseum.

I will confess my voice went up an octave. "Hear that roar? That's how the zoo sounds at feeding time. And it looks like he's missed a few meals."

The lion got a whiff of us. He did that open-mouthed thing that our family cat used to do when she was about to attack a lizard. He loped toward us.

"Ohhh, poor kitty!" said Ariyl, genuinely concerned. She put out a calming hand toward the animal. I grabbed her wrist and tried to pull her back.

"Remember Oscar night, 1948? When you put away two pounds of prime rib?"

"Eww, don't remind me!" she frowned.

"Remember how you wolfed it down?"

"You pick *now* to make me feel guilty about eating that poor cow? I was starving!"

The lion roared so loud it made my ears ring.

"Well, so is he! And that kitty *won't* feel guilty about eating you! Or me!"

"So what do you expect me to do, David?" she asked, exasperated. "Kill a poor hungry lion?"

"You mean that's an *option*?"

Not waiting for Ariyl's answer, the beast leapt for me.

Four hundred pounds of muscle, fur, and claw knocked me to the sand. One of those talons dug into my forearm and I gasped in pain. Hot breath with the reek of decayed flesh and a leonine gut going into ketosis blasted my face. But what was going to happen to me next I knew would make this moment seem pleasant.

I heard some faint-hearted screams, but mostly the mob was howling for my blood. Well, at least I would be spared the big Preston family meeting back in Brentwood.

Suddenly the lion pulled back. Or rather, he *was* pulled back. Ariyl had her hands under the beast's shoulders. She hefted his weight off me and slung him aside.

The audience gasped in astonishment.

The lion skidded on the sand then whirled back to face us. It tensed for a leap and let out another shield-rattling roar.

"No!" she commanded, pointing her finger as you might train a cocker spaniel.

Now the audience began cracking up.

The lion bellowed like no doggie you ever heard and slashed at Ariyl with his paw. One second, those knife-sharp talons were speeding toward her pristine face...the next second, it was just air his claws raked. Damn, she had reflexes.

"I SAID NO!" shouted Ariyl.

Leo didn't listen. He leapt for her.

She caught him by his forepaws and held him up. It reminded me of Beauty and the Beast dancing, right up until the moment this beast tried to bite off the beauty's face. She ducked the snap and the next one. She was simply too fast for him.

The Colosseum crowd was in hysterics.

Leo then tried to eat the hands holding his forepaws, but again, she was too fast, letting go as his jaws tried to close on her wrists then grabbing his paw somewhere else. He gave a mighty bellow, but still she held her ground. And his paws.

"Now, calm down, and I'll let go," she said soothingly. She was speaking classical Latin, though I doubted he was a Roman lion, or in any way domesticated; her words could mean nothing to him. But that calm tone of voice seemed to bewilder him. I doubt he'd ever attacked any creature that showed less fear.

The audience was guffawing.

Leo knew he was stuck. He calmed down, and Ariyl released his paws. The instant his paws hit the sand, he gave up on Ariyl and came after me again. I stumbled backward and fell on my ass.

"Ariyl!" I shouted. Oh, let's be honest, I was screaming at that point.

"I'm on it," she said, leaping into the lion's path. This time she ducked under his belly, leveraged the predator's momentum over her shoulder, and flipped Leo onto his back on the sand.

He immediately rolled onto his side, but as he got up, she straddled his back, clamped her leg around each flank, and grabbed his mane.

The lion went bonkers—roaring, writhing, trying to chase his own tail. It was an unforgettable spectacle. Through it all, Ariyl kept her grip, glued to Leo like a rider on a bucking bronco. The lion rolled onto his back, trying to dislodge her, but Ariyl kept her legs wrapped around his chest. His ribcage was too big for her to lock her ankles around it, but she didn't need to—she just held on and kept compressing his chest.

I ran to the post and tried to pull out one of the *gladii* that Ariyl had embedded there, but it was like trying to pry up a nail without a claw hammer.

Leo finally managed to get his rear paw up, and his claws deeply raked Ariyl's thigh. I nearly fainted at the sight of fresh blood welling up from those gashes, but Ariyl merely grunted in discomfort. The big cat thrashed around, dragging her on the ground. Sand caked her wounds.

Through the grit, the spectators could not see what I knew was taking place on that wounded leg: Within a minute, that incredible gene-tooled healing asserted itself. Her bleeding stopped as wounds scarred over; the scars crusting into scabs that then flaked off.

Meanwhile, the irresistible pressure of her mighty thighs was making it impossible for the lion to inhale. He couldn't even roar anymore. He might as well have been caught in the coils of a boa constrictor: Those rippling quads of hers slowly, implacably squeezed the wind from his lungs. His struggles grew feeble. Within a minute the king of beasts went limp between her legs.

Ariyl released her scissor hold and slid her leg out from under his immobile bulk, then stood.

The Colosseum crowd went nuts.

She knelt by the beast and put her ear to his heart. Then she smiled and nodded at me. The lion was fine—she'd just put him out.

One of the *venators* approached the senseless beast with his sword drawn but halted in his tracks when Ariyl stepped between him and the lion.

"Give me that," she said, holding out her hand. The animal handler gripped his weapon tighter. Ariyl scowled and took a step toward him. His survival instinct kicked in, and he surrendered it, handle first.

She jammed his sword into the post beside the others, but burying it only halfway. I figured I could get that one out, but then her powerful arm swelled as she bent the blade sideways.

She turned back to the *venator*. "Get this animal some food. Now."

"My orders—"

Ariyl grabbed the Roman by his leather tunic and flipped him upside-down, dangling his face against the unconscious lion's mouth.

"Give him something to eat, or I will," she promised.

"I shall do as you say!" stammered the *venator*.

Ariyl set him back on his feet, and he dashed to the elevator, climbed inside, and pulled up the cage door, to the vast amusement of the crowd. He yelped orders to the men below. The elevator descended rapidly.

Ariyl now strode around the arena, acknowledging the Romans' wild ovation, clenching her fists over her head, and flexing her biceps in triumph. The cheering went on and on.

Commodus glared stonily from the imperial box.

Half a minute later, the elevator rose back up to the arena level; the *venator* and one of his assistants schlepped a large basket of fresh hunks of meat partway across the sand.

"I'll take that," said Ariyl. She wrinkled her nose in disgust but lugged the gory load over to set beside the lion. The great predator inhaled and awoke with a start.

The lion wranglers tripped over each other dashing for the elevator. They stomped and yelled urgently until they were lowered to safety.

The lion sniffed the carcass in the basket. He looked at Ariyl, wary.

"Go on," she said gently.

He tried a piece, looked at her once more, then devoured the rest ravenously—with just one sideward glance to be sure Ariyl wasn't climbing back in the saddle.

As he sated his appetite, Ariyl walked up and stroked his mane. Apparently grateful, Leo let her...and kept chewing.

The audience was also eating it up. Laughing. Applauding. Cheering. And chanting:

"Invicta! Invicta!"

23

THE INVINCIBLE WOMAN

"Now can I challenge him?" Ariyl asked, with a superior smile. I knew her question was rhetorical.

"I'm telling you, he could kill you!"

"David, I've fought *Commodus the Crazy* a hundred times. He's not that great a swordsman."

"Yeah, well, for accuracy, between your vidz and Gibbon, I'll take Gibbon and his eyewitness. One mistake and Commodus will chop you up like a sushi chef!"

"What if I promise to let him win?"

I stared at her for a second.

"Would you really do that?"

She looked at the athletic Commodus, now standing at the edge of the imperial box. "Well, I wouldn't kill him, in any case." She folded her brawny arms, still pumped from all the exercise she'd just had. "But just out of curiosity, what could he *do* if I defeated him?"

"They can just keep releasing lions until one gets lucky. You can't put 'em all out. They could have a hundred lions down there."

"Yeah, right," she snorted.

"I'm not exaggerating. According to Gibbon, in one day,

Commodus killed a hund..." I suddenly realized this depressing statistic would not result in Ariyl playing nice.

"He killed *what?*" she asked.

"He killed a Hun."

"No, he didn't."

"I mean it."

"Don't bullshit me, David. That's not what you were starting to say."

"It was a Hun," I insisted.

She stared at me unconvinced.

"Commodus killed a very famous Hun."

She kept staring.

"Attila the First." I was still a crappy liar, and my gaze strayed toward the animal elevator.

She put a gentle finger to my jaw and turned me back to look her in the eye. She was getting angrier with every word, and she'd been furious when she started. "You were going to say he killed a hundred. *Was that a hundred lions?*"

"It's history, Ariyl. It's over with. It's nothing we can change, if we want to get back to our own timeline."

"Well, maybe I don't care about that right now!"

"Then care about us. You may be as strong as a dozen men—"

"Stronger."

"—but even *you* can't take on the Praetorian Guard with thirty archers and forty swords and spears. So just ask him for the honor of fighting him."

"Oh, I want that honor all right," she seethed. "I'll be honored to kick his ass in front of the whole city of Rome."

"You can't do that. I'm not going to arrange your suicide. You have to let him win."

"Really," she said flatly.

"That's the rule. Commodus always won. The upside is, he always let his opponents live."

"Always?" she said, skeptical. "That's not how it is in the vidz. In *Commodus the Crazy*, he kills a bunch of guys in private matches. Did you hear that from your pal Baboon?"

"Gibbon. Yeah, he said the same thing."

Ariyl hmphed, satisfied.

"The point is, Commodus won't kill you in *public*. It would turn the people against him."

"Haven't you figured out yet, it's not a question of whether he'll kill me? It's, will I kill him, or just turn him over my knee?"

I was stunned. "You...you can't do that."

"Sure, I can. You've seen me."

Yeah. That big cop in the Nazi Los Angeles. Poor bastard couldn't stop her. And he had a shotgun.

"Ariyl, things like that didn't happen in ancient Rome."

"Which is why this place is so fucked up. Assholes like Commodus get away with murder. Maybe it's time it *did* happen."

"Let me explain this very carefully. If you paddle the ass of a famous emperor like Commodus, it cannot fail to go down in history. We are going to find our home eras *wildly* different."

The head of the Praetorian Guard was saying something in Commodus's ear. The emperor nodded, and the officer strode over to his archers. Each one drew an arrow from his quiver and nocked it in his bowstring.

Ariyl noticed this too.

"David, we have to make a decision here. The only way we get out of here alive is if I give the crowd the show it wants. Right?"

I hated to admit it, but she was right. "Okay, we'll ask him. But remember, you *lose*. And please, let me do the talking."

She was already marching over to stand before the imperial box. I ran to catch up, a bit out of breath.

"O mighty Caesar, the gladiatrix Ariyl, champion of the *Britainnae*, begs the honor of public combat with the heir to Marcus Aurelius, first emperor born to the purple and divine incarnation of the god Hercules."

(Born to the purple meant Commodus had been the first emperor born the son of a reigning emperor.)

Commodus stared at Ariyl. "Barbarian, do you understand what that means?"

She nodded. "That I have to let you wi—"

"—wield your godly powers to prevail in the end," I interpreted.

"Exactly what I was going to say," said Ariyl dryly.

Commodus looked deeply suspicious. Lucian eyed Ariyl then murmured to him, "This must be the one Octavius prophesized."

A prophet named Octavius? I'd never come across the name in my reading, but then, not many soothsayers make it into the history books. Except the one who warned Julius Caesar about the Ides of March. Hmm.

I could no longer deny that Octavius and Eight-Fingers were connected. Someone was leaking information from the future to the past. I hoped that we'd be on speaking terms with the emperor when this was all over so I could ask him where to find this soothsayer.

I saw Commodus give Lucian a significant look.

"We shall have the cups, that you may drink to each other's health," announced the editor.

"Indeed," said the emperor. "And bring her up here. And him."

In short order, a phalanx of Praetorians escorted us up a stairway and into the emperor's luxury box. The Guard were on their most welcoming behavior, weapons sheathed or slung over their shoulders.

Lucian beckoned over two slaves, one bearing a wineskin, the other two golden goblets.

Something felt off here. I'd never heard of gladiators toasting Commodus, or any other emperor, before they fought.

The slaves filled the cups. Lucian handed the emperor the first goblet and brought Ariyl the second. I gave her a subtle headshake.

Ariyl didn't take the cup. "No, thank you. Not before a fight."

"You dare refuse to drink to the emperor?" sputtered Lucian.

Out of the corner of my eye, I could see Praetorian archers reaching toward their quivers.

"Mighty Caesar, my cousin and I hail from your distant colony of Britannia," I explained. "It is our custom there for strangers to trade cups before drinking."

Commodus grinned wryly. "A wise custom. Perhaps the Britons are not so different from us. Let us all make the barbarian giantess feel at home."

Ariyl got a funny smile and murmured to me, "Not now, David. Later."

"What are you talking about?" I muttered back.

"You didn't just squeeze my butt?" she asked.

I shook my head and looked back. A smirking young man, apparently part of the entourage, had been the one copping the feel. Ariyl looked back and scowled but wisely did not make a scene. When in Rome...

Commodus gestured, and the slaves poured more wine in the cups of the rest of the imperial retinue. No one seemed to relish the invitation. No doubt all of them were well aware of the time-honored role poison played in imperial succession.

Meanwhile, Commodus handed his goblet to a slave, who conveyed it to Ariyl and took hers to give to the emperor.

Someone thoughtfully offered me my own chalice from the palace.

I shook my head. "I'm the chariot driver."

The Praetorian beside me, unamused by anachronistic quips, put his hand on his sword handle.

"Well, I guess one won't hurt," I conceded, taking hold of the cup.

But still, no one else was drinking. I felt reasonably confident Commodus wouldn't poison his entire entourage just to get Ariyl. I wondered if we were supposed to clink cups, or what the holdup was.

Then the slave—the same one who'd felt Ariyl's ass minutes ago —was brought forward by one of the Guard.

The slave took the emperor's brimming cup and dutifully took a healthy slug. He started to set it down, but the Praetorian's glare told him he wasn't done. So he drained half of the emperor's goblet before the Praetorian let him hand it back.

Everyone then watched him like a hawk, or possibly a Roman eagle. And why not? He was the wine taster.

A few minutes ticked by, and you could sense everyone relaxing, especially the taster. These people knew how long the standard poisons took to kick in.

Lucian at last dismissed the taster with a wave.

The lad moved behind Ariyl, apparently to get a better view of what he'd admired earlier.

With a contemptuous chuckle, the emperor raised his goblet to the rest and downed the wine.

I gave Ariyl a why-not look, and we partook as well.

Now everyone else took a big gulp.

Meanwhile, the wine taster, apparently feeling bold, decided to feel Ariyl as well. The instant he grabbed her ass, she delivered a sharp elbow to his diaphragm, so subtly that no one but me noticed.

But everyone else noticed when the wine taster fell to the ground holding his belly.

Most of the retinue sprayed out their wine, choking and coughing in panic.

I'm fairly sure it was Rome's first recorded instance of a mass spit-take.

* * *

WE WERE HUSTLED BACK toward the arena, where I would be allowed to watch from the fifty-yard line as Ariyl met Commodus in combat.

Ariyl paused at a doorway by the final steps leading to the arena. She told me to wait for her downstairs. A few minutes later, she emerged wearing, over her tunic, a wide, brass-studded leather belt and a pair of padded iron *manicae*, tightly strapped to her upper arms. She also carried some mid-thigh length iron *greaves*—which I was pretty sure belonged to the *murmillo*. Well, he wouldn't need them during his recuperation. But instead of putting them on, she bent the top part of each *greave* outward.

"Since when do *you* need armor?" I asked.

"You're sweet," she said, with a weary smile. "Since I saw all those archers. And since my SmartFab's gone flaky." She touched her shoulder and said, "Full armor, ancient Rome." Nothing happened to her SmartFab outfit.

"First the Time Crystals go hinky, now this?" I muttered. Our luck was now suspiciously bad.

"I asked them for these so I'd look the part. But really, you're right...we can't trust that guy." Ariyl's hands flew as she tied the *greaves* on upside-down, so the bent ends now covered the tops of her feet.

"Hey, that's smart!" I said.

"As opposed to most of my ideas?" she snapped. She was having trouble tying the last part.

"No, of course not. Uh, you need a hand?"

She shook her head. "Fingers are just kinda numb, like I slept on them." She licked her lips. "My mouth too."

"Ariyl, are you okay?"

"I'm fine!" She stood up but gave a little grunt of discomfort. Now I could see her hands were trembling.

"No, there's something wrong with you. Hey, they didn't give you any more wine when you were getting that armor?"

"No!"

I grabbed her wrist and put two fingers over the artery.

"Ariyl, your hand's like ice, and your pulse is going crazy...did they stick you with something? A little knife prick maybe?"

"No, nothing! What, you think I've been poisoned?"

"You're sure you didn't have any wine?"

"I'm not that stupid, David! Just some water. I was really dehyd—"

"Shit! They must've poisoned your water!"

"Why?"

"So Commodus can kill you in the arena!"

"You said he'd never *do* that!"

"He also never had to fight a woman, much less one that mopped the floor with every gladiator in town. And put a sleeper hold on a lion. He must want to make an example of you! Goddamn me, why did I let you challenge him?"

"David, I don't want to die!"

"Can you tickle your throat, maybe throw it up?"

She tried. "My throat is numb!" she said, her voice rising in panic. "David, you have to give me this." She reached down into her

163

cleavage and pulled out a familiar-looking device. "I can't stand the idea of needles."

It was one of the self-sterilizing syringes that Jon Ludlo had used to drug three actors so that they would attack the 1948 Oscars: "Demon shots", as they were colloquially known, were a potent medication of the pre-Change 2030s that could heal devastating injuries and gave users superhuman strength. But it also tended to drive them insane with rage.

"Oh, God! Have you ever had a demon shot before?"

"N-Tec doesn't allow drugs, you know that! We don't need meds!"

"Are you sure it will counteract poison?"

"No, I'm not."

"Then how do we know it's safe to use?"

"I figure it's safer than the *poison* I just took!"

From one of the tunnels came a shout, the snapping of reins, the crack of a whip, and the thudding of hooves. Two beautiful white Arabian steeds burst into the sunlight, driven by an armored, whip-wielding *essedarius* in a gaudily painted war chariot. The reins were wrapped around his wrist for better grip as he lashed the horses.

Behind him, brandishing a long sword, stood Commodus, in that lion-headed robe meant to link him to Hercules' mythical slaying of the Nemean lion. If he'd been trying to enrage Ariyl, he couldn't have picked a better outfit.

She handed me the hypodermic. "Do it fast!"

I tried. I've given shots before. But it turned out that her skin, which felt so soft and silky, was as tough as rhino hide when it came to needles. Another genetic marvel.

"Hurry up!"

"I can't get it to go in!" I cried, pushing with all my might.

"It's a needle! How hard can it be to shove it in?"

"This has never happened to me before!"

The chariot charged toward us. The ground shook from the galloping hooves.

"Give it to me!" she ordered. I did but her trembling fingers dropped it in the sand.

"Shit!" I yelled, falling to my knees and feeling through the grains.

I finally found it. I rose and dropped it into Ariyl's hand—an instant before she threw me from the chariot's path. I arced into the air and tumbled onto the sand yards away. I looked back in horror as the horses stampeded over Ariyl and she disappeared under the wheels of the chariot.

I shrieked her name.

She couldn't have had time to give herself the shot.

The dust kicked up by the chariot was everywhere. I couldn't even see where she'd fallen.

The chariot turned and as it thundered around me, through the settling cloud of dust, I saw Ariyl again—holding onto the back of the chariot. She was dirty and bruised, but not in terrible shape for someone who had just been trampled by the horses that were now dragging her at a fast gallop.

The audience was yelling at the emperor and the *essedarius* and pointing behind them. Commodus finally figured out where his opponent was. He smacked the driver, who reined the horses to a halt, turned to Ariyl, and raised his whip.

That was all the time she needed to grip the axle like a barbell and hoist the chariot—driver, emperor, and all—over her head. The draught-pole between the horses cracked loudly and broke. The chariot tipped forward: the *essedarius* tumbled out beside the steeds' hooves, but Commodus managed to cling onto the chariot box like Ben-Hur.

Undeterred, Ariyl shook the chariot up and down and vigorously rocked it left and right. Commodus held on valiantly, until she finally dumped the emperor out on his ass.

She dropped the vehicle with a thud. The Arabians bolted in panic, taking the broken draught pole with them. Unfortunately for the driver, the reins were still wrapped around his wrist and he was dragged along with them. The organist played him out with a peppy, minor-key ditty.

The chariot portion of the entertainment was over.

. . .

EMPEROR HERCULES LAY DAZED on the arena sand. He got up, shaking his head. Then he became aware of the one sound on this earth that he could not abide—scornful laughter. Gales of it.

He leapt to his feet and glared murderously at the assembled citizens of Colonia Lucia Annia Commodiana, who all fell silent.

No one wanted to end up like the giraffe.

Ariyl dusted herself off. The lion claw scars had healed, leaving only whitish traces along her muscular leg, and those were fading by the minute.

Commodus charged at her, sword held high, ready to lop her head off.

But as he got closer, he stopped—noticing that the irises of her eyes were bright red. "By the gods!" he whispered.

Ariyl shook her head with a manic grin. "All your gods can't save you now, 'Hercules'."

Commodus swung to behead her. She caught the blade in one hand, took the handle in her other, and snapped the steel in two. She backhanded him and he fell supine at her feet.

As ordered, the Praetorian archers nocked their shafts and drew them back.

"Pick him up!" I cried. "Use him for a shield!" I confess I had no other advice at this point.

She seized his belt buckle and raised him over her head. Then she twirled him in her fingers like a baton.

The archers now wavered, unable to draw a bead through a moving obstacle. Kind of like the windmill at mini-golf.

The crowd went insane with glee.

The girl was a genius at this.

"Ariyl, keep spinning him!" I yelled. "They won't shoot their emperor!"

"Oh, is this like how he won't kill me in public? Is this more brilliant advice like that, David?" She sounded really pissed, and I was glad it was Commodus she had her hands on at the moment.

Then Commodus's belt broke and he dropped from her grip.

"Kill her!" he bellowed as he scrambled for the safety of the imperial box. The Praetorians drew their arrows back, ready to unleash their lethal barrage.

24

THE ARROWS OF TIME

"RUN FOR THE TUNNEL!" I HOLLERED.

Instead, Ariyl tucked me under one arm and bolted with me to the capsized chariot. As she tilted it up and we crouched beneath it, a centurion barked the order to the archers. The Praetorian Guard let loose a flight of arrows which we could hear embed in the chariot's base. Each one sounded like pfffft-THOCK.

"Now what?" I asked. Pfffft-THOCK.

"I give them a chance to surrender," she shrugged. Pfffft-THOCK! Pfffft-THOCK!

"You're joking, right?"

Ariyl lifted the chariot a crack: "I order you to stop!" shouted Ariyl. "Any man who lays down his arms, I will spare his life!"

Pfffft-THOCK! Pfffft-THOCK! Pfffft-THOCK! Pfffft-THOCK! Pfffft-THOCK! went the second flight.

Mocking laughter from the stands.

"Apparently, you have no takers," I observed. "Did you even have a plan for what would happen once you kicked the emperor's ass?"

"Get off my back!" she snarled. Then inspiration struck. "No wait, get on it."

"What do you mean?"

"Piggyback!"

"Are you kidding?"

"Again with the macho pride? *Move it!*" Even in the shade of the overturned chariot, I could see the red in her eyes. It was not a good idea to argue with her in this state.

There was now a steady rain of Pfffft-THOCK-Pfffft-THOCK! A lucky shot impaled her foot, which began leaking blood. "Agggh, shit!" she growled and yanked it out. The wound immediately began closing. "Climb on, unless you want arrows in *your* feet!" she commanded.

Her logic was unassailable. I put my arms around her neck. She stood up, holding the chariot a few inches off the ground. I locked my ankles around her waist and rode her piggyback. I felt a perfect ass, as Hugh Grant might have said.

Carrying this shell, she walked us over to the post where the *murmillo* had dropped his tall shield.

The hail of arrows kept thocking on the chariot.

The audience was growing bored and started to boo us.

"No offense, Ariyl...but what's the plan here? You're just going to trot us out of the Colosseum with a chariot over us and melt into the city?"

"Just hang on," said Ariyl.

Like I had a choice.

As soon as she stepped over that big rectangular *scutum*, she knelt down on it. She gripped the ends of the shield. The interior wood splintered, and the bronze covering groaned as she bent it upward on both sides. "Grab it," she told me.

I dutifully reached down with one hand.

Then she stood up with the chariot again. An arrow clanked off the *greave* covering her left ankle.

"What's this for?" I wondered, trying to keep a grip on the U-shaped shield.

"You'll see," she said, walking the chariot to where the Amazon's helmet lay.

Ariyl squatted again and held the chariot up a little bit on one side. "Okay, climb down now and grab the helmet."

I didn't yet grasp this plan, but already I hated it. An arrowhead scratched my hand as I snatched the helm and dragged it under the chariot. Ariyl had the now bent shield covering her back, and she folded the creaking bronze around her chest—her makeshift body armor.

Now I knew what the plan was.

"Ariyl, you can't go out there. There must be thirty archers! They'll kill you!"

"Other way around," she growled—then she shut the Samnite helmet. "Stay here till I tell you it's safe," she said from within the bronze grille.

She ducked out the open back of the chariot. Another flight of arrows hit the chariot atop me and all around me—

Pfffft-THOCK to the tenth power.

I heard her curse—one of those arrows had made it past her impromptu armor. Then she took a running leap over the chariot, and I heard her land heavily in the imperial box behind me.

I scrambled out of the back of the chariot—I couldn't let her do this alone. By rights an arrow should have gotten me in the first second.

Except there was no more pfft-thocking. Ariyl was now too close for archery. The air was filled with the angry shouts and panicked cries of the cream of the Praetorian Guard, fist impacts, the thud of falling bodies—the sounds I have come to associate with Ariyl manhandling a pack of overmatched men.

I climbed onto the overturned chariot, which wasn't easy because it now resembled a porcupine with feathered quills. I grabbed the hanging drapery and pulled myself up into the emperor's luxury box. Several Praetorians flew hollering past me on their way to the arena below.

Once topside, the first thing I saw was a dozen cold-cocked archers littering the mosaic floor. Ariyl was a fast blur, taking them out two at a time—snatching away the archers' bows, breaking them in two, grabbing their owners and tossing them onto a pair of Praetorians farther back. Those rear archers had only time for one more arrow apiece—one hit an airborne comrade, the other found its way into Ariyl's thigh, to go with the two in her left arm. She swore again, but kept moving without missing a beat, or a beatdown.

Half a dozen archers who had fallen back to the tunnel after the first flight were frantically nocking shafts. She cast off her helmet, picked up an eight-foot marble bench—three hundred pounds if it was an ounce—then bulldozed all of them against the tunnel wall.

The look on that beautiful face was ferocious. I'd never seen her like this, her eyes blazing red...her biceps and quadriceps swelling bigger than I'd ever seen—as she flexed harder, the *manica* popped its straps on one arm, then the other. Her expanding thighs burst the armor off her legs. Not that she needed armor at this point.

She kept pressing the slab against the kicking, groaning men until their breastplates buckled and the last of them went limp. I felt very sorry for them, but they were in Herculisa's hands now.

She cast aside the bench, and they crumpled in a moaning pile. Now she yanked the arrows out of her body.

Fffft-THUCK! One more arrow hit from behind, just above the bent shield, between her shoulder blades. One of the fallen archers had been faking unconsciousness. Instead of collapsing, she wheeled around and made for him, murder in her eyes.

He screamed and sprang backward, only to topple over the rim of the imperial box to the arena. Ariyl laughed. But then she winced at a sharp twinge.

"Agh! Get that outta me!" She turned to show me her back: The arrow was buried right between her shoulder blades, half an inch from her spine.

It took a really hard tug to get it out of her. Blood spurted then slowed as the puncture scabbed over.

"Ahh, thanks," she grunted in relief, like I'd just given her a backrub.

Suddenly she pulled me down flat on the deck, as a flight of spears sliced through the air just over our hairlines.

"Goddamnit!" she growled. From a crouch she charged the remainder of the Praetorian Guard. Most didn't have time to draw their swords before she went through their line, knocking them every which way like a bowling ball in a perfect strike.

Ariyl was fury personified—no man could stand against her fists. Those who managed to get their swords out had no time to use them before she flattened their owners or flung them aside. And the few who managed to strike her found their weapons useless. She simply healed too fast.

Their centurion, who at least managed to draw blood from Ariyl with one slashing stroke, was horrified to see her wound seal itself in seconds, while she bent his sword blade double, grinning with pure animal pleasure at her power.

"Fall back!" bellowed the centurion.

"Yeah, you *better* run," agreed Ariyl, her eyes on fire.

But these were still soldiers, trained to instinctively follow their commander. Commodus hurried behind a phalanx of his bravest Praetorians. The centurion barked, "Protect the emperor!"

The remaining Guard—a score of them—had nowhere to retreat to. Commodus had left them no escape route unless they climbed the rear wall of the imperial box.

"*Testudo!*" the centurion commanded. The front line of ten instantly lined up their shields and knelt behind them with blades protruding, while behind them, each of the other ten held his shield over himself and the man in front, forming a tortoise-like shell to protect from incoming spears or arrows.

But that was no use against Ariyl's incoming fists, as she battered the first two shields into scrap metal and tossed them aside.

"Peekaboo!" she growled as she seized the pair of exposed soldiers and hurled them hollering into the arena behind her. Two swords jabbed into unprotected skin on her arms but she yanked their owners into the air and smacked their helmets together with a sickening clunk then chucked them aside. By that time the sword slashes had already healed—that demon shot was working overtime.

"You can't hide from me, boys," she seethed as she bashed her way through the rest of the shields. She punched down into the huddled soldiers; more and more legs fell limp to the ground beneath the shattered *testudo*.

Two brave souls came at her with swords; she caught them in the crooks of her arms and choked them senseless.

"Didn't I tell you to run?" she demanded, then she let them fall.

She cornered two more soldiers, threw her arms around them, lifted them off their feet, and crushed them mercilessly against her chest. *"Didn't I tell you?"*

Guttural croaking was the only answer they could give.

"Ariyl, maybe you shouldn't..."

"Shut up, David," she snapped. She gave them a last crushing squeeze. I heard ribs crack, and she dropped them.

But Commodus was nowhere to be seen. He'd disappeared amid the litter of her victims. Ariyl cast the moaning bodies aside, digging through her human wreckage until she found Caesar himself, beneath a badly beaten Praetorian; Commodus was wearing the man's helmet and playing dead. Ariyl ripped the helm off him, revealing the curly-bearded coward.

"Oh, no, you don't!" she snarled, as she flattened the helmet between her palms. "You don't get off that easy, O mighty hunter."

She grabbed his breastplate with one fist, hoisted him into the air, and shook him like an Etch-a-Sketch with a dirty word on it.

"A hundred lions in one day?"

"Centurion!" bleated Commodus, his voice a tremolo.

"He can't help you. He's busy bleeding," Ariyl said.

"Guards!" he cried. "Stop her!"

"Weren't you watching?" she asked. "I just flattened your whole Praetorian Guard. Now it's just you and me, babe."

"Okay, Ariyl," I said. "You've made your point!"

She instantly lifted me with her other hand and gave me the spray-can treatment. *"Don't tell me what to do!"*

I could see from her crimson irises that I was not dealing with a rational person. But I had to try. "Ariyl, you can't do this to history!"

She plopped me down on the emperor's throne.

"No? Watch closely!"

I didn't have much choice. She was drunk with her own power. I wondered how long it would take for the demon-shot rage to leave her.

Ariyl tucked Commodus under one arm and leaped down to the arena floor. She let him drop face first onto the sand. As he tried to get up, she kicked him in the butt flipping him end over end. That got a huge laugh.

He got up and staggered down the sidelines to address the Colosseum crowd in desperation: "Citizens of Rome! Defend your emperor!"

Ariyl bellowed to the mob with a voice that didn't need a megaphone. "You all hear that? He now calls your city Rome again! What happened to Colonia Lucia Annia Commodiana?"

The audience laughed louder.

Commodus reached under his breastplate and pulled a dagger. He tried to cut Ariyl's throat, but she ripped it from his hand, put the blade between her teeth, and bit it off.

The audience screamed in hilarity.

Commodus sputtered with rage: "You cannot do this to me! I am the divine emperor! The most powerful man on earth!"

"Not any more, sweetie," said Ariyl, lifting him over her head. "From now on, you're just my toy. And it's playtime." She threw him thirty feet. The landing knocked the wind out of him, but he struggled dazed to his feet, as she strode toward him.

There was a discarded spear next to a discarded Praetorian in the sand. Commodus snatched it up and ran at her with it. She grabbed it, and with one easy motion, threw him over her shoulder with it. She snapped the spear over her knee, and then broke both halves again.

"Now you're gonna find out how every one of your victims felt. How those poor animals felt." She grabbed his armor. "Hurt!" She slapped him so hard he was knocked off his feet. She bent down and yanked him upright. "Helpless!" She smacked him ten feet in the other direction. "Doomed!" She pimp-slapped him three more times. This time he was smart enough to stay down. But that wouldn't save him.

She stood over him, hooked one finger into his breastplate, and pulled him up nose-to-nose.

"Except you're not gonna die, Commodus. You're just gonna wish you could."

* * *

SVEN BERGSTROM WOULD PROBABLY TELL you that the beginning of the end of patriarchy in the modern United States was in 2017, with a confessed sexual assailant leading the Free World while the women (and men) of the #MeToo movement arose to cry "Time's up!"

I might quibble with that date: I'd say America's reckoning with its legacy of rape began when an accusation against our favorite sitcom dad went viral in 2014, destroying the legendary comic's legacy and encouraging a parade of victims who shamed scores of other powerful and respected men, of greater or lesser culpability. Whether it's an irreversible sea-change, only time will tell. You're all heading into that future, and good luck.

However, in the metropolis briefly known as Colonia Lucia Annia Commodiana, patriarchy died on a cloudy day in 192 A.D., in a far more physical fashion, as the first emperor ever born to the purple wound up purple with impotent rage—tossed and twirled and slapped and spanked and otherwise utterly degraded by a woman for an hour while the Roman populace whom he'd terrorized for a decade laughed at him and cheered his humiliation.

25

EMPRESSIVE

A FEW DAYS LATER, ROMAN SOCIETY WAS NOT exactly back to normal. Oh, the city *was* called Rome again; and all the other institutions once branded by Commodus, including the months of the calendar, were back to their original names.

And one historic event was still more or less on track: Commodus's likeness, which had been set atop the Colossus Neronis, was removed with all the efficiency for which Roman construction was justly renowned.

Except, it came down a few months early. Also, in the first draft of history, a Statue-of-Liberty diadem of sunrays would have been placed on Nero's head, morphing history's most notorious firebug into the more-acceptable Sol (a.k.a. Apollo).

However, in our newly minted timeline, Rome's leading artists and smiths, working around the sundial and then some, had fashioned a new identity for it: Ariyl's gleaming copper face, fifteen feet high, with Roman-coiled hair, and some monumental knockers—in a bronze bra that I'd estimate as 45 (feet) EE. This shiny addition was raised by an elephant-powered crane and then clamped in place on the statue to transform Nero's Colossus into a voluptuous Titaness.

Her full Roman name, awarded by a grateful Roman Senate, was inscribed on its base: *Arial* (they insisted on a Latin spelling) *Fortis Achilles Invicta Caesar.*

No doubt the bronze facelift/boob job would look more convincing when it oxidized to the Lady Liberty-green of the original statue, a decade or two hence. I wondered if we would be around to see it.

I had watched the gigantic project from a few miles away, on the top floor of Commodus's palatial estate, the Villa of the Quintilii, while keeping guard over Ariyl as she slept off the demon shot. The villa was named for two brothers who built it half a century earlier. It was famed for its thermal baths and luxurious grounds.

Around sundown on the second day, she finally awoke.

"Ohhh...David. Where am I?"

"Commodus's old house. Which is now yours."

"God, I feel like hammered dog crap."

I peered into her once-red demon eyes. Their original purple color was slowly taking over again. "Well, now we know: demon shots leave a hangover."

"And I'm sooo hungry..."

I snapped my finger at the head servant, who hurried off to get the food served. "I took the liberty of having the kitchen prepare an ovo-lacto-vegetarian feast for a dozen people."

"I don't want to see a bunch of people tonight!" she groaned.

"It's for you."

She stared at me a moment. "You know me so well." She gave me a kiss.

Then she gasped. "Your Time Crystal! Did you...?"

I pulled down my tunic to show it safely around my neck.

"How'd you get it back?"

I pointed out her distant statue, gleaming in the last rays of sunset. "Now that you've been named Empress Arial, I used your influence to get my property back from that thieving *lorarius*. He was all apologies."

Then I pointed to a familiar (in fact, too familiar) young man who walked into the room. "I also got you back your food taster."

"He's the one who grabbed my ass!"

"Well, now maybe he'll save it. Make sure he takes a bite of everything before you eat it."

The plates and tureens and trays and ewers began arriving.

The food taster slunk past the empress, bowing and scraping. "O, mighty Empress Arial, I beg your forgiveness for..."

"It's fine. Just dig in, okay?"

The taster sat down and started picking at the first dish, with all the enthusiasm of a five-year-old confronting his first plate of broccoli.

"Will you hurry up?" she wailed. "I'm starving!"

Nervous, the young man took a healthy (we hoped) bite.

"Why do I need a food taster?" asked Ariyl. "Wasn't I a hit with the crowd? Who would want to poison me now?"

"Well, you could start with any one of the five men who would have succeeded Commodus next year: Pertinax, Didius Julianus, Pescennius Niger, Clodius Albinus and Septimius Severus. Historians actually call it the Year of the Five Emperors. Life expectancy for Roman rulers was extremely low in this era."

"What if I have all five of them banished?"

"There's still all their scheming relatives and other dependents. Rome now is nothing but military factions fighting for power. And as far as your potential poisoners, don't forget the families of the fifty-odd Praetorian Guards whom you tore apart. You have any idea what the death toll was from your little tantrum?"

Her eyes went wide. "*Death* toll? Seriously?" Then they narrowed suspiciously. "Wait a sec, I didn't kill anyone. Did I?"

"No, you didn't," I admitted. "It looks like they'll all recover. My point is, you weren't sure."

"I wasn't exactly gentle with them, was I?"

I shook my head.

She shuddered. "I was so enraged. I am never taking that shit again."

"Promise?"

She nodded.

"Hey, what do you mean *again?*" I asked. "You have more demon shots?"

She shrugged.

"You saved a bunch from the land yacht in 1948, didn't you?"

Another shrug.

"And you gave *me* a hard time about holding onto that dram!"

"David, what happened to Commodus?"

"I'm afraid what's left of the Praetorian Guard slew him on the spot. He didn't exactly distinguish himself in the battle against you the other day."

Ariyl was heartsick. "Oh, no. I just wanted to teach him a lesson!"

"And it was one he'd never forget. Arguably, they did him a favor." She looked distraught. I put a hand on her shoulder. "I couldn't stop them. You were ready to keel over, and I needed to get you out of view. If they knew you weren't in fighting condition, they'd have left us in the same heap as Commodus."

"Oh, David, I would *never* have killed..."

"I know. Don't blame yourself. The Praetorians were already plotting his assassination before we showed up. I convinced their prefect, Quintus Laetus, that you'd be a generous emperor, so they threw their support to you. The Senate immediately ratified it."

"So that's why I'm emperor?"

"Or empress. Whatever title you wish, O mighty Caesar."

Ariyl turned to her food taster. "How do you feel?"

"My stomach aches," he admitted.

"*What?*" she exclaimed.

"From your elbow, mighty empress. Which I fully deserved. The stew is fine."

She moved him aside. "Okay, what's your name?"

"Titus."

"Tight-ass?"

"Ti-tuss," I enunciated for her.

She couldn't suppress a laugh. "Okay, Titus, try the casserole thingy next. That one."

Ariyl started wolfing down the stew in the first tureen.

The head servant of the villa announced the arrival of Cassius Dio.

"Who's he again?" she asked between mouthfuls.

"A great historian. Edward Gibbon's source on Commodus. He's been senator, consul, proconsul...Dio knows Rome inside out. He's a reasonably honest public servant without any known murders to his name. After the Praetorians proclaimed you emperor, I took the liberty of appointing Dio your chief adviser and liaison to the Senate."

"Oh, you did? And who are you, my prince consort?" she wondered, wiping her fingers on a napkin.

"As the only one around here who doesn't have a motive to poison you, I appointed myself your chamberlain."

"Why did you do all this?" she said, her mouth full.

"Because the fastest way to get yourself killed in ancient Rome is to be in a power vacuum at the top. I was just keeping us safe until you woke up and we could jump out of here."

"Well, I'm not ready for that yet."

"That's what I figured." I turned to the servant. "Bring in Dio. And summon Quintus Laetus."

The servant bowed and hurried out.

"How's that one?" she asked Titus about the next dish.

He gave her the so-so gesture.

"I don't mean how does it taste. Would it kill me to try it?"

He shook his head. He offered her a little dish of silvery powder. "But it could use a little lead, for flavor."

He went to sprinkle some on the food.

Ariyl stopped him. "Lay off the lead, Titus. You'll live longer." Then she scarfed down the casserole or whatever it was.

"Mmm," she commented and turned to Titus. "You're crazy. This is delicious. Try some more."

He started to, then she remembered.

"Wait, let's not spoil your appetite. Finish tasting the other stuff."

Cassius Dio entered. He was in his late thirties, stout, bearded...he looked a fair amount like Zach Galifianakis.

"O, mighty Empress Arial, I am honored to be in your service," he began. "A female of your prowess has not been seen in this empire since the days of Boadicea of Britain."

"Oh, I know her! *Bodacious Boadicea* is one of my favorite vidz," she said, shoveling in food.

"The empress means Boadicea is her ancestor," I explained.

Dio nodded, suitably impressed. "Empress Arial, if I might be so bold, we need to discuss matters of finance."

"Oh, man. Money again?" she turned to me. "How far back in history do we have to go before people stop obsessing about money?"

"Prehistoric times. That's the thing about sticking around and rewriting history," I told her. "Money is how empires have been run since time began."

"Well, where did Commodus get his money? How did he buy this place?"

"He did not, my empress," Dio explained. "He found a pretext to have the Quintilii executed and took their estate."

"Commodus is dead and his property and money are forfeit to his conqueror," I asserted. "And I understand his fee in the arena was one million *sesterces*."

"Yes. The Senate saw fit to award everything to Empress Arial. Commodus left no heirs."

"He didn't have a lot of friends either, did he?" I observed.

"No. Our greatest Caesars, from Augustus to Hadrian, from Trajan to Marcus Aurelius, were not born to power. They were adopted. Virtue, not birth, made their fortunes. Commodus's curse was that he was born to power, and such advantage will usually warp character rather than forge it."

"Machiavelli said the same thing," I replied.

"Who?" said Ariyl and Dio.

"He was before your time," I told her, "and after yours."

"Be that as it may, Empress Arial—"

"Prefect Quintus Laetus!" announced the servant.

Laetus, arrayed in his best brass armor and purple-crested helmet, arrived and saluted the empress with an arm to his chest.

"You summoned me, empress?"

"Uh, yeah. David?" She was going to let me handle this.

I had my own agenda to pursue with Dio. "I can think of no man in Rome who could answer this better than you, Cassius: Where can we find Octavius, the soothsayer?"

"I know his house well. Should I invite him to come for an audience?"

"No," I said. "Tell the prefect where it is. The empress wants him arrested and brought here immediately."

"I know the house," said Laetus, who apparently had his own sources.

"Take twice as many men as you think you'll need to surround the place," I told Laetus.

He saluted again and strode out.

Ariyl peered closely at Dio. "Hey, now I remember! I talked to you at the Colosseum!"

"Flavian Amphitheater," I put in.

"Yeah, what he said," she agreed.

"Yes, my empress. After my appointment, you ordered me to free all the prisoners in the arena."

Ariyl put her lips to my ear. "Did I do that?"

I murmured back, "About two minutes before you passed out."

"And did you do it?" she asked Dio.

"Of course, my empress. Then you ordered me to send all the lions and other animals from the amphitheater back to where they had been captured and set them free."

I nodded.

"That sounds like me," she said. "How's that going?"

Dio consulted the markings in a wax tablet he was carrying.

"Well, it does take time to charter a galley and find enough slaves to row it."

"No. No slaves," said Ariyl.

Cassius Dio tried a polite laugh, but Ariyl didn't join in. "I mean it. Take it out of my million *sesterces*, but hire people to pull the oars. No more slaves."

"On just this galley or on any galley?"

"In the Roman Empire. If I'm emperor, then that's my decree."

Dio began to sputter. "But, empress, slaves are part of the wealth of every well-to-do Roman household. If you were to free all slaves, you would impoverish a hundred thousand Romans. You would make a hundred thousand enemies!"

"I don't care! Rome is royally screwed up, and this slavery thing is at the heart of it. I'm changing that."

Titus brought her a bowl of fruit.

Ariyl looked disgusted. "Did you have to take a bite of each one?"

"That is my job, empress."

Ariyl rolled her eyes but began chowing down on the fruit.

"May I point out, Empress Arial, that your food taster is a slave?" said Dio, trying to keep his temper.

"He is?"

Dio nodded.

I nodded.

She turned to Titus. "You are?"

"Of course, empress. Why else would I bite into food that might well be poisoned?"

"They don't pay you?"

"No."

"Then why do you stay?"

"I am a slave in this house. Besides, the food here is excellent."

Ariyl couldn't believe her ears. "Well, now it's *my* house, and I'm giving you your freedom, right now."

Titus flung himself down on the floor and began kissing her feet in gratitude.

"Okay, knock it off, or I'm going to make you pay *me*," she told him.

Titus leapt up and backed toward the door bowing and singing her praises.

"Wait, you didn't finish tasting the food!" she said.

"You could not *pay* me to do that job," said Titus.

"Oh," said Ariyl, deflated.

"But that third tray, with the skewers? I tried that one. I still feel fine."

"Thanks."

"O, generous empress, may I take some pastries with me?"

"Sure. I don't eat a lot of bread."

Titus eagerly grabbed a basket of pastry and hurried out, no doubt worried she'd change her mind if he lingered.

"Every general in Rome will oppose you," warned Dio.

"Good. Announce that the next games at the Flavian Amphitheater will be me, naked, against any ten generals who think they can take me on with the weapon of their choice. Aw, hell, make it twenty. And by the way, my fee will be two million *sesterces* for that little comedy."

Cassius Dio was beside himself. "If you do this mad thing, you will have all Rome rise up in revolt against you!"

Ariyl rose up herself, towering over Dio. "You just make sure every last one of those lions and giraffes and elephants gets back to Africa, you understand? Or my next Amphitheater gig will be a special performance as a juggler, and I'll be juggling *you*."

Dio's eyes went wide. "They shall sail on the morning tide, empress!" he stammered. He bowed then hurried out.

ONCE CASSIUS DIO was out of earshot, I turned to Ariyl. "Are you sure that demon shot has worn off? Because you still sound crazy to me!"

"They're putting up a giant statue of me, David. I have whatcha-call it...political capital. Why not use it? Why not create a Rome where they don't *need* slaves? Let's use some of that knowledge you have stored up in that handsome head of yours."

"Like how?"

"Like, build them robots to do their work."

"I don't do robots," I said. But I knew what she was getting at. "You mean like steam engines?"

She nodded. "You're Mr. Science, right?"

I considered it. "Well, the Romans have known about steam power for a couple centuries, since Hero of Alexandria. And they understand gears, going back three centuries to the Antikythera Mechanism."

"What's that?"

"A clockwork device that the Greeks built to predict astronomical events. So all we'd have to do is show them how to combine their existing tech to build steam-powered machines. For farming, construction, transportation, manufacturing...it would free up a lot of human labor."

"And a society with machines, that says slavery is wrong and sadistic butchery in the arena is wrong," she enthused, "...maybe *that* Rome never has to fall. With no dark ages or middle-evil whatever!" she enthused.

As a plan, it was insanely optimistic. But the implications, I had to admit, were fascinating. "With our guidance, Western civilization could skip a thousand wasted years," I mused. "Go right into the Renaissance and the scientific method. They might be ready for space travel around the time Leif Erikson was setting sail for Vinland."

Ariyl slipped her arms around me and leaned in for a long, long kiss. "When you talk about changing history, you get me so hot," she said at last.

We sat up half the night talking about how the reform of the Roman Empire might be accomplished, by the strategic introduction of the scientific method and edicts setting forth human rights and democratic processes.

I won't tell you how we spent the other half of the night.

* * *

THE NEXT MORNING, the empress insisted on taking a chariot down to the docks to inspect what I was calling Ariyl's Ark—actually, four different triremes which would ferry a zoo's worth of exotic fauna back to Africa.

Ariyl found the most grateful passenger was Leo, who didn't need a thorn plucked from his paw to recognize his benefactress. He licked her hand happily.

"Awww!" cooed Ariyl. She gave him a big hug and cried some. "I'm gonna miss you."

Once she was satisfied that the animals were properly fed (I didn't want to point out they were eating Commodus's less fortunate prey) and that the oarsmen where also humanely treated, with everyone paid a fair wage and no whips and no one chained to an oar, we went ashore and waved goodbye, and the galleys rowed off down the Tiber to the sea.

Cassius Dio, relieved that the Arks were no longer his responsibility, agreed to meet us back at the Villa of the Quintilii to discuss Empress Arial's reforms.

* * *

UPON OUR ARRIVAL at the villa, Quintus Laetus informed us regretfully that Octavius the soothsayer was dead. His son had slain two of Laetus's men and escaped, leaving behind the body of his father. Laetus reported the father had a broken neck.

"You're sure your men didn't do that?" I asked.

Laetus drew himself up, offended. "The Praetorian Guard does not slay men of such advanced years. He was dead on the floor when we broke into the house."

Laetus had thoughtfully brought back the old man's corpse for our inspection. Octavius the soothsayer was indeed very old—I estimated ninety at least. Which was not unheard of for members of the well-fed ruling class in Rome—if you didn't die in childbirth, nor contract plague or water-borne illnesses, and avoided military service and stuck to a strict low-lead diet, you stood as good a chance as any modern person of reaching your nineties.

According to Dio, the Octavius clan was secretive but very wealthy. They had moved to Rome from Pompeii a century earlier, shortly before that city had been destroyed by the eruption of Vesuvius.

"Such foresight established the family's traditional occupation as soothsayers to the imperial court," noted Dio.

Only two injuries marred Octavius the Elder's otherwise remarkable preservation: Like his namesakes from the nineteenth and twentieth centuries, he wore a leather patch over his right eye and was missing his right middle and ring fingers.

Obviously, it was a *very* old family name.

"Tell me about his son," I said.

"Octavius the Younger?" replied Dio. "I have only briefly glimpsed him in his father's home. He, too, had only eight fingers. It is rumored that each eldest son of their clan must cut off those fingers as a sign of loyalty, to claim his patrimony."

"Does he wear an eye patch like his father?" I asked.

"Yes."

Ariyl grimaced but couldn't resist peeking under the old man's eye patch. Her mouth dropped open in surprise. "David...why would someone wear an eye patch when he has a perfectly good eye?"

"Maybe that right eye was partly blind...maybe he saw better with it covered," I suggested.

But I had another suspicion I decided to keep to myself for now. It was too outlandish to tell Ariyl just yet.

26

DECLINE AND WINTER

CASSIUS DIO PLAINLY CONSIDERED OUR PLANS for the Empire's future impractical and borderline nuts, but compared to the emperor Ariyl had just replaced, it was an improvement. At least everything could keep its old name.

Dio promised to do his best to shepherd the empress's reforms through the Senate, though he could not guarantee there would not be a bloody revolt. In fact, he all but promised there would be. Especially the part about women serving in the Roman Senate.

"Well, do your best," said Ariyl, sending him on his way.

AT THE VILLA of the Quintilii, Ariyl finally was able to get in what she considered a decent workout, now accomplished with gym equipment that included bronze statues, boulders, and millstones connected with stout logs.

She then adjourned to the kitchen to eat a lunch that would have fed an orgy, which was cooked in front of us and eaten by the cooks before we had a bite. For all the delay and nervousness, it was quite tasty.

Then we took a nice long soak in one of the villa's excellent, steamy baths.

"All right, you might as well tell me," she said.

"What?" I hedged.

"I can always tell when you're building up to say something you know I'll hate. Let's get it out there."

"Okay. We've made very specific plans for this alternate timeline. Much more specific than we did with Lincoln and Reconstruction. And the fact that right now, you're the absolute ruler of the Roman Empire and probably the most assassination-proof emperor in Rome's history makes the odds more than fifty-fifty that a lot of it will get done."

"We're not at the part I hate yet."

"I'm coming to that. I think we need to test Sven's theory about whether we're creating a new timeline in an unlimited multiverse, or whether we're altering the same, single timeline over and over again."

"I thought we were testing that in 1933."

"Except for some crazy reason, we wound up in 192 A.D. instead."

"Go on," she said, drawing me close to her in the water.

"I can't concentrate on a logical explanation when you hold me close to you."

"All you have to do is say no, and I'll let you alone."

"I'm not saying no..."

"I noticed."

"I'm saying listen to me for a sec."

"Go."

"If this is a multiverse, we shouldn't be able to jump to 2109—or any date in between—that our actions will affect. Because it will now be *our* future, which is by definition unknowable. And *that* will mean we will have established a new, viable, alternate future where Rome did not fall in 476 A.D."

"That's logical," she said, nuzzling my neck.

"So before we spend any more—oooh, yeah, babe, but hold on— spend any more time trying to turn the most fascist, martial empire in history into a warm-and-fuzzy technological democracy...let's see if we have a chance of making it work."

"But if I'm following you, we won't *get* a positive answer—we just won't be able to travel into our changed future because we'll still be *changing* it," she pouted. "In fact, the only successful travel to 2109 we would be able to do would be if it's a greenhouse planet or nuked ruins or an ice age—some disaster with humans extinct. Which will prove Sven's right, and in the end, we have a single, changeable timeline."

"Yep. One where we have to restore your N-Tec world exactly for humanity to have a prayer of survival."

She thought it over. "I hate it."

"Thought you would."

* * *

An hour later, we were dry and dressed (just to be safe) in the warmest Roman clothes and boots we could find. We were ready to learn the fate of humankind. Ariyl's Crystal had fully recharged, so we held hands, reasonably sure there would not be the separation effect that mine had produced.

"The Colosseum, Rome, noon, June fourth, 2109 A.D."

The flickering carnival ride sensation went on for quite a bit.

Then we stood, still holding hands, on a frozen tundra, from which only the top third of the Colosseum, and Ariyl's giant green-bronze face, protruded above the snowdrifts.

"*GODDAMNIT!*" screamed Ariyl, furious.

I shouted over the whistling wind.

"Look, take us back to the same spot, but June fourth, 1000 A.D.!"

"Why then?"

"Leif Erikson! Just do it!"

Ariyl said the coordinates. We flipped through hyperspace and hypertime and wound up on the same frozen plain, though Ariyl's statue was exposed up to the waist.

"Well, that's a little better!" she said.

"Yeah, but it's still an ice age! Leif Erikson could've *walked* to Newfoundland! Try 800 A.D.!"

Nothing. We were now freezing our asses off, trying later dates, until we finally discovered that 869 A.D., was the earliest future we could visit. Sometime after 192 and before 869, something put Empress Arial's capital, and the rest of planet Earth, into a permanent deep freeze.

WE RETURNED to the Villa of the Quintilii shivering, and got back into the warm waters as fast as we could.

A tear rolled down Ariyl's cheek. I kissed it away.

"Hey, now. Your statue lasted a lot longer than Nero's did. But in the end, something happened that destroyed the climate. It's nothing we could have prevented if we'd stayed and reformed Rome."

"It's not that. I just...I really loved being empress."

"Ariyl, my love...you were the best, most badass empress any empire ever had."

She kissed me.

Then a servant girl came in, weeping.

Titus the freedman had been found just outside the grounds of the villa, poisoned.

Apparently, by one of the pastries he'd taken with him.

Ariyl set her jaw, grim. "First thing in the morning, we get the hell out of this insane asylum."

* * *

SHE WOKE me up later that night, but it wasn't for sex. She wanted to hold me and be held. She wanted answers. I didn't have any.

"But I know one thing," I told her. "Octavius the Younger got away from us in Rome because of my mistake. I was drunk with your power. I sent the Praetorians to arrest him, when we should have gone after him ourselves. We can't make that mistake again."

"Do you really think this ice age is Octavius's doing? In both timelines?"

"I only know we have one more chance to find out. In 1933."

* * *

TO BACK ourselves out of the Empress Arial timeline, we had to do the same doppelganger routine, stopping our past selves from entering the Colosseum. They both obediently disappeared to wherever potential versions of ourselves go when they're no longer on the timeline.

I had liberated some gold coins from Commodus's coffers. Now Ariyl told her Crystal to take us to Miracle Mile Coins at ten in the morning on the day of Harold Lloyd's party, in 1933.

I quietly prayed that we wouldn't wind up in another global blizzard, or on the losing side of the Siege of Los Angeles in 1846, or stuck in the La Brea tar pits as a saber- toothed tiger closed in on us.

27

MR. KOBAYASHI

W E ARRIVED OUTSIDE THE COIN SHOP AT exactly ten on the correct day and year. With me in my fancy tunic and sandals and with Ariyl attired in an empress's silks, we looked like dress extras from *Roman Scandals*.

Ariyl's SmartFab was still not following orders: It simply morphed into 1933 underwear. Although the Motion Picture Code would allow negligees and other risqué attire in movies until mid-1934, it would never do as streetwear.

We were lucky our locale was Hollywood-adjacent. The owner of Miracle Mile Coins had apparently seen wilder outfits on showbiz customers; he was happy to exchange our gleaming, mint-condition *aurei* for folding money.

Ariyl decided we'd go shopping at Bullocks Wilshire, a classic Moderne structure with a tower detailed in green copper (the place is now a law library, believe it or not). She bought herself a flattering sundress to wear around town, and a slinky white cocktail dress for the party, plus the usual incidentals.

Meanwhile, I had a linen suit fitted for me in the men's department. I then walked down the street to a gun store and bought a snub-nose .38 and ammunition. I would not tell Ariyl about this purchase, knowing her visceral, destructive, and thoroughly impractical dislike of firearms.

I met Ariyl in the Bullocks lobby at noon. We hailed a cab and headed downtown to the Richfield Building. I needed to check up on the Octavius Corporation.

* * *

THIS TIME, I was in for a surprise: The brass plate on Suite 1200 indicated that in 1933, the top floor was the headquarters of Nippon Petroleum.

"Excuse me," I said. "Do you know where I can find the offices of Octavius Corporation?"

The receptionist looked up...and up some more...at Ariyl. Her eyes went wide in wonder.

"Miss?" I asked again.

She was still staring.

"Ariyl, would you mind waiting downstairs? This'll go faster if I don't have to explain you."

"I'm a big woman! What's to explain?"

The receptionist was still gaping.

"Please," I urged.

"Fine!" said Ariyl, turning on her heel and heading back to the elevator.

"The Octavius Corporation?" I repeated.

The receptionist shook off her surprise. She spoke perfect English with a California accent.

"I-I'm sorry, sir. I don't know that firm."

"Do you know how long Nippon Petroleum has been in this office?"

"I just started here. But not long, I think." She seemed ill at ease.

"Is it possible Nippon is leasing this space?"

She had no idea. "Perhaps you would like to speak with our vice president, Mr. Kobayashi?" she finally asked.

"Yes, I would."

She looked like that was not a great idea but wasn't about to say it. "Have a seat, please," she said. She gestured to a sofa opposite her desk. I sat and she pushed her intercom button. She then conversed in Japanese to a voice in the next office. She reported my interest in the Octavius Corporation. He gave her a local number to call, to report my presence, after admitting me.

"*Hai*," she replied. Then, to me: "You may go in."

She opened the door for me into a large corner office, with a spectacular view of adolescent Los Angeles, stretching west down newly widened Wilshire Boulevard to Beverly Hills, and thence to Santa Monica and the sea. And precious little smog to obstruct the view.

Mr. Kobayashi stood and bowed. He was in his mid-twenties, tall and wiry, with close-cropped hair and a big square Easter Island head.

"Miss Fujitaki, you will take your lunch hour now."

"But...who will answer the phone?"

"I will," he snapped, impatient. "Leave us."

"Just as you say, sir." Miss Fujitaki meekly gathered up her things.

Kobayashi closed the door behind me.

On the wall behind his desk hung two antique curved swords—one shorter, the other longer—in beautifully decorated sheaths.

I introduced myself as Professor David Preston of UCLA and inquired if he knew of the Octavius Corporation. He politely answered in the negative. He had a low growl of a voice, heavily accented—he sounded like Toshiro Mifune. Or maybe Paul Frees dubbing Mifune.

It seemed a little suspicious that Kobayashi had just dismissed the only potential witness to my presence here. But if Johnson did not show up at Lloyd's party tonight, this was my only other lead. I looked up at the swords again.

"You admire my *daishō*," he observed.

"Yes, they're very beautiful. The symbol of the samurai, am I correct?"

He nodded. "The shorter blade is the *wakizashi*. And the longer..."

"The *katana*?"

"You know something of Japanese culture."

"Only what I learned from Kurosawa," I quipped.

"Who?"

Damn, I needed be careful about stupid anachronous jokes. Back in the early Thirties, Akira Kurosawa wasn't directing samurai classics. He was a failed young painter hoping for work at what would someday become Toho Studios.

"Uh, Fred Kurosawa. Friend at UCLA. You don't know him."

Kobayashi's phone rang. He picked up. "Kobayashi." He listened. "Very well," was all he said. Then he hung up and turned back to me.

"Professor, I believe in being direct. I can see you are wearing something around your neck, under your shirt. I believe it is a crystal. My employer has been seeking such a gem for many years. You would save us both a lot of trouble if you would hand it over."

Oh, God. I'd walked right into the lion's den. Again. "What if I refuse?"

"You force me to take it."

I jumped up and pulled out my gun, but his foot, fast as lightning, kicked it from my fingers. I ran to the door. It was locked. Kobayashi leapt over his desk and came at me.

I grabbed his lamp and swung it at him. He deftly caught my arm and used my momentum to toss me over his shoulder against the wall. I landed on the twin swords, knocking them to the floor. I grabbed the handle of one and yanked it from its scabbard. He did the same with the other.

Just my luck, I had the *wakizashi*. He had the *katana*.

He swung, moving like lightning. I barely had time to parry the blow.

With a growl, he charged me. CLANK-CLANK-CLANG! He backed me up, but I was still holding my own with an unfamiliar blade.

He gave a slight bow, admiring my parries.

"Most men would be dead by now."

"But you've got the longer blade. Doesn't seem quite fair, does it?"

"If you had no sword, I would still kill you." CLANK-CLANG!

"Okay. Explains Pearl Harbor."

"What is that?"

"Another anachronism. Sorry."

The doors rattled. "David, are you in there?"

CLANK-CLANK-CLANG!

"Yeah!"

CLANG!

"Why are the doors locked?"

"So he can kill me!"

BAM! Ariyl broke open the door.

Kobayashi whirled, swinging his blade laterally to decapitate her. She was even faster. She clapped her hands on either side of his blade, trapping it—then yanked it out of his hands. He gaped in astonishment.

She took hold of either end.

"Don't bend it," I urged. "Please. It's an irreplaceable antique!"

"So's your head, sweetie."

She dropped it as Kobayashi came at her with a spinning karate kick. She seized his foot, spun him around once, and tossed him hard against the far wall. He slid to the floor—out cold.

"I can't leave you alone for a minute, can I?" she sighed.

"I guess not. Thanks for not waiting downstairs."

"When he sent the secretary down, I got suspicious. Did you find out anything about Octavius?"

"Pretty sure this guy Kobayashi works for him. Whoever his boss is, wants my Crystal."

"Okay, I guess you were right," she conceded. "Someone from the future is tipping these guys off."

I pointed to the outer office. "Uh, do me a favor, and grab me a business card from the reception desk?"

While she did that, I retrieved the .38 that Kobayashi had kicked from my hand, and pocketed it before she could see it.

"What's this for?" she asked, handing me the card.

"In my time, it's customary to exchange business cards."

"Aren't you going to leave one?"

I glanced at the unconscious samurai. "Nah. You left yours."

We heard a distant siren.

"Is that coming for us?" wondered Ariyl.

"Let's not wait around to find out."

ON OUR WAY out of the building, we passed Miss Fujitaki eating a sandwich on a bench. "Did you find the Octavius Corporation, sir?" she asked.

"No. Your Mr. Kobayashi is not a nice man."

She avoided my gaze. "No, sir. He's not," she said with a trembling voice. "He frightens me."

"Listen to your instincts. Don't come back from lunch."

She nodded. "Thank you," she said quietly.

We started to leave then I went back. "Also, please consider moving away from the West Coast. The Midwest, somewhere. Before March 1942."

She stared at me, uncomprehending.

I was taking a risk even telling her that much. I hoped it might keep her out of Manzanar.

28

THE CHAPLIN STUDIO, 1933

W E HAD A VEGETARIAN LUNCH IN OLD Chinatown. Ariyl
wanted to tour this vanished neighborhood, which would
soon be relocated to the west to make room for Union Station in 1939
—the structure that would house the Time Travel Agency in 2109.

As the sun lowered, it was time for our next stop, this one in
Hollywood proper: a collection of buildings in English cottage style
at the corner of Sunset and La Brea. The north end of the property
featured a private home, tennis courts, and a swimming pool; the
south end was a working movie studio.

In later years, TV's Superman, Red Skelton, Perry Mason, Herb
Alpert and his Tijuana Brass, and finally Jim Henson's Muppets
would all hang their hats here; but the original (and current) hat was
the derby belonging to Charles Spencer Chaplin.

Using Department of Investigation ID card Sven had made, I got
us in to see Mr. Reeves, the manager of the studio. I told him we
were investigating a certain Octavius Johnson and wished to question Mr. Chaplin about what he might know of him. Mr. Reeves
informed us Mr. Chaplin was not on the lot today. I had promised
Ariyl she could play federal agent too, but at this point, she said

she'd always been curious about movie lots and asked if it would be okay to look around. Mr. Reeves told her it would be all right, as long as she didn't go into any buildings where the red light was on.

Chaplin's lifelong distrust of policemen (the butt of much of his comedy) and his brushes with the law over his two underage wives (now ex-wives) meant his studio manager treated me with a great deal of mistrust.

But that worked in my favor. I informed the manager that the Bureau had reliable information Mr. Chaplin might be in danger if he were to attend the party at Harold Lloyd's house tonight, and we were advising him not to go. Mr. Reeves said Mr. Chaplin had already sent his regrets.

So, mission accomplished.

I went outside and saw Ariyl exiting a soundstage, waving goodbye to someone inside. The door shut and the red light went on.

"Did you enjoy your studio tour?" I asked.

"Oh, it was wonderful. I met Charlie Chaplin!"

"What? They said he wasn't on the lot!"

"They lied. He was rehearsing a scene. On roller skates! He invited me to stay and watch, but I said we had to get to the party. He said he'd try and make it, then."

"Ariyl, Chaplin had sent his regrets. You just changed his mind—now he's going to the party!"

"So we just made it more awesome."

"But Octavius Johnson is going to be there! He might try something!"

"Well...maybe Charlie won't show up."

"After seeing you? Not if I know Chaplin."

"David, you *don't* know Chaplin."

"But I've read about him!"

"Look, I'll keep an eye on him. If Johnson tries anything, I'll be there to protect him."

"That sounds reasonable," I admitted. "Which scares me."

"C'mon, let's get to the party!" she said

"Well, we've got one more thing to arrange."

"Like what?"

"Like a car. This is Hollywood. We need to make an entrance, and after these clothes and, uh, incidentals, we haven't got much left to rent a suitable ride."

"Leave the negotiations to me," she smiled.

29

GREENACRES IS THE PLACE TO BE

W E ROLLED UP THE LONG, LONG CYPRESS-LINED driveway in a long, long touring car that Ariyl had charmed a salesman on Hollywood Boulevard into letting her take for a spin. He was so besotted with her, we probably had a long, long time before he got worried enough to call the cops.

I pulled out the invitation. "Just let me do all the talking."

"Why don't we just flash the FBI IDs?" she asked.

"First off, it's DOI, not FBI. And second, everybody would be afraid to talk to us. Prohibition doesn't end till December. For the moment, better if we're just some guests nobody's ever heard of."

I didn't want to hurt her feelings, but I also privately thought a six-foot-three amazon was just not going to be believable as a G-Man in 1933.

We parked the car near the top of the drive, and I walked up to a burly doorman who was dressed to the nines. I gave him the invitation, which was pretty beat up from its time in my pocket in ancient Rome.

He looked skeptical. "Name?" he asked.

Uh-oh. Security was tight here.

I got huffy. "You don't recognize me?"

"No, sir, I don't," said the doorman, apologetic. "I only see a pitcher show once a week."

With what I hope passed for movie star attitude, I ran my finger down the names on his clipboard, while scanning for names that were not crossed off. I noticed Chaplin had not arrived. But there was only one name on the list I thought I had a prayer of pulling off, partly because he wasn't that big a star yet. I tapped the name impatiently.

"Thet's mey."

He frowned at his clipboard. "You're Cary Grant?"

"Thet's rawight," I said, doing my best clipped Cary impression. I pointed to Ariyl. "And this is Ju-dee. She's mawy plus-one."

The bouncer looked up at her. "At least."

I was on my toes. Literally. Because I'd seen Grant and he was more than two inches taller than me. He was also at least two inches handsomer than me, but there was a passing resemblance.

"Sorry, Mr. Grant. It's just, ya kinda sound different in the movies," said the doorman.

Ariyl snorted.

The doorman shrugged and crossed Cary off the list.

"Say, has mawy friend Octavius *John*son shewed up yet?" I inquired.

He flipped to the second page of the clipboard. "No, Mr. Grant. Johnson sent an RSVP that he can't make it."

After all this, was our quarry not going to show himself?

The other tuxedoed bouncer angled a cauliflower ear in our direction, and in gravelly tones informed his coworker, "You're lookin' at Chic Johnson. Y'know, Olsen and Johnson? Dis guy wants *Octavius* Johnson."

"Oh, right! Yeah, he's already here."

"Came in ten minutes ago," said the gravel-guy.

Well, Harold didn't hire these guys for their clerical skills, but they turned out to be pretty helpful. They waved us in.

The next guy up to the clipboard announced himself.

"Good evening. I'm Cary Grant."

I urged Ariyl up the steps as fast as I could, leaving the disagreement fading in the distance:

"No, you ain't."

"I assure you, my good man, I am."

"You already arrived."

"Listen, one of us has *déjà vu*."

"You don't sound one bit like him."

"Look, there's Mae West, you can ask her."

"If you're Cary Grant, then who's your date?"

"This is my pal, Randolph Scott."

"Hiya," said Randy.

By that time, we were in the house.

STROLLING through the jester's palace, we beheld a glittering court of comedy nobility, everyone from Al Ritz to ZaSu Pitts. Out on a patio, a jazz band was playing, and Eddie Cantor was singing and capering and earning his nickname "Banjo Eyes"—rolling his orbs with every innuendo in "Yes, Yes, My Honey Said Yes, Yes."

I didn't see any Marxes but spotted several of their recent costars: majestic Margaret Dumont, sweet Thelma Todd, exotic Raquel Torres, and slow-burn man Edgar Kennedy.

"Wow," said Ariyl, taking in the opulent setting. "Should we introduce ourselves to our host?"

"Not just yet. We could run into Johnson any second. We need a little life insurance."

She looked at me, puzzled.

* * *

WE WALKED DOWNHILL from the villa, along a palm-lined path split by a series of cascading fountains, to Harold's golf course. It was dusk and the last golfers were calling it a day.

I walked to the nearest sand trap, took off my Time Crystal, and held out my hand to Ariyl for hers. She hesitated.

"David, we might need it to escape!"

"We can't escape what's going to happen tonight. We have to find out how Octavius knows what he knows."

"But *you're* the one who keeps getting his Time Crystal stolen! I think Rome makes it three times, right?"

(Actually four, if you count Miss Black Belt briefly giving it to Harold Lloyd. But no need to bring that up.)

"You're making my point for me. It's a sure bet Octavius Johnson wants these Crystals."

"Why can't I just hide mine in my hair, like I did last time?"

"You can't count on people being too dumb to look there. We got lucky once. Don't push it."

"But..."

"If they pull guns on us, one way or the other, they'll get the Crystals. But if we don't have them on us, we still have leverage."

"And what if they kill us both anyway?"

"I'm counting on you to prevent that."

"That's sweet. But what if?"

"In twenty hours, the Crystals auto-return to 2109, whatever that future looks like. It can't be any worse than if a killer like Octavius gets hold of one."

"Okay. Fine." She handed me her Crystal.

I dug deep into the sand. We heard voices.

"See who's coming," I said.

Ariyl squinted at the figures. "Just a fat guy and a skinny guy out golfing. But wait a sec..." She kept watching them. It was impossible not to. The duo were quite a ways downhill, but their voices carried well across the twilit course. We could hear them quibbling.

"We're the last ones *out* here!" exclaimed the thin one with a lantern jaw and a lispy English accent, peering into the dusk. He didn't notice he'd just caused his golf partner to miss a four-inch putt.

The Englishman turned back to the green, to find the large man with a tiny mustache glaring at him.

"Do you *mind* not talking while I putt?" fumed the hefty Southerner.

His partner shrugged, innocent.

The big man's final tap sank the ball. He retrieved it. "That's *four* for me," he said, giving his partner one last reproachful look.

"Okay, you win. I give up, all right?" said the thin one.

"It's certainly not all right! That's not how you play golf," declared the fat one.

"How do you play golf when it's too dark to see the ball?"

"We'd have been here an hour earlier if you hadn't made me shoot all those close-ups!"

"It's just, you look so exasperated when you're itching to get to the golf links. It's hysterical."

"Listen, I have been waiting for years for an invitation to play Harold's course. If you think I'm going to pass up my one chance just because *you* don't golf..."

"I don't golf because I'm at the studio, writing gags and watching dailies and cutting the pictures! I only agreed to visit this private amusement park because Roach said Harold desperately wanted us here. I'm sorry, Babe, but I don't have time for golf!"

"Oh, never mind," the big man said in a long-suffering tone. "Anytime I want to have fun, I'll *always* do it with someone else."

"You know, that's not a bad line," chuckled the Englishman.

"Mmh!" grunted the big Southerner in disgust as he threw down his bag of clubs. He marched up the hill toward the house.

"Hey, wait, don't be like that..." said his partner, following him.

Watching them in amusement, Ariyl hadn't seen me pull the Crystals out of the sand and stick them in my pocket. I smoothed the sand over the hole. I felt bad about deceiving her, but I had ample reason.

* * *

RETURNING TO THE HOUSE, Ariyl and I found Harold Lloyd and his lovely wife (and ex-leading lady) Mildred Davis receiving guests.

At forty, Harold was in his prime—handsome, athletic, confident. It was disheartening to think he would make only four more movies before his career was over.

"It's so wonderful to see Greenacres looking so...new," I told him.

"To see what now?" asked Harold.

"Greenacres. Isn't that what you..." I trailed off, suddenly realizing that Harold might not have named his estate that yet.

Harold looked at me skeptically. "I'm afraid you have the advantage of me, Mister...?"

"Grant," said Ariyl, before I could stop her. "And I'm Ju-dee."

Harold glanced up at her, nervous. "How do you do?" Then he frowned at me. "Did you say Grant? But the only Grant I invited..."

Mildred tugged at his sleeve.

"What is it, Mid?"

"I'm told two old friends of yours have arrived."

"Oh, thanks! Excuse me!" said Harold, hurrying off.

"Keep an eye out for Chaplin," I told Ariyl. "We have to keep him away from Octavius Johnson."

"Maybe we should split up, cover more territory?"

"Okay, but if you see Johnson, don't talk to him. Come find me right away. And whatever you do, don't take a drink from *anyone*."

"Aww!"

"Not one drop. We can't take any chances."

Ariyl went outside while I prowled the house.

I peeked into the sunken living room and discovered my favorite comedian of all time was sitting there. The diminutive, handsome, sad-eyed clown was pretty sunken himself. He was dressed in a dinner jacket that was a size too big, drinking a highball all alone, dwarfed by the room with its huge stone fireplace and giant pipe organ.

Suddenly, a raucous laugh cut through the room, so sharp it threatened to flake the gold leaf off the high ceiling.

"Hahaha! Buster!"

I shrank back into an alcove, to keep spying on my idol, Buster Keaton.

Jimmy Durante's huge nose entered the room, followed a moment later by the rest of him. "How ya doin', chum?" He pumped Keaton's hand eagerly.

Buster managed not to spill a drop of his highball as he carefully set it down. "Hiya, Jimmy."

"Whadaya doin' in here by yourself? You should be out mingling. Working the crowd! *What, No Beer?* is our biggest hit yet! We gotta do another one!"

"You'll do plenty more, Jimmy. Just not with me."

"Don't say that! We're a team!"

"Not according to the front office."

Durante grew serious. He put an arm around Keaton's shoulder. "Ya gotta stop drownin' your sorrows, kid. You're due for a comeback."

"Well, thanks for saying so, Jim. Break a leg."

Durante leapt up, pointing at Buster. "I'll be back later with a big producer. Keep ya chin up." And he blew out of the room as fast as he blew in.

Buster pulled a nickel-plated hip flask from his back pocket, put it to his lips, and kept his chin up for a nice long pull.

I knew that in 1933, he was at the nadir of his career, his greatest days behind him. I was a huge Buster Keaton fan, and I wanted to tell him how insanely great his silent comedies were. But I lost my chance when another clown crept into the room. Buster, staring gloomily into the hearth, didn't seem to notice until the Little Tramp sat next to him.

Then he did a perfect double take.

"Hello, old friend," said Chaplin.

Keaton almost cracked a smile at seeing Chaplin in his signature makeup and clothing.

"Hiya, Charlie. Too bad this isn't a costume party. You'da won first prize, easy."

"That he would!" laughed Lloyd as he entered the room. He shook hands with them. "I'm so glad you could both make it. Say, what's the occasion?" he asked, eyeing Chaplin's outfit.

"Actually, I came straight from the studio."

"Hey, I got my hat with me," volunteered Buster. He reached in back of his dinner jacket and pulled out his famous flat pork pie hat and slapped it on his head. "I always have my hat. 'Cause you never know. We should get a picture of the three of us!"

"Why not? Harold, where are your glasses?" asked Charlie.

"Safely put away. This is a night for relaxation, not publicity photos."

"Yeah, maybe it's too late. We really shoulda taken one of the *four* of us. Poor Roscoe," sighed Keaton.

Harold and Charlie grew somber.

"I heard about it," said Lloyd. "Heart attack, huh?"

"That's not what killed Arbuckle. He was killed by a lynch mob of liars and blue-nosed hypocrites," said Chaplin bitterly. "You know that last jury actually apologized to him for how he'd been framed."

Keaton nodded.

"I can't believe that was ten years ago," sighed Lloyd. "I heard the day he died, he'd just signed a contract with Warner Brothers. He was finally back in pictures."

"Which just goes to show you, there's one thing worse than being out of work," said Keaton.

"Here's to Roscoe," said Chaplin.

The men all clinked glasses and toasted their friend's memory.

"Harold said you weren't coming, Charlie. What changed your mind?"

"To be perfectly honest, Buster, a lovely young woman stopped by my studio this afternoon while I was shooting a test. She was on her way here, and I promised I'd show her the roller skate routine I've been working up."

"You were in costume?"

"No. I was just practicing skating...and she didn't recognize me until I introduced myself. She thought I was just a spry old man."

"Kids don't know us anymore," said Buster.

"Oh, but she knew *Chaplin*. She loved *City Lights*. But me, out of makeup...I don't think I impressed her much."

"So you put on the costume just for this girl?" marveled Harold.

"Was she beautiful?" inquired Buster.

"Spectacular."

"Oh, you mean Blondie! Yeah, I saw her when she came in." Buster gave an admiring whistle.

"So she *is* here?" said Chaplin. "Harold, do you have somewhere a little private here, with room enough for me to skate?"

His host looked skeptical. "And by 'skate', you mean...?"

Charlie held up a pair of old-time lace-up roller skates.

Harold nodded, sheepish. "Ah. Well, the dance pavilion is down the hill. It'll be perfect."

"I was hoping for a little more privacy. I don't want everyone in town to see this bit. The movie won't be done for another year."

"Or three, if I know you," said Keaton.

"I don't work *that* slow. You should come down to the studio, Buster. In fact, I think you and I should do a film together. Actually, all three of us. How about it, fellows?"

"I'd like that," nodded Buster. "In fact, I have an idea..."

Chaplin went on, "I think it might be funny if we played some old has-been vaudevillians. Past our prime."

Harold shook his head. "Not for me. Nobody wants to see a guy who's over the hill."

"But don't you see, that's where the pathos comes from. Old clowns. Down on their luck. Alcoholic."

Harold gave a disapproving look meant just for Charlie.

But Buster didn't notice. Or if he did, he took no offense: "Uh, sure. I'll do whatever you want, Charlie. Sounds kinda arty. But I bet they'd love it in Europe."

"And Asia! Last May, I toured Japan and showed them *City Lights*."

My ears pricked up at that.

"They laughed at all the right places. And cried."

"I heard you had some trouble over there," said Harold.

"Well, yes, if you call murder 'trouble'. The night after I arrived, my host, Prime Minister Inukai was shot dead by fascists. And it was a lucky thing I decided to take in a sumo match, because *I* was supposed to be assassinated at the same banquet!"

(Uh-oh. I owed Ariyl an apology.)

"Huh. Well, me, I liked *City Lights*," said Buster, deadpan.

Chaplin raised an eyebrow. "Just for that, *your* character shall wear an enormous mustache."

"Whatever you say," said Buster, glumly. He polished off his whiskey. "I should get going." He stood up a bit too fast and listed to starboard as if on a storm-tossed ship.

Charlie hooked him with his cane and righted him. "You're in no condition to drive."

"I'll walk."

"You're in no condition to walk," said Harold. "I'll have my man take you home. Winston!" he called.

There was no reply.

"My Rolls is right out front," said Harold. "Just wait outside, and I'll send out my chauffeur."

Buster went out the front door, yawning his assent.

Harold took Charlie's arm. "You can use my private den. It has a lovely view of Benedict Canyon, and there's a floor you can skate on. I'll show you the way."

I tailed them discreetly as Harold walked Charlie through the house and down some stairs to a long tunnel lined with stars' photographs. "It's at the far end," I heard Harold say. "I'll ask your young lady to meet you down there."

"You know the one?"

"I could hardly miss her, Charles."

I sprinted back up the steps before Harold could see me.

I FOUND Ariyl out by a table laden with desserts.

"You were right."

"As usual," she smirked, licking whipped cream off her fingers. "About what?"

"Octavius Johnson! That picture we saw of him wasn't at

Yamashiro's Restaurant. It was taken in Japan, the day the military assassinated the prime minister...and tried to kill Chaplin too!"

"What'd I tell you?"

"C'mon, Harold just sent Charlie downstairs to some private clubhouse of his. To meet you. You have to convince him to get out of here!"

"That I can do," she winked.

I saw Harold walk out the front door.

"We're gonna want some backup," I told her. "Just wait here a sec. Don't go off with anyone, okay?"

"Okay!"

I CAUGHT up to Harold and tapped his shoulder. "Mr. Lloyd?"

"Please, it's Harold," he said pleasantly. "And you are...?"

"Agent David Preston."

"I thought you said your name was Grant."

"I'm with the federal government, Department of Investigation. For two years, we've been tailing a man who's on your guest list, Octavius Johnson. We have reason to believe that he's part of a Japanese spy ring."

Harold gave me the side-eye.

"A federal agent. Really." It wasn't even a question, just the most skeptical restatement of my words possible. "May I see your identification?"

I handed him the identification card Sven had Photoshopped for me. It was a pretty damned convincing job and my billfold had luckily protected it from getting soiled by the muck of the Colosseum.

Lloyd was still on the fence, though. "And that lady wrestler you brought to my party?"

"Special Agent Ariyl Moro."

"Really." As I feared, he wasn't buying it. "I don't suppose your office is open tonight, so I can check your references?"

"Unfortunately, Mr. Lloyd, it's not."

"Why didn't you contact me earlier?"

"Because it was only an hour ago we learned Johnson and Charlie Chaplin would both be at your home tonight. There was no time to go through channels."

"Chaplin? I don't understand."

"How did you come to invite Mr. Johnson to your party?"

"I don't think that's any of your business."

I sighed regretfully, as if the matter were now out of my hands. I took out my notepad and pencil and jotted it down so he could read it over my shoulder. As he did:

"Subject Lloyd refused to cooperate with investigation."

"What do you mean 'subject' Lloyd?"

"Don't worry, you're not a suspect. At least not yet. But Mr. Hoover insists on knowing the names of everyone I question in this matter, and how helpful they are."

"Hoover? You mean, J. Edgar Hoover?" His voice slid into its upper register.

"I don't mean the vacuum cleaner."

"Well, I am cooperating!" he insisted. "Look, it wasn't my idea to invite Johnson. The executives at Paramount asked me to do it as a favor. Apparently Octavius Johnson has some, er, Chicago connections and has, uh, influence in labor disputes."

"In other words, he's mobbed up."

Harold loosened his tie. "That's my understanding. I did not want to invite that man here. I knew there was something off about him the minute we met. I've been nervous as a cat all night."

He looked off over the crowd on the lawn, then frowned, worried. "Oh, for heaven's sake!"

I followed his gaze to a column at the far end of the front lawn, with four lions facing the compass points. Smoke was coming out of their mouths.

"What is that?" I asked.

"The chimney for my private den. But who on earth would build a fire on a summer night?" I already knew Chaplin was in there, and I had an idea who he might want a cheery romantic blaze for.

Perturbed, Lloyd started back into the house, but I buttonholed him and showed him the photos of Johnson with Zangara and FDR.

"That's your guest, Octavius Johnson, with the man who killed Mayor Cermak and, very nearly, our president."

Harold gave a low whistle.

Then I showed him the printout of the photo of Johnson in Tokyo behind Chaplin. "You're familiar with what almost happened to Mr. Chaplin in Japan last year?"

Harold nodded, squinting at the printout.

I tapped the photo: "Here's Johnson again, lurking near Chaplin and Prime Minister Inukai just hours before Inukai was assassinated."

"Agent Preston, forgive me. I don't know what to say except...how can I be of help?" Then Harold held the printouts up to the light, intrigued. "Say, what kind of photo paper is this? I know a fair bit about photography, and I've never seen anything like it."

Oops. Of course not, xerography wouldn't be invented for another decade.

"It's experimental," I vamped. "Only being used by the Bureau, for the time being. The point is, I have information that Johnson is at your party to kidnap and possibly kill Mr. Chaplin."

"This is incredible. I knew there was something I didn't like about that man. Now you tell me he's a gangster and a kidnapper and a murderer? I just can't believe it!"

"You have armed security men here?"

"Yes, I do."

"Can I count on them to protect us from Mr. Johnson while we escort Mr. Chaplin to safety?"

He stood up, fire in his eyes. "Never mind all that. I'm going to find that man and throw him off my property!"

"Sir, let the Bureau handle this. You don't want a scene!"

"Actually," said Harold with grim bravado, "I wouldn't mind one."

He strode out on the driveway and ran into a cowboy in evening clothes.

"Will, have you seen that guy Johnson, with the eye patch?"

"Overheard him bein' rude to a lady a little bit ago. I once said I never met a man I didn't like, but in that feller's case, I'd make an exception."

"That makes two of us. Let me know if you see him, please." Lloyd did a taxi-whistle to summon his four tuxedoed bouncers and gave them their marching orders.

MEANWHILE, Ariyl had vanished again.

I looked back at the smoke coming from the lions' mouths and had a pretty good idea where I'd find her.

30

THE GAMBLING DEN

I MADE MY WAY DOWN THE TUNNEL. I HEARD music. I opened the door to Harold's private two-story den.

Ariyl sat at the piano, next to a dapper, wavy-haired man about my age, with a nose that followed straight down from his brow, and a pleasant tenor voice; he was crooning her a very familiar song. I'd last heard it on our visit to 1948: the Bert Kalmar/Harry Ruby tune, "Keep On Doin' What You're Doin'."

He was making lots of eye contact with her, which made me want to sock him. He was, of course, oblivious to the irony of singing Ariyl a song that rhymed "arms to hold me tight" with "flirtin' with dynamite." If he only knew.

I cleared my throat. "Ariyl, I'm told Charlie Chaplin's downstairs."

"Oh, great! Come on!" She took the crooner's hand and led him down the stairs, where the air was blue with cigar smoke and (I assume) indecent wisecracks.

A QUINTET of 1933's top movie comics were playing poker around Lloyd's table: Three Marx Brothers (who were almost unrecognizable without their respective wigs, hats, and greasepaint mustache), plus the now all-but-forgotten duo of Bert Wheeler, a curly-haired juvenile type, and jockey-sized wiseguy Robert Woolsey, with a big cigar and horn-rims like Harold's, except Bob's had lenses.

There was a blazing fire in the hearth, along with some opened-up wire coat hangers and a bag of marshmallows. No doubt imported by the brothers Marx.

Woolsey spotted Ariyl first.

"*Whoa*-oh!" exclaimed Bob, his cigar almost flying from his mouth.

Then the first Marx brother looked up at her, and his jaw went slack as he stared.

"Close your mouth, Harpo. I can see bats escaping," cracked his younger brother.

Ariyl stopped at the bottom of the stairs and indicated the crooner to me: "Oh, forgive me. David, meet Zippo Marx."

The comedians all cracked up.

"It's Zeppo," corrected the straight man with a martyred smile.

"Oh, my bad, *Zeppo!* That was a wonderful song. Thank you!"

"It's my big number in *Duck Soup*."

"It's your only number in *Duck Soup*," said Chico, sorting his hand.

"Gee, I love that song," said Bert. "I wish we had it in our picture."

"Why can't we?" asked Bob.

"Well, the Marxes are already doing it."

"When has that ever stopped you?" asked Groucho, ashing his stogie. "I'll take two."

"Deal me in the next hand," Zeppo said, pulling two chairs over to the table. He turned to Ariyl and turned on the charm. "Ariyl, have you ever considered a career in the movies?"

Ariyl snickered. Jack Warner had made her the same offer in 1945. "Don't tell me *you* run a studio."

"Oh, no. I'm an actor."

"You couldn't prove it by me," said Groucho.

"But I have a lot of contacts with agents. My brother Gummo, for one."

"Zeppo, who is this tall drink of water?" leered the former Julius Marx.

"My name is Ariyl Moro."

"Well, an aerial this tall always gets a great reception. I'm Groucho," he said, rising and putting out his hand.

The rest of the comics each politely stood, gave their names, and shook her hand. All except Harpo, who was still gaping. Groucho passed his palm up and down before his brother's eyes.

"This is why we never give him any lines," remarked Groucho.

"And I'm David Preston," I said, to no one's great interest.

"I bet you weren't invited," said Chico, without looking up.

"I was invited like you're Italian," I replied.

He let loose a belly laugh and dropped into dialect. "'Atsa some good joke, boss!"

"That's not his line; it's from *Animal Crackers*," snapped Groucho. "Don't you remember your old scripts?"

"I can barely remember the new one," shot back Chico. "I'll take one."

A figure standing at the far window turned around and tipped his derby. "Miss Moro! I'm delighted to see you again!"

"Charlie!" she exclaimed in delight. "You came to the party after all!"

Groucho shook his head. "And here I was hoping he was just an imitator Lloyd hired. Why don't you sit down and play a few hands, Charles?"

"Thank you, Groucho, but I don't enjoy gambling."

"Says the man who's still producing silent movies," replied Marx.

Charlie let that go by and gestured to the pair of roller skates he was wearing. "As promised!"

Ariyl beamed. "Oh, are you going to show me your routine?"

"Yes, well, I was hoping it would be a bit more private in here. Perhaps we could adjourn to another part of the estate, with not so many prying eyes."

I gave her a nod—whatever he says, agree.

"Sure!" she said brightly.

"A little elderly for you, isn't she, Charles?" asked Woolsey. "She must be at least nineteen."

Charlie chuckled and twirled his cane. "Goodnight, gentlemen!"

The cane tip hit Woolsey's ashtray and dumped the brimming contents in his lap.

"Hey!"

Chaplin tipped his hat in apology as he exited with Ariyl.

"Well, he sure made an ash of you," said Wheeler.

Harpo was still gawping.

CHARLIE WENT up the steps wearing skates without a single misstep —an impressive feat. At the top step, he suddenly windmilled his arms, skates slipping wildly. Then he instantly regained his balance. Ariyl burst out laughing. He really was a hilarious acrobat.

I beckoned to her. She leaned toward me, and I murmured in her ear. "Take him out to the driveway. Lloyd's armed bouncers should be able to handle Octavius if he tries anything."

She nodded and went on ahead, arm-in-arm with Charlie.

AS THEY ENTERED the tunnel back to the house, Ariyl and Charlie passed three more cigar-puffing men, all a foot shorter than Ariyl. They parted for her like the Red Sea.

"Hiya, toots!" said the fat one with a shaved head.

Ariyl and Chaplin breezed on by them.

"Ehh, too stuck-up for me," said the curly-haired one.

The one with a black mop of hair gave them both a push toward the private den. "I can't take you two anywhere. *C'mon!*"

I FOLLOWED AT A DISTANCE. But when I got outside to the driveway, Ariyl and Charlie were nowhere to be seen. The bouncers with the clipboard hadn't seen either one. What the hell? She knew where the driveway was—she just hadn't gone there.

I had a bad feeling.

I WENT into Harold's sitting room. Aside from the lit-up Christmas tree (in August!) the room was empty. I hung the Time Crystals amid the huge ornaments then went back outside.

WHERE WAS ARIYL? I had to find her. But the estate was vast—forty-four acres. My big worry was that she and Charlie had run into Octavius. If he was after the Time Crystals, he'd try to force her to tell where we'd hidden them. Except they weren't there now. I checked the load on my .38 and shoved it back in my pocket.

I was dashing down the hill toward the golf course when I encountered Octavius, eye patch and all, braced by a pair of burly doormen.

"Mr. Lloyd says to throw you off the grounds," one told Octavius. "How hard we do it, is up to you."

Octavius spotted me. "You must be Professor Preston," he said, putting out his three-fingered right hand. I didn't shake it. "Dad described you pretty well. Said I should keep an eye out for you. And here you are."

"And who exactly is 'Dad'?"

"Octavius Johnson II, of course."

"What else did he tell you about me?"

"That you have some property of his."

I looked at the white grit stuck to Octavius's shiny leather wingtips.

"Not exactly golf shoes, are those?"

"No," said Octavius.

"So what were you doing in a sand trap?"

"Looking for two crystals."

That knocked me back a bit. "Wow. No verbal fencing? You just come right out and admit it?"

"I more than admit it. My father wants those two crystals by ten

P.M. tonight. Bring them to Nippon Petroleum. And no cops, unless they bring plenty of toe-tags."

"I have the number. I'll call if I can't make it."

"Oh, you'll make it, Preston. Or the world will lose its favorite movie star. And you'll lose your giant girlfriend."

"Where's Ariyl?" I snarled, grabbing his lapels.

"She's safe," he said.

"Whoa, mister!" said a bouncer, trying to intervene.

"*Now*, Ariyl!" shouted Octavius.

Ariyl came crashing out of the bushes. She caught the first bouncer unaware and knocked him out with one punch. The other drew his gun, but she caught his hand and forced it up as he fired once. Then Ariyl socked him to the far end of dreamland.

"Like I said, she's in no danger," commented Octavius. "Give me their guns."

She complied.

"Ariyl, what are you doing?" I yelled.

"Just what she's told," said Octavius. "Grab him."

Ariyl seized my belt buckle.

"Ariyl, stop! Don't do it!"

"I can't help it! He made me tell him about the sand trap. But they weren't there!"

"Frisk him," said Octavius. "I want those crystals."

Ariyl patted me down and found my .38. She squeezed it in her hand, slightly bending the barrel. Old habits die hard.

"I didn't tell you to do that," said Octavius, disturbed. He may not have understood till this moment just how strong she was.

"You didn't tell me *not* to."

"Just do what I say. Lift him way up high."

She obediently raised me over her head, but looked up at me, helpless. "David, I'm scared!"

"*You're* scared? What have you got her on, Johnson? Pentol?"

"You know about Pentol? Dad was right, you're no dope."

"Ariyl, you *didn't* drink...?"

Ariyl shook her head. "I think it was in the *profiterole* Cary Grant asked me to try," she admitted, guiltily.

"That's right," said Octavius. "I bet the pretty boy a hundred bucks he couldn't charm her into eating it."

"He had two of them, David, but the big man from the golf course ate the other one!"

"Oliver Hardy?" I said.

Octavius nodded, amused. "Fat boy got in my hair. Thought I was being rude to Ariyl, so I told *him* to go sit in the water hazard for an hour. And when he's done, he's going to slap the ass of the first woman he sees and call her 'sugar.' Wish we could stick around for that, but we have to go."

"Leave Ariyl out of this!"

He gave a nasty laugh. "Pentol's amazing. Perfect hypnotic drug. I could tell your lover-girl to break you in two and she'd do it."

He let that hang in the air a bit. Along with me. "But that wouldn't get those crystals to us by ten. Don't be late, Professor." Then he gestured at Ariyl. "Just leave him there."

She hooked my belt onto the ornamental iron of a light pole.

"What is going *on* out here?" demanded Lloyd, striding down the driveway. "I said to toss this cheap hood out on his coattails!" Then he saw his employees sprawled on the grass.

"Guess what, Harold? I'm telling her to toss *you* out," grinned Octavius. "Do it!"

Ariyl picked Lloyd up by his shirtfront and tossed him backwards. He broke the windshield of that black-and-brass Rolls-Royce Phantom and landed in the open-air driver seat, one knee over the steering wheel.

"I am sooo sorry, Harold!" said Ariyl.

"Shut up and go get Chaplin," Octavius muttered to her. He and Ariyl vanished into the bushes farther down the drive.

"Somebody help!" I shouted.

The first person to arrive was a highly lubricated W. C. Fields. He flinched at seeing Harold's predicament. "Holy Jumping Jesus, what happened to you?"

"Nothing," said Harold, still in a daze.

"That was going to be my first guess," drawled Fields, "that nothing propelled you through your own windscreen."

He delicately tossed a triangle of broken glass aside, and helped the dizzy Lloyd out of the front seat of his Rolls. "What a beautiful automobile that used to be. Your insurance agent is going to have conniptions," observed Fields.

The two bouncers with the clipboard rushed down the steps to assist their employer. Harold waved them off. "I'm fine. Get Agent Preston down from the light post."

The pair of them unhooked my belt and lifted me down.

"Hey," growled the first one, remembering my face. "You ain't Cary Grant!"

"And you're no William Powell," I said, flashing my ID. That shut him up.

Meanwhile, the two doormen Ariyl had decked were coming to.

"Help those two inside," Lloyd told the clipboard team.

Then for the benefit of his fellow comedian, he tried to laugh off the incident: "Heh, well, I thought that gag would get a bigger laugh than it did."

"In my experience, Harold," Fields intoned, "it is funnier to damage a car that's already a little banged up. And it's funnier bending a thing, than breaking it."

"I'll try to remember, Bill," said Harold dryly, still brushing shards off his jacket.

"If I were you, I'd be trying to forget," muttered Fields.

A pretty Negro waitress glided by with a tray of highballs. "Here, dear, let me help you with those," he said, falling into step alongside.

"Do you believe me now?" I asked Lloyd.

"I believe you're both out of your minds! And you have one minute to get yourself and that madwoman off my property, because I'm calling the police and that's how long they'll take to get here."

He turned on his heel and marched back toward his house.

At that moment, Ariyl and Octavius emerged from the bushes down the drive. She had an unconscious man slung over her shoulder. He was wearing skates.

"Harold, look!" I shouted.

Lloyd strode back down the drive, ready to punch me in the nose. Then he saw Ariyl dump Charlie into the back of Octavius's car.

"Hey!" He dashed to the car, but Octavius pulled out with a screech of rubber. Harold almost caught up, but when Octavius circled the fountain, Harold broke off his pursuit, yelling, "Stop! Don't circle that fountain! *It's bad luck!*"

Octavius ignored him, his tires squealing around the far side of the waterworks. Lloyd cut across the drive to catch Octavius as he sped downhill. Harold just missed grabbing the passing car door; he kept running, but it soon outdistanced him.

Lloyd ran back over to me. "Octavius just kidnapped Chaplin!"

"Just like I said he would!"

"Yeah, you did," he admitted. "Well, I'm calling the police!"

I grabbed his arm. "Don't you get it? Everything I told you has come true. Now I'm telling you that Octavius drugged Ariyl. She's under his control. There aren't enough cops in L.A. to hold her if he tells her to fight. They'll have to kill her. And in the meantime, he'll kill Charlie!"

"Why would he do that?"

"The same reason he almost killed Charlie in Japan a year ago. To start a war with America!"

Lloyd was stunned, but somehow he sensed I wasn't lying about that. "Well, we can't just do nothing!"

"I know where he's headed. If you and I can get there first, we can take them unaware. But we have to leave *now!*"

"You're cuckoo!" he said.

"Fine, if you're afraid, I'll go by myself!"

"What do you mean, afraid?" he bristled.

My problem was, the car I'd arrived in was blocked by another parked auto. So I jumped in his Rolls. "Where are the keys? Or is it a starter?"

"You're not driving this car! You'll scratch it!" he said. He pushed me over and got behind the wheel. Then he saw the spiderweb of broken glass that still covered most of the windshield. He wrenched the frame back and forth till it tore loose, then he dumped it on the drive.

Then he backed us down the driveway at forty miles an hour.

We passed Oliver Hardy sitting in the water hazard, checking his wristwatch, and heaving a huge sigh.

31

DESIGNATED DRIVER

HAROLD MERGED WITH BENEDICT CANYON IN reverse, garnering a honk and screamed epithet from the southbound motorist he almost hit.

"Go left on Sunset!" I shouted. Harold hung a screeching turn and roared east.

"Where are we going?" he shouted back. We were both squinting into the wind, no longer having a windshield.

"Richfield Building on Flower!"

"I hope you're right. I don't see them up ahead!"

"Probably took Wilshire! Hey, do you have a gun?" I asked belatedly.

"There's one in the glove box," he said.

I opened the compartment and found a revolver loaded with six rounds. I hoped that would be enough.

There was also a pair of the famous lensless horn-rims.

"What are these for?"

"Personal appearances." He took a beat. "I want one thing understood: I'm helping you because Charlie Chaplin is a friend, a colleague, and a guest at my home. Not for Hoover, or you, or your lady friend, whatever your crazy story is."

"Look, I'm sorry about Ariyl throwing you like that. She wasn't in her right mind."

"That I can believe."

"If you met her under better circumstances, I know you'd love her."

"She actually reminds me of my mother. A formidable woman," Harold replied.

"Well, there you go."

"No, there I don't go. I keep as far away from Mother as I can."

I heard a body slide against the door in the passenger compartment. I looked back.

Buster Keaton sat up in the rear compartment. With a jolt, I realized he'd never gotten his ride home. He'd just climbed into the back of the Rolls and passed out. I watched as Buster blinked and tried to focus his bleary eyes.

Like most L.A. streets in 1933, Sunset had light poles every couple hundred feet, providing only a small pool of illumination.

Buster apparently couldn't see Harold or me in the open-air driver seat. We'd be silhouettes at best. All he could tell from the light globes flashing past was that he was in a vehicle doing about sixty miles per hour.

Harold swerved left around a car that was too slow to jackrabbit the green light. A horn honked.

The swerve slammed Buster against the side of the compartment.

Electrified, Buster grabbed the air in front of him, then felt all around the front window of the compartment, groping madly for a steering wheel that wasn't there. He looked down, stomping everywhere for a brake pedal that didn't exist.

I saw all this played out in absolute silence. It would have been hilarious if I wasn't worried we'd be too late to save Ariyl.

Finally, I found a map light on the dashboard that I flicked on, and now Buster could see us. He looked relieved not to be driving. I was equally glad he wasn't.

He gestured at me with palms up—what's going on?

Maybe a master of pantomime could have communicated the

idea better, but all I could do was wave my palms downward, like he should sit back and be patient.

"What's going on?" asked Harold, noticing my activity. He almost clipped a streetcar.

"Just keep your eyes on the road! I'll tell you later!"

We were now whipping through the Sunset Strip, doing twice the legal limit.

"Harold, slow down! We can't afford to get stopped by a cop."

"Maybe we could *use* an escort!" he said. "Maybe get a hundred angry cops following us!"

"If we pull up with sirens wailing, Octavius will hear it and kill them both!"

"I still say..."

"You don't even know what office they're in. I do. We do this my way!"

Harold set his jaw, fuming.

I glanced back and realized the reason I didn't see Buster in the rear compartment was that he had stepped out onto the passenger side running board!

"All right, I'll slow down," said Harold, hitting the brake.

Buster nearly fell off the running board. He grabbed the brass mirror.

"No!" I cried.

Somehow Buster held onto both the car and his hat.

"Well, make up your mind!" snapped Harold, punching the gas again.

Buster lurched backward. The mirror bent.

Harold heard the metal creak—that's when he saw Buster's hand clinging to the distending brass fixture. "Buster, what are you doing here?"

In an amazing feat of acrobatic strength, Buster flipped himself one-handed into the seat between me and Harold.

"Waiting for my ride home," he croaked. He offered Harold the mirror that had just wrenched off in his hand.

Harold remembered to look ahead—just in time to avoid an oncoming truck. With a PING, he lost his driver side mirror.

"I think maybe I better walk," said Buster. He rose to get back out on the running board, but Harold and I pulled him down again.

"Why'd you pull a crazy stunt like that?" demanded Harold.

"I've seen you do worse," said Buster. "I wanna know what's going on!"

"You could've called me on the phone!" Harold unhooked his driver's telephone and showed it to Buster. Buster blinked in surprise, then looked back at the compartment. Sure enough, there was a phone set hanging back there.

"Hey, that's swell!" he said, impressed. "I don't even have one of those in my home!"

Then we heard the siren.

Buster looked ready to climb out of the car again.

"Just pull over and stay calm," I advised.

The motorcycle cop parked behind the Rolls and walked up to Lloyd.

"How fast was I going, officer?" Harold asked with a nervous smile.

"Thirty, same as me. That's not why I pulled you over."

"Oh. Then why?"

"Do you ever clean your windshield?"

Lloyd looked, and gave an embarrassed chuckle. "Oh, that. That just happened."

"I didn't touch that part," announced Buster, pointing with the broken mirror.

"Let me see your license."

Harold dug it out of the glove box. I considered jumping out and running the rest of the way, but it seemed like a great way to get shot.

The cop frowned. "Lloyd. I feel like I know that name." With an eye-roll, Harold pulled out the Glasses and put them on.

The cop lit up like Harold's Christmas tree. "Oh, Mr. Lloyd! Of course! Aw, I love your movies!"

"Thank you."

"If you'd wear them glasses all the time, you'll never get a ticket," chuckled the cop.

"About the windshield..."

"I bet you're rehearsing something for your next thrill picture, huh?"

"Er, yes!"

"How about that? Harold Lloyd! Well, I won't keep you gentlemen," he said, folding up his ticket book and stuffing it in his back pocket. "Hey, aren't you Buster Keaton?"

"Pleased to meet you," said Buster, tipping his pork pie.

"Pleasure's all mine," said the cop, putting out his hand. Keaton handed him the busted mirror.

"Goodnight, officer!" said Harold, throwing the car into gear.

We sped on to 555 Flower Street.

32

RICHFIELD TOWER

H AROLD AGREED WE SHOULD NOT PARK IN sight of the building.
Once apprised of the situation, Buster refused to wait for us
at the car on Fourth Street. He insisted on helping us rescue Charlie
and "Blondie."

We all hurried down Flower Street toward the Richfield Building.
By night, it was even more spectacular: an ebony-gilt petroleum
palace, topped by the glowing neon RICHFIELD sign on the oil-
derrick tower.

But we found the palace guarded by gunmen.

Not the uniformed building security that I had seen earlier today,
and on my visit in 1954. These guys looked like mob muscle. Their
overcoats worn on a warm summer night were a dead giveaway that
they came from a much colder town, and no doubt were supposed to
disguise weaponry that couldn't fit into a pocket; I presumed sawed-
off shotguns and/or tommy guns.

I saw only one uniformed security guard, and he was out front
waiting at the bus stop.

"Excuse me, is Richfield Tower open to visitors tonight?" I
asked him.

"Brother, it isn't even open to me," said the guard. "A buncha garlic-eaters took over the place at five o'clock. Building manager was sweating bullets. He said they have a big confidential meeting upstairs, and ordered out all the staff. Even the janitors. Said it's our night off. And, mister, with what they're packing, I wasn't gonna argue."

His bus pulled up before I could continue the interview.

I reported back to Harold and Buster.

"Okay, what's the suite number?" asked Harold.

I told him 1200.

"That figures," sighed Harold. "It *would* be the top floor."

Harold eyeballed the side of the building then led us around the back (western) side. "No brick. It's a difficult climb. That slick terra-cotta wraps around all four sides. But there *are* a lot of details and chevrons. And it looks like no one's watching the rear side, on Figueroa."

I couldn't believe my ears. "Climb? Harold, *Safety Last* was a movie. We can't do the human fly routine in real life."

"Why not? I already have. And I bet Buster can too."

"Who, me?" slurred Buster.

"Well, maybe not this time," decided Harold.

"You can climb twelve *stories?*" I said, incredulous.

"Well, I climbed three stories on a real building. Let's hope I find an open window by then."

"This is crazy."

"We could still call the police," he suggested.

I shook my head. "Let's do it."

Harold took off his prosthetic glove. No one was going to film this climb, and it just got in the way. But he neglected to remove the Glasses. Maybe it felt more natural doing a stunt with them on.

Carefully, but with admirable speed, his eight fingers took hold of the crannies in the architecture, his polished dress shoes found footholds, and he ascended to the second story.

Keaton handed me his pork pie hat. "Don't lose it. These things cost me two bucks apiece." Then he pulled out his nickel-plated hip flask, took a snort of brandy, and handed that to me as well. He started up then came back down and reclaimed his hat. He put it on.

"It helps me balance." Then he clambered up after Harold.

"Buster, are you sure you can climb this?" I whispered up.

"Sure, I got two more fingers than Harold does," he said, now two stories up.

"You also drank four fingers more!"

"Well, if I fall, I'll be loose and it won't hurt as much," said Buster. By this time, he was three stories up and Harold was scaling the fourth.

I followed. It wasn't as hard as it looked. I managed to get one story high before I slipped and fell. I landed on my feet then my ass, but not quite hard enough to break anything.

"Buster, I got another idea!" I hissed. "Toss me your cigs!"

Keaton tossed me down his pack of Lucky Strikes. I walked around to the front of the building again.

A POLICE CAR pulled up to the side of the building. I resisted the urge to ask him for help. I knew why that wouldn't work. But I was also terrified that he would drive around the back side and see the two figures clambering up the building—now at the fifth and sixth floors. Luckily, in their dark clothes against the black terracotta, they were hard to spot. Finally, the cop drove on.

I lit the first cigarette that I'd tried since I was eight, and then strolled back toward Flower Street, puffing casually and trying not to cough my lungs out. The city had thoughtfully provided a big steel wastepaper basket near the bus stop. It was brimming with trash. As I passed it, I splashed half the open brandy flask into it, then discarded my lit cig, and kept walking.

It took a few seconds for the bonfire to start. For a while, it was touch and go whether it would set the nearby Italian cypress on fire. Vigilant thugs poured out of the lobby, kicked over the basket, and upended brass-and-copper extinguishers, spraying the hoses on it. Eventually, everyone from the lobby was fighting the fire.

Tellingly, nobody bothered to call the fire department.

Before the blaze was knocked down, I had slipped into the lobby, those amazing Deco elevator doors had closed on me, and I was on my way to the twelfth floor.

THE DOORS OPENED. Two burly mouthbreathers in topcoats made my plan to enter Suite 1200 a non-starter. They glowered at me, but in my nice suit, I looked too respectable to rough up.

"Wrong floor," one of them informed me with polite menace.

"You betcha!" I said, imitating movie drunk Jack Norton.

I let the doors close, and I went down one story. More guards. I went down one more.

The tenth floor was dark and unguarded. It seemed like my only chance to get to the Nippon Petroleum office was to climb up to the penthouse and hope to find an open window.

I was no Harold Lloyd, but I wasn't about to let Octavius Johnson kill my girl. So I opened the window and nearly knocked Harold off the side of the building.

"WHOA—" he yelped as the gun fell out of his waistband and he tottered backward.

"Shh!" I hissed, grabbing his hand. With every ounce of strength I had, I pulled him inside. Meanwhile, the gun clattered on the street far below. At least it didn't go off.

Lloyd was panting from exertion, surprise, and vertigo. So was I, for that matter.

"He's got armed guards on both floors above us," I whispered.

"And now we're *un*armed. How did you get up here?" he demanded.

I pointed to the elevator. He looked like he could cheerfully break my neck. Considering I'd nearly broken his, that was understandable.

"Where's Buster?" I mouthed.

Harold reacted in alarm and looked behind him. I leaned past him. No Buster. But no broken body on the pavement a hundred feet below, either. We looked at each other, perplexed, then looked down again.

"Who are we looking for?" said a voice behind me, leaning over us for a good look.

Startled, Harold and I nearly fell out, but Buster pulled us back in to safety.

"You boys better be careful," he advised.

"Don't tell me *you* took the elevator," muttered Harold.

"Naw, I saw that open window on the south side," Keaton said, pointing across the hallway. "And there's an open window on the top floor and the room is dark. It's right above this one."

He started to climb out the same window I'd just pulled Harold in. Then he stopped, and gave us a polite "after-you" gesture. Harold gave me a dubious look.

"It's just two stories. I can do that much," I said. I started to climb out.

Harold pulled me back. "You'd better stay behind."

"I'm going," I insisted.

"Then you better stay behind *us*," said Harold.

"Thanks a lot."

"I'm just being practical. If you go first and fall, you'll take us with you."

"Hey!" Buster came running out of a janitor's closet, with a pair of heavy twelve-foot extension cords. "We can tie him between us. Like we're mountain climbing."

He expertly hitched the cord to my belt, and then tied it to his.

"I can barely hold *myself* on this building!" said Harold, exasperatedly showing Buster his mangled right hand.

"All the more reason." Buster looped the other cord through Harold's belt. "If *any* of us slips, there's still four hands to hold him." He looked at Harold's hand again. "Three-and-a-half, anyway." By that time, he'd finished knotting the other end of Harold's cord to my belt.

We went up two more floors, to the penthouse. Harold first, then me, then Buster.

A stiff evening breeze was whipping our clothes, but nobody slipped. Harold helped me over the final ledge. I stood up, trying not to let my jacket catch the wind. The ledge was only a foot wide, but it felt like my favorite easy chair compared to climbing without a net. Buster was last. Harold helped him up and got a whiff of Buster's breath.

"I can't believe you did that climb drunk!" said Harold.

"I hope you don't think I'm dumb enough to try it sober," said Buster.

The lights went on in the windows of the corner office behind us. We instantly crouched, cowering out of view. Finally, I rose up just high enough to sneak a look over the window sill.

Someone had entered the office, but he stood at a bookcase with his back to me. He was tall and black-haired, but it wasn't Octavius; he was dressed in a gray business suit.

I felt a tug on my cord. Harold motioned to us to move down the ledge.

We crept on hands and knees past another lit window. I ventured another look:

It was the outer office I'd been in that morning, with the receptionist's desk. Ariyl stood obediently before the desk, while Octavius stared at the telephone and checked his watch. He picked up the phone and dialed someone (I assumed) in the lobby.

"Nothing yet, huh? Call me the minute he gets here." Then he hung up and walked over to Ariyl.

"Honey, when this is all over, you and I are going to have some real fun. And you're not going to do a thing to stop me, are you?"

She shook her head. He grabbed her and kissed her, hard. She didn't resist, but she didn't respond either. He backed away, scowling in frustration.

"It's like kissing a mannequin. Act like you love it!"

"How would I do that? I don't."

"Kiss me back, goddamnit!"

He kissed her again, and she kissed back, but I could tell her heart wasn't in it. I could've kicked myself for making Harold drop his gun. Finally, Octavius backed off.

"We're gonna have to experiment with this Pentol stuff," he growled. "Maybe write you a script to follow, girlie."

"God, you're repulsive," she said.

"No more talk, sweetheart," he told her.

She shut up.

He checked his watch again.

I ducked down. I didn't have a watch, but I looked southeast to the lit-up clock on the Eastern Columbia Building: it was five minutes to ten.

Harold led us crawling along the ledge to a darker set of windows.

This time Buster reconnoitered then ducked down. "It's the elevator lobby," he whispered. "Window's open. Charlie's there. He's still passed out. But there's three guys watching him."

Keeping low, I peered in the window. Curiosity overcame Harold, who looked in as well.

Our angle was from behind Kobayashi, but I would have recognized his buzz-cut, squared-off head, even if he wasn't holding his sheathed samurai blade. There was a big bump on the back of his skull that hadn't been there before Ariyl threw him across the room.

Two of the mob button-men each had Charlie by an arm; they literally wheeled the unconscious Chaplin over to a sofa. It was easy, because he still had the roller skates on. He had a cloth bag over his head.

"You gonna take the skates off this guy?" wondered one thug.

"We do not wish them removed," said Kobayashi. He took out a small knife and sliced the loops of the roller skate laces. That did not bode well for Charlie's future.

One thug frowned at the familiar costume the unconscious man was wearing.

"Who *is* this guy?"

"That is none of your concern," said Kobayashi. "You will leave us now."

The gunman took offense. "Nerts to you, Confucius." He ripped the bag off Charlie's head and did a big double take.

"It's Charlie Chaplin!" gasped the other thug.

"Say, what the hell's going on here?" demanded the first one. "I didn't sign up to kidnap no movie star!" He reached for his gun.

"Me neither!" said his associate, pulling his weapon. "Mr. Nitti ain't gonna like it!"

Kobayashi's next move was so fast, I almost missed it by blinking.

He unsheathed his sword, swung it past both their throats, then watched as the astonished men dropped to their knees, their heads toppling from their bodies.

We immediately ducked. I was ready to vomit again. Harold and Buster were as pale as if they were wearing pancake makeup.

"Oh, my God," gasped Harold. Then Buster did throw up.

"I should have let Ariyl destroy the damned thing," I muttered.

"Well," gulped Buster, "on the bright side, at least there's only one guy now." He looked at Harold. "I say we rush him. He can't kill all three of us."

Harold hissed back, "He can kill at least two of us!"

I put my finger to my lips. I could hear Octavius stepping out into the lobby.

"Kobayashi? What the hell?!"

"They did not wish to be a part of this. They were going to call their Mr. Nitti," said Kobayashi. "I had no choice."

"No, I guess not. Shit. Well, in an hour, it won't make any difference. The world will be at war. Ariyl!"

I had to take a peek. I saw Ariyl come into the lobby. She saw the bodies and opened her mouth to scream.

"Don't make a sound," Octavius said, pointing at her.

She shut her mouth.

"Just calm down."

The horrified look left her face. The first time that command ever actually worked. It seemed this early version of Pentol couldn't create emotions that weren't there, but it suppressed inconvenient ones like revulsion. She stared blankly at the two headless bodies.

"Put 'em down the trash chute."

She obeyed.

"The heads too."

Down they went.

"And their guns."

She did.

Octavius grimaced at the blood now staining her dress. "You're a mess." He opened a janitor's closet, handed her a rag and a can of turpentine. "Now...clean yourself up. Then come back in."

He went into the receptionist's office.

Ariyl poured turpentine onto the rag and tried to clean the blood off her dress. It just made a larger red smear. She set down the can and shed her dress, exposing her bloodstained SmartFab negligee.

Ariyl touched her shoulder and said, "Clean up." The blood immediately dried and flaked off her scanties. (Octavius apparently had no idea what SmartFab was.) She touched her shoulder and tried again: "White cocktail dress, 1933." She tapped her shoulder a few times and tried again.

This time, the old "bang it a few times" method worked; the underwear morphed, and she was back in an approximation of her party dress.

Then she rejoined Octavius.

I felt a tug on my cord. Harold was motioning me to get down. But I put up my palm—Charlie was coming out of his stupor. Harold and Buster took a peek as well.

Kobayashi cleaned the blood from his *katana* with Ariyl's rag.

Groggy from whatever mickey Octavius had slipped him, Chaplin's eyes focused first on that sword. He seemed mesmerized by the gleaming, lethal perfection of the blade. Kobayashi sheathed it again.

"Such an amazing culture you have," Chaplin said, slurring somewhat. "You know, I was nearly killed in your country."

Kobayashi nodded, impassive.

Chaplin continued, "My host, Inukai Tsuyoshi, was shot dead in his own home by a bunch of young naval officers. I'm told as he lay dying, he told them, 'If I could speak, you would understand.'"

Charlie paused, searching Kobayashi's face. "I sincerely believe if you and I could speak, I could make you understand..." he wagged his finger drunkenly "...that I am not your enemy."

"Do you know how Inukai's killers answered him?" Kobayashi asked.

Chaplin cogitated a moment, then shook his head, which just made him dizzier. "Haven't the foggiest."

"They said, 'Dialogue is meaningless.'"

Chaplin considered that. "Well, then it's probably a good thing I didn't make any talkies."

Charlie's gaze wandered and refocused on Buster and Harold outside the window. He blinked and shook his head to dispel the hallucination.

By the time he opened his eyes, we'd all ducked down.

WE UNTIED the cords from our belts. With Octavius Johnson III in the outer office and Kobayashi in the lobby, I was burning to know who the big shot was in that corner office. I now had a strong hunch as to the identity of Octavius Johnson II. So I carefully went around Buster and crept along the ledge, then stuck my nose over the sill of the corner office.

My hunch was right.

I'd refused to admit to myself, much less Ariyl. But ever since Rome, I'd known it in my gut.

The black-haired man with a patch over his right eye checked the load of his revolver, then spun the chamber and flicked it closed.

It was Jon Ludlo.

33

CORNERED

I T COULDN'T BE. THAT QUARTER-TON television camera, thrown from seven stories had crushed Ludlo so fatally, so definitively, so R-rated-violently that the 1954 timeline he'd worked so hard to create had dissolved because he would never return to 1948 to cause it.

And the only reason he'd been alive in that 1948 timeline was that I'd accidentally diverted him from going through with his *original* timeline, in which he'd drowned under the tsunami that destroyed Atlantis.

Yet there he sat, rocking back in a fancy Art Deco office chair as if he owned the place. And knowing Ludlo, I bet he did.

No doubt Sven could explain the time travel logic, if I lived long enough to ask him.

The suspicion I'd hatched back at the Villa of the Quintilii was now confirmed: Roman soothsayer Octavius the Elder, and all the Octavius Johnsons we'd found since, were getting their tips on the future from the unkillable Jon Ludlo.

. . .

HE LOOKED STRANGELY DIFFERENT, though. Meaner. Leaner. More rugged. Maybe he'd been working out like Ariyl?

He set the pistol down by the intercom. As he swiveled the chair around, I ducked out of sight.

I whispered to Harold and Buster, "This is the boss. I need to talk to this guy."

"*Talk?*" croaked Buster.

"Shh!" I put a finger to my lips. "He's got a gun. And we can't let him see you two, or the jig is up. But I have an idea how to keep him *and* Octavius busy for five minutes."

"With talk," repeated Buster, dubious.

"While I do that, can you two take out that samurai in the lobby, then take Charlie in the elevator to the tenth floor, barricade yourselves in an office, and call the cops?"

"Two men against one man with a sword," repeated Harold, incredulous. "Only this time it's two men *without* guns?"

"I don't see why we can't handle him," said Buster, matter-of-factly.

"Oh, don't you?" said Harold. "Well, count me out. I'm climbing back down to the tenth floor and calling the police." He started to crawl back to our route up.

"We don't have time!" I whispered.

"Then I'll handle him," said Buster.

"You can't do that alone," I told him. "And *you* can't let Buster jump into the Big Nehama all by himself," I told Harold.

Harold's eyes grew wide. "Who told you about my dog?" he breathed.

"You did," I said.

Harold sat back on the ledge, stunned.

"I need my flask back," Buster told me.

I handed it to him. He could tell it was lighter and gave me a suspicious look.

"I set something on fire," I explained.

For some reason, that answer satisfied Buster. He pulled off one shoe, then peeled off his long sock. (Harold and I exchanged an embarrassed look as we realized the toe needed darning.) Buster stuffed the flask into the sock, and then whirled his makeshift black-jack experimentally. He accidentally clipped his own chin.

"Definitely works," muttered Keaton, rubbing his jaw. He put his shoe back on his bare foot and tied it. "Harold, you go in first and distract him. When he comes after you, I'll sap him."

Harold took the sock-blackjack. "If you don't sap yourself first. How about *you* distract him?"

Buster shrugged. "Okay. But don't lose the flask. It was a gift from Natalie."

"Your ex-wife? Well, that's appropriate."

"Guys," I hissed. I got their attention. "Give me a slow count of sixty, then go for it."

THE CORNER WINDOW WAS OPEN. I made my way down to it and crawled in. I was super quiet. Unfortunately, some ass on the street below chose that moment to blare his horn.

Ludlo looked over as I dove for the gun on his desk.

He was too damned fast and got in front of me in a second. I pulled his hair, trying to yank him back while I grabbed for the gun.

He flung me aside with ease and turned the gun on me. "Get up!"

I obeyed.

Then he recognized me, glanced at the window, and almost laughed. "Well, if isn't David Preston, human fly!" He kept the gun on me as he patted me down.

Octavius burst in the door, gun at the ready. "How'd he get in here?"

"David here sees too many old movies," said Ludlo. "Wait outside. We have some catching up to do."

Octavius didn't like the idea, but he obeyed orders and shut the door.

"You came all the way up here, without a gun?"

"Dropped it on the way up."

This time, he did laugh. "Bad luck, old man. Well, well...it's been a long time."

"Not long enough, far as I'm concerned."

"No, it's been much too long. Three-and-a-half millennia," he said with an edge.

Of course, I realized. The patch was on his right eye, where I'd shot him in ancient Atlantis. If this were the other Ludlo, who'd had my gun explode in his hand in 1948, he'd be missing his left eye.

I had to ask. "How the hell did you survive that tsunami?"

"Call it a triumph of genetic engineering over a trillion tons of brine. I only know that when I came to, I had washed up on the shores of Rhodes. Thanks to you, I was missing my right eye, and had nearly lost my left. But that one healed. I'd also lost these two fingers to what I'm guessing was a shark.

"For the first decade or so, I had complete amnesia. A homeless idiot beggar subsisting on the Rhodians' charity. But I began to remember bits and pieces of my past. By the time I had lived a century on Rhodes, I remembered who I am. And who Ariyl is. And who you are. I knew that I had been a time traveler and was now stranded thousands of years in the past."

"With no way to get home except stay alive. How tragic."

He ignored my sarcasm. "Of course, by then most of my neighbors and acquaintances on Rhodes were dead, and their descendants considered me a sorcerer or an ageless demon. I learned not to spend too much time in any one region."

I leaned forward across the desk, putting my fists in front of the intercom. I prayed that Ludlo didn't see me flick the intercom on with my little finger.

"And who's this prick who calls himself Octavius Johnson III? Your son?"

"Yes. Not biological, though. I'm sterile. I married more women than I can count, but never sired a child. And watching a beautiful young wife grow old and ugly and bitter became tiresome. In time, I realized that I didn't need a wife. But I did need an heir. Someone who could inherit my property when I supposedly died."

"So all this Octavius Johnson stuff is about an immortal trying to hold onto his money?"

"I adopted an Octavius in every era I lived through. An adolescent boy who knew I was immortal, who resembled me enough to be believable as my son. In time he would grow too old, and I'd have to replace him. Literally. Because by then, my son was starting to look older than me."

"So you'd liquidate your holdings, relocate, and in your new city *he* would play Octavius the Elder, and you became the young Octavius. And when he died—or you killed him—you'd play Octavius the Elder again and adopt a new son."

"Bravo. It's almost like you met me back then."

"I just missed you in ancient Rome."

From the direction of the elevator lobby, I heard a soft thunk. I prayed it was Harold sapping Kobayashi.

"So you cut off Octavius's fingers to match yours, you son of a bitch!" I abruptly shouted. I had to keep Octavius listening to us.

"And to prove his loyalty. Find a kid who's young enough and hungry enough, he'll do anything to be rich. But, hey, I didn't make them lose an eye. Just wear a patch like mine. And they all agreed never to marry or have families. Loyalty to me had to be absolute."

Yet Octavius III wears a gold band, I thought to myself. Then I noticed a black smear on my own fingers, and suddenly, I knew what had happened.

"Ludlo, if you're immortal, why do you look older than me?"

He shrugged. "You can't spend thirty-five centuries living mainly outdoors and not look a little rugged. Don't worry; there'll be plenty of time for rest and soft living once I get my Crystal back."

"You look at least forty. How many of your so-called sons made it past that age?"

He gave me that killer smile. "Well, obviously, not every bright boy has the makings of a fine father. With those who became discontented with our bargain, or couldn't keep my secret, I had to skip that step."

"While they skipped the rest of their lives."

"Of course."

"And you feel no guilt about all those murders."

Ludlo shook his head, weary. "There have been so many, I literally can't remember most of their faces. But this one...he's different."

This was *not* what I wanted. I didn't want Octavius hearing how much Daddy approved of him.

"He's disposable, like all the rest," I snapped.

Ludlo permitted himself a smile. "You're wrong. He's learned so much from me."

"Like how to use Pentol?"

"A primitive form of the drug that never found a use in its discoverer's lifetime. It'll be a century before it's properly understood and refined. But it's quite adequate for our purposes."

"Yeah, kidnapping and murder. Your boy's a real chip off the old block."

"True. I really feel Octavius *is* my son, in all the important ways."

"So you let him marry and have kids. Yeah, I saw the wedding band on his finger."

Ludlo winced. "I warned him not to wear that. It exposes a weakness. But yes, I decided he should have a stake in the future I'm working to ensure."

"And that was your mistake, Ludlo. You should have read Machiavelli and stuck with adoption. You went soft and let your boy start a dynasty. You might have gotten by with it in a time when no one questioned the divine right of kings and robber barons. But this is the twentieth century."

"Or as I call it, the beginning of the end," he said sardonically.

"You let Octavius have heirs...and he took it hard that they would not inherit all of his billions, because of the inheritance taxes that liberal democracies began passing around the turn of the century."

"Exactly why democracy is so dangerous," nodded Ludlo. "The greedy, ignorant poor always outnumber their betters."

"So a decade ago, Octavius began helping destroy those democracies by financing the competition. He used his wealth to support Mussolini and the fascists in Italy, because they were friendly to the rich and the big corporations. He's been backing Hitler in Germany for the same reason."

"Big deal. That's not illegal."

"But conspiracy in assassination *is* illegal." I showed him the pictures of Octavius in Miami. "Your son on February fifteenth, with a deranged loner named Giuseppe Zangara. I think he groomed Zangara—no doubt using Pentol—to shoot FDR before his New Deal could *really* raise taxes on you."

"What you think and what you can prove are two entirely different things."

"But Zangara's bullet missed FDR and killed Mayor Cermak."

"So?"

"So, your son does sloppy work."

"Well, my friend Frank Nitti is convinced it was no mistake. Cermak was out to get Nitti, as you may know. Sent cops to kill him. So Frank was really grateful."

"So now the Chicago Outfit owes the Johnson family a favor. That explains all the legbreakers guarding this place. You don't miss a trick, do you, Ludlo?"

"I can't afford to. I can't jump out of an inconvenient era like you can." He gestured in my direction with his gun. "At least not yet."

I showed him the photo of Octavius with Chaplin. "Here's your boy in Tokyo, May fifteenth, 1932: the day a military *junta* assassinated Japan's last democratic leader. And almost got Chaplin."

Ludlo's smirk vanished.

"He didn't tell you about that little project, did he?" I asked.

"Coincidence," said Ludlo.

"Yeah, right. I'm sure J. Edgar Hoover is gonna believe that. Look, I get it. Octavius wants the fascists to win in any country. It keeps his taxes low. But why does he want to kill Charlie, too?"

"Chaplin is a leftist, which is reason enough in my book. But it's not just that." Ludlo actually sounded sad. "Octavius doesn't know the future like we do."

"Why not, Ludlo? Why not just tell your son the future you and I both know has to happen? Tell him you're a time traveler, like me!"

"He wouldn't believe me. And if he did, he'd feel betrayed for my not telling him what the Crystals are for."

"And he might get ideas. Like keeping one for himself."

"No. He won't."

"He's already got some very inconvenient ideas. Like killing FDR. Like killing Chaplin. We know neither of them can die in 1933."

"Well," Ludlo conceded sadly, "you can only teach a son so much. Then he strikes out on his own, to become his own man. Octavius thinks, like his friends in Japan did, that killing America's most beloved movie star will spark a war with the United States, which Japan would win with its superior military."

"And that's why you're here tonight. You suspected what he was up to."

Ludlo leaned forward, face to face with me. "That's why you need to turn over the Time Crystals to me, Preston. If we leave tonight up to Octavius, his pal Kobayashi will behead Chaplin, and then commit *seppuku*, like a true samurai. It'll be in every paper in America. And there's your war. Now, you don't want that, do you?"

"No. Because *that* war is supposed to be fought eight years from now," I replied. "And by then it will be too late for Japan to beat America. But the thing is, *you* can't afford for Japan to win. You've figured out that you can't allow any big change in history until N-Tec is invented."

Ludlo sat back in his chair, keeping the gun leveled at me. "I don't know what you're talking about," he said coolly.

"Sure you do." I held up my blackened fingers. "You're dyeing your hair. That craggy face isn't just the result of a hard outdoor life. You're not really immortal! It's taken thirty-five centuries, but you're getting *old*."

Ludlo shook his head but didn't waste his breath denying it.

"I estimate you're aging at least a year every century," I went on. "Probably more. I bet if we washed that black out, your hair would be whiter than Chaplin's. That's why you need to keep history intact until N-Tec is invented. You need N-Tec...at least till it clones you a new, young body."

Ludlo gave a mirthless chuckle. "Well, Ariyl always did like guys with brains. Regrettably, I'll have to do something about yours now." He aimed his pistol at my forehead. "Last chance. Where are the Crystals?"

"You're desperate to escape this era. I don't blame you. You can't control your boy Octavius anymore. Assassination, treason, and a few minutes ago, two of Nitti's men murdered...he'll lead the law right to you. And I won't give you the Crystals. So you *know* you have to kill your boy tonight."

Ludlo gave a reluctant sigh. "I know...but you first."

He cocked his gun.

The door burst open. It was Octavius, his pistol pointed at Ludlo. Heard it all on the intercom. Tears in his eyes. "Lying son of a bitch!"

"Shoot him now—he's faster than you!" I said as I hit the floor.

Gunfire erupted over my head.

34

LIKE FATHER, UNLIKE SON

A STRAY BULLET EXPLODED THE OVERHEAD light fixture, plunging the room into darkness. There were eleven or twelve shots. I lost count because I was too busy crawling toward the door. Then an eerie silence settled on the room.

I reached up, opened the door, and saw Ariyl crouching behind the desk.

"You okay?" I mouthed.

She nodded.

Behind me all was still.

"Ludlo!" I called. "Still want those Crystals?"

No answer.

"Octavius?"

Still nothing.

Harold and Buster ran into the outer office.

"Get down!" I hissed.

They dropped behind the desk, with Ariyl.

"You okay, Blondie?" asked Buster.

"Yeah. But I could sure use a drink," she said.

Buster reached in his pocket and pulled out his flask and

removed the sock. "Aw, look," he said in dismay. "That big jerk dented it."

"Kobayashi?" I asked.

"Out like a light," said Harold.

"But it took a few tries," said Buster, inspecting the damage to his flask.

I motioned everyone else to stay down and pushed the door wide open. Light from the outer office spilled into the corner suite. The first thing I saw was Octavius lying on the floor, a bullet hole drilled through the center of his forehead; he was also leaking from several other less-lethal holes in his arms and side.

Harold shook his head. "I warned him not to circle that fountain."

Ludlo's feet stretched out from behind his desk. I kicked him. He didn't stir.

I checked Octavius's gun—six spent shells. Apparently, at least one had done the job on his adoptive dad.

I picked up Ludlo's gun and opened the chamber. There was one unfired round. I snapped it back.

Abruptly, I felt the back of my neck caught in a steel vise, while a powerful hand snatched the gun from my hand, and pointed it at Ariyl.

If Ludlo was unconscious a second ago, he was now awake—weakened, but homicidal as ever.

"Forgive the cliché, but everybody, hands up," said Ludlo. "Now, back up, nice and slow. Nobody do anything stupid or the girl gets it first."

Ariyl, Buster, and Harold complied.

My feet were barely touching the floor as Ludlo held me by the scruff. He walked me into the lobby. I saw Kobayashi sprawled face-down near the elevators, blood trickling from a big knot on his temple. There was more blood by the trash chute, and the lobby smelled of turpentine.

Ludlo was bleeding profusely from two gunshot wounds in his chest, which were soaking his shirt, but since they'd missed his heart, I had the sinking feeling that he was going to recover.

"Let David go, Ludlo," pleaded Ariyl.

"Never tell me what to do," he said calmly.

She immediately shut up.

"She doesn't know where the Crystals are," I told him, wincing in pain. "Hurt her and I promise you'll never see them again."

"I can live with that," he hissed at me. "I'm almost home. Another century and a half, and I can get a new body. My problem is the same as yours right now: how to put history back together so nothing interferes with N-Tec. That entails wiping some memories."

"Maybe we can help each other," I suggested. Then I groaned as he tightened his grip.

"You just forced me to kill my favorite son," seethed Ludlo. "So you need to shut up right now. It's taking all my patience not to snap your scrawny neck like a twig."

He looked at the three comedians: Lloyd and Keaton, both glancing around, no doubt looking for something, anything to use against Ludlo; and Chaplin, weaving even while standing still.

"Well, Chaplin's flying high on that mickey. He's not going to remember this," said Ludlo. He peered into Buster's semi-bleary eyes. "Keaton, I need you to sober up a bit before the Pentol will work on you. Lloyd, hold these for me."

Ludlo dug a glass pill bottle out of his coat. He stuffed it into Harold's breast pocket, while keeping his gun on Ariyl. "Remember what I said, boys."

He punched the call button for the elevator, then backed into the office, picked up the phone, and spoke to some mope in the lobby. "This is the senior Mr. Johnson. I'm sending three genuine movie stars down in the elevator. Be polite but keep your guns on them till I get there."

With a chime, the elevator opened. I nodded at Buster and Harold. Whatever I tried now with Ludlo, it would be better if they and Charlie were out of harm's way.

Keaton and Lloyd took Chaplin's arms and rolled him into the elevator. Ludlo punched the button for the lobby.

Charlie looked at Buster and Harold. "You're not going to leave that poor girl up here?" he protested, as the doors slid shut.

Ludlo threw me at Ariyl, who caught me from falling and put me back on my feet.

"Now, I'm quite sure you two are unnecessary to the invention of N-Tec," said Ludlo. "I've waited three thousand, five hundred long, lonely years for this moment. The only problem I have is, how do I kill the two people I loathe the most with only one bullet?"

"You think you're lonely now? You think you'll feel better if you kill the only people who know what you've been through?" asked Ariyl.

"Oh, I'm sure of it, sweetheart."

"But you don't hate Ariyl, Ludlo," I said. "It's me you hate. I wrecked all your plans. Shoot me."

"Ah, how noble," he sneered. "No doubt that's why she chose you. And that's why *she* gets the bullet. But not before she gives me some compensation for all I've suffered at both your hands."

"Jesus, every time I think you can't sink lower..." I spat.

"Oh, you think I'm going to rape her? Or torture her?"

"Wouldn't it be pretty to think that you're above those things," I said.

"You lack imagination, Preston. I got over my lust for Ariyl ages ago. And as for torture, mere pain is nothing compared to guilt, grief, and horror. So Ariyl: since my poor, unfortunate son Octavius died after giving you Pentol, I want you to beat his killer, your lover David, to death. With your bare hands."

"No! Please don't make me!" said Ariyl, aghast.

"Yes. And I want it to be slow. Don't rush it. Break every bone in his body, but start small and work your way up. Pace yourself."

I launched myself at Ludlo. Better a bullet than let him do this to her.

Ariyl shoved me into the outer office before Ludlo had a chance to shoot me. He smiled to see me in a heap on the floor.

Ariyl slowly came toward me as I got up.

"Ariyl, this isn't you!"

"I know it isn't! But I can't stop! I have to do what he says!"

"No you don't!" I yelled, as I slammed the heavy wood door and threw the bolt.

"Yes, she does," said Ludlo.

"Yes, I do!" Her fist smashed through the oak door. She battered it to splinters.

I grabbed a wooden hatrack, thinking I could knock the wind out of her long enough to get by her. I rammed it into her stomach.

She barely grunted. Then she broke the hatrack in two.

I dove under the desk—a second later, she flung it aside, grabbed my collar and thigh, raised me over her head, stepped through the doorway, and threw me across the elevator lobby.

I bounced off the sofa and skidded to a halt near the mobsters' bloodstain.

Ariyl came stalking toward me.

"Ariyl, you're not his puppet!"

"But I am, David! I'm sorry!"

I threw the chrome ashtray at her—she batted it aside.

"Fight him!" I threw a chair at her.

She smacked it into kindling.

I knew it was pointless, but I broke the next chair against her. "Tell him no!"

She kept coming.

"Enough with breaking furniture," said Ludlo. "Start in on his fingers."

I turned to run—God knows where—and suddenly I saw what Ariyl was marching toward. What she'd thrown me toward.

The turpentine can.

I turned back, and she winked at me. She'd gotten that swig of Keaton's flask after all!

I "tripped" backward and fell right next to the can. I hoped this worked.

Ariyl reached down to grab me, but grabbed the open can instead. Then she turned and splashed it in Ludlo's face. He screamed, clutched at his one good eye, and fired blindly at Ariyl.

The flame from the muzzle ignited the turpentine.

Ludlo suddenly looked like the Human Torch. Or maybe just Ghost Rider. Still screaming, he charged Ariyl, grabbed her throat in a stranglehold, and slammed her against the wall. Flames leapt from his head to hanging curtains, and ignited the turpentine spills on his pant leg and the floor.

I leapt up, grabbing the broken chrome ashtray to crack Ludlo's skull, if I could.

Then I heard a guttural growl and turned to see Kobayashi coming at me with his *katana* raised. I blocked his first swing with the ashtray. But it was a clumsy club against a samurai blade.

Ding! The elevator doors opened. Harold and Buster were back—they'd only gone down partway. They left Charlie in the elevator as they ran to my aid.

Buster swung the flask in his sock like David warming up for Goliath. Caught between us, Kobayashi retreated a step and took aim at Buster.

"The place is on fire!" yelled Harold.

The fire raced along the turpentine spill into the janitor's closet, which must have been packed with solvents. There was an explosion and a fireball that turned the closet into a bonfire.

Ariyl broke Ludlo's chokehold, picked up a metal table, and used it to push the still-flaming Ludlo against the wall.

Buster and I kept double-teaming Kobayashi.

Harold grabbed the fire hose nozzle and tried to crank the valve wheel. Which wouldn't budge.

Though completely blotto, Charlie helpfully rolled over to Harold, and held the nozzle for him while Harold strained with both hands to turn the valve. At last it gave with a loud squeak. The hose stiffened, then came alive with pressure.

Harold had forgotten Charlie was in skates, and the hose pressure began whipsawing the Tramp back and forth.

The torrent hit Ludlo, extinguishing his flames. He threw Ariyl back from him, then plunged through the wall of fire coming from the closet. I couldn't see him after that—he was on the other side of an impassable barrier of flame.

The floor was slick with water. Charlie's uncontrolled torrent hit Harold in the face and knocked him down. Then me.

I heard a feral roar. As I wiped the water from my eyes, I saw Kobayashi come at Charlie, sword raised. Buster grabbed the back of the hose and used it to whip Charlie out of Kobayashi's path. The *katana* sliced down on the hose instead, right at the standpipe.

The gush of water threw Kobayashi against the window, shattering the glass. Partway out, Kobayashi clung to the frame with his left hand. Harold grabbed his right hand and tried to peel the sword from his fingers. Kobayashi wrenched his hand away from Harold and raised his blade to decapitate the comic.

Meanwhile, Charlie politely picked up Kobayashi's dropped scabbard—not seeing the cord that was looped around the man's heel. When Chaplin handed it to him, it yanked the samurai's foot up. Kobayashi toppled backward out the window with a vanishing scream.

Charlie looked around, holding the sheath and wondering where its owner had gone.

I smashed the glass on the fire alarm and pulled the handle. Lacking a viable fire hose, we could not fight the raging inferno that was blocking us from the elevators and the stairway.

"We've got to get down to the tenth floor!" shouted Harold.

Buster took the slashed hose and knotted it around the standpipe. "Ladies first," he said gallantly.

Ariyl tugged the hose hard to be sure it would hold, then grabbed Charlie and slung him over her shoulder. She climbed out the window, and with one hand gripping the hose, slid down to the tenth floor and climbed in the window.

Buster and Harold watched her go, jaws slack.

"Wish I could find a girl like yours," Buster told me.

"You will in about seven years," I told him.

"You next!" said Harold.

I didn't argue. I went down the hose, and Ariyl pulled me in. Buster came next, speeding up suddenly as the knot slipped half a foot.

"I don't think that knot's gonna hold!" he shouted up to Harold.

"Guess I'll find out!" said Harold, ducking below flames that roared out the top floor window. He scrambled out and slid down. At that instant, the knot came undone, the hose came loose, and Harold fell.

35

MOPPING UP

AROLD LANDED IN ARIYL'S OUTSTRETCHED hands, outside the tenth floor window.

"Safe as in your mother's arms," she smiled, bringing him inside.

"Safer," he gasped. "Thank you, Miss Moro. Now, please...put me down."

Fire engine sirens came wailing down Flower Street.

* * *

WE TOOK the stairs down to the street, emerging at the back of the building. It was just the five of us, no witnesses.

"Harold, Buster," I began. "About what you overheard on Octavius's intercom..."

"I wasn't listening," Buster assured us. "Especially that part about time travel."

"Time *what* now?" hiccupped Charlie.

Harold stared at me and Ariyl. "I don't know which story is more fantastic," said Harold. "You two as G-Men or you two coming from the future. Frankly, I liked it better when you were just a couple of gate crashers. At least nobody would fit me for a straitjacket if I told them that."

"I think your instinct is sound," I replied. "That's all you need to tell them. Now we'd better get back to the party, before you're missed."

"I'll go get the car," said Harold. "Buster, watch Charlie."

Buster nodded, then hurried after Charlie, who was slowly rolling backwards toward Figueroa Street.

"Be right back," I told Ariyl.

I HURRIED around the front of the building, where the Los Angeles Fire Department was on the scene.

From what I overheard, their ladders were too short, but an intrepid team had gone up the stairs on the far side of the fire and were already knocking down the flames with the fire hose from that side of the building. White steam now replaced the black smoke pouring out of the twelfth floor windows.

A uniformed police captain was talking to a curly-haired, sharp-featured young woman in a sailor frock with anchor insignia, as they watched the mop-up operation. The legbreakers came out of the lobby, each accompanied by a pair of burly plainclothes LAPD in fedoras.

"Strictly off the record, these hoods work for Frank Nitti," he told her. "My boys are giving them an escort to the depot. Just to make sure they don't miss their train back to Chicago."

"What about the Japanese guy who fell out the window?"

"The G-Men just took charge of him. My guess is he was a spy, but of course, you can't quote me."

"Captain, at least can I get pictures of the blaze?"

"What blaze, Aggie?"

My God—this was a younger Agness Underwood, the reporter Ariyl and I had met in 1954. My instinct was to turn away so she wouldn't recognize me; then I realized not only was that two decades in the future, but that meeting was in the 1954 that we had erased.

"You can't cover all this up, Captain!" Agness asserted. "I heard one of those mopes say there are still six men missing in that building."

"Aggie, you're new to this game. I could be a big help to you, but you need to learn how to play ball. The Richfield Oil Company is a major employer in this town, and they don't want to read about every little trashcan fire in their headquarters. Or any mob scandals."

"We'll see what the editor of the *Record* has to say about that."

"I already phoned the *publisher*, Aggie. But you go ahead and talk to your boss. Have a good night."

I GOT BACK TO BUSTER, Charlie, and Ariyl.

"They're going to cover it up," I told Ariyl. "It won't even make the papers. The only problem is the six missing men."

The stairwell door burst off its hinges, thanks to a very large black woman slamming her butt against it. This was understandable, since she had her hands full: she had a topcoat-wearing mook draped over each shoulder, and another tucked under each arm.

Buster's jaw dropped as she backed out onto the street carrying the four men, then laid them on the sidewalk.

"Make that just two missing men," said Dylila Duprae.

"Dylila! When did you get here?" gasped Ariyl.

"Not soon enough, obviously," she said. "I couldn't get to the fire. I had to carry these goons down eleven flights."

I checked the groaning men—they were bruised, but not burned. "Smoke inhalation?" I asked.

"Attitude adjustment. I told them to evacuate. They picked the wrong time to lay hands on me. Not after a night of rich white folks copping a 'tude with me."

I looked at Dylila and realized she was wearing a maid's uniform. "You were at Harold Lloyd's party? As a maid?"

"Only way I could get in without causing a riot. Didn't even notice me, did you, Davy?"

"Well, I wasn't really paying attention to the help...uh, the servan..."

"Stop digging, David," suggested Ariyl.

"...uh, no I didn't see you."

"Typical." She touched her shoulder. "*French* maid's outfit." SmartFab shrank her demure hemline to miniskirt level and her neckline receded, revealing Dylila's epic bust and sculpted legs. She looked like a Frederick's of Hollywood catalogue. She smiled teasingly. "Bet you'd have noticed me in this."

Buster was still gaping, as was Charlie, who started rolling backwards again. Buster caught him without taking his eyes off Dylila.

"Anyway, I saw *you*, just before you took off in Lloyd's car. By the time I could grab my own ride, you had quite a head start. So what happened here?"

"David owes you an apology, that's what happened," put in Ariyl.

"I thought you were the one who was tipping off the Octavius Johnson family about where to invest," I admitted.

"Why would I do that?"

"Okay, I was wrong! Sorry! It was Jon Ludlo. He survived the Atlantis tsunami. He lived the last thirty-five hundred years quietly profiting off his knowledge of the future."

"And where is he now?"

"He got away during the fire."

"Goddamnit, David!"

"Why is he still part of history? You told me you'd erased his trip!"

"I did! I took him back to 2109. N-Tec was fine. We erased Ludlo's trip and put a freeze on all further Time Crystal trips. But when I went for the lost plays of Sophocles and returned—bam. N-Tec was gone again. Ice age. Maybe there are no stable futures where Ludlo didn't travel in time. But you weren't need-to-know on that. I just needed you to stop Ariyl."

"Why did you send me to *save* Lincoln, then?" demanded Ariyl. "That history ends in an ice age, too!"

"Because I was desperate, girl. I still am. It's like nothing we do stops that ice age, and I don't know how it starts."

"We tried a third timeline where Ariyl became emperor of Rome in 192 A.D.," I told her. "Our idea was to ban slavery and introduce industrialization and human rights. But sometime before 869 A.D., the ice age began."

"That's more than a thousand years early! Were these both nuclear winter?" asked Dylila.

"Not in the history where Lincoln lived. Not enough radioactivity," I replied.

"And I would never have allowed nuclear weapons in *my* Rome," said Ariyl.

Dylila gave a slow smile. "192 A.D., huh? Did you kick Commodus's ass?"

Ariyl grinned.

"Honey, I knew you would," chuckled Dylila.

"Seriously? You two are talking about using time travel to relive your favorite vidz?"

"Says the man who can't keep away from Flat-flix Hollywood," laughed Ariyl.

"Not just favorite vidz, favorite activities," smirked Dylila.

Whatever the hell that meant.

The fire was now out, and the first engine company was packing up their hoses and equipment.

Dylila gazed up at the Art Deco treasure and shook her head in admiration.

"Quite a gem, huh?" I asked. I couldn't resist tweaking her. "Even rich white folks can produce a work of art now and then."

"And you saved it tonight," she said. "But in 1969, your people will take a wrecking ball to it."

I gave a philosophical shrug. "It was a miracle it lasted forty years. This town treats its great buildings like old sets cluttering up the backlot. So in its place, we now have a couple of giant glass stereo speakers."

"The rich men who run your oil firms don't give a shit about a sustainable climate. So don't be surprised they'd smash a beautiful jewel."

I didn't argue. She was right.

"You know, this is right where I found Khutulun," remarked

Dylila. "She ran all the way from the hospital. Almost a mile. But this —she just stopped and stared. Classic Stendhal Syndrome."

"Well, L.A.'s not exactly Florence, but coming from the yurts of Mongolia, it must have blown her mind." I paused. "Did she...?"

"Don't ask. I took her where she belongs."

"Dylila, why don't you trust me a little bit? If I'd known you were here, I'd have asked for your help. As it was, we wound up risking the lives of three irreplaceable geniuses."

Keaton looked around, then at Chaplin. "Who, us?"

Harold pulled up and honked. Then he did a huge take at Dylila's spectacular version of a French maid.

Dylila nodded, "Who now need their memories wiped."

36

THE PARTY'S OVER

H AROLD GOT US BACK TO HIS ESTATE BEFORE IT was time to bid his guests goodnight. Everyone was having such a great time that nobody realized their host had been gone, which if you ask me, is the mark of a truly excellent party.

No one was at the front of the house when we pulled up. It seemed they were all out on the patio; we could hear Eddie Cantor singing "My Baby Just Cares For Me."

Lloyd let us out of his Rolls. Dylila (now back to her more period-appropriate uniform) tried to return her borrowed car to its original spot. Alas, someone had parked behind her and there was barely room.

"If you don't know how to parallel park, I'd be happy to guide you," I said condescendingly.

"No need, thank you," said Dylila, lifting the rear of the car off the ground and setting it against the curb, then doing the same for the front end.

I thought Lloyd was going to faint. After witnessing that feat, he was more than eager to give Ariyl the bottle of Pentol pills from Ludlo. From a passing waiter, Ariyl took two more *profiteroles*; she crushed the pills and inserted the drug into the cream filling.

All the exercise and tossing his cookies had largely sobered up Keaton. Chaplin, on the other hand, was still looped on whatever Octavius had given him.

"Don't worry about Charlie," I told Ariyl and Dylila. "He won't recall a thing." I was so sure, that I said it right in front of him.

Charlie nodded in sad agreement. "No, I expect I won't," he slurred. He kissed Ariyl's hand. "You shall be the exquisite dream I will never quite recall."

"Aww!" said Ariyl.

I thought it was a safe assumption W. C. Fields—who was dozing peacefully sitting on a bench—would be in the same blackout condition. The rest of the guests hadn't seen enough to affect history.

Winston, Lloyd's chauffeur, helped Charlie into the passenger compartment of the Rolls. Eddie Cantor walked by the Tramp and did a double take.

"Chaplin was here in makeup? Say, maybe I should have done my numbers in blackface!"

Then he turned and found himself looking up at Dylila. Now those banjo eyes were more like bass fiddles.

"On second thought, I should have done them on the radio. Goodnight!" He hurried off into the dark.

So I was pretty sure it was only to Harold and Buster we needed to slip the Pentol. Ariyl coaxed them both into sampling a dessert for her. "Just one bite and I promise I'll leave you alone from now on."

Harold immediately gobbled one. "It's a deal."

"Now, wasn't that tasty?"

"Sure was, Blondie," said Buster. "But you don't have to leave *me* alone." Then he yawned. "I need to get home and get some sleep."

Harold again offered him a ride home.

Buster demurred, "Naah, it's just three blocks down on Sunset."

"When did you buy a home in Beverly Hills?" asked Harold, surprised.

"I didn't buy it in Beverly Hills. I bought it in Culver City. I just parked it in Beverly Hills."

"Buster...you're living in a trailer?"

"It's a motor home. And a nice one," insisted Buster. "I just hope it hasn't gotten a ticket. The cops in this town are pretty strict."

"How long has this been going on?"

"Since MGM gave me the boot. You know, Natalie got the house."

"Oh, Buster. I'm so sorry. I wish you'd listened to me instead of giving up your studio. Those money-grubbers at Metro haven't a clue about how to make comedy."

"Charlie gave me the same advice. I didn't listen. I couldn't believe that MGM, with so many smart, talented people, would try to stop me from doing what I know how to do. I got tired of fighting 'em, Harold. So now, I just fight for someplace I can park my home."

"Not anymore, you don't," said Harold. "You bring it up the drive and park it right here at Greenacres, for as long as you want."

Moved, Buster took his hand. "Thanks, pal."

A moment later both began to look dizzy. The Pentol was kicking in.

Ariyl put her arms on their shoulders.

"You two will have nothing more to drink tonight. You will forget about everything about David and me and Dylila, the fire at the Richfield Building, Mr. Kobayashi, and Octavius Johnson. You never left the party. You had a wonderful time...and of course, Harold just invited Buster to park his trailer here."

They both nodded obediently. Then Ariyl came over to Dylila and me.

I still had the nagging feeling I was forgetting someone.

"Look, David..." began Dylila.

"Yes?"

Just then Lloyd walked past the three of us and gave us a puzzled look. "Are you off duty?" he asked Dylila.

"Yes, sir," she said quietly.

"Well, then pick up your wages at the kitchen." Then he gave Ariyl and me a polite, clueless smile. "So nice to see you," he said, moving on.

"These *people*," fumed Dylila, shaking her head. "I have had it with twentieth-century male arrogance."

. . .

DYLILA BECKONED TO US, and we walked into a secluded grove of trees on the slope leading to the golf course.

"As I was saying before we were so rudely interrupted, I only recruited you, David, because I was hard up. But I underestimated you. For a pre-Changer, you did all right."

"Speaking as a man born in the twentieth century, I thank you," I said dryly. "How did you track us down, anyway?"

"After I sent you to 1865, I decided to see if the Crystal would now let me travel any later than November 2016. I wound up at your apartment house in March 2018. I just missed your visit by one day, but I ran into your neighbor, Professor Bergstrom. Apparently, you'd described me pretty closely," she said with a knowing look.

I wondered if Sven told her about my books; it didn't seem prudent to ask.

"Now, I need you to give back your Time Crystal," said Dylila, putting out her palm. "Both of you."

"We don't have them," admitted Ariyl. "David hid them."

"Well, then he better unhide them," said Dylila.

"I'd rather not, just yet," I said.

Her temper rising, Dylila did that thing where she moved her head sideways on her neck. "You'd 'rather not'?"

"Until we come to an understanding. I think you're going to need my help, and I can do that a lot more effectively without having to constantly hitch a ride and have my opinion discounted because I'm a man."

"*David...*" warned Ariyl, quietly.

"Are you telling me how to do my job?" Dylila asked, incredulous.

"Not at all. But I think you'll find I'm a lot more useful as a full partner in this situation, than as some lackey you drag into service as a last resort."

"How about I just drag your ass all over this golf course and teach you some manners?"

"Physically, I couldn't stop you."

266

"You are so right, little man."

"But you already tried dangling me over a seven-story drop, and that didn't make me cooperate."

"Dylila, he did help me find Octavius Johnson. I couldn't have done it without him," put in Ariyl. "And he found Ludlo."

"You want this pre-Change male working with us? As an equal?" demanded Dylila.

Ariyl slipped her arm around my waist. "Yes. I want him."

Dylila was fuming mad. Her eyes drilled into me. "This is payback for me tossing you around at Château Élysée, isn't it?"

"Well, maybe a little. And payback is a bit—"

Ariyl's eyes widened, and Dylila's narrowed.

"—of a bastard," I said. A last second-edit seemed wise.

"All right," she rumbled, fists on hips. "Get the Crystals, before I change my mind."

"Happy to. You won't regret this, Dylila."

"I already do."

At that moment, Oliver Hardy, his lower half soaking wet, came stalking angrily through the grove. Soon as he saw Dylila, he smacked her loudly on her ass and said, "Hiya, sugah!"

She turned to him, and a look of horror crossed his face as he realized what he'd done.

"Oh, no, I didn't mean...whoooaaaa! Ohhh, Stan, ooooohh, hellllp!"

Hardy's tenor howls carried across the estate as Dylila threw him around over her head like a street performer spinning one of those arrow ad signs.

A MINUTE LATER, having explained to Dylila the comedian's Pentol-fueled misbehavior, Ariyl ministered to a very dizzy Hardy.

"I've never been so embarrassed in my life. I don't understand why I did it," the comedian told Ariyl. "I didn't touch a drop tonight."

"That's why," said Ariyl.

"Huh?" said Hardy.

"Don't worry, in a little while it'll be like it never happened," she soothed. "By the way, I saw *The Music Box*. I think you and Mr. Laurel are the funniest men I've ever seen in my life."

Mr. Hardy beamed and twiddled his tie.

I went into the house to retrieve the Time Crystals from Harold Lloyd's Christmas tree.

As I came out, I joined a parade of stellar guests heading to their cars: Gary Cooper, Marlene Dietrich, Ronald Colman, Jack Benny, Mae West, Joe E. Brown, Edward Everett Horton...

Dylila gently tapped me on the shoulder.

"Pick me up at the bus stop down on Sunset," said Dylila. "And don't make me have to track you down again." She waited a moment, then added with a trace of a smile, "Please."

She strode down the drive, passing two men who didn't even notice her. The big one was squishing and leaving wet footprints with every step.

"You wiped Hardy's memory, right?" I whispered to Ariyl.

"And told him what to say if anyone asked about tonight."

As if on cue, we heard Stan Laurel ask his partner, "Say, what were you howling about? And how'd you get all wet?"

Hardy replied loftily, "I have *nothing* to say."

Stan started to laugh. He was going to use that line.

ARIYL PUT her hand out to me. "Car key, please. If we're putting the future back together right, we can't let that poor salesman lose his job." She walked down to the car, while I lingered, eavesdropping on Lloyd and Keaton.

Buster pointed down the driveway and told Harold, "I'll just go get my home and be right back." He turned on his heel and marched off toward Sunset Boulevard.

"He'll be all right," I said. "Eventually." I left out the fact that Buster would endure another seven years of blackout drinking and one more bad marriage, be put in a mental hospital to dry out, and literally escape from a straitjacket...before he found happiness and married Eleanor Norris.

Harold nodded, but he wasn't really paying attention to me.

His wife came over to him. "Greenacres," he mused to Mildred. "What do you think of that for a name?"

She squeezed his hand. "I'll drink to that."

A petite, pretty brunette tugged on Harold's sleeve and chirped in a high voice. "Harold, Mildred, thank you so much for having us! We had such a wonderful time!"

The brunette's husband took out his cigar. "Say, who was that giant blonde I saw out here an hour ago? I glimpsed her from across the lawn when she lifted a man over her head. With one hand," he added, incredulous.

Harold frowned, bewildered. "I have no idea who you're talking about."

I gave an innocent shrug.

"Oh, George, you just had too much to drink. I better drive," said his wife, taking his car key.

"Maybe you better. I saw a lot of strongwoman acts in vaudeville, but I never saw a woman pick up a man so easy."

"Well, *sure* you have," smiled his wife. "Me!"

He blinked at us. "Say goodnight, Gracie."

"Goodnight!"

37

THE SINGLE CHANGEABLE TIMELINE

J UNE EIGHTEENTH, 1954. WE WERE IN ANOTHER borrowed auto. Rented, actually. The best we could afford was a compact Nash Rambler convertible.

From the lower gate, we buzzed for entry. Harold Lloyd was at home. In fact, he answered the buzzer. "I'd be happy to see you again, David. As long as you leave your matches at the gate."

So he remembered my previous visit. But the acid test was yet to come.

"It's a deal," I replied. "I brought along a couple of lady friends. I took them to see *Girl Shy*, and they can't wait to meet you."

"That's peachy! The more the merrier. I'll buzz you in."

With a hum, the electric gate opened.

The Nash wound its way up the long drive. But when we parked, I asked Ariyl and Dylila to wait in the car while I rang the bell.

Harold, now sixty-one, opened his own door and smiled at seeing me and shook my hand with his left.

"Well, if it isn't my young fan!" Then he gave me an odd look. "David...have we met before?"

"Yes. Three days ago."

"Oh, I remember that, believe me. The Lady and the Tiger. But before then, perhaps? Were you ever here for a party?" I started to answer, then he shook his head. "Naah. You're too young. You just have one of those faces." He looked at the car. "Please, invite your lady friends in!"

I waved to the car. "Thanks, Harold. They're huge fans."

Ariyl and Dylila unfolded their mile-long legs from the small car and bounded up the steps. Harold looked up at them, awed.

"You weren't kidding."

"*Girl Shy* was hilarious!" said Ariyl.

"I loved *Speedy*," said Dylila. "It's like a trip back in time to old Manhattan."

"Speaking of a Manhattan, could I offer you ladies a drink?"

"I'd like an Orange Blossom," said Ariyl, as the amazons each took one of Harold's arms.

"You know it's funny...that was Charlie Chaplin's favorite drink," said Harold. "Do you know who he was?"

"Of course!" laughed Dylila.

"*And* Buster Keaton," said Ariyl.

* * *

WE HAD A LOVELY VISIT. The ladies kept dropping hints about the events of that night, but though Harold kept staring at them in that *déjà vu* way, it was clear he didn't have any conscious memory of them.

Harold was quite the charmer. He pulled a coin out of Dylila's ear (he was an expert magician) and when he mentioned being a handball champion, Ariyl said she'd love to play him. I gave her a please-don't look, and she let it drop.

I mentioned the Marx Brothers, W. C. Fields, Laurel and Hardy, Burns and Allen...eliciting only Harold's fond professional admiration, but no memories regarding his *Duck Soup* party.

Finally, I asked him directly if he had any further dreams about Octavius Johnson.

He got a funny smile on his face.

"I had one just the other night. But it wasn't terrifying like the others. It was like the end to a really thrilling picture. I actually woke up feeling relieved. Exhilarated, even."

I made excuses that we had to leave. Lloyd was sad to see the visit end. He asked if the ladies would consider posing for him sometime. Oh, no, I thought, bracing myself for the feminist backlash.

"That's very flattering, Harold," smiled Dylila. "I know you've had some important stars pose for you. We'll see."

Whew.

As he walked us to the door, Harold looked out his window and down at the drive. "Oh, Ferdinand brought back the Rolls," Harold noted. "He's blocked you. I'll get him to move it."

Dylila took a gander. "It's okay. I can handle it."

All at once, Harold looked spooked. "I'm sure you can." Then he shook it off. "But please remember..."

"Don't drive around the fountain," we all said in unison.

On the way out, Ariyl nudged Dylila and pointed to a framed nude that I recognized as my Little Miss Black Belt. Ariyl whispered something to Dylila, and they both cracked up as they went out the door.

"What?" I demanded, following them out.

"Move it, Mr. Movie Buff, we have to get this car back to Hertz!" said Ariyl, hurrying down the steps.

"Oh, come on, this isn't fair. At least give me a hint who she is!" I said as they ran to the car, leaving me farther behind.

"Faster, pussycat!" laughed Dylila, getting behind the wheel.

I managed to jump in the back seat as she backed and filled perfectly in one try...then went down the driveway in reverse at fifty miles an hour.

* * *

WITH OCTAVIUS JOHNSON III having died in 1933, the Time Crystals seemed to be functioning at top efficiency again, delivering us to Sven's apartment as directed, just one day after we'd left him, on

March sixteenth, 2018. Two days before the big Preston family meeting.

"I only got a brief look," I reported to Sven. "But I know for sure the Rolls had a different color windscreen frame and mirrors. They were chrome replacements, not the brass originals that were on the car when Ferdinand gave me a lift just three days earlier."

"See? The universe changed. And yet, Harold Lloyd remembered you. Just as I remember every detail of your last visit. And yours, Miss Duprae," said Sven.

"But Harold didn't remember us being at the party," Ariyl pointed out.

"Only because you used Pentol to erase his memory. He still dreamed of Octavius, and even his dream has changed. I think the three of you have conclusively proved that we are dealing with a single changeable timeline," concluded the old physicist.

"Which ends with this world under a glacier," said Ariyl gloomily.

"Not necessarily, Ariyl. You now know that Jon Ludlo is the fly in the ointment. We must assume that he's still alive, throughout history. And something he does between 1933 and 2016 leads to the new ice age. Would you like my advice?"

My instinct was to say, "Hell yes!" But I was walking on eggshells with Dylila, who I knew was not happy with sharing her time cop role with me and Ariyl. It didn't seem smart to usurp her authority.

So I turned to her. As did Ariyl.

After a moment, Dylila nodded. "Go on, Professor."

"Please, call me Sven."

"What do you recommend, Sven?"

"Actually, it's two-fold. First, you need to carefully explore the twentieth and twenty-first centuries, and see if you can figure out the exact act by Ludlo that triggers the ice age and prevent it."

"Are we sure it was Ludlo?" asked Dylila.

"Well, how many Time Crystals are there in existence?" asked Sven.

"Only three. Two for travel, one for Quality Control. And they are all in this room."

"Good. David tells me we can trust you, Dylila, and that's good enough for me. So who else would be warping history for his own ends? It has to be Ludlo, the one time traveler whose actions we can't account for. Even without a Time Crystal, Ludlo's foreknowledge gives him the power to change history."

"I'm still trying to figure out how Dylila can cancel his trip, and yet he's still back in time."

"There are now two competing timelines, David. One where Ludlo's trip was canceled so he never left 2109, and one where he did go, got stuck back in 1628 B.C., and is still alive today. It's just like Schrödinger's cat. But in this single changeable timeline, eventually the probability wave collapses. We want it to collapse into a viable future."

"What's the second part of your advice?" asked Dylila.

"If you can't identify and prevent the ice age disaster, you will have one very risky tactic left to you: track down Ludlo in some era that you have not yet visited, and kill him. Probably somewhere in ancient times would be best."

"But...that would erase everything we just did in 1933," I said. "You won't even remember what we did or why we had to go."

"I'm not important. I'm not a time traveler. You three will still have your memories," said Sven. "But you must never again revisit any era you have already traveled to."

"But we already did that," said Ariyl. "Twice. Saving Lincoln, then letting him die again...and overthrowing Commodus, then erasing that."

"Those were unavoidable; you had to undo your changes to the timestream. But interacting with your past selves is unspeakably dangerous. You might injure or kill them by accident. Or deliberately, as you did to Ludlo."

"Yeah, yeah, I vaporized an entire timeline! No one is *ever* going to let me live that down," Ariyl pouted.

"Okay," I ticked off on my fingers. "No changing major historical events, and no revisiting our own past selves. Anything else?"

"I can't think of anything at the moment."

"So what do we do next?" I asked Dylila.

"We're no longer under the gun, timewise," she said. "Ludlo has no Time Crystal, so whatever he's done is already done. I think we all need some rest."

"And I'd like a couple days to settle my affairs," I said.

What I meant was, I had that damn family meeting Sunday night, where I planned to alleviate my parents' concerns prior to our departure. But also, before we left I would dictate a narrative of our latest travels for Sven.

Not that I wanted Dylila to know that.

"Could we just do something fun today? Like see Disneyland?" said Ariyl.

"Um...sure," I said. What I really wanted to do was sleep for a week. "I have to warn you, it's the start of a weekend. And it's almost noon. The crowds will be insane."

"I was thinking a little earlier," said Dylila, who was apparently inviting herself along.

"We can't get there before noon," I said.

"I'm thinking a lot earlier. Like around 1961. That was when they opened their new Tomorrowland," said Dylila. "I always wanted to try the Flying Saucers."

"Oh, yeah," I said. "I heard about those. Like bumper cars, only on a cushion of air."

"David, you look wiped," said Ariyl. "You sure you're up for a day at Disneyland?"

"Oh, sure. I mean, the crowds back then were so much smaller. Even if the rides were kinda low-tech. Besides, I promised you."

"Ohh, David!" she said, kissing me happily.

* * *

IT TURNED OUT, these girls were champing at the bit to do the Magic Kingdom old-school style. We were first in line at nine A.M., which was when I thought the place opened. We actually had to wait till ten when they dropped the rope at Main Street and everyone dashed to the Submarine Voyage or the Rocket Jets or, in our case, the Flying Saucers. Unlike modern visitors, for each ride we needed tickets which came from our admission booklet, and this was the ultimate E-ticket ride (fifty whole cents!)

There were fourteen "saucers" with open-air seats and seatbelts, clustered together alongside a big mechanical boom. We each sat on one and belted ourselves in.

Big underground fans hummed and my saucer rose on a cushion of compressed air. The boom swept open and I went cruising out onto a circular field, pocked with air valves that opened as I passed over them; it really was ingenious. By leaning in my preferred direction of travel, I glided on air, picking up speed. I was a human air hockey puck. I had fun bouncing off several other merry riders.

Then came a burst of laugher from Ariyl and Dylila. I turned back and saw they hadn't left the starting position. A couple of high-school-age attendants were puzzling over the fact their saucers weren't rising, despite quite a bit of compressed air venting out of the rubber bases.

"I don't understand," said one pimply youth. "We had a guy out here last week who weighed three hundred pounds, and he could ride this thing. Sorta." He appraised Ariyl. "There's no way you weigh more than three hundred pounds."

"Yeah, no way," deadpanned Dylila. That brought a fresh round of guffaws from the girls, who laughed themselves sick as they exited the ride.

Well, now I had some idea how much each of them weighed. They were only six-three, but their muscular density had to be double mine.

"Sorry, we broke the Flying Saucers!" giggled Dylila to the waiting crowd.

"They're not broke, folks," protested the young attendant.

We hit a few other long-vanished attractions like the Mine Train and the Monsanto House of the Future—which they found hilariously quaint. I pointed out that we should really come back in eight years to experience the famous audio-animatronic rides like the

Haunted Mansion and Pirates of the Caribbean. But the gals were having too much fun with the ancient 1961 tech.

I hadn't slept since we left imperial Rome. I'd gone through a strenuous day and night in 1933, and then a long visit to 1954, and then our chat with Sven in 2018. Three hours in the hot Anaheim sun finally did me in. I actually nodded off on the Matterhorn Bobsleds. I could have happily left the park, but the girls wanted to stick around for the fireworks that night.

We rode the Monorail over to the Disneyland Hotel, where we checked into two rooms. At least, I think we did. One minute I was waiting on a couch in the lobby, and the next minute I felt Ariyl laying me down in the bed like a tuckered-out tot.

I slept for fourteen hours.

38

MEET THE FAMILY

W HEN I FINALLY AWOKE, ARIYL AND DYLILA had a room service breakfast waiting for me. I showered, then we returned together to Sven Bergstrom's apartment on March seventeenth, 2018. It was one day later for him, as well.

For a few hours, Ariyl and Dylila planted themselves in front of Sven's big screen TV. They bypassed the entertainment offerings but were fascinated by a world where there was news 24/7, even if the lurid, violent headlines were ancient history to them.

"Well, with seven billion people in this world, I guess they make a lot of news," opined Ariyl.

* * *

THE NEXT COUPLE days while I was bunking at Sven's, Ariyl and I didn't make love. Apart from my quotidian concerns about the expense of getting a hotel room for privacy, I was laser-focused on leaving behind my record of our travels. So while I dictated my narrative for Sven to transcribe, Ariyl spent the better part of those days shopping, exploring, and bar-hopping with Dylila, who somehow was paying for a nearby hotel room for them. And no, I didn't let Dylila in on the fact I was again writing my memoirs.

Sven was my *de facto* editor now. I did make him promise not to publish anything unless, you know, we didn't come back in a reasonable period.

"Define a reasonable period," said Sven. "Your last few trips, the Time Crystals have brought you back a day after you left."

"Yeah, but you know these Crystals. The least little paradox makes them go haywire."

"Don't wait too long to see me again, David. I'm ninety-two, for God's sake."

"Okay, Sven, make it a month. If I'm not back to file my taxes by April seventeenth...you can assume I'm in a lot bigger trouble than the IRS can cook up for me, and you can publish it."

"And maybe you'll have some royalties to pay taxes on next time," he said.

"Knock wood," I replied.

Sven had thoughtfully saved the contents of my old apartment's closet. Lacking the morphing SmartFab attire of my traveling companions, I'd decided on black combat boots, Levis, a cotton T-shirt, and a nondescript dark flannel shirt—an outfit that would not look out of place anytime from 1900 on; not exactly formal dress, but not alien either, and adaptable to a range of temperatures.

* * *

THE AFTERNOON before our scheduled departure, Sven showed me the diagrams he'd made of our altered timelines. I pointed to one that featured my path into the twenty-second century.

"So you agree, a traveler can check out his own future as long as he avoids places that he might have any effect on?" I asked.

"You proved that when you went to the Cavendish Lab. So pick someplace remote, where people never go. Like the Australian outback. Start with 2109, and work your way back in time from there. Our first step must be to find out the date when this ice age began."

"Sounds right."

Abruptly, Sven frowned and reached into my hair. "What's this?"

"I dunno, lather? I just showered."

Sven showed me the bee-sized dram with its tiny red light on.

"This thing really does look like a firefly. I guess that's why none of you noticed it," he mused.

"How long has that been hanging around me?"

"I don't think you ever turned off the dram when you left for 1933. It must've gone with you. This little thing must have an excellent video recording of your time travels to Commodus's Rome, the ice age in 2109, plus 1933, 1954, and 1961."

"Well, I'll be damned," I said. "Wait a sec, you mean that was still on all those times I was alone with Ariyl?"

"Unless you turned it off."

"I didn't know it was on. I didn't know it was there!"

I looked around to make sure Ariyl and Dylila weren't overhearing.

"Sven, I need to find the erase button on this thing. Or else a flyswatter."

"David, a good scientist cannot be a prude," lectured Sven. "You must preserve the data, regardless of your feelings about it."

"Well, I'll be happy to show you the historical record, but the personal stuff is off-limits, Sven."

"I'd expect no less of a gentleman. But consider that posterity has a right to know everything when you're gone."

"That does it," I said dryly. "I'm taking the damn thing with me."

* * *

THE NIGHT before we were due to leave for Australia, I went to Brannigan's Steakhouse on San Vicente, to allay my parents' fears. I wore the same outfit I'd picked out for traveling. I figured I wasn't going to get it dirty in one evening.

Mom hugged and kissed me and even Dad, not a big hugger, embraced me. We sat down at a table for six.

"Ben said he'd be a bit late, but go ahead and order. His treat," said Mom.

"That's very generous of him," I said.

"Well, he can afford it," said Dad. "He picked a good job."

And with that subtle opener, we were off to the races.

We were about ten minutes into a loving but stern lecture on financial and personal responsibility from Dad, interspersed with messages from Mom about the joys of settling down with the right girl, when Ben breezed in. He put me in a mocking headlock.

"Don't ever do that to us again, bro!" he said, holding me longer than was necessary to make the point.

"I changed my mind, I will have that wine," I told the waiter. Otherwise, I'd never make it to dessert.

"Cindy has a thing tonight, but she sends her love," Ben reported; I suspected his wife just couldn't be bothered with me.

Ben snapped his fingers. The waiter immediately came, and took his order for the full rack of ribs, no sauce. Ben was taller and beefier than me, but there wasn't an ounce of fat on him. "And tell the bartender we need the TV turned down," he said.

I'd pretty much tuned out the news program, but Ben was a guy who could be annoyed by things others barely noticed. However, my ears pricked up when I heard the anchorwoman report:

"...in a wild St. Patrick's Day brawl last night that sent a dozen patrons of the famed Calabasas biker bar to the hospital. It got so violent that several motorcycles were hurled onto the highway. Police are seeking two persons of interest who some witnesses blamed for the disturbance. They are described as two women, both well over six feet tall, one blond, the other Afric—"

The barman muted the TV.

"Wait, can I hear the end of that?" I called out.

"Dave, c'mon. Focus up here," said Ben. "I'm gonna address the elephant in the room. Are you on drugs?"

"Oh, Ben..." clucked Mom.

"Of course not! Do I look like I'm on drugs?" I rolled up my sleeves. "No track marks, okay?" I opened my eyes wide. "Normal pupils." I bared my perfect teeth. "No meth mouth."

Then I gulped my wine, peeved.

"Your brother has your best interests at heart, Davy," said Dad. "We all do. We want you to be happy and productive."

"I *am* productive!"

Mom vouched for me. "Of course you are! But are you happy?"

"Dave, your word's good enough for me," Ben assured me. "But I had to ask you that, before making you this offer."

"Offer?"

"My brokerage is looking for a new account exec, and I want to put you up for it. You're a shoo-in."

"Me? Ben, I've never sold anything in my life."

"Dude, it's not brain surgery. Anyone with a head for figures and a friendly phone voice can do this job. You're overqualified. You start at forty thou, and the sky's the limit."

"You have so much talent, and you're such a good person," Mom added. "I just feel like you need some stability in your life."

"*David?*" came a voice from across the room.

The last person I expected or wanted to see just then came over to our table.

Moira Shea. My beautiful ex-fiancée, who'd given me the bounce on my return from Santorini in 2013. She looked even lovelier than she did five years ago.

She kissed my parents and Ben on the cheek, and everyone exchanged pleasantries.

I rose to dutifully kiss her cheek, but she turned at the last second and I got lips.

"Why don't you join us, dear?" said Mom.

"Oh, I don't want to intrude."

"Don't be silly, you're practically family!"

"Well, thanks, Jenny!" Moira sat across from me.

I signaled the waiter for a refill.

Moira told us all how she'd loved her job in D.C. but after her boss the congressman lost his reelection bid, she realized how much she missed her hometown. Then she looked at me. "And everyone here."

Oh. My. God.

This little family gathering was starting to feel like a cross between a come-to-Jesus meeting and an arranged match, with Mom as Yenta.

But maybe I was being an ingrate. These people all loved me and wanted the best for me. After all, I'd come here to set their minds at ease. If I pulled another disappearing act now, they might never get over it.

Moira gazed at me fondly and squeezed my hand. "David, I want you to know I think the way the Greek government treated you was outrageous. I still have contacts in Washington, and if you like, I could work them for you. You deserve credit for your find!"

"Moira, that's really sweet of you," I said.

"Tell her your good news," urged Mom.

"About...?"

"The job with your brother!" Mom said.

"You're going to be a stockbroker?" marveled Moira.

"Well, I haven't really decided..."

"That's so exciting!" she cooed.

"I'm going to have two rich sons," chuckled Dad, clapping me on the shoulder. "I'll never have to pay for another meal."

"George!" chided Mom.

By the time I had finished my second glass of wine, I was basking in the glow of unaccustomed approval from everyone at the table. Ben might have been an overbearing big brother, but cushy desk jobs that start at forty grand were not the worst way to earn a living, especially for an assistant professor whose career had crashed and burned.

It was a pleasant surprise to have Moira taking an interest in my work. Maybe she really could get my find on Santorini out of bureaucratic limbo. Maybe I could sell stocks and do archaeology in my spare time, the way Ben does his mountain climbing. Maybe I didn't always have to be the black sheep of...

"David!" came another voice from across the room.

I was wrong before. *This* was the last person I expected or wanted to see just then...coming over to our table.

"There you are! Oh, I'm so glad to finally meet you all!" said

Ariyl. She was wearing khaki short-shorts and a tank top that revealed more than WikiLeaks.

"Oh, boy," I murmured to myself.

The waiter passed by, and I signaled him urgently with my empty glass.

Ariyl put out her hand to Mom. "Ariyl Moro, Mrs. Preston. David's told me so much about you! You're the reason he knows how to dance so well!"

Mom shook hands, nonplussed.

Ariyl then shook Dad's hand. "And, Mr. Preston! Oh, you *have* to show me your video collection someday. I'm a major Boris Karloff fan!"

Dad's jaw dropped.

"And you must be big brother Ben! David told me all about how you used to play with him." She clasped Ben's hand firmly.

He winced.

Not waiting for an invitation, Ariyl sat in the empty chair beside me, facing Moira. There was an awkward pause. Moira put out her hand, with a frosty smile. "I'm Moira."

"Ooh, what a memorable name!" said Ariyl, admiringly. She turned and swatted my shoulder with feigned indignation. "You didn't tell me you had a sister!"

Ben choked a bit on his drink.

Moira looked daggers (or maybe steak knives) at Ariyl.

"Moira was my fiancée five years ago," I said quietly.

"Oh! I *am* sorry," Ariyl told her. She smiled at me. "You are just full of secrets."

"How do you and David know each other?" wondered Mom.

"You wouldn't believe it in three thousand years," I muttered.

"Through the Bureau," said Ariyl.

"What bureau's that?" asked Ben.

"The FBI, what else?" she smiled.

Again, I looked for a crack in the floorboards I could sink through, but there was none.

"We met while David was undercover..." Ariyl trailed off as I widened my eyes at her. "Oh, I am so stupid. Of course you don't know. You see, all these months, David couldn't tell you about the case he was working on for us, or contact you in any way."

My third glass of wine arrived while Ariyl spun her elaborate fiction. I was quite sure I would need it.

"I told him that's all right, now that we've made the arrests. But your son is so cautious where his family's safety is concerned. But really, you're all perfectly safe. We dropped the net on the whole cartel, and there is no way there will be any reprisals."

"Reprisals?" gulped Ben, color draining from his face.

Dad narrowed his eyes at me. "David, is this true? You've been undercover for the FBI?"

I took another slug of wine. Might as well be hanged for a wolf as a black sheep. "That's right, Dad."

Mom stared at me saucer-eyed. I felt a pang of conscience. "It wasn't a drug cartel or anything dangerous, Mom. It was a, uh, antiquities smuggling cartel."

"Oh! They have those?" she asked, surprised.

"Well, this puts a different complexion on things," said Dad. "My son, an FBI agent!" He shook his head, amazed.

"You know, Davy, I've always wanted to see a real FBI ID. May I?" said Ben eagerly, holding out his hand.

I smelled the skepticism behind the smile.

"Uh, you don't carry ID when you're an undercover agent," Ariyl said, condescendingly.

I relaxed a bit.

"But here's mine," she said, showing Ben her fake 1933 ID. I cringed.

"Black-and-white?" said Ben, squinting at it. "I thought these had a color photo and 'FBI' in big blue letters."

"Only on *The X-Files*," I said with a forced chuckle, snatching the card out of his hand and passing it back to Ariyl.

The waiter brought Ariyl a menu. She opened it. "I'm starved! What's good here?"

"The salads," I quickly said, closing her menu and handing it to the waiter. "She'll have the Cobb salad," and here I dropped my voice to a murmur, "...hold the chicken and the bacon."

"Someone's on a diet," smiled Moira.

Ariyl pointed to the big bowl of salad someone was eating at the next table. "Are they *that* size?"

The waiter nodded.

"Better bring me three," she said.

"In fact," I told the waiter, "we've changed our minds. We'll all have the salad."

"What?" exclaimed Dad.

I turned to Mom. "You're always after Dad to eat healthier. Let's set a good example!"

"David's right," shrugged Mom.

"I didn't come to a steakhouse to graze!" protested Ben. "Just bring what I ordered," he told the waiter.

"So what are you, David's supervisor or something?" Dad asked Ariyl.

"Oh, David, you didn't tell them yet?" She squeezed my arm. "Your son is so considerate. He didn't want me to miss the big announcement."

"Announcement?" blinked Dad.

"We're engaged!" gushed Ariyl, showing off a sparkling diamond ring.

Moira dropped her glass with a crash while I choked my wine all over the tablecloth. Ariyl thumped my back heartily.

"Excuse me!" I coughed, heading toward the restroom.

Ariyl came with me.

"What are you doing here?" I gasped. "And where'd you get that ring? Wait, I don't want to know!"

"Sven told me all about this little intervention."

"He and I need to have a talk about discretion. And boundaries," I rasped.

The bartender, who was watching us, along with most of the restaurant, handed me a glass of water. That was when I noticed on the silent TV behind him: "Biker Brawl Update" supered over the anchor's face, followed by a sketch labeled "Police Seek Suspect." The drawing was a perfect likeness of Ariyl.

"You should thank Sven," Ariyl told me. "Your relationship with your family needed some fixing."

I looked back at our table. Everyone was staring at Ariyl, who stood unaware beneath her police sketch on the TV.

"Oh, you fixed things, all right!" I whispered. "Now they think I'm an FBI agent who's engaged to a wanted criminal!"

"A perfect explanation for why you disappear for months at a time. You'd rather they think you're a loser who flips out every few years?"

"Of course not, but..."

Ariyl pulled me back to the table and told my astonished family, "We're actually starting a new assignment tomorrow, so I hope you'll all be understanding of..."

Her voice trailed off as she stared in revulsion at the rack of ribs on Ben's plate. Ariyl grabbed my brother by his lapels, lifted him in the air, and shook him like a jug of orange juice: "What the fuck are you eating, you monster?"

Dylila burst in the front door, hand gripping her Time Crystal. We could hear police sirens wailing into the parking lot behind her. "We need to go, *now!*" she said to Ariyl. Then she dashed out the back way.

Ariyl tossed Ben ten feet onto the dessert cart.

My mom screamed and fainted. Dad caught her as she fell out of her chair.

"Ariyl, for God's sake!" I yelled. "Are you crazy?"

Ariyl gently lifted me up eye to eye. "First, let's get one thing straight between us," she said. Then, as the whole restaurant gaped at us, she wrapped her arms around me and kissed me passionately.

At last, she smiled at me: "And there it is."

HISTORICAL NOTES

I have tried in the non-altered timelines, to hew as close as possible to established history.

The Lincoln conspiracy is factual, including John Wilkes Booth's decision to assassinate the president upon hearing Abraham Lincoln's speech on April eleventh, 1865, which endorsed giving the vote to black men.

Charlie Chaplin's tour of Japan and near-assassination in May 1932 is also factual; Chaplin wound up going to a sumo match instead of the banquet at which he was marked for death; his host, Prime Minister Inukai Tsuyoshi, was killed. This coup ended civilian control of the Japanese military until the close of World War II.

Harold Lloyd's fabled estate Greenacres stood intact for some time after the comedian's death in 1971; the villa itself remains, but 39 of the acres surrounding it were sold at auction in 1975 and subdivided into 14 home sites.

The scenes and conversations with time travelers are fiction, but based on research into the lives of the famous people depicted.

ACKNOWLEDGMENTS

MY GRATITUDE for reading, notes, proofing, suggestions, kind words, support or invaluable advice: Jim Casaburi, Deirdre Molitor, Barry Galef, Bob Leonard, Randy Cook, Gary M. Black, David Larmore; Art Eisenson for his expertise on weaponry. Bobbie Metevier for her keen eyes and Christiana Miller.

Deepest thanks to Barry and Ellen, Marty Rudoy, Robin Stein and Ginny Scott, friends indeed.

And Sue and Deirdre, for enduring it all again.

ABOUT THE AUTHOR

DOUG MOLITOR is an L.A. native who has written for comedies (*Sledge Hammer!, Lohman & Barkley, You Can't Take It With You, Police Academy*) and sci-fi/fantasy adventure series (*Sliders, Mission: Genesis, Adventure Inc., Young Hercules, F/X*) and the western comedy *Lucky Luke*.

In animation, he was co-writer of the feature *SpacePOP*, and writer and/or story editor for over 200 episodes of such series as *The Wizard of Oz, Happily Ever After, X-Men, The Future Is Wild, Bill & Ted's Excellent Adventures, Sinbad, Where on Earth is Carmen Sandiego?, Class of the Titans, Roswell Conspiracies, Sabrina, Beetlejuice* and *Captain Planet*. For the latter, he won two Environmental Media Awards and was nominated for the Humanitas Prize. His 2008 musical election spoof, with Hillary and Obama singing "Anything You Can Do, I Can Do Better" had 2.4 million hits on YouTube.

Doug is also a former *Jeopardy* Champ, appearing a total of 13 days on two versions of the show.

To be notified of Doug's next book, please send your email address to TheAltadenaPress@gmail.com

You can also connect with him on social media or on the website thealtadenapress.com

PREVIEW: CHRONICLES OF A TIME TRAVELER

TIME AMAZON — BOOK 4

COMPARED TO THE HUMILIATING CHAOS THAT was the Preston family dinner in Los Angeles in 2018, I actually found it a relief to end up in the ice-locked Australian outback in the summer of 2109 A.D. (We had made the time-leap from the back alley behind the steakhouse, as cops banged on the locked door whose knob had been snapped off by one of the girls.)

We saw nothing but deep snow and freezing gray skies. Jumping back a decade at a time, we found the same frigid vista in 2099, 2089, 2079, and 2069.

However, January first, 2059, we were in a typical Aussie hot spell, albeit cranked up to fifty-six degrees Celsius by mid-century global warming.

No, we didn't bring a smart phone to ask for the weather, as it seemed likely the software and satellite links of a 2018 phone would be utterly obsolete in the latter twenty-first century. We only knew the temperature because my mentor, physicist Sven Bergstrom, had supplied me with his old mercury thermometer.

Time Travel Agent Dylila Duprae tried 2065, then 2060, then June 2059, but at each date, the shift to the ice age had already begun. So it was back to a broiling New Year's Day 2059, and then moving forward day by day, until January sixth, when the Crystal refused to move us to the next date, or even to midnight. That meant the date of the apocalypse was today: January sixth, 2059 A.D.

After the sub-zero chill, it was a pleasure to experience the hot red dryness of the Gibson Desert, a hundred miles east of Kiwirrkurra Community. At least for the first ten seconds or so, until the wall of stifling hot air, the sizzling sand, and the searing sun went to work on me; I began sweating from every pore, especially under my hair.

I stripped off my flannel shirt and tied the sleeves around my head, with the back of the shirt protecting my neck, kind of a half-assed *kaffiyeh*. Meanwhile Dylila and my love, Ariyl Moro, morphed their SmartFab dresses into bikinis, and their jackets into beach towels.

Yes, the girls were actually going to sunbathe while we waited for Armageddon in arguably the remotest spot on earth. And believe me, I'd have been delighted to view their lush expanses of pulchritude if my entire body was not feeling like a match head being whipped across a rough surface.

We had arrived at noon. In Fahrenheit terms, it was a hundred and thirty in the shade. And there was no shade. I would not survive till sundown in this inferno.

I begged Dylila to jump us ahead a few hours.

"David, we seriously depleted the Time Crystals' charge with all this time-hopping. We need enough power left to escape when the war starts."

"Well, my bet is that Kiwirrkurra Community is on no one's nuclear target list. Unless Queensland joined the H-bomb club."

"Can you just cool your jets for ten minutes while we soak up some rays?" asked Ariyl, who undoubtedly was as immune to melanoma as she was to clubs, swords, and minor flesh wounds.

"I can't cool anything in this incinerator," I snapped. "If we can't jump to sunset, then just kill me now."

In answer, an enormous fireball appeared in the southern sky, trailed by a fast-rising roar and then a sonic boom that almost knocked me over.

"What the hell?" I exclaimed. "Who started this war, Antarctica?"

"That's no missile!" shouted Dylila.

"It looks just like the asteroid in *Planet Killer!*" yelled Ariyl.

"That's what it is!" hollered Dylila, taking hold of her Crystal.

The roar of the blinding white object tore apart the sky, leaving a spreading vapor trail of superheated clouds.

"Link Crystals—return to start point!" bellowed Dylila.

Nothing happened.

"Goddamn it, return to start point!" Dylila screamed over the ear-splitting din. She whacked her Crystal.

Still nothing happened.

All of our Crystals were flickering like a porch light about to fail.

"Shut your eyes!" Dylila shrieked. "Don't look!"

Then something really happened.

Even through closed eyelids, we could see the entire northwest sky turn as bright as the sun. We waited for seconds that seemed an eternity, and then the three of us were violently thrown to the scorching sand as the desert floor began to writhe like an angry sea. A blast-furnace gale howled till I thought it would pop my eardrums. The Earth was a giant gong just struck by the hardest hammer in the Universe.

Then everything went black.

Read the rest of the story in
Chronicles of a Time Traveler

ALSO BY DOUG MOLITOR

Time Amazon Series

Memoirs of a Time Traveler

Confessions of a Time Traveler

Revelations of a Time Traveler

Chronicles of a Time Traveler

Adventures of a Time Traveler

Full Moon Fever Series

Monster, He Wrote

Pure Silver

Short Stories in Anthologies

Love and Other Distractions

Hell Comes to Hollywood II

www.ingramcontent.com/pod-product-compliance
Lightning Source LLC
Chambersburg PA
CBHW020432030726
47495CB00006B/1762